Capitol Hell

by Jayne J. Jones and Alicia M. Long

BEAVER'S POND
PRESS

ISBN 13: 978-1-59298-536-4

LIBRARY OF CONGRESS CATALOG NUMBER: 2012912489
PRINTED IN THE UNITED STATES OF AMERICA
FIRST PRINTING: 2012
16 15 14 13 12   5 4 3 2 1

COVER AND INTERIOR DESIGN BY TIFFANY LASCHINGER
BEAVER'S POND PRESS, INC.
7108 OHMS LANE
EDINA, MN 55439-2129

(952) 829-8818
WWW.BEAVERSPONDPRESS.COM

HTTP://WWW.CAPITOLHELLBOOK.COM/

TO ORDER, VISIT WWW.BOOKHOUSEFULFILLMENT.COM
OR CALL 1-800-901-3480. RESELLER
DISCOUNTS AVAILABLE.

1
Allison's Inaugural Day

As I approached the enormous white marble building that loomed menacingly in front of me, I paused to draw a deep breath and closed my eyes for a moment. These were my best efforts to get my wits about me. Could this really be happening? Surely not. How was it possible that a small-town girl from South Dakota was standing in front of the Russell Senate Office Building, the oldest and most prestigious Senate building on Capitol Hill? I was about to embark on my first day as a Capitol Hill staffer. It was a dream come true.

That I had just gotten lost in the subterranean maze known as

the Metro and now had two enormous blisters forming on the heels of both feet no longer mattered. My attempt to try and navigate to work on my own had taught me three valuable lessons. First, high heels and public transportation do not mix. Second, a black suit is considered appropriate work attire; my hot pink skirt suit fresh off the Target clearance rack was not. Third, escalator etiquette is key. Despite these setbacks, though, I had arrived. And I was on time.

Still, it was difficult to forget how I had been berated by several Washingtonians for failing to adhere to the unwritten rules of the escalator. How was a small-town girl to know that the right side of the escalator is for standing and the left side for walking? Surely it was not a mistake I'd make again! I vowed that would be the last time I was called a stupid tourist. I was no tourist—I was a bona fide Capitol Hill staffer! I gathered my courage and declared it aloud, "Allison, you are a Capitol Hill staffer!"

I took another deep breath, clicked my hot pink heels together, and ascended the imposing marble steps, ready to embark on the opportunity of a lifetime! As I walked through the large metal door, I was immediately greeted by a bald, middle-aged Capitol Police officer who barked in a New York accent, "Staff ID, please!"

"Oh," I stammered, taken aback, "I don't have a staff ID yet. Today is my first day. I'm going to work for—"

"If you don't have a staff ID, you can't use this entrance. Go around and use the visitors' entrance," he snapped in his rude New York tone, cutting me off.

"Oh. Well, where is the visitors' entrance?"

"You newbies don't know anything," he replied tersely. "Follow the building around to the left and go in the next entrance off Constitution."

"Thanks!" I offered.

He smiled and said, "Good luck." Then he muttered under his breath, "You're gonna need it!" as his short, skinny sidekick snickered. I had no idea how right he was.

Still undeterred by the day's minor setbacks, I hustled toward the visitors' entrance. As I rounded the corner of the Russell Building, I was stunned to see a very long line of what appeared to be middle school students. As I drew nearer, out of breath, I realized that they too were waiting to get into the Senate building. I glanced at my watch nervously—ten minutes to spare before nine o'clock. Thank God I had left extra early. I wondered how long it takes fifty middle school students to go through a metal detector. I got my answer thirty minutes later when I finally entered the building after watching an endless parade of backpacks and computer games being screened.

Once I got through the second set of metal doors, I was greeted by a burly African American police officer who sneered at me from behind a metal detector.

"Place your bag on the belt and remove all metal items from your person," she instructed.

This part I had down; even in South Dakota we knew this drill! I had been through airport security at least half-a-dozen times. I confidently placed my fashionable bright purple purse on the belt and stepped through the magnetometer. It immediately began to shriek and flash.

"Take off your shoes!" the burly police officer blared.

"Seriously?" I asked. "None of the middle school kids had to remove their shoes."

"Do I look like I'm kidding?" she replied. "Take off your damn shoes!"

Irritated, I removed my shoes, placed them on the belt, and walked through the metal detector.

"Nice blisters," the officer remarked with a smirk.

"Yeah," I said as I grabbed the rest of my belongings, shoes included, and made my way to the nearest set of elevators. I offered up a silent prayer that I wouldn't be in too much trouble for being late on my very first day.

Senator Anders Nathaniel McDermott III was the type of

senator every staffer dreamed of working for, or so I thought. I had joined his campaign—brimming with hope and expectations—as a full-time volunteer almost a year earlier. He was handsome, eloquent, thoughtful, and truly wanted what was best for the people of the state of Minnesota. I had just started my senior year of college at the University of Minnesota when I joined the campaign. Like many others, women in particular, Anders captivated me. He seemed to embody all the values and sentiments one would want in a leader. To top it off, he was surrounded by a beautiful family who wholeheartedly supported his campaign for a better Minnesota.

The months I spent on his campaign were filled with travels all around the state. My hands suffered countless paper cuts from literature dropping and blisters from pounding in lawn signs. My elbow endured multiple encouraging pinches from Anders as he passed by, and I gained about twenty pounds from the endless pancake socials and barbecues we were forced to attend. I had also marched in countless parades, rarely slept more than four or five hours a night, and had been sworn at over the phone more than I cared to remember. But I knew it was all worth it when, after an overwhelming victory, Anders was elected a member of the United States Senate and he became Senator McDermott.

I realized just how much my hard work had paid off when I received a phone call from the senator's chief of staff, Charles Stanford. He asked me to be Senator McDermott's personal scheduler. I was stunned, excited, and almost speechless. I told Charles I'd be honored to serve in such a prestigious position, but then asked where Rose was going.

Rose had been the senator's personal scheduler for well over ten years, throughout his entire political career, which started when he won a seat in the Minnesota State Legislature. I couldn't imagine her leaving his side. Rose knew exactly what he'd order at any restaurant, his shoe size, and what type of makeup he wore (only for television appearances, of course!).

Charles just laughed, "Oh Allison, no worries. Rose isn't going anywhere. We're promoting her to deputy chief of staff. She'll be there to help you transition into your new position."

I was ecstatic. Not only was I being offered my dream job, but Rose would be there to help me with any questions or concerns I had. Things couldn't be better! With a setup like this, there was no way I'd fail. I accepted the position immediately, without even considering the challenges of moving across the country, the salary, or the high housing costs in Washington, DC. Visions of the Capitol Building, the White House, the Washington Monument, and other notable DC landmarks began swirling around in my head. I was deliriously happy, and could not wait to embark on my new adventure!

Within a few short months I was ready to go. I found a tiny apartment located right on Capitol Hill, courtesy of Craigslist, and I couldn't wait to meet my new roommate, whom I knew very little about. I decided to sell my car since I'd be only a short Metro ride or quick walk from work, which I found absolutely exciting. It was my first opportunity to use such an extensive mass transit system. Senator McDermott's office had even agreed to help pay some of my moving expenses. I was on my way! The only small setback was my salary. I was informed that I would be making a paltry $24,000 per year. But since I was accustomed to living on student loans and part-time jobs throughout college, I was determined to make it work. I thought the cost of living in DC couldn't be that high... could it? Plus, a salary of $24,000 in South Dakota was almost like being rich!

Four days after I graduated from college, I was riding in a U-Haul across the country with my parents. They were both so proud of me. When my dad expressed serious concerns about me being able to survive alone in DC on $24,000 a year, I assured him it was the opportunity of a lifetime—which is what everyone had told me. Little did he know my purse was full of credit card applications and buy-one-get-one-free coupons. I already had a boatload of student loans, what was a little more debt? I reassured my dad that there would be opportunities for raises and with all the valuable experience I'd gain,

Capitol Hell

I could land more lucrative jobs in the future. He reluctantly agreed, but grumbled that he still thought law school would've been a better option.

I shrugged my shoulders at the thought of staying in Minnesota or South Dakota. I was a city girl, and I wanted to take my *Sex in the City* attitude straight to 1600 Pennsylvania Avenue. I didn't let my father's doubts or worries dissuade me. I was about to be a Capitol Hill staffer, complete with hot pink heels!

After two days of nearly nonstop driving, we had a bumpy arrival at our destination: our nation's capital, Washington, DC! We were nearly arrested by the Capitol Police for driving our U-Haul a little too close to the Capitol. But after some sweet-talking by Mom, we made our way safely to the Senate side of Capitol Hill, where my new home was going to be. As we drove past the numerous row houses, I couldn't wait to see my new apartment. I was certain that for the $800 in rent I was paying each month, it would be gorgeous! Surely a $1,600 two-bedroom apartment, smack dab in the middle of DC, would be glamorous. After all, it was practically the equivalent of my parents' monthly mortgage payment in South Dakota.

My daydreams about all the grown-up DC things I'd do in my glamorous apartment were interrupted as Dad pulled the U-Haul to a halt. He mumbled, "We're here."

I looked out the window and saw a small, shabby, drab yellow brick apartment building with metal bars affixed to all the windows. This couldn't be my apartment. *My* apartment was supposed to be glamorous. After all, I was paying $800 a month for it. Dad must have gotten it wrong.

"Dad, I don't think this is right. Are you sure we aren't in the wrong quadrant? DC consists of four quadrants, you know," I said, quoting my mini DC travel guide. "Maybe we're in the Southeast quadrant, that's closer to the House side. We're supposed to be in the Northeast quadrant, which is closer to the Senate side. It can get very confusing. I'm sure we're just in the wrong quadrant," I rattled on.

"Allison, I am not confused," my dad said gruffly. "While I might be from South Dakota, I can read a map, and this is the correct address. Now come on, let's see what you've gotten yourself into. Did you sign a lease already?"

"Errmm...," I started to mumble. Thankfully Dad's attention was drawn elsewhere when, as soon as we stepped out of the U-Haul, a scruffy-looking toothless man asked him for money. My mom looked on from the car window. She looked terrified.

"Get out of here," he shooed, and then quickly turned to me. "Allison! You've got beggars right outside of your apartment! Are you sure this area is safe?"

"Safe?" I responded, "Umm, there are bars on the windows. And, well, it is still on Capitol Hill, which means the area is under surveillance by the Capitol Police, so I'm sure it's safe, Dad. If Bill and George can live here, I can too."

He looked at me doubtfully and said, "They had the protection of the Secret Service; you don't. Come on, let's go inside."

At the doorway I anxiously pressed the buzzer for apartment 2B. I couldn't wait—I was about to meet my new roommate and see my new apartment for the very first time. After a few seconds without a response, I pressed the button again and listened. Nothing. It appeared the buzzer was broken. I spied an open window and yelled, "Hello?"

A perky blonde girl poked her head out of the window and called down, "Are you Allison?"

"Yes! You must be Veronica!"

"I'm so excited that you're here! I'll be right down." A few moments later she opened the door and said, "Come on up! It isn't much, but it'll do."

As we walked up the single flight of dirty stairs my apprehension grew. Then we entered my "new" apartment. The entire thing was painted a sterile white, including the bookshelves that extended the length of the living room. The carpet was tattered and stained, and

the kitchen looked like it hadn't been updated since the 1950s. It was also remarkably bare. This was far from the glamorous girl-meets-city apartment I had envisioned.

Sensing my concern, Veronica piped up, "I know it isn't great, but don't worry—my furniture is supposed to arrive today and then I just know we can make this place feel like home."

I was comforted by her enthusiasm and offered her a half smile. I had concerns about our apartment, but I could tell Veronica and I would be fast friends.

After I unloaded the U-Haul and said goodbye to my parents, I went to bed and prayed, prayed again, and then prayed some more. I was about to embark on my dream job, and I couldn't fall asleep. I kept hearing scary scratching noises from overhead—mice crawling through the walls and ceilings. As if that wasn't enough, I began to hear loud sex noises from the upstairs neighbors. It was going to be a long night.

✳   ✳   ✳   ✳   ✳   ✳   ✳

As I stepped off the elevator onto the third floor of the Russell Building, I remembered how hard I prayed that first night in DC and began to pray again. This time I prayed no one would notice my first-day tardiness or the getting-worse-by-the-minute run in my nylons. I rarely opted to wear nylons, but Rose had informed me that Senator McDermott's office had imposed a strict rule: when female staffer's wore skirts or dresses to the office, nylons were mandatory. As I walked down the hallway, covertly fidgeting with my nylons, the corresponding numbers next to the large mahogany doors began to shrink: 385, 383, 380—I was getting close—377, 375, and finally, 373.

I had arrived.

I immediately noticed the crisp American flag and the comforting Minnesota flag straddling either side of the entrance. I took a confident step across the threshold and was promptly ignored by the two receptionists, a young man and a woman, who sat behind adjacent desks. Atop their desks were bowls full of Land O'Lakes coffee creamers and miniature Pearson Salted Nut Rolls. Nothing like a little taste of home for visiting constituents, I thought.

"Good morning, excuse me—" I started, only to be stopped by an upraised finger indicating I should wait. The female assistant had performed the maneuver without so much as a glance in my direction. I was starving, and snatched a quick nibble from the Minnesota candy dish. It hit the spot and made me think of home.

"Senator McDermott's office, please hold," the woman said quickly, as she pushed one of the many lit buttons on her expansive phone. "Senator McDermott's office, please hold," she repeated to another constituent, and again: "Senator McDermott's office, please hold."

It seemed this was going to go on forever, so I turned slightly to the male receptionist and quickly realized I wasn't going to get any help from him either. He appeared to be trapped on the phone with an angry constituent. I could faintly hear screaming coming from the headset he was wearing. I couldn't tell what the call was about, though, because he just kept responding, "Mmm hmm, uh huh, okay, yes, sir. I will pass that along, sir. No, really, I will pass your concerns along." After another ten minutes and a seemingly endless flurry of phone calls, the female receptionist tossed her long brown hair over her shoulder and asked in her nasally voice, "Can I help you?"

"Yes," I replied. "My name is Allison Amundson. Today is my first day. I—"

"You're almost an hour late," she snapped. "I hope you know you're missing the Monday morning staff meeting. Charles is not happy. Senator McDermott has been walking around looking for his daily folder, which you should have provided by now. You'd better get in there," she snapped as she hopped up and rounded the corner of her desk. "Follow me!"

Great. It was only my first day, and I had already managed to piss off the chief of staff and the senator.

I followed her through one of the office's interior doorways and was greeted by twenty-five blank stares.

"She's finally here," the snobby receptionist announced to the room, which consisted of all of my coworkers. They were almost all under the age of thirty and were seated around an enormous cherrywood table.

"Nice of you to join us," the chief of staff said sarcastically. "Have a seat, Allison."

I immediately sat in the nearest chair and tried to make my presence unknown. Only then did I realize that not only did the DC staff see me walk in late, but there was a teleconference going on with the state office as well. I had managed to make a fool of myself in front of McDermott's entire staff. I was mortified.

Charles proceeded with the meeting and asked Morgan, the legislative director, for a quick update from the "leg shop" (pronouced "ledge shop"), the slang term used around Capitol Hill for the legislative division of any Senate or House office. It's the job of the leg shop to pay attention to all the bills pending before Congress and to draft legislation for the senator. As Morgan began to drone on about the Farm Bill and why the US should be trading with Cuba, I began to silently curse the fifty middle schoolers who had made me late. I was picturing ways I could torture each and every one of them when I suddenly heard my name.

"Allison, do you have that information for us?" Charles asked.

"Excuse me?" I stammered.

"Really, Allison, if you aren't going to show up prepared and on time, you really shouldn't bother coming to the staff meetings at all. I asked if the senator has ten minutes today to do an interview with CNBC about the amendment to the transportation bill we're pushing."

"Umm… I'm sorry, sir," I stammered. "I haven't even gotten my computer or BlackBerry yet. I don't have that information, but I will check into it right after the meeting." The room was silent and I felt like a complete idiot. But then, after a painful eternity, Rose piped up.

"The senator is available at 1:15 p.m. today. I'll set it up," she offered helpfully.

"Thanks, Rose," Charles said. "I can always count on you."

I sighed in relief and vowed never to daydream during a staff meeting again. After concluding that Morgan could talk circles around any issue and would win a professional rambling contest hands down, I decided I'd need to find a way to stay focused despite the inevitable boredom.

After the staff meeting ended, Rose greeted me warmly, "Allison, so nice to have you on board. I love the pink suit. Talbots?" Before I could answer, she continued without taking a breath, "Why were you late today?"

"I am so sorry!" I exclaimed. "I left my house an hour early and thought I had plenty of time." I started to regale her with the story of the three-ring circus that had been my morning.

"No worries," she smiled. "Let's just get back on task." Rose spent the morning acclimating me to life in the Senate. First up was employment paperwork that more closely resembled a book. Not only was I expected to fill out the customary W-2, employment forms, and direct deposit slips, I also had to pick a health insurance plan and enroll in something called the Thrift Savings Plan, which apparently has something to do with retirement. I was utterly clueless. I had filled out basic employment forms before, but never anything relating to health insurance or retirement!

I had just graduated from college and was still on my parents' health insurance plan. Plus, I was only twenty-two. I had been able to legally drink for less than a year. What did I know about retirement? Retirement is for old people—why should I care about that now? But I did my best to complete the necessary forms with occasional advice from Rose. Then we traveled the maze of the Senate office buildings to submit the forms and get my official Senate ID badge.

I hadn't realized that the US Senate occupies three Senate office buildings. The oldest and most prestigious was the Russell Senate

Building, where Senator McDermott's office was. It's also the prettiest of the three. Its walls and floors are all marble, and it's dimly lit by immaculate gold and silver chandeliers, all of which enhanced the building's Senatorial feel. As we walked, I peered into other offices in the Russell Building and noticed thick draperies covering large windows and richly painted walls covered with gorgeous portraits and political memorabilia.

We took an elevator to the basement and walked down a long hall, which I was told ran underground to the Senate Dirksen Building, the middle Senate building. Not only does the Dirksen Building sit in between the newest and oldest buildings, it was the second of the three to be built. And it's definitely the least trendy of the Senate buildings. Apparently constructing a building over a span of thirty years—the 1950s to the 1980s—isn't a great idea. The building appeared to contain the epitome of tackiness from each of those decades. I thought the gross pink-speckled tile on the floor was bad until I noticed the gross green-speckled tile on the rest of it. I could find nothing dignified about the Dirksen Building. Its dingy white walls and speckled floors suggested a mental institution more than corridors of power.

I learned the Dirksen Building is where most committee hearings take place and that most senators don't have official offices there. I surmised that its décor probably had a lot to do with that. After all, I wouldn't want to have an office in that tacky building! As we continued, Rose pointed out the Senate cafeteria and told me about the tremendous takeout salad bar that helped her stay on track with the Atkins diet, and noted the convenience of being able to eat at her desk. We took the elevators just outside the cafeteria and walked toward the Senate Hart Building to the disbursing office to drop off my new employee paperwork.

The Senate Hart Building is the newest of the three buildings and certainly the most modern. Its Senate offices were constructed around a nine-story atrium that houses an imposing contemporary metal sculpture by Alexander Calder called *Mountains and Clouds*. The offices overlooking the atrium have glass walls and windows and the ceiling has skylights to allow in extra light. The floors and walls are a polished white and pink marble, which are spectacular on their own. I was noticing how very different the three Senate buildings were when we arrived at the disbursing office.

I turned in my paperwork and was sworn in. I had never felt so official! We left disbursing and headed back into the Senate Dirksen Building to the Sergeant at Arms Office to get my Senate ID. I couldn't wait! Those police officers wouldn't be able to stop me now! As I approached the woman who would process my ID, I began having DMV flashbacks. I just hoped this photo would turn out better than that one had. It didn't.

When the ID was printed, I looked at it anxiously. I couldn't believe how close up the picture was or how horrible I looked. Maybe I should join Rose's diet plan. I looked like a swollen teenager who'd just had her wisdom teeth pulled. My hair was a frizzy mess—it wasn't responding well to the DC humidity. But it didn't matter. The important thing was that I was now an *official* Senate staffer!

The rest of my first day was much less eventful since the senator had left for Florida to have a fundraising dinner with wealthy Minnesota retirees. Rose showed me around the office and introduced me to my coworkers, who all seemed perfectly normal, welcoming, and friendly—at the time. Then she got me set up at my desk, right outside the senator's office, where she had kindly placed a box labeled "Allison's supplies." The box was filled to the brim with a hodgepodge of items: blue markers, five small bottles of hand sanitizer, a cell phone charger, pencils, and, of course, my BlackBerry. That BlackBerry would soon serve as my electronic dog leash to the office.

There was also an orange index card with an array of personal information about the McDermott family: the children's birthdays, each family member's social security number, the senator's best friend's assistant's phone number, and Mrs. McDermott's height and weight.

The back of the card was full of interesting but odd information, such as favorite sandwich (crushed egg salad on toasted rye bread with one tomato slice, cut into squares); one teaspoon of Red Owl honey per two lemon-flavored tea bags; and never forget to call poker night friends each Tuesday to remind them of the weekly game. I noticed that the card also listed the frequent-flier numbers and associated passcodes for the senator's family and Charles's family. I couldn't imagine why I would need the chief of staff's children's frequent-flier numbers.

I snickered at the outrageous card and wondered why the sacred orange card didn't also include the direct number to Barack Obama? Or maybe God himself? With the clock edging toward six, I threw the card into my top desk drawer and emptied the rest of the box quickly. I was set and ready for day two. Rose passed by my desk before leaving for the day, warning me that the senator would be arriving at 6:30 a.m., and I should be at my desk to greet him. Then I overheard her tell Charles that she'd be late tomorrow because she was flying up to New York to assist Mrs. McDermott as she guest-hosted *Live! with Kelly*. Charles laughed and said, "Oh, Rose, when will we ever learn?"

As more of my new coworkers started passing my desk and filing out the office door, I realized I was the only soul left. My rocky morning had quickly turned into a productive day of settling in and diving into work. I didn't know then that my first day would be the least eventful day in my career as a Senate staffer.

2
The Teapot Dome Scandal

I woke up to my alarm clock screaming in my ear at 4:58 a.m. I was confused and disoriented. Why was my alarm going off at such an ungodly hour? I finally came to my senses and realized that I wasn't in my college apartment in Minnesota—I was in Washington, DC! And today was going to be my second day of work as a Capitol Hill staffer!

I dragged myself out of bed and into a hot shower. Then I chose a sensible navy skirt with a white button-up top and gray blazer, rather than something over the top. I even left yesterday's hot pink stilettos in the closet and opted for standard black high heels

instead. I looked myself over in the mirror one last time, thinking I looked just like any other dull, drab, cookie-cutter Washington bureaucrat. This wasn't me. To add a little flare and style to my boring outfit, I inserted a silver hoop earring into each ear. They were fresh off the Target clearance rack and instantly provided a glam difference. It's amazing what bargain-priced earrings could do for an outfit. I then topped everything off with some bright red lipstick and instantly felt better.

To ensure that I wouldn't be confused by the Metro again, I decided to walk to work that morning. I grabbed my bag and threw open the door, nearly forgetting my BlackBerry. But then I remembered Rose's admonishment from the day before: "Never—ever—forget to bring your BlackBerry with you. *Ever!* It's the only way the senator knows how to reach you. If you forget it, he may not be able to do that and then you've failed at your job." I was determined not to disappoint. I whipped around, grabbed my BlackBerry off the coffee table, and bounded out the door.

I began to walk at a brisk pace down the sidewalk. I knew exactly where I was going because I had successfully executed a practice walk the night before. I had it down. My usual brisk, but not too brisk, pace would get me to work in twenty-five minutes. Currently, it was 5:55 a.m. I had gotten ready in record time and left myself plenty of time to get to the office. I wasn't going to be late today!

As I was walked along, I realized that the first rule I had learned in DC—high heels and public transportation do not mix—also applied to a walking commute. Although I had opted for my more practical and broken-in black heels, they were still no match for DC sidewalks.

DC sidewalks aren't the sensible sidewalks found in South Dakota or Minnesota. They're uneven bricks grouted together with large, heel-grabbing gaps in between. After five blocks I'd already lost the fight with the sidewalk three times. Every time I stumbled it was an embarrassing spectacle. First, my shoe would get stuck in a sidewalk crack, which would cause me to trip. Luckily, I was just clumsy enough to have had plenty of past experience in balance recovery. Those painful growth-spurts that led to my 5'10" frame and clumsiness were finally paying off. That hard-won skill was the only thing that prevented me from falling flat on my face each time my shoe got stuck. Then, after my less-than-graceful recoveries, I'd hop on my shoed foot back to my other shoe, bend over, yank it out of the sidewalk, and place it back on my foot while real Washingtonians watched my antics and snickered. Day two wasn't going well so far.

I focused on choosing my steps more carefully. I felt like a child trying to avoid all of the cracks. "Step on a crack and you'll break you mother's back," I muttered to myself. Thirty-five minutes later I arrived at work. Right on time. I took a deep breath, thanked the good Lord for getting me to work on time, and prayed for a successful day. I was armed with my new official Senate ID and had no trouble whisking through the employees-only entrance. When I arrived at the McDermott office, I noticed the interior lights were on, which was odd, since Rose told me I would be the first to arrive.. Maybe she had decided to come in after all?

I walked through the main office back toward my desk outside the senator's office. I heard a voice ask, "Rose, is that you? It's unlike you to be late."

Late? "Umm, no…" I called out, as I continued to my desk. "It's me, Allison."

Just then Senator McDermott came around the corner. "Allison? What are you doing here?" he asked.

"Oh," I hesitated, caught off guard. "Well, Rose said she was going to be in late today because she flew up to New York to assist Karma while she co-hosts *Live! with Kelly*."

"Karma's in New York? Maybe I could fly in for dinner. When we spoke last week, I don't remember her telling me about New York. Is that today?" the senator asked. "Allison, why is she co-hosting again?"

"I'm sorry, sir, I'm not sure, but I can find out," I replied.

"Oh, no matter, she's always up to one harebrained scheme or another. But that still doesn't explain why you're here."

"Oh," I said, taken aback. "Well, since I'm going to be your new scheduler, Rose thought it might be good for me to get used to coming in early to make sure you have everything you need. Senator, I'm so excited to be in DC working for you. You really are the best and thank you so much for this opportunity!"

Senator McDermott looked at me with his wide smile and mumbled, "It's always good to see you. Good to see you. How are your folks?" Before I could answer, he pinched my elbow and continued, "Next time, you had better be on time."

"I'm sorry, sir. I thought I was supposed to be here at 6:30."

"Right. 6:30 not 6:34," he said, glancing at his BlackBerry. "Allison, never forget rule number one. You need to pay attention to detail. ATD, I like to call it. Never forget ATD."

"Yes, sir," I replied. "Sorry, sir."

"Now how about some tea, Allison?"

"Yes, sir. Right away, sir," I replied. I scurried off to the kitchen as the senator retired to his office. As I approached the coffee machine I realized that it looked more like some sort of NASA spaceship than a regular coffee maker. It had all kinds of knobs and spouts, and I had no idea where to even pour the water. Okay, plan B: the microwave. I quickly filled the senator's cup with tap water and popped it in the staff microwave, which looked as though it had never seen a sponge in its life. I pressed two minutes on the keypad and waited. When I took it out, I dropped not one, but two, tea bags into the steaming water and stirred in a teaspoon of honey, just as the orange card instructed. I proudly brought it on a coaster into Senator McDermott's office, knocking slightly before entering. He barely glanced up from the *Roll Call* newspaper he was reading. I placed the mug on his desk and quietly exited his office to get ready for the day.

After my awkward morning greeting from the senator, I thought things were looking up. As I turned on my computer, though, I was interrupted by the sound of Senator McDermott gagging and coughing. "Oh dear God!" I thought. "He's choking!" I immediately leapt up from my seat and ran into the senator's office. "Are you alright, sir?" I asked frantically as I tried to remember the Heimlich maneuver. Step one: Squeeze his nose. Step two: Tilt his chin back. Step three: Oh shit! No, that's CPR!

"Alright? Am I alright? No, I most certainly am not alright. This is the worst cup of tea I've ever tasted. What did you do to it?" he yelled.

"Umm, I don't know what you mean, sir," I said. "I just warmed up the water and put two tea bags in along with one teaspoon of honey, just as you like."

"Did you use the Jura Capresso Impressa Z6 Automatic Coffee Center to warm the water? It doesn't taste like you did. You didn't warm this in the staff microwave, did you?"

How on earth could he tell the difference between water warmed in the espresso machine and water warmed in the microwave? Senators must have a direct line to the water gods or something. Hot water was hot water, wasn't it? I quickly contemplated lying, but figured that probably wouldn't be the best idea since the espresso machine wasn't even turned on, and I hadn't the faintest idea how to do so.

"I'm sorry, sir. No, I did not use the espresso machine. I used the microwave," I admitted. "Is that a problem?" I asked innocently.

"A problem? Well, you tell me," he responded angrily. "You opted to use a dirty microwave the staff uses to heat up their old leftovers, which gives off rays that cause cancer, rather than the $3,000 espresso machine that's here for the sole purpose of making me hot beverages. Does that sound like a damn problem to you?"

"I guess I see your point," I said, shocked. "It's just that I'm not familiar with how to use the espresso machine, and I knew you wanted your tea. So I thought using the microwave would be okay."

"Well, it most certainly is not okay. When Lindsay gets here, have her show you how to use the espresso machine so that this *never*

happens again," he snapped. Then he turned his attention back to his newspaper. "Also, have her come see me when she gets in. You, on the other hand, should not disturb me," he said without looking up.

Lindsay was the senator's executive assistant. She was only about a year older than me, and had only been in the office for about six months. Apparently she knew how to make one helluva cup of tea.

Just before I made it out the door, Senator McDermott volleyed one last shot. "And, Allison, lose those earrings before Secretary Fatia comes in today and wipe off that lipstick! I need my staff looking at least halfway professional, not like they just got home from the bar. Please shut the door."

I stood there stunned, unable to decide what to do. Did I dare apologize? Maybe I should run downstairs to the cafeteria and buy some tea for him. Did he really just comment on my appearance? Should I try to use the espresso machine? But he did say it cost $3,000—what if I broke it? I decided to do nothing, and closed his office door. He told me not to disturb him, so I wouldn't disturb him. After all, he was a fifty-year-old man. If he wanted his tea that damned bad, surely he could get it for himself, right? I mean, he was a United States Senator after all. If he was capable of drafting federal laws, he could secure a cup of tea on his own if the one I provided was unsatisfactory.

I sat at my desk and continued to stew. He could have stopped at Starbucks on his morning commute like the rest of America. It would have required little effort, since he had a driver and all. I finally decided to use this time to prepare for the day and stopped obsessing about the Teapot Dome Scandal I had created.

Within a matter of minutes, the senator was pacing in front of my desk, brushing his fingers through his hair. He ordered, "Allison, call Karma and set up dinner with her. Also, make sure you call Trista and have her set up drinks with a donor beforehand—maybe Al—so the campaign will cover things. And make sure to call what's-his-name, you know my good, good friend on 22nd Street, and tell him I want my suit altered. There's a great seafood place on the corner of Broadway and… what block is that again? Just get dinner scheduled, and I like an aisle seat. That's all for now, Allison. Always great to see you."

I sat there stunned and confused and unsure of how to proceed. Was this man bipolar? What was he talking about? One minute he was irate about a damn cup of tea and the next it was great to see me? And what the hell had he asked me to do? Maybe he did really need his cup of tea in the morning to be capable of making sense.

I looked down at the notes I'd scribbled on my hot pink Post-it notepad that had luckily been at hand when the senator came out of his office rambling orders. I tried to make sense of my chicken scratches so I could decide where to begin deciphering what he was talking about. I read the first line: "Set up dinner with Karma." Okay, that makes sense. I can handle that. But does he mean tonight? Oh no, that couldn't be. She's in New York and we're in DC.

Maybe some of these other notes would help clarify the situation. My next line read: "Call Trista, set up drinks with donor, 'Al?' Campaign pay." What the hell did that mean? I knew Trista was the senator's longtime campaign aide. She was a whiz in the fundraising and finance departments. In fact, that woman was better at squeezing dollars out of donors than I was at squeezing oranges for my morning juice. It was clear he wanted me to set up drinks with a donor, but tonight? And who was Al? And what did he want the campaign to pay for? The drinks?

The third line read: "22nd St., good friend, suit altered." Okay, now I was really lost. 22nd Street in DC? Minnesota? New York City? Good friend? Why would his good friend care that he wanted his suit altered? And for that matter, which suit? He must own at least a couple dozen. The more I dissected my notes, the more confused I became. None of it made sense.

My final scribble was: "Seafood place, Broadway, dinner, aisle." So he wanted to have dinner at some seafood place *on* Broadway, and the only Broadway I was familiar with was *the* Broadway in NYC. But there must be a Broadway in Washington, DC. After all, it was

the middle of session, a Tuesday. There would likely be votes early the following morning, or at least some lively debate. Not to mention the committee hearings he had scheduled. And what was this about the aisle? Did he want to sit in a certain aisle of the restaurant? Did restaurants have aisles? Did he mean an aisle seat on a plane?

I decided to turn to my one and only friend in the office for help: Google. Google always had the answers. First I googled *Broadway* and *Washington, DC*. No promising results. I was directed to links for Broadway Pizza and Broadway shows, but it appeared there wasn't a street called Broadway in Washington, DC. So I googled *Broadway, New York*, and *seafood*. And there it was, staring me right in the face: Blue Fin, 1567 Broadway, New York, New York. One of the ten best seafood restaurants in New York. Dammit! Did he really mean he wanted to travel to NYC tonight for dinner with Karma? And to meet with some donor named Al? I debated whether or not to call Trista at such an early hour—it was only 6:53 a.m. in DC, and back home in Minnesota it was an hour earlier. I knew Trista worked like a madwoman, but I thought 5:53 a.m. might be just a bit too early to call, even if it directly concerned the senator. As I contemplated my next move, Lindsay burst through the doors in a frenzy.

"What did you do?!" she hissed.

"Excuse me?" I responded.

"The senator," she cried. "He BlackBerried me and told me to get here immediately. He said things were 'out of control' and that he'd been poisoned."

"Poisoned!" I laughed. Surely she couldn't be serious. But I could tell from the look on her face that she was.

"Why are you laughing?" she snapped. "You've really upset the senator. What did you do?!"

I composed myself before replying. "Lindsay, it really wasn't a big deal. I wasn't sure how to use the espresso machine, so I warmed up the water for his tea in the microwave."

She gasped. "You NEVER EVER use the staff microwave for the

senator's food. He doesn't like being exposed to all those cancer rays! Are you trying to kill him?"

"Umm, I really don't think microwaves are that bad. Everyone in America has one—"

"How dare you," she cut me off. "First you try to poison the senator, and now you won't even take responsibility for it! No wonder he's so upset! And who doesn't know how to use an espresso machine? Seriously, what is wrong with you?"

Just as I was about to respond, Blair Bloomberg II, the senator's press secretary, came blowing in. "I need to see the senator *now*," he demanded.

"Good morning, Blair. You're looking very sharp today in your bright pink button-down," I replied jokingly.

"Allison, this is no laughing matter," he snapped. "Let me see him NOW!"

"I'm sorry, Blair. The senator has asked to be left alone for a few minutes before Secretary Fatia arrives. Maybe I can help you."

"I need to speak with him immediately. We've got trouble. Trouble with a capital T. And this is one crisis I can't handle before my morning yoga. Where is Charles? He's going to love this one! Karma is up to her old antics," Blair said, out of breath. He looked stressed.

"Charles came in early this morning for the chief of staffs' breakfast meeting and should be back in ten minutes," Lindsay piped in.

"Thank you, Lindsay, you are always so professional and polite," Blair said as he stared at the senator's closed door. "Allison, when Charles gets in, come get me," he ordered as he stomped away.

A few minutes later Charles arrived with his usual skip in his step. He was decked out in an orange dress shirt and lime green tie and was chatting noisily in baby talk to one of his children on his BlackBerry. "I love you too, give Mommy a big kiss for me and try to not hang from the chandelier today, honey. I will see you Friday afternoon and I'll have a special toy from the space museum. Be good!" Charles intoned as he ended the call and gave me a wink. After a deep breath, he asked,

"What do we have going on today, ladies? Is Anders in?"

I quickly replied, "Apparently Blair thinks we have a C-R-I-S-I-S with a capital C."

"What kind of crisis?" Charles questioned inquisitively, then asked me to get Blair and to come into his office immediately.

"I'll let Blair fill you in on the details," I said. "We'll be right there."

I quickly grabbed a notebook and hurried to alert Blair that Charles was waiting for us in his office. As I approached Blair's spotless desk, his ergonomic chair was turned and I couldn't see his face. "Blair, Charles would like to see us right away," I said calmly but assertively. As he spun his chair around, I could see he was spritzing water on his face. I started to laugh and asked, "What are you doing?"

"Allison, just because you don't care about your appearance doesn't mean I shouldn't care about mine," he said as he looked at me and my drab outfit in disgust. "I'll share my beauty secret with you. Every morning, I use an Evian water spritzer to cleanse my face and soul. Unlike you, I need to be ready to face the press at a moment's notice. My job is to represent Senator McDermott, and I can't represent him to his best if I don't look my best. Allison, I am called to serve. Called to serve, Allison," he mumbled as he poured himself a cup of coffee from his personal Keurig coffeepot.

"Okay, Blair, whatever you say!" I said as I rolled my eyes. "Charles wants us to meet with him now in his office. I can't wait to hear about this morning's emergency. And, Blair, did daddy pick up that personal coffee maker for you in Paris?" I asked, only half joking.

I had met Blair when I started on the campaign. It was common knowledge that his father was a maxed-out donor to the senator's campaign. He had also donated generously to the senator's recently created PAC. It was no secret how Blair had gotten his job. And it was annoying that he actually seemed to be good at it, despite his irritating personality.

"Good one, Allison," he smirked back. "You're just jealous that you didn't have the privileged upbringing that I did. Apparently they don't teach refinement or etiquette in South Dakota," he snarked.

As we approached Charles's office, Morgan, the legislative director, came bounding in. He was skipping and singing the theme song to *Cheers*. He looked at us quizzically and asked, "What's up, friends?"

Blair responded as though reporting a national emergency, "You've got to hear this. Come with us to meet with Charles. We have trouble!"

As we all packed ourselves tightly into Charles's jammed office, which was adorned with his children's latest artwork, he bluntly inquired, "Blair, what is it now?"

After drawing a heavy breath, Blair said in a gossipy tone, "Today, while co-hosting *Live! with Kelly*, Karma—on *live* national, morning television—declared to the world that not only is she living in LA, but that any monkey could run for office and be president. And *then* she started an off-the-cuff impersonation of the president as a monkey! To top it off, she suggested that we don't really need any certain type of leader to run the country, that anyone is fit for the job."

"Come again?" Charles asked as all the blood drained from his face, leaving him deathly pale.

Morgan, apparently unaware that Charles had understood what had happened but didn't want to believe it, started to rephrase Blair's report. Charles quickly cut him off, "Morgan, I get it. This is why I have so many gray hairs at the age of thirty-eight. When will I ever convince Karma to get a real job, and when will she learn to keep her mouth shut?" Charles fired out. "Allison, what does his morning look like?"

"Umm, he has an 8:30 with Secretary Fatia, and then he has two school groups to visit with before his International Relations Committee mark-up, which I've been told he actually needs to attend to vote," I answered. "Oh, and he asked me this morning to set up dinner with Karma in New York tonight. He wants to get out of DC by 1:00 p.m. and return by 10:00 p.m.," I said, knowing I still needed to figure out how to pull off such a feat.

Charles shook his head, threw his arms in the air, and ordered, "Back at it, team. Let's get back to work. Allison, be sure to squeeze

me in some time with him this morning. And, Blair, do some damage control until I can kill this with a good story. We can't have people thinking the senator would compare the president to a monkey!"

As we left Charles's office, Blair and Morgan brushed me off like an ugly stepsister and went on their way, laughing about Karma's monkey impression of the president. Back at my desk, Lindsay kept staring at me without saying a word. I finally asked, "What?"

"Oh nothing." Then, in the same breath, she mumbled, "Rose *always* kept me in the loop and told me everything that was going on."

I ignored her as I looked at the endless list of the last-minute New York planning I had to do before the senator's office meetings started. I didn't have time to gossip.

It was almost 7:00 a.m. in Minnesota, so I decided to give Trista a wake-up call to inform her about the unexpected New York trip. She assured me the campaign would come up with a way to cover the trip and that she'd find an appropriate dinner guest for the senator. "Just another Anders excursion," she said. I thanked her profusely, and told her I'd make airline and dinner reservations and call Karma. Trista, in her business-like tone, said we'd touch base later.

Just as I hung up the telephone with Trista, the senator emerged from his office. "Allison, did you say Karma was on that show today?" he asked a bit nervously.

"Yes, sir, this morning. I think it's still on ABC if you'd like me to change your office television to the correct channel, sir," I offered.

"I'm a United States Senator, Allison," he stated arrogantly. "I don't have time to watch how to bake cookies and do craft projects and crap. I need you to draft a quick email to Karma. Just tell her she did a superb job and looked glamorous," he ordered. Then he mumbled to himself, "That should get me some guaranteed sex tonight before I fly back—well worth the trip."

As my face turned bright red, I drafted a quick message. "Dear Karma, you are the love of my life and you were magnificent today. I'm so proud to call you my better half. You're still as hot as the day we met.

Let's have dinner tonight and then hit the sheets! XOXOX, Anders."

Before I hit the send button, I erased the entire thing and opted for something more bland. "Karma, you were superb and looked glamorous today. Anders." As I stared at the screen, I prayed that someday my knight-in-shining-armor husband would send his own messages rather than ask his young, underpaid, unmarried personal assistant to do it for him. I hit send and wondered how things would play out after the senator heard about the monkey impression. I thought it was best to leave delivering that news to Charles.

It was approaching 8:30 a.m. and Secretary Fatia was first on the senator's schedule. Lindsay knocked on his door to alert him to the time and went back to her desk. My desk was already buried in papers, my phone was ringing off the hook, and my fax machine kept spitting out scheduling requests. I still needed to call to arrange flights for the senator and was feeling generally overwhelmed. I couldn't help but shoot a jealous look at Lindsay as she counted the senator's supply of tea bags and wiped off the top of the honey container. Must be rough.

I was able to reserve and confirm a last-minute round-trip flight to New York and even remembered that he had asked for aisle seats. My ATD must be working today, I laughed to myself. It was 8:45 a.m., and Lindsay kept looking at her watch. Senator McDermott came out of his office in a fury asking, "Where is Fatia? Was I supposed to go to her office? Get Fatia on the phone."

Without skipping a beat, Lindsay looked at me and said, "I have Secretary Fatia's phone number right here, Senator!"

"I have it, too, Lindsay. Afterall, I am the scheduler. I'm sure she's just running a little late this morning," I said, trying to downplay the situation. "But I'll call her office right away," I offered, as I performed an internal eye roll.

"Hi there," I said cheerfully. "This is Allison calling from Senator McDermott's office. I could be wrong, but this morning I had an 8:30 a.m. set up with Secretary Fatia. She hasn't arrived, so I just wanted to confirm."

"The secretary made an emergency trip to Haiti this morning," her assistant replied. "I left a message on your voice mail this morning at 6:00 a.m."

"Oh… thanks," I replied. The shit was about to hit the fan. I hadn't had time to check my voice mail. I took a deep breath and went into the senator's office. "Sir, the secretary's office informed me that she needed to cancel your meeting today. An emergency cropped up in Haiti that she needed to attend to."

"It sure would have been nice if her office would have called to inform a United States Senator at least five minutes before the scheduled time, don't you think, Allison?" the senator asked.

"Well, sir," I stammered, "the secretary's office did call this morning and left a message at 6:00 a.m., but I just haven't had time to check my voice mail until now," I quietly replied.

"Allison, ATD!" the senator snapped.

"Yes, sir, I am sorry, sir," I mumbled. "I'll start coming in fifteen minutes early every morning to check my voice mail, sir," I assured him.

Just then, Lindsay conveniently popped her head into the senator's office. She carried a camera and a trusty cup of hot tea. "Senator, we have two school groups ready to see you, and I thought you'd appreciate a cup of tea before seeing them."

"Thank you, Lindsay!" replied the senator.

As I walked away, ready to barf, Morgan approached me and asked if I knew the lyrics to the *Laverne & Shirley* theme song. I laughed at his odd but funny sense of humor. I sang a bar of the song for him and got back to work. Those late-night reruns on TV Land had paid off.

At my desk I prepared to call Karma about dinner reservations for the evening. First, I went into the senator's email account and made sure "his" message hadn't bounced back, and saw that Karma had already replied: "Went well." That seemed fittingly personal. I decided to print the message for the senator. As he left his office to see the school kids, I gracefully shoved Karma's message in front of him as he passed. Without reading it, he tossed it into the nearest garbage can, which was right next to the office paper recycling bin. As he headed out the back door, he swatted the backs of all the interns working for him and shared his usual, "Good to see you. What a treat—what a treat."

Morgan walked by my desk again, this time humming the theme to *Happy Days*. I laughed and wondered how he ever got any work done. As I settled in, I checked my email and saw that Blair had emailed me eight times already that morning. I quickly read his messages and was dumbfounded. Who was this guy? Didn't they teach any manners at the fancy prep school he attended? As I scrolled through all my unread messages, Blair came running up to my desk.

"I need to schedule Fox News at 9:30 a.m.," he ordered.

"Excuse me?" I asked.

"Allison, look. I need to schedule a Fox News interview at 9:30 a.m. He'll be on for fifteen minutes. They want to talk about Haitian adoptions and Secretary Fatia's visit. This will be a tremendous story to kill Karma's silliness today. See that open space on his calendar? Just type in 'Fox News Interview,' Allison," hurried Blair.

"Did you ask Charles about this?" I questioned.

"Allison, I'm the senator's go-to person for press. I just got him an excellent interview on national television, I'm stressed out, and I don't need any heckling from you. Just fill in his calendar and change the background color so it looks like he has an appointment. Really, there is nothing to your job, Allison. Any monkey can do it, just ask Karma!"

"I can't just fill in his calendar, Blair. You know the rules. It's the same process you used with Rose. We need Charles's permission before scheduling anything, including your press interviews," I reminded him.

"Do whatever you must, Allison," he said as he shook his head and gave Morgan a high five as he passed. "Hey, Morgan, do you know the theme song to *Allison's Island?*" he asked. They both snickered as Blair walked away.

Charles agreed to the interview and the day flew by, as did the senator. He was on his way to New York City, and I could catch up on some work. Just before the senator left with his driver to catch his

flight, I reminded him for the third time, "Senator, remember that the flight you're on out of New York is the *last* flight. If you don't catch it, you'll miss tomorrow morning's votes. The first available flight out tomorrow isn't until 9:00 a.m., which means you wouldn't arrive here until around 10:30 a.m."

"Stop worrying, Allison," the senator corrected. "I am, after all, a grown man!" I waved to him as he left and hunkered down to finish my pile of work.

As I walked home from the office around 7:00 p.m., I amused myself remembering the day's events—Karma's monkey comment, Blair's cocky attitude, Lindsay's no-real-work-required job, and Morgan's television theme songs. What a political circus. I hoped after my first-week jitters it would all start to make sense and calm down. It must, I thought.

When I got home, Veronica greeted me with a cold beer and an oven-baked pizza. I fell into the couch and told her about my day. It was refreshing to have a voice of reason around to keep things in some kind of perspective. I started to doze off on the couch, but was abruptly awakened by my BlackBerry.

Damn! I had missed five messages from Charles. The most recent was, "Let's go for a walk. I'll meet you at the corner of 5th and Constitution in ten." Even though I much preferred a night of reality television, I quickly changed clothes, grabbed my running shoes, and headed out—duty calls!

As I approached Charles, I noticed that he looked worn out, not his usual self. We started walking at a fast pace, and he told me that power walking the streets of DC in the evenings always helped him make sense of the city's craziness. Charles was a good man. I had wholeheartedly trusted him from the day we met during the senator's campaign. I always knew Charles had my best interests at heart, and that he would never put me into a situation I couldn't handle.

I didn't say a word on our walk, just listened as he talked. As we power walked down the National Mall, Charles began to carelessly share his thoughts about everyone in the office. It was clear that Charles had his favorites. It felt like I needed a scorecard to keep track of who was in and out of favor.

Charles's List:
Heidi—legislative assistant, drunken diabetic, office instigator, recently hooked up with a Tennessee intern.
Blair—press secretary, over-the-top spoiled brat, Senator owes his father for significant campaign support, needs a good kick in the ass.
Raquel—receptionist and intern coordinator, aka drama queen, steals candy bars from office supply, cheats on time cards, and allegedly used forty hours of sick time during a recent bout of chicken pox.
Morgan—legislative director, brilliant but wacky, everyone knows why he's never been married or even on a date with a woman, and picks office favorites, usually good-looking younger men.
Cam—legislative assistant, smart farm kid from Minnesota who wants to run the Agriculture Committee someday, workaholic, single, and needs to learn to unwind or get laid.
Rose—trusty advisor and the go-to gal for anything.

Charles walked me home and thanked me for coming to DC to help him and the senator. He reassured me that within a few weeks, I'd catch on to the job. He reminded me that I was still in the learning stages, and if I needed anything I could ask for Rose's help. He guaranteed me that they both wanted me to succeed. After a quick hug, Charles went back to his weekly hotel room, and I went to my new apartment.

My head spun from the last hour of gossiping with the chief of staff. I was tired and ready for a good night's sleep. I got into bed and found myself worrying about the senator catching his evening flight

back from New York City. I hoped he got some last-minute action from Karma! Maybe it would put him in a better mood.

In the middle of my nightly prayers, my BlackBerry started to chirp. Beep. Beep. Beep. I had seven email messages, all from the senator. I read the first message and the others quickly:

"What time is my flight?"

"Where is my confirmation number?"

"Hello are you there?"

"Hurry up."

"Need to change my flight. Traffic. Will not make it."

"Number for Senator Owen?"

And, finally:

"Just get me the Delta phone number and I will call myself. You are a horrible travel agent."

I couldn't reply fast enough; his messages kept flooding in! What an idiot. Why didn't he make his flight? For crying out loud, he was a grown man. The tantalizing potential for a reasonable bedtime was ruined. Now I'd need to book an early flight for the senator and a hotel reservation for tonight (Lord knows, he couldn't think of staying with Karma). Tears began to roll down my face as my BlackBerry started to ring.

"Hi, Senator," I said, after looking at the screen.

"Did you get me a new flight yet? I need to be back to DC by 6:30 a.m. to play tennis with Senator Ortega," the senator stated angrily.

"Sir, I'm sorry, I haven't. I'm trying to book a new flight on my personal cell phone while I have you on my BlackBerry. I'm also looking online, and it seems there's only one flight, sir, and you'd arrive in DC at 10:30 a.m.," I answered.

"That won't do!" he exclaimed.

"Sir, I need to call you back. I can't juggle two conversations at once. I'll call you right back."

"Allison, just forget it, I'll call Rose!" screamed the senator. Then he hung up on me.

Devastated, I didn't know what to do, so I did the only thing I could—continued to hold for a Delta agent's assistance. After what felt like hours, a cheerful Delta agent greeted me on the phone. "Delta Airlines. How can I help you?" I anxiously explained who I was and the crisis I was trying to avert for Senator McDermott. "Oh, you work for Senator McDermott?!" the agent exclaimed. "I just adore him, and I know he's one of our frequent fliers. I'll see what I can do." She placed me on hold, and a few minutes later she was back on the line. "You're in luck. One of our earlier flights from New York to DC was delayed due to mechanical issues. That flight is scheduled to leave in thirty minutes. Can he make it?"

"I think so! Can I book that flight now?"

"You sure can," she said. "All I need is your credit card number."

Credit card number. Shit! But then I remembered the emergency Senate-issued travel credit card Rose had given me for just such an occasion. Thankfully, I hadn't left it at the office. As I rummaged through my messy purse, the Delta agent told me how great my boss was and asked for a signed photo. I assured her that if she got the senator on the last flight, she could have a hundred signed photos.

Within a few minutes the senator's flight was rebooked and I called him with the good news. He picked up after the first ring. "What is it, Allison? Have you ruined any more travel plans? Has Rose cleaned up your mess yet?"

"Actually, Senator, I solved the problem on my own. There's a flight that was delayed earlier and is now scheduled to leaves in thirty minutes from JFK. Can you make it?" I asked.

"Can I make it?! Well, I am at JFK and I've been ready to get on a flight, you just didn't book one for me."

Instead of arguing about the unjust accusation, I just gave the senator the gate and terminal information and hung up the phone. Hopefully he wouldn't get lost before boarding. At that point my anger was about to boil over. Not only had the man not listened to the specific warning I gave him earlier about not being late for his

Capitol Hell

flight because it was the last one out of New York, but then he had the audacity to act as though I had never even booked him a return flight! Where was the nice, down-to-earth man I had campaigned so hard for? Had Washington really changed him that much and that quickly? Maybe he was just having a bad week. He couldn't really be this difficult, could he? How was it possible that he could act one way with his constituents and completely opposite with his staff? As it turned out, he could.

3

Payday! Payday!

-$126.89
-$126.89
-$126.89

I had to read my online checking account balance three times before it finally sunk in. There was no better way to say it: I was flat broke. After two weeks of McDermott Senate Office drama and new job jitters, I anticipated celebrating my first payday by having margaritas at Tortilla Coast, one of my favorite Hill bars, with

my new roomie Veronica and her Senate Office cronies. Instead, I was shocked and nauseous. How could this possibly be, I wondered as I stared at the computer screen, puzzled. How could I have just gotten paid and have a negative checking account balance?

So the start of what was to be a long, relaxing weekend (a three-day break from Senator McDermott) began with a finance-induced stomachache. I started to list my bills on my notepad:

Rent:	$800
Student loans:	$300
Credit cards:	$150
TOTAL:	**$1,250 per month**

I added them together again. And again. Then I stared at the computer screen, dumbfounded. As the first to arrive in the office today, I discovered my biweekly net pay was a whopping $749.99. My stomachache began to get the best of me. And it only worsened when I realized that I forgot to include my cell phone bill in the budget I had constructed! That was another $50 per month I couldn't afford. I quickly prayed my parents would forget to ask me to reimburse them for the bill since it was still being sent to their address. I felt tears well up, but refused to let them out.

Thankfully, I was alone in the office so the others wouldn't see my state of panic. I totaled my bills over and over again, and the total remained the same. I had $200 each month for essentials—groceries, toilet paper, shampoo, and, rarely, a clearance find from Target. That was only $50 per week. Clearly I was going to have to give up the shopping habit I had honed in college.

I desperately wanted to treat Veronica to a margarita as thanks for being so supportive in my first few weeks, and for keeping me sane and grounded. It looked like it was either going to be tampons or margaritas this month. Tortilla Coast and the margaritas win, I decided as I contemplated ways to steal tampons out of the public bathrooms in the Senate office buildings. Maybe I could swipe a few off the cleaning lady's cart in the hallway when she goes in to clean the bathroom.

I wondered how much I had made per hour in the past two weeks. It couldn't have been much. I tried to mentally add up all the hours I worked from home. Almost every night the buzzing of my BlackBerry woke me up as it signaled new messages. And, of course, I dutifully responded each and every time. I spent the Metro commute time running through the senator's schedule. Every time I was out with Veronica and her friends I was interrupted by at least one call from the office. And there was no way to factor in the blood, sweat, and tears I had invested. I took a deep breath and thought of the phrase my parents often used: "Hard work always pays off." Easy for them to say. Maybe in South Dakota that was true, but apparently it didn't hold up in the halls of the United States Senate!

My cell phone began to ring and the caller ID flashed *Dad*. I let his call go to voice mail. I couldn't tell him I was flat broke and about to live on my credit card for the next two weeks, especially since I had just gotten paid! My financial decisions and actions would be such a disappointment. He'd already expressed his doubts about me being able to survive in DC on such a paltry salary. I could already hear his speech about "being responsible" and "paying for only necessities." Then he would toss around terms like "retirement fund" and "financial planning" and a bunch of other things I really didn't care about. Retirement fund! If only he had a plan for a way to create a margarita fund. Then maybe we'd finally see eye-to-eye about financial planning. I felt alone for the first time since moving to DC.

Lindsay arrived and I quickly opened a new window on my computer screen as her wandering eye checked out what I was doing. We rarely talked, and today, with the senator out, I was curious to see what work she would do. It's sure going to be hard to serve hot tea to the senator while he's home in Minnesota. Lindsay started to complain about how tired she was after the past week and how she

was in "desperate need of a vacation." I couldn't even look at her with a straight face. Her "work" was a joke.

Just then, Trista called and asked if the senator's remarks for tomorrow's Farm Bill event were ready. The senator was getting antsy and had asked for them. I relayed the question to Lindsay and without hesitating Lindsay said, "If the senator's event is in Minnesota, the state office is on the hook for it." I couldn't believe her lack of teamwork.

Trista gracefully disagreed and asked me to intervene and email the agriculture remarks and talking points ASAP. I empathized with the pressure Trista felt and without any Lindsay-esque pushback, I emailed Morgan and asked him about the remarks. Just as I pressed *send,* Morgan arrived proudly wearing a faded denim shirt, crisp blue jeans, and ostrich cowboy boots. He informed me this was his casual Friday outfit, and told me I should be prepared to see it each and every week. While Morgan lacked fashion sense, his commitment to old-fashioned living made him truly one of a kind. He was a devout Catholic and still used *afghan* to refer to a small blanket rather than someone or something from Afghanistan. He was a likeable soul who never raised his voice to female staffers. Actually, Morgan was uncomfortable around women in general. And somehow I always managed to end up alone with him.

Morgan complimented me on surviving the first two weeks in the DC office and asked if I knew the theme song for *Good Times*.

"Little before my time," I told him cheerfully.

"Allison, we need to think of a good theme to use as our song— just you and me, kid," he replied.

"I'll work on that. But first, maybe you can help me with something. Trista just called and the senator is looking for his remarks for tomorrow's Farm Bill event. Will you email them to me?" I asked.

"Talk to Cam. And let me know if you need anything else for the boss today. Right now, I'm going to my office and shutting the door so I can write a letter to the Pope," he shared in a serious voice.

"Put in a good word for me, Morgan," I replied.

"Will do. Not a problem, Allison," he said as he walked down the hallway. I shook my head and wondered if he was really going to write a letter to the Pope. It seemed nothing was beyond the realm of possibility with Morgan.

My next stop was Cam, the senator's agriculture legislative assistant. He was very shy and kept to himself instead of getting involved in the office hoopla. Of all the legislative staffers, he was always the first to arrive and the last to leave. He was loyal, studious, and one of the most polite men I had ever met. And at six foot three with his curly dark brown hair, he was the epitome of tall, dark, and handsome.

As I approached his cubicle, my stomachache transformed into butterflies. This had a tendency to happen anytime I approached Cam. "Hey, Cam, the senator is requesting his remarks for tomorrow. Have you written them yet?" I asked.

"Oh, hi, Allison, I'm writing them now. It'll probably be another half hour or so," he replied, barely looking me in the eye.

"Sounds fantastic. Oh, is that a picture of your family?" I asked, pointing to a frame on his file cabinet.

"Ah, yes," he said, half smiling.

"Nice-looking family! I see where you get it!" I said flirtatiously.

"Thanks, Allison," he responded, blushing. "I'll get you the speech as soon as possible," he said, all business.

I walked away smiling. Cam was handsome and the total package. He was smart, kind, personable, and charming. I had developed a schoolgirl crush on him. Thankfully, he was single. If only I could get past his shyness. I knew he had a personality in there somewhere. I just had to dig for it.

When I got back to my desk, I overheard Lindsay talking to Heidi, the senator's education legislative assistant. Heidi was one of the shrewdest women I had ever met. She had a high-pitched nasally voice. But what really set her apart was her distinctive southern drawl. Well that, and the fact that she had little regard for anyone but herself. She and Lindsay were making crucial lunch plans and gossiping. "Can

you believe Janet is coming to work in the DC office as our health legislative assistant? Charles really likes her but she has no experience. This will be interesting," she snarled.

"I have no idea how she's ever going to learn how to do what we do!" added Lindsay.

I wanted to jump into their conversation but decided to stay out of it. Charles had already told me, in confidence, that Janet was coming to the DC office to add her Minnesota touch. Janet became a close friend during the campaign. I knew she'd work her ass off for the senator to whom she had undeniable loyalty. Her only hang-up would be leaving behind her cherished Minnesota for a job across the country. Also, she was stepping into the position with the highest turnover rate in the office. I didn't have the heart to tell her how horrible my first two weeks had been. She was excited and, selfishly, I knew having her in the office and in DC would be a blessing to me. But this wasn't Minnesota, and I was afraid the DC environment would be a rude awakening for her.

As I started to work on scheduling the senator's appointments for the following week, Blair scurried over to Lindsay and Heidi. "Did you read 'Heard on the Hill' today? We made the list!" he announced.

"For the top 100 hottest Senate staffers?" asked Heidi.

"Hardly," he continued, and proceeded to quote the column. "'Senator McDermott is number one for the most turnover in Senate staff for last year. Just ahead of Senator T-C-H and we know what she's all about!'"

"Heard on the Hill" is the gossip column for Capitol Hill. It's published every morning in *Roll Call* and is filled with juicy tidbits about the people living and working on the Hill. You could find out which senator was spotted dining with which lobbyist, which congressman had narrowly avoided being arrested for drinking and driving, or which celebrity was likely to make an appearance on the Hill that week. It was always chock full of good stuff. And that day was no exception.

"Let me see that!" Lindsay said as she snatched the newspaper from Blair to read the article.

"Just what I need today, another media crisis to kill!" whined Blair. "My job is never ending. It's Friday and I planned to chill out while the senator is in Minnesota. How am I supposed to learn new techniques to center my chi when I have to deal with things like this?" It was apparent he wanted to remind us that he'd just started a new yoga class. "I guess I'll be working another twelve-hour day today," he whined. "Hey, Allison can you even count to twelve?"

Before I could respond to his snarky comment, Heidi cut in, "Do you think we really have the highest turnover for a Senate Office?" she asked. "We're such a great staff and we're all such terrific friends," she added.

I almost choked on the coffee I was drinking. She must still be drunk from last night. Or maybe she'd been working in a different Senate Office than I had for the past two weeks.

"Well, when you add up all the riffraff who've come through those doors and who don't understand the senator's priorities and needs, then we do have a long list of names," answered Blair. "Not everyone understands the senator's needs like we do," he added, looking only at Lindsay and Heidi. "Which is unfortunate, because when others can't meet the senator's needs like we can, it puts so much more pressure on us. My back hurts from carrying the weight of everyone else's jobs! Actually, Allison, since you've arrived my back has been particularly sore. You're a heavy load!"

"Thanks, Blair," I replied. "Watch out. The next time you need a press interview scheduled, you're going to need a chiropractor!" I was only half joking. Just then, Morgan came out of his office and joined in the conversation as Blair was hamming it up, holding his back in pain.

"Blair, did you hurt your back?" asked Morgan.

"Just carrying Allison's workload, sir," he responded. "And it's starting to be awfully painful!"

"I just wrote a letter to the Pope," Morgan stated proudly.

"That's cool," remarked Blair.

I didn't say a word. Was I the only one who found it totally odd

that our legislative director had spent the past hour writing a letter to the Pope rather than working on legislative issues?

"I wanted to tell him how much he's influenced my life. I just needed time to reflect on that and tell him personally," Morgan said softly.

"Hey, Morgan, did you see we made 'Heard on the Hill'?" Heidi questioned loudly.

"No, what's in it today?"

"We have the highest staff turnover!" answered Heidi.

"That figures!" Morgan said.

"Yeah, if we keep hiring South Dakota cowgirls we'll make number one again next year!" Blair said as he hit my arm.

"Allison, you're a cowgirl?" asked Morgan, stunned.

"Ha, ha. No. My only claim to fame about South Dakota will be when my head is carved in stone, right next to George, Tom, Teddy, and Abe," I replied.

"Yeah, more like next to Crazy Horse!" answered Blair.

Everyone laughed, and I said, "Okay, Blair. Truce. That was a good one."

Morgan asked, "When and where are we going to lunch today, Heidi?"

"Capital Grille at 12:45," Heidi said as she winked at Morgan.

"We'll tell you later," Lindsay said with a don't-talk-about-it-now gesture.

"Okay, 12:45 it is," Blair said. "Until then I have some more heavy lifting—I mean work—to do." He walked down the hallway to his office.

"Allison, think of our theme song yet?" asked Morgan.

I laughed and said, "Nope, not yet. But I will!"

Just then I got an email from Cam. I opened it, excited to read his message: "Allison, the senator's remarks for tomorrow. Per your request. Cam."

I wrote back: "Thank you, Cam! They're amazing. Well done!

Thanks again! Allison." Then I forwarded the remarks to Trista.

Soon it was 12:45 p.m. and Blair, Morgan, Heidi, and Lindsay gathered in front of my desk. They left for lunch without inviting me. I was hurt, but also relieved they hadn't invited me because I didn't have a dime to my name, let alone forty bucks to pay for some extravagant lunch.

I was just about to start preparing for my dreaded weekly scheduling meeting with the senator when my phone rang. I recognized Charles's home number and answered the call quickly, "Hey Charles, how's Minnesota?"

"It's good. Cold and wet," he replied, and then added, "but I'm taking the kids garage-saling today to find birthday presents for Malaree. Is Morgan around?"

"Nope, he just went to lunch with Blair, Heidi, and Lindsay," I answered.

"Okay, when he gets back, the two of you need to call me right away. I'll have my BlackBerry on," he ordered.

I wondered what Charles needed and then, as the time passed, what was taking Morgan and company so long to return. I knew Fridays were a long-lunch-hour day, but Morgan had already been gone for ninety minutes. I had sent him a couple of BlackBerry messages, but hadn't received a reply. My phone rang and it was Charles again. "Allison, I asked you to call me with Morgan," he stated angrily.

"I know. I'm so sorry, Charles. Morgan isn't back yet from lunch, and I've sent him three emails," I answered.

"Ask around the office and find out where they went to lunch. Then call the restaurant and tell Morgan he needs to get his ass back to the office now," ordered Charles.

"Got it," I stated.

As I walked around the office, I was greeted with silence and blank stares about where Morgan and the crew went to lunch. When I asked Cam, he got a weird look on his face. "What is it, Cam? Do you know where they went to lunch?" I asked.

"They went to see *The Avengers*," he said. "It was released today

and they wanted to beat the evening rush with a matinee," answered Cam. "But you didn't hear that from me."

"Oh my God. They went to a movie during the work day!?"

"They disappear for three-hour lunches all the time when Charles and the senator are out of town."

"Let me guess that they don't use vacation time," I laughed.

"Right," he mumbled, rolling his eyes. "My favorite was the lunch hour Morgan hosted for the office staff that lasted a whole day. We had our very own Senate bar with an eight-hour happy hour. Heidi was dancing on Morgan's desk and the interns were doing shots in his office. Charles was a little pissed that time!" he said, shaking his head.

I returned to my desk, stunned. I didn't know what to tell Charles, if anything. Should I rat out my new colleagues or take the bullet for them? Blair wouldn't have hesitated to throw me under the nearest bus, but Morgan seemed like a great person. I finally decided to tell Charles the truth. I emailed him the news: "They're at *The Avengers*." My phone rang within seconds.

"They are *where*?" asked Charles.

"Apparently they went to a movie," I answered.

"Oh dear God, what on earth are they thinking? Just what we need—a picture and headline showing McDermott's staffers walking out of a movie theater eating popcorn while on the taxpayers' dime," Charles said fiercely. "When they return, tell them to call me together from my office. Thanks, Allison. I hope you do something fun this weekend. Get out and start making some friends."

I wanted to answer, "Sure, no problem, I have a whole dollar in my pocket, and no time on my hands, Charles." Instead, I kept my mouth shut. Another hour passed and the movie bunch came through the office doors talking about how slow their waiter had been. "Charles would like you all to call him from his office," I said, which seemed to dampen their mood.

"Did he say what it's about, Allison?" questioned Morgan.

"I'm not sure," I answered.

"I'll handle this one," Blair stated confidently.

They closed the door but I could still hear the laughter coming from Charles's office. Since they all came out smiling and laughing, I thought Blair must have the magic touch when it came to Charles after all. Maybe he had just told Charles that his dad had signed another check to the new PAC.

"Allison, I'm going to work with Cam on rewording some of tomorrow's remarks for the boss. How late will you be around tonight?" asked Morgan.

"I was planning on leaving at six. I have a date with a large margarita tonight."

"Huh. Well, the date might have to wait a few hours. We'll need you to get the senator's remarks to Trista tonight after I spend some time on them with Cam."

"Okay, I understand, Morgan," I answered.

Soon enough it was 7:00 p.m. I was tired and sick to death of staring at my computer screen. I was organizing my notes for the painful weekly scheduling meeting—for the third time. Morgan and Cam were the only ones in the office. Morgan came to my desk and said, "I'm going to take Cam to dinner at the Monocle. We'll be back to finish up the remarks. Did you think of a theme song yet?"

"Not yet, Morgan, but many options are starting to make the list."

"Sounds great, Allison. And thanks for all you do. Hold down the fort," he said as he put his arm around Cam and hurried out the door.

There was an eerie sound and feeling in the building as I turned on the television in my cubicle to watch the senator's interview on MSNBC. These high-profile interviews were becoming something of a habit for the senator since his election. Charles had started referring to him as the "Senate Flavor of the Month." Senator McDermott was captivating and charismatic—and easy on the eyes, with a charming smile. From fundraisers around the country to interview after interview, everyone wanted a piece of him. I thought about my

frustration and about my piddling salary and decided I was going to adjust my attitude. This job, as Charles often reminded me, was one of the most sought-after positions in America, and I shouldn't take it lightly. The senator was terrific in the MSNBC interview. Feeling proud to call him my boss, I decided to drop him a quick email message of congratulations: "Hi Senator, I just saw you on MSNBC and you were super! Have a great weekend in Minnesota with Karma and the kids. Allison."

Within a matter of seconds he replied: "You are simply the best. Million thanks. Did you get my speech for tomorrow yet?"

I wrote back: "Morgan and Cam are working on it. I'll send it to you and Trista ASAP."

He replied: "I needed it two days ago. Do you have the number for Kim Kardashian?"

"I'm sorry about the remarks, but we'll get them to you ASAP. I don't seem to see Kim Kardashian in your contact list, sir. Do you need her number this weekend?"

"Of course, I need her number tonight or I wouldn't be asking, would I?"

"Got it. I will check and get back to you. Stay tuned."

I took a deep breath. Why does he want Kim Kardashian's phone number? Particularly late on a Friday evening? I began to panic about how I was going to manage this request. It wasn't as if I could find Kim Kardashian's number in the White Pages. I decided to email Lindsay, Rose, Trista, and Charles for their advice—and to alert them to this entertaining request.

"Hi all. The senator is requesting Kim Kardashian's phone number this evening. Do you have it? Thanks, Allison." The responses were amusing and summed up their personalities and work ethic.

Lindsay replied first with: "Nope, sorry."

Then Trista responded: "You've got to be kidding me! Let me think about who might have her number, and I'll check with our donor list. Right now I'm putting the kids to bed, but then I'm on it! Why are you still working?"

Charles was the third to chime in: "He didn't. This smells like Karma. I'm heading over to his house to talk about some other things. Let me see what he's really wanting with this one."

Rose replied fourth: "Good luck!"

As I was shaking my head from Rose's email, Cam and Morgan returned from dinner. "Hey, Allison, thanks for holding down the fort! Anything earth shattering happen?" Morgan asked.

"Ah, well, the senator is looking for Kim Kardashian's telephone number!" I laughed.

"Who?" asked Morgan.

"Kim Kardashian!"

"Who?" asked Morgan, looking confused.

"Kardashian. Kim Kardashian!" I exclaimed again.

"Oh, which office does she work for?"

"Morgan, she's like the most photographed star right now!" I corrected him. For someone who's so into old TV show theme songs, he really wasn't very up on pop culture and celebrity gossip.

"Oh. Well, good luck, Allison. Did you by chance think of our theme song?" he questioned again.

Cam jumped in, "I get the feeling that searching for Kim Kardashian's telephone number is on the top of her list right now. Not searching top television theme songs on the Internet."

Morgan and Cam walked away laughing.

I took a deep breath, wondering who would know Kim Kardashian. Just then, Trista emailed me Kim's contact information. I instantly replied, "Oh, you're a lifesaver! Thank you! Thank you! Thank you!" I had no idea how she'd gotten it, and I didn't care. I was just glad to have Trista in my corner. I forwarded the information to the senator and didn't hear a word back.

A few minutes passed, and Charles called. "Allison, got the remarks yet?"

"Not yet, but Cam and Morgan are working on them."

"Great. He's getting antsy. Oh, by the way, Kim Kardashian's number is about coming to his daughter's sweet-sixteen party. Send me the remarks when you get them."

"Right on it," I assured him.

It was approaching 9:00 p.m. and it had been nearly a thirteen-hour day. I chuckled as I thought about Blair's comment that I didn't know how to count to twelve. Little did anyone know that I worked around the clock for Senator McDermott and was the lowest-paid staffer on his team. I started to daydream about how my life had changed in the past two weeks. I began to worry again about having no money and wondered how I was going to make ends meet. Could a regular kid from South Dakota make it as a Hill staffer? I was still up for the challenge, but I missed home more and more.

Then a message came in from Cam with the finished remarks, and I quickly forwarded them to Trista, Charles, and the senator. I turned off my computer, said good night to Cam and Morgan, and started to walk home. It was dark outside, and I talked to Janet on my cell phone as I walked. As I approached my last corner, my BlackBerry started to buzz repeatedly. Shit. Does this job ever end? Couldn't I please just have thirty minutes to myself?

I checked my BlackBerry and saw that I had five unread messages from Rose, including her last one: "We need to talk immediately on Monday! Have a great weekend, and please copy me on all your messages to and from the senator and Trista."

I wondered what I had done wrong now. I got the senator Kim Kardashian's number (thanks to Trista), and had sent him the remarks as soon as they were available. Next time, maybe I should rent a private plane and hand deliver them with a pitcher of margaritas since I'd never see a payday margarita again. I got home and collapsed on my bed, but couldn't fall asleep. My mind was rapidly spinning. Why did Rose want to speak with me on Monday morning? Why couldn't she just tell me what was up now, instead of waiting?

The weekend passed too quickly. On Monday morning Rose

scolded me for my failure to pay more attention to detail on the senator's schedule and my lack of urgency. She informed me that I'd need to start doing all my work in pencil and handed me a box of freshly sharpened No. 2 pencils. She said maybe the erasers would prevent me from making mistake after mistake. I was to have meetings with her twice a day so she could monitor my performance. Apparently I really needed to grow up and dedicate myself to this position, she said.

When she was the senator's scheduler, she never recalled this many problems, certainly not distressed calls from Anders himself. I tried not to get upset and promised Rose I would rededicate myself to the senator and my work.

This job just didn't seem to be getting any easier.

4

Retreat! Retreat! Staff Retreat!

A few paydays had come and gone, just like all the cash in my checking account. I had burned through a pencil sharpener at work, and I had a new motto written in bright red lipstick on my bathroom mirror: ATD, Allison. Every morning, I said a quick attention-to-detail prayer: "Dear God, let me have ATD today."

Rose and I met twice a day to review the senator's schedule and to double, triple, and quadruple check my work. She had an amazing talent for going over the schedule with a fine-tooth comb, asking unthinkable questions like, "When the senator is dropped off at the

restaurant, on which side of the door will the hostess be standing?" And, "Which hostess is working that night and what's her name?" Then she'd double check that I had faxed the senator's headshot to the hostess to ensure she could "greet him properly" when he arrived. Senator McDermott hated it when people didn't recognize him.

Rose's ATD was tremendous, and I was jealous. I honestly believed that if Rose put something on the schedule with enough detail, the senator would simply do it without even thinking about it. Honestly, I think if we had written *Senator's Bathroom Break*, he'd use the designated time to pee on cue. A few times, when I was feeling extra gutsy, I wanted to put *Sex with Karma* on the schedule just to see his reaction. But I always chickened out. He would probably have sent a gazillion emails asking me to define S-E-X. I'm sure that if I didn't write down the exact positions he was supposed to use, he would have bungled it and blamed me the next morning. A scheduler's work is never done.

One skill I had definitely gained over the past few months was the ability to give any travel agent a run for her money. Watch out, Orbitz and Expedia—Allison Amundson was in town! I was a flight-booking expert extraordinaire. I could recite backwards and forwards the flight times from MSP to DCA, from DCA to MSP, and even a few flight times from DCA to JFK. I had also memorized the flights between MSP and LAX because I had begun booking more and more travel for Karma. I was starting to wonder who I worked for. Although I worked for Senator McDermott, I realized very quickly that I needed to ask "How high?" when Karma said, "Jump," which was happening more and more frequently. It took talent to get all of those stupid airline times down. I thought someday I might audition for Letterman's stupid human tricks. I could go on national late-night TV to display my wacky skill—reciting flight times while standing on one foot, BlackBerrying, and erasing my mistakes from the schedule with my worn-out pencil eraser, all at the same time. Who knew my college degree would come in so handy?!

I was thankful I still had my sense of humor at least. That was partially due to the addition of Janet to the DC office. We had bonded a ton in the past few weeks and escaped from the office together as much as possible. Unfortunately, not as much as we both would have liked. It seemed that when Senator McDermott was in town, I was tied to my desk, and she was always running off to attend a committee hearing, listening to some crazy constituents, or trying to scrounge up some money from the appropriations committee for sick kids. I was working incredibly long and hectic hours, but I had to give Janet credit—she came in a close second. While my job entailed making sure the senator knew the names of the people coming in for his next meeting, Janet seemed to actually be getting things accomplished.

When we did get to steal a few moments away, we laughed about the craziness of the office, gossiped like mad, and began to wonder if we were actually the crazy ones amidst all the madness. I would have pinched myself to see if it was all a bad dream, but I had gotten enough elbow pinches from the senator that my body had developed an immunity.

After my talk with Rose, I followed through on my promise and made a new commitment to my thankless job. I took her words to heart and put all my focus and dedication into being the best scheduler I could possibly be. After all, I was the scheduler for a senator, and jobs on Capitol Hill were highly coveted. I was his gatekeeper, or as everyone else in the office referred to me, I was the senator's bitch. But I didn't let it get to me.

My closet was full of bright colors and trendy skirts. This was due in large part to the credit line that Macy's Visa had graciously extended. One day I decided to spice things up in the office—a new attitude deserved a new look! I replaced my standard navy suit with a tight brown, above-the-knee pencil skirt, a cream satin camisole trimmed with lace, a thin, fitted cream cardigan to match, brown sling-back pumps, and a long pearl necklace to top it all off. I felt sexy;

I felt like my old self. I was ready to hit the Senate floor, and I was taking no prisoners. Succeed or fail, I was ready.

As I walked to work my new sling-backs got stuck in the sidewalks, causing a few heads to turn as I passed by. But I didn't care. Today was Monday and the senator would be in the office all week with a jam-packed schedule until early Friday morning. Karma was scheduled to arrive in DC on Thursday evening, and on Friday morning, they would depart together on a military congressional delegation, or CODEL, with three other senators and their spouses to Iraq and Afghanistan for a weekend trip to visit National Guard members from Minnesota. A CODEL is a government-funded trip abroad for members, designed to give lawmakers firsthand knowledge about matters that are relevant to legislation or national policy.

With the senator traveling, Charles and Rose had planned a mandatory staff retreat in Annapolis, and I was looking forward to seeing Maryland's state capital and all of its historical landmarks. But I was most excited about seeing the cadets that were attending the Naval Academy. I had always been a sucker for a man in a military uniform. As if that weren't enough, I knew the retreat was going to allow me to spend all weekend flirting—I mean working—with Cam, and visiting with Trista in person to swap horror stories. Plus, the senator supposedly wouldn't have BlackBerry reception during his overseas trip, which meant that even though I was to spend the whole weekend working, it actually was going to be a much-needed respite. Or so I thought.

But my Annapolis and Cam daydreaming had to wait. First I needed to survive the next four days without any slip-ups. The senator was scheduled to play tennis at 6:30 a.m. on his regularly reserved Senate tennis court against Senator Marv Starr of Tennessee. Senator Starr was the chairman of the Appropriations Committee and the chief deputy whip. He had a no-nonsense approach, was a media hog, and according to the rumor mill, wasn't very keen on Senator McDermott's instant ego or claim to fame as the "Senate Flavor of the

Month." It had taken me weeks to get their match planned because Starr's scheduler kept avoiding my emails and phone calls. But finally Starr had agreed and McDermott wasn't one to miss an opportunity, even if it occurred over a match of tennis.

I was certain that while he was sweating from chasing and whacking tennis balls, he was going to volley Starr for special Minnesota earmarks. And I was quite sure he was going to offer up some massive campaign donations from his recently formed PAC in exchange. I wondered if our new fundraiser knew of this frequent tactic of his. My guess was she didn't. I was curious to see who'd win the competitive tennis match, the young McDermott or the almost retired Starr. My money was on Starr.

Just as I was about to turn on my computer, the senator came flying in the office, out of breath, in his white T-shirt and shorts, "I can't find my keys! Where are my keys? Keys. Keys. I need my keys," he shouted.

"Sir, can I help?" I asked as I tried not to stare at his overly skinny white legs.

"Tennis keys. Tennis court keys. Where are my keys?" he asked as he tore through his desk drawers, causing papers to fly in all directions.

"Sir, I put the keys in your daily folder in the inside pocket, just as I do each Tuesday morning," I reminded him.

"What? Why would you do a stupid thing like that?" he asked.

"Sir, ah, Rose told me to," I stated.

"Rose isn't that foolish. Find me the keys. Keys. Keys. I need those keys," he mumbled as he reached for his cell phone.

"Rose isn't answering. Rose pick up. Rose," he yelled as he dialed and slammed his phone down.

"Sir, I believe we have an extra set in Lindsay's desk. I'll get them for you," I told him.

"Brilliant, Allison. ATD working today? ATD, Allison? Why didn't you tell me that ten minutes ago?" he asked.

"Here you go, sir," I said, ignoring his latest rude remark. "Good luck."

He snatched the keys from my hand and ran out the door in a huff. "Don't let the door hit you on the way out." I muttered under my breath as I shook my head. He was such an ass.

Within seconds he emailed me, "I'll be late for Starr. This can never ever happen again. Please start to care about my life. I don't appreciate it when you make me late."

I didn't reply, but couldn't stop myself from drafting a response in my head. "If you would look in your daily folder you'd see the keys taped in the same spot they are every Tuesday. Would you like me to wipe your ass for you as well, sir?" Instead I sent an apology, promising it wouldn't happen again.

I shook my head and tried to not let McDermott get to me. Janet arrived, and I told her I needed a coffee break soon. When we returned I felt better, even though Lindsay gave me her typical I-do-all-the-work look. I ignored her immaturity.

As I started to focus on the senator's schedule, Blair came into the office. "Wow, good morning, Allison. Get dressed by Senator Jenkins this morning?" he asked as he passed by my cubicle.

Senator Jenkins was blind and had the distinction of being the youngest senator ever elected to the Senate. And, coincidentally, Janet had developed a C-SPAN crush on him. He also happened to be the Chairman of the Senate Budget Committee, a highly sought-after position. She marveled at how Jenkins would speak from the Senate floor without any notes. According to Janet he had "old-fashioned prestige." The crush had gotten bad. It had started with Janet alerting me whenever he spoke on the Senate floor. But things had gotten worse.

Under the guise of work, she had conned his healthcare legislative assistant into sending her Jenkins's daily clips. All members have their press shop send all the newspaper clippings that feature them around to their staff so they can see what's playing well in the press. By reading Jenkins's clips, Janet learned what issues he was focusing on and where he might be at certain times. She also began memorizing his committee meetings schedule and locations. Janet would plant herself close to the entrance of each committee room, hoping Jenkins would bump into her with his hard cane. So far the tactic hadn't worked, and I thought a few of his staffers were getting suspicious. "Where there's a will, there's a way," I'd tell her each time she'd return to the office defeated.

As I sat thinking about Janet and all of her secret ploys to get Senator Jenkins to fall in love with her, I received an email that made me wish I was a gambler. If I'd bet my hard-earned money on the McDermott-Starr tennis match my bank account balance would have been above a hundred dollars for the first time in weeks. Starr had slaughtered the senator, winning every game in the match. Starr's scheduler was requesting that no more tennis matches be played between our bosses again. "My boss likes his tennis matches to be competitive," the email read. I chuckled and saved the message for future reference. I anticipated needing it for my defense when Rose was called into action by the senator to ask why I never schedule tennis with Starr.

Monday through Wednesday flew by. Thirteen-hour days were starting to feel normal, and I had come to terms with how things were in the office. Lindsay did an excellent job of stirring the senator's tea and never failed to knock on his door to keep him on schedule. Blair was Blair and had zero regard for anyone who didn't come from a wealthy family or whose job title was lower than his. Heidi created more drama in the office than a Broadway show, and Morgan asked me every day if I had found our television theme song. He asked me about that far more often than any other work-related question. Cam kept to himself, but would give me an occasional wink after witnessing some foolish or pompous display by one of our colleagues.

My work life was going more smoothly. Charles told me he was seeing significant improvement in my performance. He encouraged me to continue to improve and learn from Rose. I was incredibly grateful for the sympathetic ears of Trista, Veronica, and Janet—all of whom had common sense, wit, and a bit of welcomed midwestern humility.

Senator McDermott kept a very busy and tight schedule, often

working from 6:00 a.m. to 10:00 p.m. each day. He was tireless in his attempt to become an increasingly prominent member of the Senate. He never missed an opportunity to jump into the spotlight, which was most certainly at the expense of his family life. As I witnessed his antics, I hoped I'd never marry a man like him. I hoped my future husband would take at least ten minutes out of each day to pick up the telephone to call me. I felt sure Karma would have settled for a BlackBerry message. Lord knows, Senator McDermott had those down pat! But it seemed he never called or emailed his family unless someone asked how they were doing, and even then, only as an afterthought. I guess when it came to family, his ATD wasn't working properly.

On Thursday morning I arrived at the office early. I wanted a jump start on the day because I knew everyone would be stressed with the senator and Karma departing on the military CODEL the next morning and with the mandatory staff retreat fast approaching. While it was a mandatory staff retreat, getting Senate staffers to break away from their DC computers for a weekend was all but impossible. Staffers like Cam spent their weekends catching up on their daily work and preparing for the upcoming week.

Just as I was digging in, my telephone rang. I recognized the Minnesota area code and thought it was awfully early for a constituent to be calling in. I answered the call, only to regretfully learn that it was Margot, the McDermott's nanny and Karma's personal assistant. Margot was in her late thirties and still single, and it was quite clear why. She was a firecracker who acted like she was on speed all the time. She was constantly saying inappropriate things to people and often got herself into precarious situations. She also was extremely friendly. After a few drinks you could get Margot to dish out all the McDermott household gossip without holding back. She cared deeply about the McDermott family, but didn't have basic memory, organizational skills, or common sense. She also had a hard time knowing when she was crossing the fat line between campaign and public ethics. Margot took it upon herself to become "close personal friends" with the senator's male donors. She made sure the return on their financial donations was nothing less than orgasmic.

"Hi Allison! It's Margot. I need your help right now. Drop everything!" she exclaimed.

I was becoming accustomed to these "emergency" calls from Margot. It seemed there was always some drama that she needed assistance with. Her last emergency call was when she and Colonel, the senator's live-in father, got in an argument over who lost the remote control. Both Margot and Colonel liked to toss back a few happy hour drinks, and this often resulted in some sort of dispute that would have to be handled by some unlucky staffer. Most of the time, I was the unlucky staffer. Margot could be incredibly hard to deal with, and I had started to believe the rumors that she was a user of what was euphemistically called "nose candy."

"Hi Margot, how can I help you today?" I asked, biting my lower lip.

"Karma can't find her passport for tomorrow's trip!" she exclaimed frantically.

"Margot, I emailed you a few weeks ago and specifically asked about Karma's passport because a military CODEL requires an official government passport. Are you saying Karma can't find her official government passport?"

"Ah, ah, I don't know. She just emailed me at 3:00 a.m. It says: 'I can't find my passport. Help! Call Allison!'"

"Um, where is Karma right now?" I asked.

"She's been in Los Angeles since last week. Tonight she'll fly straight from LA to DC," she answered.

"Crap!" I answered. "Well, let me see what we can do."

"Thanks, Allison! I'm going to bring Colonel to the VA today," she said, "but I'll have my phone on," she added.

I took a deep breath and decided I would first email the CODEL's trip coordinator assigned by the military and beg for forgiveness. Next, to cover my tracks, I emailed the following message to Charles, Rose,

Trista, and Lindsay: "Hi all, Margot called and said Karma can't find her official passport. I have sent the CODEL coordinator a message requesting assistance. Stay tuned. Allison."

Just like clockwork their responses started to fly in, and soon I was overwhelmed with BlackBerry messages. Did they sleep with their BlackBerrys? Have sex with their BlackBerrys? *Oh, I'm sorry, honey, it's a message from Allison. Hold on to that thought and hard-on please.*

Charles was straightforward: "Need to get it resolved immediately."

Then there was the typical Rose reply: "I asked you to make sure Karma had her passport for this trip last week. Why didn't you do this?" To which I replied: "I did check with Margot last week and she confirmed all was okay." To which she replied: "Did you follow up with Margot since last week?" To which I replied: "Umm, no, I assumed it was okay." To which she replied: "Next time, you must follow up and be attentive to detail, Allison."

Trista's message made me laugh: "Oh Lordy!"

Lindsay showcased her true team mentality: "Good luck!"

I received a follow-up message from the CODEL trip coordinator. "We can issue a new passport for tomorrow morning if you get us Mrs. McDermott's birth certificate, two passport photos, and her completed application by 5:00 p.m. today."

Without skipping a beat, I called Margot. "Hi Margot, we can get Karma a new passport for tomorrow morning but I need you to get me her birth certificate, two passport photos, and her completed application by this afternoon. I think some of the Minnesota office staff will be flying out here this afternoon for the retreat. They could bring those materials with them, and I'll hand it to an intern to hand-deliver it to be processed."

"Okay, back up, Allison. What type of photos do you need?" she asked.

"Passport pictures that are wallet-sized close-ups of her face. You can have them taken at any post office," I answered.

"I'll just use some of her modeling shots," she answered.

"Um, okay, we can try that," I said, thinking there was no way those would work for a government-issued ID. I began searching through the Karma folders Rose had given me to see if perhaps there were extra passport photos from the first time Karma lost her passport. Luckily, there were. I breathed a sigh of relief. This was one less thing for Margot to worry about. "How about the passport application? Can you get Karma to fax a signed, completed one to you?" I asked.

"Oh, great idea, Allison. Will you fill out her application and fax it to her?"

"Um, well, I don't have any of Karma's personal information, and the senator will arrive at the office in fifteen minutes," I answered.

"Oh, I'll call Anders and tell him what happened. He'll understand that you need to correct your mistake," she generously offered.

"Margot, I asked you about this a week ago," I corrected her.

"Allison, we can't live each day worrying about our past mistakes. Today, we must focus on today," she lectured. I wanted to ask what she was taking today, and if she could spare any.

"Oh, just forget it, Margot. I'll see what I can do," I said, ending the call.

I printed out the passport application and was stuck on line one. I decided to scan and email Karma the application. I asked her to print it out and fax it back to both Trista and me. Next, I called Karma and got her voice mail. I left her detailed instructions. I emailed Trista asking if she minded packing the necessary paperwork in her DC-bound suitcase. Trista reassured me that there was no problem, and we made arrangements to meet outside the Senate Hart Building in the late afternoon. I called Margot again and told her to get the passport paperwork and Karma's birth certificate to Trista ASAP.

A few hours passed and I was able to perform my duties without much drama. And then Blair came to my desk. "Allison, Allison, I need to get a press interview scheduled before the senator departs for Iraq and you're not returning my emails," he said angrily.

"Blair, we've been through this same drill a hundred times. You

know Charles has the final say. I forwarded your messages to him, and I'm waiting for his response."

"Allison, this interview is paramount! The senator is going off to Iraq to serve steaks to Minnesota guardsmen, and we need to get the headlines," he pompously informed me.

"I understand, but I need to let Charles make that decision," I corrected him.

Charles came out of his office and said, "Let's try and get him scheduled for an interview this evening, timed for coverage live for the 6:00 p.m. newscasts, Blair."

"Allison, did you hear that or do I need to speak in sign language since it looks like Jenkins chose your wardrobe today," he laughed. Blair was always so compassionate and politically correct. A legacy of all that expensive private education, I guess.

"Ah, I have one sign for you!" I said, barely holding back the urge to flip him off. "Blair, I'll hold time between 6:30 p.m. and 7:00 p.m. for you. Please let me know the details."

He gave me a thumbs-up and walked over to Lindsay's desk. "Okay, who should do the press advance for the interview?" she asked.

"How about Janet since she knows about organizing the steak feed with the military?" Blair suggested.

"I'll go tell her," laughed Lindsay.

"Janet, I need an advance memo written for the senator's interview at 6:30 p.m. tonight by 1:30 p.m. today," she said in a fierce tone.

"Ah… I have constituent policy meetings booked every fifteen minutes until 6:00 p.m.," Janet told her.

"Well, it's your issue. You're responsible," stated Lindsay. "Get it done," she ordered as if she had any sort of authority.

"He's doing a health care interview about Iraq today?" questioned Janet.

"No, it's about the steaks-to-soldiers event," Lindsay replied as she walked away, rolling her eyes.

"Oh, boy!" Janet said as she got her legislative correspondent to cover her constituent meetings. I knew how much it bothered Janet to have Minnesota health care leaders travel to DC for policy meetings expecting to speak with her or the senator and instead getting her legislative correspondent. Not only was he less qualified than Janet, but many of them had never met him. But she passed off her meetings and finished the advance memo and sent it to Blair and Lindsay.

Moments later Blair came running down the hallway, "Janet, where are the questions and answers?"

"What?" asked Janet.

"You didn't write up all the possible questions the senator might get asked by the reporters and your answers to them," Blair said in a panic.

"I need to draft answers to *all the possible questions* the reporters might ask about Iraq right now?" Janet asked.

"Ahh, yes, Janet," he responded sarcastically. "Welcome to DC and Iraq!"

Lindsay, who always had one ear on everyone else's conversations, decided to step in to intervene. "Janet, you're the staff person assigned. You'll need to redo your advance memo to include any possible question that might get asked," Lindsay informed her.

"Easy for you to say!" Janet stated. A few minutes later she sent me a quick email: "How am I supposed to know anything about Iraq?"

I tried to comfort her. "You can do this. Go to the shared drive and online. Read others' talking points and answers. Look at Jenkins's stuff, and make it sound like McDermott."

Janet finished her memo without further push-back from Blair or Lindsay. But it was a rude awakening for her to realize that her cherished senator was high maintenance, and possibly a phony.

I couldn't believe my ears as I hung up the phone with Trista. She had just finished filling me in about how our little passport project was going. Margot had filled out Karma's passport information with her own personal information and then forged Karma's signature in purple crayon by tracing it from an autographed photo. Unbelievable. What a dumbass. She needed more hand-holding than a kindergartener! For

passport pictures, Margot had selected face shots of Mrs. McDermott that also showed her bare shoulders. I said a silent prayer of thanks that I had located her old passport photos, since Margot's contributions certainly would not have been accepted by the State Department. Thankfully—amazingly—the elusive birth certificate was authentic. Trista was already late leaving for the Minneapolis airport and asked me to take over Operation Karma Passport.

Full of dread, I called Margot and informed her that we would need Karma's information on the application and her signature. She told me Karma was already on a flight to DC, which was why she'd used her own information, thinking no one would notice. I wanted to remind her that we were dealing with the US State Department, that what she'd just attempted was a federal crime, and that any passport officer would have picked up on the forgery immediately. However, I kept my mouth shut. Back to square one, I thought. I called the CODEL trip coordinator again and explained the situation. He assured me that if I was able to get Karma's signed application to him by 8:00 p.m. they'd do special processing and her passport would be ready by the time the military plane took off.

To cover my ass, I went to Charles and told him what had happened. Charles just shook his head and said, "I don't want to hear any more. Karma and Margot are quite the duo. Just figure it out and keep me in the loop. Thanks, Allison."

Thankfully, Cam was the staffer designated to pick up Karma from the airport. I asked if I could tag along to get her to fill out her passport application. He was nice about it and even offered to drive me over to drop it off for processing so I wouldn't have to use the Metro.

It was almost 6:30 p.m., and Senator McDermott was getting overly anxious about his upcoming press interview. Blair was in his office, and I could see the senator pacing the floor, reading and flipping through the pages of Janet's advance memo. He was desperately trying to memorize all the talking points. Blair watched the senator in amazement with the blind adoration of a high-school crush. It made me want to vomit.

"Where is Janet?" screamed the senator as he came out of his office. Janet came around the corner and he said, "Let's go, Janet." She gave him a puzzled look. "We have an interview, don't we?"

"Oh, you bet," she answered, as Blair stared in shock that the senator invited her to attend with him.

Janet returned from the interview just before Cam and I were heading out for the next phase of Operation Karma Passport. "Okay, so basically, I think I just got bitch-slapped by the senator," she whispered.

"Uh oh, for what?" I asked.

"When we were getting on the elevators in the Capitol, I noticed it said Members Only. I didn't know if that meant I could take it or just McDermott. So I kind of stood back. McDermott yelled at me, 'Janet, this isn't Sam's Club! Get on here!'"

We both laughed and wondered if McDermott had ever stepped foot in a Sam's Club. Janet told me she was going to top off her day by walking past Jenkins's office before heading home. Just in case.

I was excited to go with Cam on Operation Karma Passport. Karma was truly a piece of work, and I knew Cam would be nervous to pick her up and drive her back to the senator's apartment. I was happy for the opportunity to go with him and help calm his nerves. Not to mention, it was nice to spend a little time alone with him. Karma's flight was scheduled to arrive on time and, thankfully, traffic was light. We arrived early and sat in short-term parking, waiting for her call.

It was the perfect opportunity to chat with Cam a little bit to learn more about him. Much to my dismay, our conversation was pretty awkward. I did all the talking and he did a lot of listening. I had a horrible habit of rambling whenever I got nervous. Finally Karma called Cam, asking to be picked up at door seven. We had almost made our way there when she called again to ask if we went to the wrong airport.

Karma was dressed in a black linen dress and a white and black hat. Her height and model-like physique made her stand out, and

she turned heads as she walked down the sidewalk. Without lifting a finger toward her luggage, she opened the car door and sat in the backseat. Cam got her luggage and carefully placed it in the trunk. We sat in silence, and I decided to break the ice with the latest news about Operation Karma Passport.

"I can't deal with all this stress! I need to have my hair blown out tonight—not worry about chasing a passport paper trail," she snapped.

"Mrs. McDermott, I'll get the passport processed, but I was hoping you'd fill out the application."

"Why am I doing this now? Don't they know who I am?" she asked.

"Everyone needs a passport, especially in today's world," Cam offered in an effort to help me out.

"What country am I going to again?" Karma asked. Before I could answer, she continued, "Did they schedule any spouse downtime activities? I really can't stand drinking tea with the other Senate spouses. They're all so drab."

"You're traveling to Afghanistan and Iraq," I reminded her. "And your schedule is very tight. I don't recall any spouse downtime."

"I hope we'll have some time to walk around the markets to do some international shopping," she said. I gave Cam a look of disbelief. I couldn't imagine Karma wearing a hijab. I wondered if she even knew there was a war going on.

Without much objection, Karma accurately completed the passport application. As we pulled up to our destination, she didn't seem to recognize the senator's apartment building. When she got out of the car she headed toward the wrong one. "It's that building," I told her, pointing in the opposite direction. "I'll email the senator when your passport is ready. I hope you have a great evening," I chirped as she walked away without even looking at me.

After she walked into the senator's building, Cam hit my shoulder and said, "I don't think she's ever been here."

"I don't think so either."

Next we went to drop off Karma's application. "Here, I think this is the building you need," Cam said as he dropped me off. "I'll wait here."

"Oh, you don't have to. This could take hours, given how everything has gone so far and Karma's luck!" I told him, hoping he'd stay anyway.

"I'll drive you back to the office. Hurry up and get that baby processed," he said, smiling.

I was only able to drop off the application and supporting documents and was told that the military CODEL staff would have Karma's passport at the flight door tomorrow morning. I decided to email the senator and copy Rose, Charles, and Lindsay with the update: "Hi Senator, Karma's passport will be hand delivered tomorrow morning to the military aircraft before departure. Allison."

He replied three hours later: "I'd like you to meet the passport staffer and get the passport directly. Then you should give it to Karma. I don't need the other senators knowing about your mistake. And I don't want it to seem like Karma didn't have a passport."

I was just heading to bed when I got his message and felt sick to my stomach. First I wondered how this had become my fault. Then I started to wonder how on earth I'd get past military security on such late notice to get Karma her prized passport. I called Cam and asked if he was ready for Operation Karma Passport, Phase Two. He laughed and agreed to pick me up at 6:30 a.m.

Morning came too quickly and I got up early to pack for the staff retreat in Annapolis. But first I needed to make sure Karma had her passport. Just as I was walking out my apartment door, my cell phone rang. I recognized the Minnesota number as the McDermotts's household line. "Hello?" I answered.

"Oh, good, Allison. It's Margot," she said, out of breath.

"What is it, Margot?" I asked.

"I can't get Colonel to take his medicine and he's running around the house chasing me with his cane," she said seriously.

"Umm, tell him to put the cane down," I suggested, not sure what she wanted from me.

"He's coming at me, Allison," she stated nervously.

"I'm about to go get Karma's passport. Can you deal with this spat between the two of you on your own?" I asked.

"No, no, don't hang up. He's a crazy old man, Allison. Thank you for all your help with Karma's passport," she said in a whiplash change of subject.

"No problem, Margot. Get some sleep!" I closed and hung up. I couldn't deal with her.

As I collapsed into Cam's front seat, I told him about Margot's phone call, and he shook his head. "Are all Senate offices this bizarre?" I asked him.

"I have no idea, but you have a hard job," he stated.

"You *think*!? It's about to get harder if I can't get past security here!" I laughed. "That is, if I even have a job after all of this."

Using my sweet midwestern charm and my official Senate ID, I was able to get Karma's passport from the military CODEL staff. I found her gazing at herself in the women's bathroom mirror. She was dressed in a red linen dress and black sandals. Her hair looked professionally blown out and her makeup was breathtaking. She looked ready for the Grammy Awards, not Operation Steak Feed in Afghanistan and Iraq.

"Oh, Allison, thank God you're here! I need your help. I'm going to practice my lines for being on the plane today. You're perfect to practice with!" she exclaimed.

"Oh, okay," I said, wondering if she knew this wasn't a movie audition.

"It's heart-wrenching to see Iraqi women and children unable to voice their opinions," she said, and then asked, "How was that? Did it sound genuine? I think so," she said to herself. I was almost embarrassed for her. "Well, don't just stand there, Allison. Help me with my luggage," she ordered as she walked out the bathroom door.

As soon as I was free from Karma's view, I hurried toward Cam's car. I didn't care that neither the senator nor Karma thanked me for the extra assistance. I just wanted to get out of there as soon as possible.

Cam dropped me off in front of the building, at a spot behind our retreat bus. I spotted Janet across the street and wondered what was going on. I walked toward her and asked, "What are you doing?"

"Shhhhhh," she said, as she waved her arms to shoo me away. Then I noticed Senator Jenkins was walking up the sidewalk. As if it had been choreographed, Janet walked straight into Jenkins and his cane. He kept walking as if he'd just run into a tree, and she looked defeated. I laughed to myself and rolled my eyes. She was really starting to get out of control, and I tried to think of a way to bring it up with her.

I got on the bus, hoping to get a seat next to Cam. Morgan was already onboard and said, "Allison, sit here, right next to me!"

"You got it, Morgan," I said, as I looked to see where Cam might sit.

I settled in, and thought sitting next to Morgan wouldn't be so bad. I couldn't help but overhear the conversation in the seat in front of me. Blair and Heidi were huddled together criticizing everyone on the bus—except themselves, of course. The two of them shared a unique talent. I had never heard any two people able to dole out so much criticism about such unimportant things.

Blair whispered, "So Heidi, did you see the tie Cam has on today? The horizontal stripes totally clash with the pinstripe suit he's wearing."

"Oh my gosh, I know!" Heidi responded. "But that's nothing compared to the shoes Lindsay's wearing this morning. I mean flats with a skirt—are you kidding me?"

As they babbled on, I thought it was no mystery why we were having a staff retreat. If this was how everyone in the office talked about one another, we certainly needed to find a way to create some cohesiveness. I wondered what they would have said about me had I not been sitting directly behind them. I was troubled that though Morgan could also hear their sniping comments, he laughed with

them rather than stopping their high-school antics. I also noticed that Janet was sitting across from Cam, and she'd somehow gotten him to chat her ear off. Janet had a way of getting anyone to speak to her, probably even a mute. Rather than getting jealous, though, I knew the setup could work to my advantage. If I knew Janet, and I did, she'd pump Cam for personal information and fill me in on all of the dirty details tonight in our shared room. And seeing as she was a smitten kitten with Senator Jenkins, I knew she was no competition. Hats off to Janet, I thought.

Annapolis was a welcome sight. I was thankful that the senator and Karma were in the hands of the US military. If anyone could handle them, it was our men and women in uniform. Also, it would be awfully hard to complain about anything from Iraq or Afghanistan via a BlackBerry. The coast was clear, and I was ready for a three-day break from the senator's nonstop demands via one-line messages.

When the bus arrived at the beautiful coastal hotel, Charles announced the evening's schedule. "Folks, we have to do a few scheduled meetings because Rose needs to be able to account for this travel as business on the books. Our first meeting is tonight over dinner, and you are all required to attend. Rose and Lindsay have created a few activities to build teamwork. I'll see you all at 6:00 p.m. sharp. Please, no drinking until 6:30 p.m.," he ordered. I was dying to get the 411 from Janet as we rushed to our room to trade stories.

"Cam is so quiet, but he really seems like a nice guy," Janet said.

"Oh, you can do much better than that!" I exclaimed, "What did you learn? Don't hold back," I ordered excitedly.

"Geez, it's hard to remember. Oh, I did get that he hasn't dated anyone in a long time. In fact, I don't think he's ever been on a date with a woman," she pondered.

"You don't think… ?" I asked.

"No, too Catholic. I think he's just shy and more focused on work," Janet answered. "Tonight at dinner, sit by him and flirt."

Janet was dreading the team-building dinner and I told her it would be fine, although I must admit I felt nauseous as hell. I couldn't let on or Janet would have bailed in a matter of seconds. "The only ice-breaking I'm planning on participating in is the ice I'll be chomping on from my Diet Coke," Janet said sarcastically as we left the room.

When we arrived for dinner, Rose was at the door sticking names of famous people onto everyone's backs and explaining the rules. "You can only ask questions to others about whose name is on your back. We tried to match celebrities with your personalities," she joyfully exclaimed.

"You've got to be kidding me," said Janet, as she rolled her eyes at me.

"Oh, come on, lose the attitude," I told her. As I turned to show Janet my name she roared in heavy laughter. "Am I a female?" I asked Janet.

"Yes!" said Charles, entering the game.

"Am I in politics?" I asked Charles.

"No!" he told me as he walked away to continue coasting around the room.

Then Morgan showed up. "Am I in movies?" I asked him.

"I have no idea!" Morgan answered.

"Hey, Blair, is Allison's person in movies?" he shouted across the room.

Blair answered loudly, "Better not be, we were trying to match up personalities. Unless it's the wicked witch from *The Wizard of Oz*!"

Great, I thought. Rose and Lindsay wrote these up; I'm doomed. Just then, Trista came over and offered, "I'll rescue you if you rescue me!"

"You got it!" I answered, as I ripped off her name piece. She did the same and handed it over to me.

"Tammy Faye Baker." I looked at it, stunned.

"Note to self: lighten up on the daily makeup," laughed Blair as he shook his head.

"I guess tonight I'll be leading the dinner prayer." I laughed to Trista.

"Now we're ready for our second icebreaker," announced Rose.

"For seating arrangements tonight, you'll sit in alphabetical order according to first names."

"Allison, you start. Blair, you're next to Allison," ordered Lindsay.

"Fantastic. Blair. Why couldn't my name be Yolanda?" I asked Charles.

"We're not finished yet. Your dinner partner tonight will be feeding you dinner," instructed Rose.

"You have got to be kidding me," Janet whined as she gave me a look of death.

"Allison, you really shouldn't be eating tonight, I mean look at you!" Blair said. I tried my hardest to ignore him. "Allison, maybe we'll just do the half salad tonight—without dressing—and skip the beef. You are getting a little heavy, and should be eating only organic."

"I prefer a full cut of manly beef, and Lord knows you'll never be able to give that to me," I retorted.

Dinner was treacherous, and I caught Janet escaping out of the room early. I would have given anything to have been that savvy. After a few more excruciating team-building exercises, I was able to join her in our room. "Oh my God, what were Rose and Lindsay thinking?" she asked while she browsed her online dating matches from eHarmony.

"I'm heading out tonight with everyone, are you coming along?" I asked.

"No, I'm going to call it an early night. I have some online research to do. I read that Jenkins is an online dater. I think maybe I can find him and we'll get matched!" she exclaimed.

She was relentless about Jenkins. I couldn't help but laugh at her plan, and then asked, "Okay, should I wake you up when I get in tonight?"

"Only if you have some good dirt to share. I just hate staff retreats and forced socialization," she whined as she continued clicking through her "matches."

"I know, I know," I replied. "But this is politics and it's all about relationships."

"Then get me a relationship with Jenkins, and I'll be all politicked out! He can punch my ballot any day!" she laughed.

"Good luck finding him. Good night!" I told her as I closed the hotel door and walked down the hallway.

*　　　*　　　*　　　*　　　*　　　*

"Here, I think it's this room," I told Cam. "Oh, the key doesn't seem to work!" I laughed.

"Try it this way!" Cam said, flipping the magnetic keycard around.

"Oh you have the magic touch!" I said as the door unlocked.

"Okay, well, I'll see you tomorrow, Allison," he said, high-fiving me as he walked away.

"Right!" I said, wishing for a goodnight kiss instead.

"Janet, wake up!" I yelled as I gave her a push.

"Unless you have major news, zip your lips and go to bed, Allison," she ordered.

"Janet, wake up!" I yelled.

"Okay, this better be good. Is there a Diet Coke?"

"Here," I said, handing her a pop. "You'll never guess what happened! Everyone was super drunk. Morgan was absolutely gone, and when Blair tried to sneak the interns into the bar, Morgan got right up in the bouncer's face and said, 'Let them in,' as he waved his fist. The bouncer called the police and Blair got kicked out before they arrived. The interns aren't even twenty-one! The police came and we all about died. Morgan told the police we were from Senator Malloy's office—and that they couldn't tell us what to do because we wrote the law!" I exclaimed without taking a breath.

"Wait, Blair got kicked out? I didn't know Edina kings got kicked out of anything!" Janet grumbled, referring to Blair's hometown.

"Yeah, it was ridiculous. He was all over an intern and tried to get her into the bar and she was underage. I think she's like nineteen years old," I said incredulously.

"Morgan must have been bombed," Janet said.

"Yes! Can you believe he told the police we were from a different Senate office?" I said, trying to wake Janet up. "There's more! You goof, sit up!" I insisted. "After the police came, Cam asked if I wanted to leave and I said yes. When we were walking back to the hotel, we could hear Heidi's annoying voice but we couldn't see her. Then—I'm not kidding—we both almost died of laughter when we saw Heidi on her knees in the middle of the hotel alley giving a blow job to that intern from Wisconsin."

"Oh, that's a very gross visual," shrieked Janet.

"She was super drunk!" I exclaimed and continued, "She was all over everyone."

"Isn't she diabetic?" asked Janet.

"I think so," I answered.

"Huh, I didn't think diabetics should be drinking."

"Well, maybe giving an intern a blow job is the cure! I'm not kidding you, it was out of control!"

"Cam walked you back?" asked Janet.

"Yeah, but it was harmless. I got a high-five at the door. Any luck matching up with Jenkins?"

"No, but I'll try and try again," she said, laughing at herself. "Damn, maybe all this hooking up will rub off on us!"

"What time do we need to set the alarm so we don't upset Charles?"

"It's already set for 7:00 a.m.! Good night!" said Janet.

The next morning, like dedicated employees, we were the first to arrive for our scheduled staff meeting. Charles opened the meeting right on time and asked where Heidi was. Lindsay and Rose offered to go knock on her door.

"I hear we need to give a round of applause to Blair," Charles said. "Gang, last night was Blair's first time getting removed from a drinking establishment," he announced. I couldn't believe it; Blair had gotten kicked out of a bar on a staff retreat and was being lauded by the chief of staff. Could this golden boy do nothing wrong? Apparently, daddy had written another check. "Son, job well done. Now, moving right along, folks, while the senator is in Iraq this weekend, we wanted to share a video message from him with all of you," informed Charles.

"This ought to be good," Trista whispered to me.

"Yeah, I wonder if he'll talk about ATD!" I laughed.

The professional video lasted just under five minutes. It was a message about the senator's priorities for the upcoming year, which included agriculture funding, housing crisis solutions, strategies for an economic recovery, and eliminating our dependence on foreign oil. Charles walked to the front of the room after the clip and said, "You all do amazing work for the boss. While he can be demanding at times, we are working for one of the most talented senators in the United States. And friends, that's why we have another ten-minute video just for you from Anders."

Lindsay and Rose opened the door and helped Heidi to a seat. She looked like death warmed over. Janet leaned over to me and said, "Diabetic shock, what an idiot!"

"I couldn't agree more," I said, and told her to hush.

As the video began, I couldn't believe what I was seeing. I sat there stunned. I gave Janet a whack under the table. Could this really be happening? Senator McDermott did have talent and was the Senate's current "Flavor of the Month," but was I hearing this video correctly? Anders had been a senator for less than one term, but the video was alluding.... As I was contemplating what I'd just heard, Charles turned the lights on and clapped. He asked us to all stand up.

"Team, we're running for President of the United States!" he yelled. "Anders and Karma are thrilled and ready for an all-hands-on-deck campaign," he continued.

My life was about to get one thousand times worse.

"Wow, that's great!" cheered Blair.

"Umm, what does this mean for our sugar beet subsidies in the Farm Bill?" panicked Morgan.

"Relax! This is major news. We'll cover all your questions later," reassured Charles. "But first, we've asked a campaign election law expert, Karl Rove, to come speak with you all today about campaign ethics," he joyfully stated.

Rose quickly added, "We'll have a celebration dinner tonight after Mr. Rove's presentation and then you're on your own to celebrate!"

I sat, stunned, through Mr. Rove's presentation, but learned the basic ethics principles: no political activity on government equipment, office space, or time. However, I could do scheduling for official and campaign events. The presentation was loaded with information, and after three long hours, we adjourned until the big celebration dinner.

Janet and I walked back to our room and crashed onto our beds. Janet was excited for the senator. I had an ultra bitch of a stomachache. As the clock struck 6:00 p.m., both Janet and I dreaded the thought of a celebration dinner. We were pleasantly surprised when dinner was much more relaxed than the previous evening and free of icebreakers. Predictably, Janet escaped dinner early and headed back to the room for Internet time.

Cam settled into her empty seat and asked me to walk the pier with him. I jumped at the opportunity. Toward the end of our walk we unfortunately ran into Blair, Heidi, and Morgan, who asked us to join them for dancing and music at the Ram's Head Tavern. Unable to gracefully decline, we followed behind them. I was pleasantly surprised when we entered the bar—it was packed with tons of boys from the Naval Academy. If nothing else, the night would be full of eye candy.

Cam, a native of small-town northern Minnesota, didn't like to dance and neither did Morgan. The two of them sat at the table and people watched. Morgan also seemed to enjoy watching the Naval cadets. While Blair strutted around the room like a peacock, I enjoyed myself with Cam and thought this was the first time I had seen him let loose a little. It was good to know that it only took a few drinks.

All the official retreat activities were completed, and our bus was leaving early in the morning. None of us cared about getting sleep so we decided to close the place down. While Blair, Heidi, and I laughed and danced to Madonna's "Like a Virgin," Morgan noticed my BlackBerry going off repeatedly and took it upon himself to read the messages. Morgan approached our self-made dance floor and said, "The senator is emailing you about his tennis game on Tuesday, Allison."

"For Christ's sake, isn't he still in Iraq?" I yelled, still dancing.

"Yes," said Morgan.

"Morgan, I don't care about his tennis game right now," I told him, bumping hips with Blair.

"Okay, I'll answer him," Morgan told me.

"Tell him to go hit his balls against Karma," I laughed, knowing I'd had too many drinks.

"Will do!" Morgan said as he walked away.

Cam helped me back to my room and left again without much more than a friendly hug. I felt defeated, but had thoroughly enjoyed my time with him, Morgan, Heidi, and even Blair.

The next morning I realized that Morgan had actually emailed the senator my line about his balls in reply to his tennis question. Shit! It was going to be a very long bus ride back to Capitol Hill, which I decided was more properly deemed Capitol Hell.

5
Boycott the BlackBerry

W̲e returned from Annapolis and I spent Sunday afternoon washing baskets full of dirty laundry and watching the *Project Runway* marathon with Veronica. Strictly out of habit, I found myself checking my BlackBerry every fifteen minutes. Surprisingly, I had received no new messages from the senator, Charles, Janet, or Rose. Veronica was getting annoyed at my compulsive need to repeatedly turn the BlackBerry off and on again to make sure it was working properly. While the silence was golden, I was surprised the senator did not have terse words for me about the tennis balls message. Or something about Karma needing a staffer to

drive her to Reagan National Airport for her early-morning flight to Minnesota. Rose would be so proud if she could see me now, anticipating their needs. The senator should finally be happy with my ATD.

Just before the *Project Runway* finale, my cell phone rang. It was Janet. "Hey, how are you?" I asked.

"Ugh, did you see the news?" she asked.

"Nope, we've been watching the entire season of *Project Runway*. What's going on?" I asked.

"Jenkins is taking aim at the senator for his lack of conservative voting and spineless politics!" she swiped.

"Oh, well, we better get used to seeing McDermott in the line of fire now that he's officially in the big race," I told her.

"Of all people, my lover Jenkins," Janet continued.

"Ah, wait a minute there, Juliet. Does Jenkins even know who you are?" I asked.

Janet giggled in her contagious manner and said, "You just wait. When I'm First Lady with my sex machine and lover, President Jenkins, you can host a reality show to redecorate the White House. Just like *Project Runway*. It'll be *Project Pennsylvania Avenue!*"

"Geez, I cannot wait to decorate for the blind president and his leopard-print-loving wife."

"I better get back online to search for Jenkins. Ugh, I do not want to work tomorrow! The weekly Sunday night stomachache strikes again," complained Janet.

"I know, I know. But look at it this way. Now at least we have options—either you'll be married to President Jenkins or we'll be President McDermott's bitches!" I laughed. "On that horrible thought, hurry up and find Jenkins online and land yourself a date!"

After I hung up Veronica asked what the call was all about. I told her, but swore her to secrecy. She was shocked. She worked as a staff assistant for Senator Thomas. He was from my home state of South Dakota. According to her stories, he seemed to be the complete opposite of Anders. She described him as kind, caring, principled, and patient. And, at six foot five with his homegrown farm-boy build, he was easy on the eyes as well. I envied her and her Senate office.

Janet was right—the late-Sunday-evening stomachache returned as I tossed restlessly in my bed. I watched the hours on the clock tick away and prayed the next week would be better. At some point, life had to get better. It couldn't get much worse.

*   *   *   *   *   *

After little sleep, I woke up before my alarm clock went off at 5:45 a.m. Without hesitating I quickly checked my BlackBerry for any overnight messages. Shit. Seventeen unread messages from McDermott. I fell back onto my bed to scroll through them. They read, in order:

1:45 a.m.	Tennis balls? LOL. Anders.
1:46 a.m.	Need home number for Chairman Jenkins.
2:15 a.m.	Hello? Are you there?
2:16 a.m.	I need Jenkins's number now.
2:19 a.m.	Jenkins! Damn it Jenkins!
2:25 a.m.	Answer me. Did you receive my messages?
2:55 a.m.	Call me.
3:30 a.m.	Rose, pls talk to Allison about being more responsive to my needs. Improvement necessary.
3:31 a.m.	Schedule lunch with Jenkins for tomorrow.
3:33 a.m.	Karma will need ride to airport.
4:00 a.m.	Anyone home? Anyone working for me? Do I pay your salary?
4:15 a.m.	Need kids' school schedule faxed to Karma.
4:55 a.m.	How many frequent-flier miles do I have? Karma? Kids' accounts?
5:12 a.m.	Apartment is out of decaffeinated coffee. Karma would like some this morning and

	prefers fresh beans. Can you have Cam drop some off?
5:15 a.m.	Allison? Allison? Earth to Allison? Come in, Allison.
5:16 a.m.	Charles, need Jenkins's number and lunch plan.
5:30 a.m.	Did not sleep well. Pls have driver pick me up at 9 and have Cam leave coffee with concierge.

And a terrific top-of-the-morning to you, Senator Asshole—I mean—Senator McDermott.

I dressed quickly and on my morning commute I tried desperately to fight back tears. Charles kept telling me that my position was one of the most sought after on Capitol Hill. According to him, it was either scheduling for McDermott, or he could help me land a job as the official Senate elevator girl. Apparently that gig had a uniform, including hat. At first, I'd thought Charles was joking, but after spending some time in DC, I realized he wasn't. Elevator girls were stuck riding up and down with senators all day. It could be worse, I thought as I approached our office.

Last to go home and first to come in, I told myself as I smuggled a handful of the Minnesota-made Salted Nut Rolls out of our reception area and turned on my computer.

Thankfully, Cam was right behind me, and I didn't waste any time. "Hey, I'm really sorry but the senator wants you to bring Karma some decaffeinated coffee beans this morning."

"What?" laughed Cam.

"Sorry, I hate to be the one to ask you. But apparently they're out of coffee. The senator emailed me and asked that you bring them fresh beans," I said with a slight smile.

"Not a problem," answered Cam.

"You're the best. Just leave the beans with the building's concierge. I'll email the senator that you're on the way!"

Cam left and the empty feel of the office returned. It was mighty quiet. Thankfully I got more accomplished when Heidi and Blair weren't around wreaking havoc. As the clock approached 8:00 a.m., the office quickly started to fill. Stories from the retreat began circulating. Heidi, dressed in her routine black suit, still looked terrible and Blair was devising his plan of attack for the senator's big media announcement.

"Good morning, team!" Morgan blurted out as he walked into the office. "Hey, Allison, got our theme song picked out yet?"

"How about 'Movin' on Up' from *The Jeffersons*?" I asked and jokingly sang, "Since we will be movin' on up to the East Side, to that deluxe White House in the sky. We finally got a piece of the pie!"

Morgan jumped in and belted, "Fish don't fry in the kitchen. Beans don't burn on the grill. We're gonna get a White House chef crew. Just as soon as we get offa this hill!"

"I like it. I like it!" I laughed, thinking that the team-building retreat might have worked.

Morgan continued to sing and grabbed Blair to dance with him. "Well, we are movin' on up to that East Side. To a deluxe White House in the sky. Yes, we are movin' on up." When Morgan continued down the hallway, Blair stopped playing around.

"Allison, I need at least a two-hour block of time this week for the senator to make his big official announcement," he demanded.

"Oh, did Charles agree?" I questioned.

"Look, Allison, I know the drill. Charles told me to work hand-in-hand with you about this announcement," he stated.

"Okay," I said.

"What do you have, Allison? What will work?" Blair asked impatiently.

"Umm, I'll need to reschedule a few appointments, talk to Trista, and email you the time," I answered.

"Oh, come on, Allison. Charles said we need to work together on this. Do you need me to find you the open time on the calendar?

Just cancel a few constituent meetings if you need to. Nothing is more important this week than the senator's announcement," Blair groused.

"If it was only that easy, Blair. Boy, do you have a lot to learn about public service. His constituents actually have to like him to elect him," I squawked back.

Blair walked away in his typical pouting manner, singing, "When we move on up to the East Side to that big White House in the sky, we'll need a new scheduler cause this one will be staying on the Hill!"

I would not let Blair get to me. To lift my spirits, I decided to send Cam a quick email message. "Thanks again for picking up coffee for Karma! You saved me! Annapolis was fun. Rudy has offered to buy me and a friend drinks and dinner at Oceanaire. Let me know if you're game! Have a great day! Allison."

Rudy was a lobbyist for many Minnesota clients, and I regularly scheduled meetings with the senator for him. Rudy seemed to appreciate my hard work and would sometimes reward me by taking me out to fancy dinners. Dinner on Rudy was basically a blank check for drinking, drinking, and big eating!

"Bingo! I think I might have found Jenkins online finally!" Janet squealed as she nabbed one of my pilfered candy bars and pulled me over to her desk.

"Really? Do tell!"

"His dating profile doesn't have a picture, but it states that he's a conservative politician who describes himself as pragmatic, perceptive, and personable. He likes to play cards, read biographies in braille, and go jet skiing! He's searching for a woman with homegrown values and bestowed faith, and who's unafraid of public exposure," Janet recited from the site.

"I think the Senator Jenkins project has reached a new level!" I said, laughing. "'Public exposure.' I wonder what that kinky guy has in mind! Go get him! Write to him," I ordered.

"Oh, I did. Right away. Now I'm checking and rechecking my email every five minutes waiting for him to reply. Nothing yet," she said, looking at her BlackBerry.

"How can a blind guy go jet skiing?" I asked.

"Trust me, I'll sail Jenkins's boat any day! Anchors away!" laughed Janet as she bounced in her chair.

Janet's made-for-TV-movie love affair with Jenkins reminded me of the senator's lunch request, so I quickly called Jenkins's office. His scheduler made it clear that the chairman not only had no time available, he also didn't want to make time for Senator McDermott. I told Lindsay and, as usual, she rolled her eyes and said, "You'll have to explain the news to the senator and Rose."

No shit, Sherlock. Sorry to disturb you while you make hot tea and stir in honey. I wanted to ask if it was rough making $45,000 a year to boil hot water, drop in two tea bags, and add a teaspoon of honey every day—sometimes even twice a day! But I managed to hold it in.

I walked into Rose's office, surprised to find her reading *What to Expect When You're Expecting*. As I tried to pretend I hadn't seen her reading about pregnancy, Rose looked up and said, "I'm late for the third straight month, my boobs are about to bust out of my shirt, and Anders will kill me if I have to go on maternity leave during his presidential campaign!" For the first time ever, I realized that Rose was a normal, hormonal woman, and she was about to break down in tears in front of me. I was a little out of my league but I tried to comfort her, "Wow, a baby! Congrats! This is so exciting!"

"Anders is going to ask how this happened," Rose said, sounding panicked.

The thought of the senator needing to ask about the birds and the bees amused me. "He'll be thrilled for you, Rose."

As Rose tried to refocus her energy back to work-related conversation, I was taken aback by her genuine worry that Anders would comment about when she decided to start a family. In addition to being offensive, wasn't that illegal?

"Did you need something, Allison?" Rose asked.

"Yes, the senator emailed and asked me to arrange lunch today

for him with Chairman Jenkins. I tried, but Jenkins's scheduler pretty much blew me off."

"Did you ask to speak to his chief of staff?" asked Rose.

"Oh, no. I didn't want to overstep my bounds, and I really get the impression Chairman Jenkins isn't interested in a lunch date with the boss."

"Why don't you talk to Charles and see if he can shake it loose for us?" Rose suggested. "Oh, and Allison, the senator seems concerned about your lack of responsiveness to him. Please make sure you copy me on all messages you send to him and all staff. Thanks!" Her mood swing was dramatic—from romper room to political war room in a matter of seconds.

Blair followed me back to my desk, most likely in an attempt to peer over my shoulder to stare at my computer screen. "ALLISON! I can't believe you!" he suddenly screeched.

"Excuse me?"

"Oh my God, are you trying to kill yourself, Allison!" he asked, panicking.

"What on earth are you talking about, Blair?"

"You did not!" he yelled, puffing out his cheeks as he gave Lindsay a pointed look.

"What?" I asked again.

"Lindsay, did you see Allison's garbage can?"

I quickly looked in my garbage can and saw papers, pencil shavings, and a few empty water bottles. "What is it, Blair?"

"We should have an office pool to see who can guess how many candy bar wrappers are in Allison's garbage can," laughed Blair.

Morgan popped out from his office to join the fun. "I wager six!"

They both laughed. Just as Blair reached for my garbage can, I lunged to stop him and, by accident, my elbow landed smack-dab in his left eye.

"Agh!" he screamed, covering his eye.

"Oh my gosh, Blair, I'm sorry," I said as Blair fell to his knees and continued to hold his eye.

Lindsay quickly ran over to my desk and yelled, "Office code blue, office code blue, office code blue!" I stared in disbelief as Rose arrived with the office first-aid kit and Heidi came running down the hallway.

"Do we need to call 911?" asked Heidi.

"Oh my God, I just put my elbow in Blair's eye," I said in disbelief.

"Allison, we're the office's code blue team. You need to remove yourself from the cubicle," directed Lindsay. I started laughing and Lindsay snapped, "Do you not understand what I just told you?"

Blair stood up and, sure enough, he had a black eye the size of Rhode Island. "Let's get an ice pack on that," ordered Rose.

"Are you feeling dizzy or like you might faint?" Lindsay asked.

I tried to keep from rolling my eyes. If the little jackass hadn't been peering into my garbage can counting the number of candy children's school bar wrappers in it, this never would have happened.

"I am slightly dizzy and the room is spinning," Blair said.

"Like a room spinning when you're drunk?" asked Heidi. Everyone laughed, and Rose told them to get back to work. She told Blair that she'd bring him an incident form to complete for liability purposes and instructed me to help him hold the ice pack on his eye.

"Blair, I'm sorry. I didn't mean to knock you out," I apologized.

"Lay off the candy bars, Allison!" Blair said as he walked away. I couldn't help but find it just a little bit funny that someone so concerned about his appearance was going to be sporting a shiner for the next couple of weeks. That should teach him to mess with me.

Senator McDermott was scheduled to arrive in the office momentarily, and I nervously anticipated a royal chewing-out over my "lack of responsiveness." I braced myself. To cover all the bases, I emailed Blair a time for the official presidential announcement. I also printed out the children's school schedules that Trista had sent, per the senator's request. I felt organized and went through my to-do list five times and double-checked each assignment.

That afternoon was the weekly scheduling meeting with the whole

entourage—the senator, Charles, Trista, Morgan, Rose, Lindsay, and sometimes Blair—to go over upcoming requests. The weekly scheduling meeting was by far my most dreaded hour each week. I always felt like I was being interrogated about every single little detail concerning each scheduling request. They asked bizarre questions about other meetings with the senator that had taken place years ago. They'd ask me questions about people I didn't know. Sometimes I wanted to give in to my urge to give a sarcastic answer. "I'm sorry, Senator, I wasn't even born yet when you had that lunch date with Bette Midler."

The scheduling meetings always left me baffled and feeling like everyone's target. When I would tell Janet about these meetings, she couldn't believe how Morgan and Charles morphed into spineless little boys when the senator was in the room. Rose would strategically only answer some of the senator's questions making her look like an unsung hero. Thankfully, I could rely on Trista, the only one who seemed to have my back. But since she participated through video conferencing, she couldn't help much.

Just then, like two prodigal sons, Cam and the senator arrived in the office, laughing as the senator patted Cam on the back. "Cam, you're the best. It's always good to see you," he said, while Cam rolled his eyes at me.

"Allison, Allison, Allison!" yelled the senator.

"Yes, sir," I replied. "That's my cue!" I peeked into his office and he said, "Get in here, Allison."

My stomach knotted as I readied myself for a rant about what he considered my lack of performance.

"Angelina Jolie is in DC lobbying for some kid-friendly legislation, maybe child abuse or something—I really don't care. In any event, see if you can schedule dinner with her tonight," he instructed. "If she's available, see if Thomas wants to join us." Senator Thomas, who was Victoria's boss, had his office next door to ours. It would be an understatement to say that Senator McDermott was fonder of Senator

Thomas than vice versa.

"Oh, and Allison, did you get lunch scheduled with Jenkins?" the senator asked as he straightened his tie.

"It doesn't look good for today, sir, but we will keep trying for another time."

"Make it happen, Allison."

"Will do, sir!" I answered, leaving his office as fast as I could.

I rushed back to my computer and was frustrated to see that Cam hadn't responded to my dinner invitation. I ran out to buy a turkey sandwich for lunch and scarfed it down at my desk while I pulled together my files for the dreaded scheduling meeting. I suddenly noticed the senator was on an unscheduled telephone call.

"Lindsay, is the senator on a personal call?" I asked.

Lindsay stopped counting the tea bags and looked up with a puzzled expression. "I'm sorry, what did you say? I was in the midst of counting this month's tea supply. Rose and I think a staffer might be stealing them."

"Not the prized tea bags." I mumbled under my breath. "Do you know if the senator is on a personal telephone call right now? I know we don't have any scheduled calls, and we're five minutes from the scheduling meeting."

Lindsay dropped the tea bags to the floor like a hot potato and scrambled to the senator's office door. "Oh, no. I thought Blair had cleared a call from Anderson Cooper of CNN with you! Mr. Cooper called while you left to get lunch, and I passed the call on to the senator," exclaimed Lindsay.

"I don't know anything about a call with Anderson Cooper, and I'm surprised you couldn't have followed our scheduling procedures for the five minutes it took me to run downstairs to grab a sandwich. Great! Do you even know what the call is about?" I asked. Lindsay just stared at me blankly.

The senator's office door remained shut, and, like a flock of sheep, everyone gathered outside his door for the scheduling meeting. Both

Capitol Hell

Lindsay and I tried to look busy and focused so no one would ask us whom the senator was speaking to. When we all finally piled into the office, I positioned myself next to Charles and directly across from Rose and the senator. In prior meetings, I sometimes felt Charles looking at my notes in an attempt to help me answer the senator's typical yet unpredictable attention-to-detail questions.

I was surprised that no one asked the senator whom he'd been speaking with when Charles started the meeting, "Okay, Allison, what do you have?" he asked.

I took a deep breath and started out with what I thought would be an easy first request. "Former Governor Jesse Ventura would like fifteen minutes on Monday to talk about changing the Senate's rules on lobbying. In particular, he's asking for you, Senator, to be the lead author on a bipartisan package."

"Ventura wants to meet with me?" the senator asked with amusement in his voice.

"Yes, sir," I answered.

"Has his PAC given us any money? Morgan, didn't we just do ethics reform? What package deal is Ventura referring to?" the senator asked and looked puzzled.

"Ah, ah, ah, sir, I believe, I believe the governor, I mean, former governor, is talking about and referring to Senate Rule 101.567 subsection (A) most notably points (1) and possibly (3)…oh and ah, ah maybe (5), deeming all gifts from lobbying principles and lobbying agents illegally receivable versus the current ban of a monetary amount of less than $250.00 and the caveats associated herein," answered Morgan.

I had no idea what he was talking about, and wondered if anyone else in the room could understand his legalese.

Charles turned beet red and snapped, "Morgan, good God, in plain English—where do we stand? Yes or no!"

Whew, at least I wasn't the only one who was lost. Just then, Blair made his usual fashionably late appearance. Of course, no one said a word about his lack of timeliness. "Wow, Blair, nice shiner!" laughed the senator.

"Watch out for the office's own Paul Bunyan, sir. Allison has quite the elbow shot," answered Blair.

"Nice. Another crack about my height," I shot back.

"Oh, yes, that reminds me, Blair, I talked with Anderson Cooper about the presidential race. It was a great conversation, and he told me it was all off the record," the senator said as he got up to straighten pictures on his office wall.

"I heard," Blair said, giving me a murderous look. "Sir, I didn't know you were talking with Anderson Cooper this afternoon. As a matter of fact, sir, right before I came to this meeting, CNN reported that you said you'd be a 99.9 percent improvement over Chairman Jenkins for president."

"What?" screeched Morgan.

Rose started to squirm noticeably in her seat and then blurted out, "I need to go. Sorry, I'm going to puke. Why do I have to be pregnant now?" She ran out of the office and Charles gave the senator the ultimate I-know-nothing look.

"I didn't say that!" yelled the senator. "Where do they get that stuff!" He began briskly pacing from wall to wall straightening his pictures.

"Sir, we'll need to clear up this quote. And, just so you know, CNN also broke that you're weighing a presidential campaign," Blair said quietly.

"Damn it. Now we're on defense instead of offense. Anders!" yelled Charles.

No one said a word. I quickly stacked my scheduling folders, anticipating an early adjournment of our meeting.

"What does Ventura want to meet about?" the senator asked me again.

All eyes turned to me as I answered him, "Gift ban ethics and you sponsoring the language, Senator."

"He can take his damn cigar and smoke it til the Cubans arrive in Minnesota for all I care," the senator mumbled as he continued his agitated pacing. "And where the hell is Rose, and what's this talk about being pregnant? Who has time for sex in this office?" he asked as he began to fidget with his royal blue tie.

"Okay, team, on that note, I think we'd better adjourn for now. Allison and Blair, let's head to my office," Charles ordered.

"Sir, would you like a cup of tea?" Lindsay asked the senator as we all began to leave his office.

"If I wanted a cup of goddamn tea, I would ask for a cup of goddamn tea! Besides, you make the worst goddamn tea in the Senate. Why did you put Anderson through to me?" shouted the senator.

Lindsay walked out of his office and burst into tears as she walked toward Heidi's cubicle.

✻   ✻   ✻   ✻   ✻   ✻

"Holy shit, friends, holy frickin' shit!" exclaimed Charles as we gathered in his tiny office and dug into his bowl of candy. I was surprised to see Blair emotionally eat piece after piece of candy without even taking a breath. "How do we get ourselves into these situations?" he questioned as he multitasked by checking his email.

"I think we need to kill the quote with good McDermott news," asserted Blair.

"Janet always has good soccer mom stuff, and I've been holding a couple of her warm, fuzzy stories from her casework days for when we needed them," remarked Charles. "I'll handle getting a story from Janet. The two of you need to work together to keep this presidential buzz quiet. Blair, draft a response for the senator to get past this 99.9 percent comment. And Allison, don't let anyone through to the senator without first running it by me." I let that slide since Lindsay had already taken a hit for her mistake.

The whole "99.9 percent better" episode made the afternoon fly by. When I received an email response from Cam about my dinner invitation, I opened it nervously and read it twice: "That sounds incredible, Allison. Just tell me when and you're on my calendar! BTW, remind me to buy you elbow pads for Christmas!"

I clicked the reply button as fast as I could and wrote, "Skip the elbow pads and make it knee pads!" I thought again about sending such a racy message so I deleted it and started over with a more politically correct response. "Awesome! I'll email Rudy and get us a date. Stay tuned. Remind me to buy Blair some balls for Christmas. Thanks again for helping me out today." I hit send and caught myself daydreaming about kissing Cam for the first time and our first official date.

Almost immediately after I contacted Rudy he replied and said he'd set up Friday evening reservations under the name Awesome Allison and everything was taken care of. I passed the news along to Cam and then told Janet as I walked with her to spy on Jenkins at his weekly Monday press conference. "Did Charles talk to you yet?" I asked.

"Nope. What about?" Janet asked, as she carefully positioned herself to get the full side view of Jenkins at the podium.

"He's going to ask you for another heartwarming story to tell about the senator. He's put his foot in his mouth again." I stopped when Janet put her finger up to her mouth, gesturing for me to be quiet. We only stayed for a minute to watch his press conference, but that was enough to give Janet her Jenkins fix.

"He's so adorable," Janet said.

"Yeah, well, I'm glad you see it because I surely don't!" I said as we both laughed and walked back into the office.

"Alright, back to the grind!" Janet said as she rolled her eyes and walked toward Charles's office.

"Hey you two, I can't imagine where you were! How's Jenkins looking today?" Charles asked mischievously, putting his arm around Janet's shoulders. "I was thinking we should try and tell one of our recent success stories. What've you got?" Apparently I wasn't the only one who had picked up on Janet's crush.

"Hmmm. Well, the senator helped a Minnesota doctor get emergency medical visas for three Haitian orphans who are dying of cancerous stomach tumors after the Embassy rejected the kids three times for not having financial ties to Haiti," Janet said.

"I like it—if we can stay away from the immigration debate on it. Write up some talking points about what the senator did. Include all the contact information and send it to me," ordered Charles.

"Will do!" Janet told him. Charles could get Janet to do just about anything for him or the senator.

"Oh, and keep me in the loop about any dates with Jenkins on the horizon!" Charles said as he gave me an it'll-never-happen wink.

"Will do!" laughed Janet.

✳   ✳   ✳   ✳   ✳   ✳

My first date in months was booked, and it was with Cam! Nine o'clock rolled around and as I walked home I decided it was a perfect night for a run. I couldn't afford the luxury of a gym membership, and I missed having time to work out each day. With a date on the calendar, though, every woman (no matter her shape or size) knows that any pre-date routine includes the sudden need to work out coupled with some quick weight loss. I was even able to twist Veronica's arm into running with me, which was a good thing because we both had packed on a few pounds from all of the Congressional receptions we had been attending.

We learned very quickly that a great way to eat and drink for free was to sneak into any of the numerous receptions that were going on within the Senate or House buildings. Lobbyists and special interest groups would host receptions to promote their various causes. They knew supplying free food and drink was a guaranteed way to get Hill staffers to show up en masse, and Veronica and I were no exception. As a scheduler, I had access to all of the receptions going on around the Hill, and we took full advantage. Our favorite receptions by far were hosted by the Wine and Spirit Wholesalers and the Beer Wholesalers, for obvious reasons.

As we were about to head out the door, I panicked about not having my BlackBerry or cell phone with me on the run. "Are you chained to McDermott?" Veronica asked.

"Good point, I'll leave them here," I answered. "But God help us both if some Karma emergency crops up while we're out trying to drop a pant size!"

We both laughed and I offered up a quick prayer that nothing would happen. Our run was tremendous, and we both made a commitment to start running at least four times a week until we both squeezed into smaller bikinis.

I was beat from another adventurous day at the office and went straight to bed when I got home. Just as I turned out the light my cell phone rang. It was Janet. "Hey, what's up?"

"He wrote back!" she screamed.

"Who wrote back?" I asked.

"Where have you been? Jenkins! Jenkins answered my initial request to communicate on eHarmony! Duh!"

"Are you sure it's him? How does a senator have time to dink around on eHarmony?" I asked.

"Still no picture in his profile," Janet said. I could hear her clicking away at her keyboard.

"Well, what did Romeo have to say?" I asked.

"I asked him to tell me one of the already written eHarmony questions about what he's most proud of in his life. And he wrote about being elected to office," Janet answered seriously.

"Oh, that narrows it down to just 100,000 available bachelors!"

"God, you never give me any credit. He's blind, elected to office, talks about being conservative. Do you need me to go on? It's totally him. How many blind politicians do you know?"

"Okay. So what's the next step?" I asked, trying to show some compassion for my best friend.

"I have to answer his questions," Janet said.

"Well, don't keep me in suspense. What did he ask?"

"How many times a week do you exercise, and what type of exercise do you do?" she told me.

"Ha! Men will never get it!" I laughed.

"Yeah, it's a pretty ridiculous first question!"

"I know. Write back and say you're the national sumo champion," I laughed. Janet cracked up. "Actually, no—say you haven't worked out in a while, but your favorite form of exercise is hitting the sheets!"

Janet laughed again and said, "We can't blow this one. I'll answer him but what should my second question back to him be about?"

"We've got to write something good!"

We talked for an hour and mustered quite an impressive list of questions ranging from his favorite sexual position, to the biblical verse most overused by politicians, to what an appropriate going rate for a prostitute is in New York City for the governor. Janet would never send those questions, though, so we settled on: Can you recognize friends by their scent? And which do you enjoy more, sex or money? We hung up and I was anxious to know what her mystery man would write back.

I fell asleep easily but was soon awakened by the annoying buzz of my BlackBerry. I rolled over and decided after the previous night's disaster I had better check it. It was a message from the senator:

12:45 a.m.   I need the telephone number of where Angelina Jolie is staying while in DC

Oh shit. I wrote back:

12:50 a.m.   Okay. Let me see what I can do.

I didn't know where to begin so I sent my increasingly frequent mass email message to the entourage:

12:51 a.m.   The senator is asking for the phone number

for where Angelina Jolie is staying while in DC. Anyone have any connections?

The senator sent another message:

12:52 a.m.   Check with Janet. She likes kids' issues.

I wrote back, assuring the senator I would check with Janet and let him know if I heard anything further. I imagined Janet was probably at her computer having cyber sex with Jenkins by now, not thinking about public policy. The senator wrote again:

12:55 a.m.   Sure would like that telephone number soon—like tonight!

I sent Janet an email to her private Yahoo! account so I wouldn't wake her with the annoying BlackBerry buzz.

12:56 a.m.   We have a horny dog senator on the loose. Do you have Angelina Jolie's contact information?

Janet replied in a matter of seconds.

12:56 a.m.   I do not. But guess who I'm talking to?

I laughed and wrote:

1:00 a.m.   Okay, make that two horny dog senators on the loose. Ha ha. What does Mr. Senator have to say?

She responded almost as quickly as before:

1:01 a.m.   He answered the questions. Yes to scent, plus their handshake. And he only enjoys money more for now because he's saving himself, just like me! Janet would likely relate on this issue here.

Capitol Hell

I was dumbfounded. I wrote back:

1:02 a.m.　What? Jenkins is a virgin? Now that's a match for you! That old guy! OMG! What are you guys talking about?

Seconds later, Janet wrote:

1:03 a.m.　I'm waiting for his answers to these three new questions: Did you have any serious accidents as a kid? Should prayer be allowed in the classroom? And define the perfect marriage.

I responded:

1:05 a.m.　Nice one on the accident! Now we'll know if it's Jenkins or not! Let me know the verdict and get some sleep tonight, Monica Lewinsky!

She wrote:

1:06 a.m.　Send a blue dress and some stain remover. Good night! Oh, email me if Anders asks for any more booty calls! Ha ha.

I thought about Janet's questions as I fell asleep and wondered how Cam would answer them. I tossed and turned throughout the night, bothered by the senator's late-night request for telephone numbers. But I told myself it could just be innocent fun, and DC was a lonely city.

＊　　　＊　　　＊　　　＊　　　＊　　　＊

TGIF! I was downright thrilled for my dinner date and alone time with Cam. But first I needed to get through a hectic Friday, which included sending the senator back to Minnesota for a three-day weekend. He'd be off my hands in a short seven hours, I thought as I started my day.

Janet's love affair with Jenkins was becoming a daily ritual of he said/she said and I was looking forward to her early morning arrival to hear the latest from the Jenkins Journal Report, the name I'd coined for the play-by-play. The two had been consistently exchanging emails, and Janet was hoping for a telephone conversation over the weekend. I thought it was cute that Janet was saving all of Jenkins's emails, and occasionally we'd read them aloud and ponder what he was thinking. That morning she arrived in the office beaming. Her face was flushed.

"Oh my God, why are you so red?" I asked.

She was out of breath and looked desperate for water. As she huffed and puffed she said, "I had to walk around the building twice this morning and my left heel broke."

"Why did you have to walk around the building twice?" I questioned.

"Jenkins was in the staff member line and I couldn't have him see me," she said nervously.

"Are you forgetting that he can't actually see you?"

"I couldn't bring myself to stand next to him, especially after last night," Janet said.

"Oh dear Lord, what happened last night in the latest episode of *The Young and the Sexless?*"

"Up—all night—all night online," she answered vaguely.

"What? You were online with Jenkins all night?" I laughed.

"Yes, all night. I did Jenkins all night long but still have the virgin badge of honor," Janet answered.

"Okay, something isn't measuring up here. Did you two lovebirds talk or did you two get all frisky with the keyboard?"

She rolled her eyes and said, "A girl can only wish. He wants to do breakfast on Wednesday! What the hell—breakfast? Ah, yes, Senator, I'll have a plump and juicy sausage with my hard-boiled eggs." We both laughed as Charles ordered our Jenkins Journal Report meeting adjourned.

With dates on the horizon, it was clear to Charles that both Janet

and I had checked out for the day, mentally and emotionally. I'm sure he suspected this TGIF was going to consist of a day of Internet searching for date outfits, watching soap operas on our cubicle televisions, and nonstop giggling and daydreaming about the new men in our lives. The day went by fast, our workloads were light, and before we knew it, the senator was out the door. Before Janet left the office, she made me promise to call her after my date with Cam to give her all the juicy details. "You got it!" I told her. "Happy online sex this weekend!"

"Virgin badge of honor, did you forget? One plump and juicy sausage," she said just loud enough for me to hear and then laughed loudly.

When I arrived home I nervously tried on five short dresses before selecting my always-reliable low-cut, just-above-the-knee black knit dress. I modeled my final look to Veronica and she said, "Someone is getting laid tonight!"

"Ah, perfect!" I answered, even though I hoped she was wrong. I liked Cam a lot, but I wasn't sure I was ready to hop into bed with him. "A kiss will do, but a handshake will hurt!" I said.

✳   ✳   ✳   ✳   ✳   ✳

Cam and I arrived at Oceanaire, my favorite seafood restaurant in DC, and we both were blown away by our choice table and first-class service. We felt like a king and queen and were thankful that our overpriced drinks and entrees were on the never-ask-how-much lobbyist tab. We didn't hold back and ordered drink after drink. Cam was quiet and I tried to keep the small talk alive. As much as I tried to not talk shop, we both found ourselves talking about the office, our coworkers, and the endless stream of unbelievable gossip. Cam was a small-town guy living in the hustle and bustle of DC's sometimes-dirty politics, and it was clear that he'd held on to his small-town values. After shoveling in several crab cakes, I noticed that I'd missed three BlackBerry messages from the senator.

"Does your job ever end?" asked Cam.

"I only wish," I laughed.

"You work very hard, Allison, and the senator takes you for granted," he said kindly.

"Thank you for noticing! That means a lot to me. I try hard, but can never seem to win!"

"Well, sometimes it's only after something good is gone that you notice how great it was!" Cam said as he gazed into my eyes. Just then my work cell phone began to ring, and I grabbed it as other patrons in the restaurant turned to glare at me.

"Ah, shit, it's him!" I squirmed.

"Take a deep breath and just tell him no!" stated Cam.

"Yeah, right!" I said, swallowing a gulp of red wine as I answered.

"Hi, Senator!" I answered.

"I emailed you three times!" Senator McDermott accused.

"I'm sorry, sir. I'm having dinner right now and wasn't checking my messages. I am sorry!"

Ignoring my apology, he continued, "I forgot my laundry in my washer."

I was silent.

"Allison, are you there?" he asked.

"Yes, I'm here, sir. You said something about your laundry, sir?" I asked, puzzled.

I heard the senator sigh. "I forgot my laundry in the washer," he repeated.

"Oh, I see, sir," I answered and shrugged at Cam.

"I need you to go and put my laundry in the dryer before it molds over the weekend," ordered the senator. "Do it tonight, and make sure to use extra dryer sheets—I don't like static cling!"

I gave Cam a look of disbelief and said, "Sir, I don't have your apartment key. Are you certain you want me to do your laundry tonight?"

"Allison, my laundry can't mold. The building concierge will let you into my apartment," he answered.

"Okay—well, I guess it's worth a try. I'll go tonight after dinner to

put your laundry in the dryer," I answered.

"Thank you, Allison. But I need you to go right now. I'm afraid of ruining my under-shirts. Karma will have my head if I continue to ruin my shirts," the senator mumbled.

"I understand. Will do!" I said as I rolled my eyes at Cam and ended the call.

"Ugh. I can't even have dinner without McDermott needing something—and he's in Minnesota!" I bitched to Cam.

"I'll go with you," he offered. "Let's take my car."

"Are you sure? It's Friday night. I know you must have much better things to do than the senator's laundry."

"We're in this together!" answered Cam as he hit my shoulder.

Before leaving for McDermott's apartment, we guzzled the final sips from our bottle of wine. "Whoa, I'm a little buzzed!" I laughed as we found Cam's car.

We pulled up to the senator's apartment building and parked in front. "It says fifteen-minute parking. Think this will be okay?" asked Cam.

"This better only take five minutes!"

The building's concierge was doing a crossword puzzle and watching *The O'Reilly Factor*. When he looked up at us I told him, "My boss, Senator McDermott, would like me to do an errand for him tonight and said you could let me into his apartment."

He just shook his head no and went back to his crossword puzzle.

"Excuse me, sir, but my boss asked me to get your help," I politely pushed.

"I can't let you in," he answered.

"Aw, shit!" I complained.

He looked up again and asked if we needed anything further.

"I need to get into McDermott's apartment or my ass is grass," I answered.

He took a big breath and asked, "Do you have a card on you?"

"No, I don't. You see, I was having dinner with my friend here when the senator called me to do his laundry," I answered.

"I can't just let you into a senator's apartment, lady. What are you, some kind of stalker?" he asked.

"What?!" I said.

Cam stepped in. "We both work for Senator McDermott and he just emailed Allison asking her to do him a personal favor."

"Oh, I see. Do you have the message?" he asked.

I showed him the senator's three emails and he gave us the apartment keys. Apparently it was easier than I thought to con your way into a senator's apartment in our nation's capital.

Cam and I entered the senator's apartment and discovered bare walls and hardly any furniture. I found my way to his washing machine and quickly threw his barely wet laundry into the dryer. "Should I pull any of this out to hang dry?" I asked Cam.

He laughed and said, "Yes. His boxers."

"Boxers, really? McDermott in boxers?"

"Oh, he's a boxer guy, I have no doubt," laughed Cam.

"I like a guy in tight briefs!" I answered.

"Good to know!" Cam yelled from the other room.

"Well—that should do it!" I said. "Hey, where are you?"

"In here—over here," answered Cam. I found him looking through the senator's nightstand and checking out his pile of hardcover books.

"Likes to *read* in bed!" I laughed.

"Hardy-har-har," Cam said.

"We better get out of here before Mr. Concierge finds us snooping around the senator's apartment," I told Cam.

As we walked out to the street we found Cam's car gone. "Holy shit, we couldn't have been in there for longer than twenty minutes max!" I shouted.

We were stunned. We went back into McDermott's apartment building.

"Our car was frickin' towed!" Cam shouted to the concierge.

"No, I'm the only one who can order cars to be towed, and I've

been here waiting for you two to leave," answered the concierge.

"Where's his car then?" I asked.

"Well, I don't know," answered the concierge. "Are you sure you two kids drove here tonight?"

I couldn't believe the question. "Of course we drove here," I answered.

"By the smell of your breath, neither of you should have been driving," he remarked.

"Fuck, Cam, your car was stolen!" I realized.

"We better report this to the DC police," the concierge said as he rolled his eyes. "They won't do much but ask you to file a report. Cars get stolen all the time in DC."

Cam reached into his pocket for his keys. "My keys are gone!"

"Either you left them in the car or they fell out of your pocket. Cars around here can be gone in a matter of minutes," the concierge told us.

Cam was shocked that the DC police wouldn't come file a stolen-car report and instead insisted that he file a report in person within forty-eight hours. "Just like that your car is stolen!" Cam said, shaking his head. "In Minnesota, at least the police show up!"

It was shaping up to be the worst date ever. Cam came to my rescue and ended up with a stolen car. I doubted he'd ever want to see me again.

I emailed the senator to tell him Cam's car was stolen while we were doing his urgent laundry. McDermott wrote back, "Thanks for doing my laundry."

"What an arrogant ass!" I exclaimed.

"What?" asked Cam.

"Oh, nothing!" I answered, not wanting Cam to see the man behind the McDermott curtain. "Well, how are we getting home?" I asked, changing the subject.

❋   ❋   ❋   ❋   ❋   ❋   ❋

Janet arrived within an hour and seemed stressed from driving in downtown DC. We dropped Cam off at his home where I got a friendly punch on the shoulder as a farewell. I decided to stay overnight at Janet's place. After we shared a pizza, she pulled out her laptop and we wrote all night to Jenkins. Between laughs, we talked about the no-lay-tonight date dress and read Jenkins's messages repeatedly. Janet was head over heels for him.

"To Wednesday's breakfast, losing the virgin badge of honor, McDermott's laundry, and finding Cam's car to make out in," we toasted before falling asleep on opposite ends of Janet's couch.

6

Congress is Out: August Recess!

E ven a young and inexperienced Senate scheduler knows that legislative session weeks make a calendar year seem to fly by, and the same was true of working for Senator McDermott and Karma the Diva.

This week our much-anticipated congressional recess was to begin, and our entire office was in the final crunch of a pre-recess vote-a-rama, meaning the senators would be stuck in back-to-back votes nearly all day long.

Thankfully, in less than four days McDermott would be headed back to Minnesota to officially announce his presidential campaign.

Although CNN and Anderson Cooper had unofficially broken the news, this event would be the official campaign announcement. It was sure to be a spectacle. His announcement would end with him cruising around Minnesota on a Zamboni, followed by a bus filled with Kool-Aid–drinking volunteers and supporters waving their McDermott hockey sticks. The whole thing was actually quite fitting since the volunteers seemed to think of politics as a sporting match—and I mean that literally.

Without question, the next four days were bound to be busy beyond belief and tension-filled. The words *pressure cooker* came to mind. I sat at my desk, wondering why I couldn't concentrate on work. After a sleepless weekend, which included the McDermott laundry fiasco and the stolen car adventure, it was hard to focus.

While I should have been worrying about the senator's tennis key, his kids' school schedule, and Karma's next spa appointment, I found that my mind was juggling real-life issues like how to pay the rent, how to get back home for a few days during recess, and most importantly, Cam. For crying out loud, when was he going to wake up and realize that his dream girl sat kitty-corner from him sixty hours a week!

I daydreamed away the entire first hour of work. My stomach was in knots from worry, which had become my new normal. It wasn't good. Janet was spot-on with her self-diagnosis of the Monday-morning sickness. The feeling was directly related to work and tended to outlast Monday. I snapped out of my daydreams when I was startled by the office intern. He barged through the office door, barely clinging on to an extremely large shipping box. Conveniently, the nervous intern dropped the box right smack in front of the senator's office door and scurried away without uttering a peep.

Nothing like breaking a four-inch heel and getting a run in my new eight-dollar pantyhose to kick-start the morning, I thought as I attempted to move the large shipping box. I laughed when I imagined Blair trying to move the box by himself. He probably would have been too concerned about ruining his new manicure or scratching a custom cufflink to even touch it.

The box was heavy and oddly shaped. I was annoyed that our intern didn't follow our mail procedures. Hopefully the box had been screened already. I took a large breath and held my nose shut as I opened the box. If anthrax was going to come pouring out, at least I was going down for the one and only Senator McDermott! Thankfully, no white powder came rushing out. Instead, I was shocked to find 250 personalized adult-sized hockey sticks. This package of campaign materials should have been sent to Minnesota to the senator's campaign office. This obvious campaign-finance violation now had my fingerprints all over it. Fuck!

I pulled out a hockey stick. They were cool; I had to give Trista credit for her clever idea. They really were quite a campaign novelty.

Next, I perfectly positioned the stick back in the box, sealed it up so it looked like new and slanted it against Lindsay's chair. I didn't have time to deal with hockey sticks this morning. Surely Lindsay could find time to stir the senator's tea and send hockey sticks back to Minnesota by Friday. I'd just have to make sure to instruct her to use campaign funds, not official Senate funds, to ship those things off. Hopefully she wouldn't screw it up.

Just in the nick of time, Lindsay and Rose came barging into the office, each carrying a cup of coffee. As was typical, my morning greeting was ignored by each of them. I couldn't fully describe the feeling of working in McDermott's office, but at times it reminded me of eighth grade with all the cliques and cattiness. One day, they're friendly; the next day, you're on top of their shit list for a week.

"Whoa, what's this box doing in my space?" Lindsay asked.

"That box arrived this morning. It's addressed to the senator," I answered as I tried to keep a poker face. As the clock struck 8:30 a.m. the office filled quickly. Janet was among the 8:30 a.m. arrivers and had a suspicious look on her face. "Oh, I know that look. You're up to something," I said as she inspected the run in my pantyhose.

"Just counting the hours," she whispered to me, pointing at the run.

"I know, I know, don't pull on it. I'm going to run to the bathroom and try to Super Glue it. Hours until what?" I asked.

"Are you kidding me? Really, you don't know?" she asked, rolling her eyes.

"Umm, not a clue," I answered.

"Maybe this will help refresh your memory," Janet said, pretending to be blind as she walked to her desk. She rammed directly into the shipping box Lindsay had just moved. The box crashed to the floor and hockey sticks spilled onto the office floor.

Blair came running. "Oh my God, is the senator being targeted? Do we need to take emergency cover and bring him to an undisclosed location?" he asked seriously.

"No, Blair, we just had a spill of hockey sticks," Rose answered.

"Cool," Blair responded as he and Janet each picked up one of the sticks.

"Holy shit!" laughed Janet as she gave me an oh-my-God-you-wouldn't-believe-it look.

"McDickmott for President!" screeched Janet.

"That's not appropriate for the office, Janet!" Rose scolded.

"I'm just reading the printing on the stick," explained Janet.

We all grabbed a hockey stick. Sure enough. Printed clearly on each of the sticks: Anders McDickmott for President. I quietly laughed to myself, as Janet tried desperately not to burst into laughter again.

"Allison, will you please call Trista right away and tell her we have a misprint. You'll also need to figure out how to ship these sticks back to the Minnesota hockey supplier," ordered Rose.

While we were still gathering up the sticks, the senator walked into the office. "What on earth is my team doing? Did we sign up for the Senate intramural hockey league? Let me guess, Blair is the coach, Morgan is our ace on the blue line, and Janet, with her wide hips, is covering the net?" the senator joked.

I could see the humiliation on Janet's face as she tried to laugh it off. We tried to quickly get the sticks back into the box without the senator seeing the typo. Our fast hands, though, weren't fast enough.

"Blair, pass me one of those sticks, I used to play a pick-up game or two. I bet I've still got fast hands," the senator said cheerfully as he reached for a stick. "These are real hard sticks," he said while checking out the stick's capabilities. As he read the printing on the stick, we all tried to focus on other work.

"Rose, did you see these sticks?" he asked.

"I didn't look closely," answered Rose. "What's up?"

Trying to not snicker out loud, I saw Janet run to her computer and begin typing quickly. I tried to not look at the senator or Rose as I sat down at my desk. All of a sudden an email popped up from Janet: "McDickmott. Sticks. What's up? Ah… see any resemblance?" I deleted her message, knowing exactly what she was thinking. For a virgin, her mind was always somehow linked to sex.

"Don't we proof prints around here?" yelled the senator. "Growing up, my dad always said measure twice, cut once," he said, walking briskly into his office and slamming the door.

I took a deep breath before I tackled my new assignment of returning campaign materials from the official Senate office. I quickly figured a way to have a delivery service come to the office, pick up the sticks, and have them shipped back to the manufacturer. It seemed like the best option to me. Of course, the answer seemed too easy, but I needed to start working on my normal scheduling duties for the busiest week of the Senate session.

The day went quickly. I didn't even look at the clock until 4:30 p.m. Missing lunch was becoming routine, but at least it was good for my waistline. Right before 5:00 p.m., the delivery service arrived to pick up the sticks. As I re-taped the box and handed it off to the delivery service, Charles stopped us in the doorway. "What's going on, Allison?" he asked.

"Oh, we're just returning the hockey sticks," I explained.

"Oh, no. We can't have some random delivery-service dude do our dirty work, Allison!" he shouted.

I was stunned at his outburst, and asked, "What?"

"We can't trust some dude off the streets. We don't know if he's a D or an R. We don't know if he's an enemy. How do we know he's not a campaign staffer dressed in a brown delivery-service uniform? How do we know he's not going to take our package and head straight to the Office of Senate Ethics? Or worse yet, Allison, how do we know he's not some scumbag reporter digging up dirt on our boss?"

After Charles rattled off scenario after random scenario, he ordered, "Tonight, you and Janet can take her car and find a shipping place. I have the utmost trust that the two of you can put your heads together and figure out where you can ship a box. Good Lord, the two of you know every cheap Chinese buffet in the District. You should be able to find a FedEx or UPS store!"

"Will do," I answered, trying to lug the box of hockey sticks back to my desk without ruining the entire pair of hose with another run. I went right over to Janet's desk. "We need to bring the hockey sticks to a shipping place tonight," I mumbled, as I snacked on her faded bowl of desk candy.

"Oh. Really? Darn it! I need to be online with Senator Blind Date by 9:00 p.m., though," she answered.

"We should be home by 9:00 p.m. for your evening of sexting! Come get me when you're ready to head out!"

When I returned to my desk, I couldn't believe it. There was an unopened delivery of what appeared to be fresh flowers in a vase. I instantly melted into a pile of mush, just like women do everywhere when flowers arrive. Before opening the attached card and envelope, I wondered who they were from. Cam came to mind first, then my dad (who knew I'd be burning the midnight oil this week), and then I realized that I secretly hoped they were from the senator. Maybe he'd finally woken up and realized everything I did for him.

I opened the envelope with a wide smile on my face. The little white card read, "Happy Birthday, My Bride! You are the nexus of our family and the only love of my life. There is no one else. See you soon.

Love, McDicky." The bouquet was magnificent, with bright colors and extremely delicate flowers. I looked at the envelope again and my name was clearly typed in black letters.

Janet came galloping over and asked, "Ready to deliver some hockey sticks?" Then she noticed the flowers. "Whoa, those are mighty pretty," she squealed, grabbing at the white card. She read the card out loud. "McDicky?" she asked.

"Which one of your guy friends is Mr. McDicky?" she asked.

"No, you goofball, these flowers aren't for *me*!" I said. "Didn't you read the card? I'm always the bridesmaid, never the bride!"

"I didn't think it was your birthday!" Janet exclaimed.

"I don't know who McDicky is. But I'm thinking it must be McDermott," I answered.

"What should I do? Drop him an email—excuse me, Senator, but your wife's birthday bouquet came to me instead of crazy Karma?"

"Gosh, I think I'm going to puke," Janet said.

"What now?" I asked. "Can't you see I'm in a bind yet again? Why can't we just work for a normal senator? Surely other senators aren't this crazy, are they?"

"Allison, I don't know how you do it, but somehow you always manage to find yourself smack dab in the middle of some drama. I'd love to help you, but I can't get the thought of Senator McDicky's tinky-winky out of my head," stated Janet.

"Grow up. I think I'll drop him a quick email. Make yourself useful and help me write it."

Janet pushed me out of my chair and began to type at her lightning pace. That woman could type even faster than she could talk. Given the fact that words poured out of her mouth at a million miles a minute, that was saying something.

"Hi Senator!! Hope you're doing great!! Wonderful to see you today—you looked mighty handsome in your three-piece pinstripe suit! Sorry again about the hockey sticks. We're having them slashed. No pun intended! :-) Say, I just wanted to drop you a quick line. I

received the birthday flowers you sent for Karma today. They certainly are pretty—you must have coughed up quite a bit of your Senate pension for them! Just wanted you to know! Have a swell night! LOVE, Allison."

Annoyed with her bizarre and unnaturally long brown-nosing message, I hit delete and made a second attempt. "Senator—we have another mix-up. No worries though. Your schedule is fine. I just received your wife's birthday flowers instead of Karma. Thought you'd want to know ASAP." I was always much more direct than Janet. But, somehow the senator seemed to gobble up the ridiculous emails she'd send him. I knew I could never get away with emails like that. After hitting send, the senator immediately called me. When he wanted something, it never ceased to amaze me how responsive and available he was.

"Hi, Senator," I answered nervously. He'd know that I learned he went by "Mr. McDicky" as his pet name at home. "Right, Senator. Sure, Senator, will do," I answered as quickly as possible to get him off the line. I could feel myself blushing, and said a quick thanks to the heavens that this conversation wasn't one I had to have in person. I hung up with a huge sigh.

"Oh shit. I know that sigh," Janet said nervously.

"The senator wants us to buy Karma a white dare-to-bare baby doll and ship it overnight with the hockey sticks," I informed her. "I barely have enough money to scrape by until our next payday, let alone buy the boss's wife lingerie," I stated.

"The boss is going to buy Karma a doll?" asked Janet.

I just shook my head and wondered if Janet was raised in a bubble in rural Minnesota. I told her I'd explain on the way. "We'd better get going so you don't miss your evening of hot online sex with Jenkins."

I swiped up my BlackBerry, cell phone, and folders of scheduling requests and we were out the door. As we left the office, we each grabbed two corners of the hockey stick box and tried to get out of the office building as quickly as possible. Janet's rusted-out car was small, and the box was twice the size of her trunk. So we perfectly positioned the box and rammed one end against the windshield and the other into the backseat. We looked like two sardines stuffed into her little Volvo. We also were the definition of hot messes with runs in our pantyhose, makeup dripping from our sweaty faces, and frizzy hair galore.

"I've had a little bit of struggle lately with Bessie starting," Janet said as she pet her little Volvo's front hood like a dog. It was clear that her car hadn't been manufactured in the current decade. I found myself cheering out loud for Bessie to start. Janet's car started right up, but then as we pulled out of the parking space we heard a loud sound like a gunshot. BANG!

"What the fuck was that?!" I asked in shock.

I looked over and noticed Janet's eyes welling up with tears. Before we could look up, our car was surrounded by three uniformed Capitol Police officers. Their guns were drawn and pointed directly at us. In the time we'd spent together, I'd become accustomed to Janet and her crying. I knew that once she started, she was unlikely to stop for quite some time. Even though I was terrified, I knew I'd need to step up and manage the situation. I gingerly rolled down my window with my right hand, holding my left in the air in the universal "I surrender" gesture. "Officer, we're so sorry. Our car just misfired and we aren't sure why."

The officer began to put away his gun and said, "You ladies alright in there? You sure are packed in."

"Yes officer, we're fine," Janet answered tearfully.

Sounding irritated, another officer said in a scolding tone, "We'll need to inspect the interior, trunk, and underside of your vehicle for any security risks. You'll both need to step out of the car, and remove all personal items from the car. We'll need to run the vehicle through our underneath mirror safety check."

Janet and I got out of the car and started to empty it one item at a time. We gathered a large pile of items, and I was embarrassed to notice the number of Senate staffers gawking at our incident. "Why do you have boxes of games in your trunk?" I asked as I took out Scrabble and Upwords.

"You never know when someone wants to play," Janet replied nonchalantly, as though I was the odd one. Some of her habits I would never understand.

After almost an hour, we received the all clear from the Capitol Police and were allowed to exit the parking lot. Janet and I both quietly said individual prayers and hoped Bessie would start without incident and keep us safe on our McDermott errands. As we drove, I could sense that we both were thinking the same thing. The two of us going to a mall together was a dangerous combination. We both loved shopping way too much and were both poor money managers. Janet had an "emergency" credit card that we occasionally (every six to nine months) used for our "emergency" shopping day. Lord knows what we'd do if a real emergency ever cropped up. The truth was her credit card would probably be maxed out by then.

"We haven't had an emergency shopping trip in a while," Janet said as she pulled into the Pentagon City mall with a devious smile.

I purposely left my BlackBerry and cell phone in the car's glove compartment since both Charles and the senator knew we were busy taking care of Operation Pack and Ship.

"I know, but tonight we need to get Karma's present and head home so you can talk with Senator Up-to-No-Good," I said with a wink, trying to distract her from overindulging in the newest trends.

"I don't even know where to start looking for a dare-to-bare nightgown," Janet said, eyeing a hot pink plaid jacket.

"Well, I may not have gotten any action in the past year," I quipped, "but I used to have a sex life. I know where to find a baby doll, I just can't believe we're buying lingerie for our boss's wife!"

As we walked into Victoria's Secret, I could see Janet's chin drop to the ground. I approached a sales associate and explained that I needed a white baby doll. I watched Janet briskly going through rack after rack of lingerie. The sales associate showed me three baby doll pieces, and I selected the most expensive one. I also thought it was the trashiest. I felt queasy about the price tag and wondered if it had an extra zero—$250 seemed a bit high for something that consisted of so little fabric. Then again, the senator had champagne taste, and I was stuck on a beer budget. I decided it was an appropriate time to use Janet's emergency credit card. No use offending the senator, I thought. The most expensive was the best bet. Karma was a diva and we didn't want to disappoint her.

I went to find Janet and noticed she was rushing into a fitting room, her arms full of lingerie. I wondered what my virgin friend could possibly need lingerie for. "Janet, what are you doing?! You know Jenkins won't be able to *see* you in any of that stuff."

She told me to shut up, and sequestered herself in a fitting room. After what seemed like twenty minutes, Janet came out of the fitting room. "What is all this?" I asked, "Holy shit, 38DD!"

"Shhhhhh, hush, please don't cause a scene. I'm already intimidated by all these sex-driven pajamas." She continued in a whisper, "I don't know how to properly measure my two watermelons.

"Well, 38DD seems a bit large. But why on earth do you need two black corsets and these exotic g-string nighties?" I asked.

"Wednesday—remember Wednesday," Janet said, as though I was the idiot.

"Whoa, wait. Are you forgetting that Wednesday is the first time you'll be meeting Jenkins, and that it's over breakfast? Breakfast!"

"Well, I just want to be prepared," Janet said as she looked at the price tags. "If I need to spend $500 to get laid, then so be it!"

"Oh, Janet, I thought Mr. Senator was saving himself!" I said as I rolled my eyes. "So you think Wednesday's breakfast might be a cherry-popping event?"

"Here's to getting some action on Wednesday," I said, grabbing our bags after we'd paid. I wanted to give her a hard time, but I could see she was serious about the lingerie. She was like an X-rated version of a kid in a candy shop—a thirty-year-old virgin in a lingerie shop.

"I need to figure out how to put on those panties. They were riding up my ass a bit awkwardly," she said.

"Let's just come back to reality for a minute, Dr. Ruth." I stated, "Are you sure you want to lose your virginity to a United States Senator?" I asked, concerned that she might be jumping into things.

"Allison!" she exclaimed. "I can think of no better person to lose my virginity to! Can you imagine!? Having sex for the first time with a senator! I consider it my patriotic duty!" she joked as we got back into her car.

"Okay, Uncle Sam. Maybe you should just point your finger and say 'I WANT YOU!' right when you meet him." She continued to giggle as I retrieved my BlackBerry from the glove compartment.

"Fuck, fuck, ffffuck!" I said as I read my emails. "That little shit. God, I can't stand him. He's only working for the senator because his daddy is loaded," I complained as my hands started to shake.

"Now who?" asked Janet as she drove to the nearest FedEx.

I didn't even answer her. I nervously reached for my scheduling folders and notepad and starting flipping through papers. Janet's car quickly transformed into my mobile office.

"He's such a little bitch. I swear he's more of a drama queen than all the women in our office combined," I said, trying to collect my thoughts. He really was a little prick, and I couldn't believe that he was trying to throw me under the bus again. I wrote him a message with the first thoughts that raced through my mind: "Blair, who the fuck do you think you are? You're not the senator nor are you his chief of staff. You're his pissant little press secretary. Your job is to write talking points and get the senator media opportunities. Learn your job and keep your nosy ass away from mine!" Send.

Two seconds later I wrote another message: "Blair, really, you find it useful to email the senator your evaluation of my job performance—and that you think I need a job evaluation pronto? Are you fuckin' kidding me? You wouldn't last more than half an hour in my position. You wouldn't have time to spritz Evian on your face. I'm busy working directly for the senator. Get a life." Send.

Amazingly, Janet drove us right to the FedEx without so much as a wrong turn. We both breathed a sigh of relief after we made sure the two packages were sent properly. I noticed that Janet was staring at the clock. It was already 9:00 p.m. and neither of us had eaten. "Thanks for your help," I told her.

"Let's go get some dinner—Chinese?" she suggested.

"Jenkins will be waiting for you!" I said as my stomach rumbled at the thought of Chinese food.

"I can pull up eHarmony on my BlackBerry and chat with him," she said.

"Chinese sounds good," I told her. "And you've got to read what that little drama queen wrote to McDermott."

We found a hole-in-the-wall cheap Chinese buffet in bumblefuck Virginia and loaded our plates full of food. As we settled into the comfy booth seats, we both reached for our BlackBerrys.

"This ought to be good," I said as I read a new message from Blair.

"Dear Allison, That kind of language only displays your lack of a vocabulary. Enjoy your evening. Blair."

I noticed that he'd conveniently cc'd Charles, Rose, Morgan and, of course, McDermott. "Shocking. I should have seen that coming."

I showed Janet all the recent Blair-related messages but she seemed disinterested. I decided to ignore Blair, but did begin to question my job performance. I thought I'd be proactive and send McDermott an email, even though I doubted he'd want to get involved in a petty interoffice squabble. "Hi Senator!" I wrote. "Shopping mission accomplished! We got a great white dare-to-bare baby doll for Karma and shipped it overnight. She should receive it first thing in the morning. See you tomorrow! Allison."

Within seconds, McDermott wrote back: "Thanks. How much?"

"It was $250 and shipping was $45 for the overnight shipping. We put everything on Janet's credit card so you can pay her cash or write a check. Thanks!" Send.

Within seconds, the senator wrote again: "Great joke. Really, how much? Hope you lovely ladies are taking in a movie and staying out of trouble tonight."

I responded: "No movie, just Chinese. Yum. Sorry, no joke. It's very pretty and classy. She'll love it!"

McDermott wrote: "Talk to Trista in the morning. Get the campaign to pay Janet. Best you two go easy on the Chinese. Maybe take a walk later."

"Ugh," I sighed in frustration. "He wants the campaign to pay for Karma's birthday present," I told Janet, who was absorbed in her BlackBerry and wasn't eating her food. "He also implied that we're both overweight," I said as I grabbed another egg roll out of spite.

"I'm sorry, what was it Blair just said?" Janet asked.

"Put down your BlackBerry and pay attention. McDermott just told me to talk with Trista to have the campaign pay for Karma's baby doll," I answered. "It's a complete violation of Senate ethics. I don't know what to do."

"I guess when your marriage is a business decision, you can figure out ways to make all family gifts campaign related," Janet answered without skipping a beat.

"Just seems so wrong." We sat in silence for a while as we both answered our emails. It had become our way of life. We constantly communicated via text and email. Life without a BlackBerry seemed foreign. "Janet, why is it that in politics the bad guys always finish first and hard workers get tossed aside?" I asked.

"My mom has always told me that hard work pays off in the long run. We can't lose sight of that," Janet responded. "Charles and the senator know we work hard. I know it will pay off. People like Blair, who are lazy, will get caught and their true colors will show through—they have to."

"What kind of lowlife randomly emails the senator to tell him I need a job evaluation?" I complained. "Who does something like that and then expects to work together as a team?"

"I know. I know. Our office can't be normal," Janet sighed. "We're dealing with immature coworkers who were raised with silver spoons in their mouths," she said.

"Well there's definitely no silver spoon in my mouth. Shit, I worked three jobs during college to pay my tuition and bills," I told her with pride.

"I know, and that shows in our work ethic and personalities," Janet said. "I think that's why Charles and the senator like us. They know we're working for them because we believe in what they believe. And they know we're the best workers in the office. I think that's why they're tougher on us," she continued. "They keep us around because we're valuable, not because our parents can write fat checks to the campaign coffers."

"I hope you're right," I told her.

"Oh, there he is!" shouted Janet, changing the subject.

"Who?" I asked, even though I could guess the answer.

Janet started smiling broadly and began to type rapidly. "Jenkins, silly!" she said.

I didn't want to disturb her texting date, so I played Words With Friends on my iPhone. Nearly ninety minutes later we finally left the restaurant.

I barely slept that night, wondering about my exchange with Blair and how the senator would respond. I desperately wanted the senator to stick up for me—just once.

*   *   *   *   *   *

I woke up early after a restless night and hurried into the office. It was only day two of the longest week of the Senate session and I was already operating on adrenaline. I knew today would be awkward because of the Blair incident, but I wasn't going to let him hold me back.

The morning flew by without many hiccups. Lindsay and I were finally in sync and serving the senator. He seemed happy going from

meeting to meeting and, amazingly, was right on schedule. I barely spoke with Janet, Charles, or Rose throughout the morning. Everyone seemed focused on their jobs.

Then, all of a sudden, Janet called me to say Charles and Rose wanted to speak with her immediately in Charles's office. I told her not to fret or worry. I was sure it was nothing. I watched Janet make her way into Charles's office and heard her ask him about his kids. Then Charles closed his office door. He also shut the blinds to his office so I couldn't see what was happening. That was not a good sign.

Just then the senator came raging out of his office, "Allison, what size baby doll did you buy for Karma?"

"Sir, I talked with the sales associate and her professional opinion was that Karma would be most comfortable in a medium," I answered politely.

"Karma is pissed. She's an extra small and gets a thrill when I have to help her strap into her high thighs," the senator told me. I was immediately uncomfortable.

"I'm sorry, sir." He walked away and didn't mention anything more.

"Did you just hear what I heard?" Lindsay asked me.

"Yes, I think we heard the same thing," I laughed back. We said, in unison, "Gross."

Almost two hours later Janet emerged from Charles's office. She looked terrible. I could tell her eyes were red and that most likely she'd been crying. She ignored me and went straight to her desk.

I sent her a message, but I didn't get a reply. Then Charles called me into his office. I thought I was going to throw up.

In a very fast fifteen-minute meeting, Charles and Rose explained that Blair had filed a hostile work environment complaint against Janet and me that morning. He had a laundry list of complaints about our behavior, and alleged that we were disruptive and prevented him from performing his official work duties.

I laughed. I thought it was a joke. Rose informed me that Blair was dead serious and he'd be speaking to a lawyer that afternoon.

Charles asked me to refrain from emailing or speaking to Blair until they could get a better sense of his concerns. I rolled my eyes and quipped, "Wait, I'm not allowed to have any contact whatsoever with Blair? No matter the outcome of this lawsuit, can we please keep that in my job description?"

Charles didn't find that funny. He suggested that Janet and I work on our attitudes and be friendlier to the staff. I couldn't believe what I'd just heard. Then he told me he was disappointed that neither of us showed up at the staff happy hour last night. I almost fell out of my chair before I responded, "Janet and I were out buying the boss's wife lingerie we couldn't afford, mailing hockey sticks for the campaign, answering emails all night long—and, to top it off, neither of us even knew about a staff happy hour. Not to mention, we couldn't afford a night of drinking!"

"Allison, knock that shit off," Charles said.

I didn't respond. I was livid.

Rose closed the meeting and informed me that they were going to try to resolve Blair's issues. She asked that Janet and I stay focused on our work. I was fuming. Unlike Janet, who had a tendency to get teary-eyed and hysterical, I had a tendency to get pissed.

I returned to my desk, stunned. How could Blair even imagine he was the victim of a hostile work environment? He must be delusional. Janet passed my desk at least five times the rest of the day and didn't mutter a word to me. I knew she'd take Blair's accusations personally, which would deflate her natural energy and passion for her work. The spoiled little snot could dish it out worse than anyone I knew. But the single time I snapped back at him, he ran off to make a formal complaint. What a baby.

Janet sent me a message asking to go for a walk. I suggested we meet outside the office door so no one would know we were walking together. She agreed, and we met up. The instant I saw her I knew she was taking things way harder than I was. She stood in the hallway, shoulders slumped, head down, shuffling her feet.

"It'll be okay," I said. "We haven't done anything wrong. If anything, you and I both easily could be filing complaints about a hostile work environment. You're the lawyer, you know his claims have absolutely no basis," I said, trying to appeal to her reason.

"I know," she said. "But you know how I get. When I get pissed and feel taken advantage of, I cry—you scream."

"Yeah, that pretty much sums it up. Don't fret, this will all blow over," I assured her.

We walked around the outside office corridor of the Hart Building like it was a racetrack, making several laps. When we returned to the office, it was empty, aside from Cam and Morgan, who were huddled over a computer.

"Hey—it's my favorite Minnesotans!" exclaimed Morgan. We both answered without our usual energetic response.

"You guys okay?" asked Cam.

"What—the gopher got your tongues?" teased Morgan as he made a lame reference to the University of Minnesota mascot.

Janet walked away without saying a word and Cam looked at me quizzically. "You want to grab a beer?" he asked.

"I thought you'd never ask."

"I'm coming too," Morgan chimed in.

Damn, there goes my shot of being alone with Cam. Why does Morgan feel the need to tag along? Why would a forty-something man want to hang with two broke twenty-somethings? He was definitely going to ruin my game.

We bellied up to the bar at Irish Times, our favorite staff pub, which was conveniently located just a few blocks from the Senate office buildings. I was whipped from my day of never-ending crises, and the Guinness I ordered tasted delicious. As it turned out, Morgan was good for something after all. He bought round after round of drinks. We shared a few laughs, and it felt great to be with Cam, even if Morgan was there chaperoning. Then Morgan left to take a phone call and never came back. Cam and I stayed and closed down the bar.

With the Guinness flowing through my veins, all I wanted to do was kiss him. But I resisted my urges.

Cam walked me to Union Station, and even though I tried to show him affection by grabbing his arm, he didn't betray any feelings. I began to think he just wasn't interested. He went into deflection mode and began to talk awkwardly about policy issues. It was further frustration on top of a difficult day. After getting off at my Metro stop, I walked home and tried to fall asleep, but I was filled with worry about Blair's stupid, out-of-the-blue accusations. Even though it was nearly 3:00 a.m., I called my dad.

"Allison!?" he answered groggily. "Are you alright? Is everything okay?" he asked. After I assured him that I was physically okay, I began to emotionally download about the stresses of the job and that I was now potentially a party in a lawsuit.

He reassured me that everything would be fine and, like a great dad, reiterated how proud of me he was. Then he told me to keep working hard and that he too thought everything would blow over. He also suggested that I take care of Blair the same way I took care of the fourth-grade boy who picked on me when I was a second-grader. I had no clue what he was talking about.

He laughed and said, "Well, when you were little, this boy was picking on you. So I told you, if he ever does that again, you grab him by both of his shoulders and head-butt him in the nose. The next day after school, I got a call from the boy's dad. He was pissed. He said he needed to talk to me, that my boy beat up his boy at school. After I told him that was impossible because my only son was two years old, he insisted that my kid beat up his kid. When I told him I had a daughter in second grade, he said to forget it and immediately hung up the phone. It sounds to me like this Blair guy needs a good head-butt," he concluded.

"You're probably right," I said. "But at this point, it's probably not a good idea to add simple assault to the charges being leveled against me." He agreed, and told me to get some sleep.

His reassurance and advice made me think of Janet and her parents. I was thankful that Janet and I were both raised in good homes with structured discipline by parents who encouraged us to study, work hard, and be involved. I was thankful my dad didn't let me settle for the typical small-town mentality, in which college wasn't an option and where getting married and pregnant by age twenty-two was the cool thing to do. I fell asleep feeling loved and blessed, with my BlackBerry cozily situated next my pillow.

*   *   *   *   *   *

I woke up to the ring and buzz of my bed buddy. I glanced over and saw it was 4:55 a.m. and Janet was calling. "Hey," I answered.

"I need your help," she announced without preamble. "I don't know how to put on this g-string corset deal."

"Where are you?" I asked.

"At home!" she said, sounding upset.

"Why are you putting on the g-string lingerie now?" I asked.

"Allison, I'm going to breakfast today with Jenkins!" she screamed.

"Settle down, I know that. But why are you wearing lingerie?" I asked her again

"Because I need to be ready in case one thing leads to another," she answered in all seriousness.

I went through step-by-step directions with her and wondered if she was in a little over her head. I couldn't imagine her wearing that crap under her clothes all day. How uncomfortable.

I lay awake after Janet's call and decided to head to the office early. When I arrived, I found the office lights on and Blair in a yoga position in the middle of the office floor.

"Good morning, Blair," I said out of habit. I didn't hear a response. I went to my desk and tried not to barf in response to seeing his little body flopped in odd positions. I tried to log on to my computer, without success. I tried every password I could remember, but each of my attempts failed. Without a computer, I couldn't work. I soon found myself staring at the senator's collection of tea bags to avoid any more contact with Blair in yoga positions. I kept wondering how Operation Senate Blind Date was going. I was anxious for Janet's recap, but I resisted the urge to BlackBerry her. I didn't want to interrupt, and she wasn't likely to respond anyway.

Rose arrived to the office shortly thereafter and I went immediately over to tell her about my computer password. "Oh, you haven't spoken with Charles yet?" she asked.

"Nope, he isn't in yet," I answered.

"Last night over dinner, we decided it would be best for Janet and you to head to Minnesota for the August recess to do the senator's campaign scheduling and advance work. This whole Blair blowup is creating turmoil in our office. We can't have the risk of a lawsuit around here, especially not with the presidential campaign ramping up. We think removing the two of you from the office would be best right now. You'll handle the senator's schedule for the next month, and Janet can assist you. Of course, you'll need to take all your DC work and responsibilities with you to Minnesota. We can't afford to replace you two for the month. So you'll be performing both your official Senate duties as well as campaign duties. You'll be paid accordingly," she finished.

"Wow, I didn't realize we'd be heading to Minnesota. Should we plan to be there starting next week and work with Trista on our airfare and hotel reservations?" I asked.

"No. We thought you two could drive Janet's car out today. You'll both be staying at the McDermotts' for the month," she said casually. "Is Janet in yet?"

Trying to cover for Janet's breakfast date, I answered, "Didn't she say something about an early morning pediatric dental group breakfast yesterday?"

"I don't really remember, nor do I care. Please be sure to keep

Lindsay in the loop. We locked both of your computers so we can go through all your emails to make sure Blair's complaint isn't warranted," said Rose.

"Okay," I answered. I frantically began to mentally catalog every inappropriate email I'd ever sent through my Senate account. It was going to be a long day.

I had really been looking forward to a break, possibly even a few vacation days, during recess. I needed time to unwind and not worry about Senator McDermott. Now, overnight, thanks to Blair's overreaction, we were headed to Minnesota to work around the clock. To make matters worse, we'd be living with Karma and the senator. Surely this couldn't be happening. I wasn't excited. In fact, the idea made me sick. I began to wonder how Janet's little Volvo would possibly make it to Minnesota without backfiring or blowing up. Janet couldn't come back to the office quickly enough. And, of course, the one morning I really needed her, she was off having breakfast with a US Senator, fulfilling her online romance. I still refrained from sending her a message or calling her. I'd let her enjoy her last few minutes of freedom.

The clock turned toward noon, and still no sign of Janet. I caved around 11:30 a.m. and tried to call her nine times. I kept getting her voice mail. I left message after message and attempted to email her. I started to worry. I pictured her murdered or raped by some crazy nut posing as Senator Jenkins online, but who was really a repeat sex offender preying on a Minnesota virgin. Just as I was about to call the police, Janet came skipping into the office. She had a glow I'd never seen before. "We've got to talk," I told her.

"Oh, yes, we do!" she said.

"No, really, we need to talk!"

"Whoa, what's your problem? Gopher got your tongue?" she asked, mocking Morgan's lame joke.

"We're hitting the highway for a road trip to Minnesota today—in your car. We're also now officially working on the presidential campaign part-time, and we'll be living at the McDermotts' while we're in Minnesota," I blurted out.

"Come again?"

"Oh, you heard me, darling. Charles and Rose agreed last night that you and I should work out of the Minnesota office for the next month. Rose told me this morning that we have to live at the McDermotts' to save money. I couldn't have made this up if I tried."

"I don't think my car will make it fifty miles, let alone a thousand miles," panicked Janet.

"At least we'll be together," I reassured her, "and thankfully we've got the emergency credit card in case we need it."

"Yes, but we just put $1,000 on there the other night and I only have a $2,000 limit," Janet said, looking scared.

"We can always call our parents. Trust me, we don't have much of a choice," I answered as I packed my folders and other paperwork.

"Well, over the next thousand miles you can hear all about my breakfast date, with Jenkins!! It was him! That reminds me, I'd better head to the bathroom and get out of this lingerie," Janet said, squirming uncomfortably.

Every time Janet or I traveled I was impressed with our ability to "pack light." This trip was no exception. Within two hours, Janet had picked me up and we were ready for our long drive to Minnesota. We were amused that our luggage consisted of only one oversized suitcase each, which were bursting with bright skirts and trendy, inexpensive shoes. Janet's backseat was filled with boxes of scheduling requests, folders of work, every possible telephone number, and contact information for everyone who was anyone. I felt sure that one sudden tap on the brakes and we'd be buried in paper.

Within six hours I had said goodbye to Veronica and we were on the road heading to Minnesota. We encouraged the rusty car in unison, "Come on, Bessie," as we patted her with love.

"The McDermotts' or bust!" we added.

7
Minnesota Bound

Janet and I were excited to leave DC behind us for the month, but we were nervous about what the time would entail. I felt frustrated about being forced to work in Minnesota and missing my first August recess. I'd been looking forward to it for a long time. I also fretted about the Cam situation. I was going to miss seeing him on a daily basis and knew that trying to flirt with him while in Minnesota would be challenging. I made a mental note to make sure that my Microsoft Outlook interoffice communicator was set up ASAP. I tried to think of ways to get his personal Gmail address so I

could Gchat with him all day. I was going to have to hit up Janet for ways to improve my online seduction techniques.

Janet didn't have to say anything for me to realize that she was fired up about working and living with the McDermotts. All I felt about that situation was dread. But she seemed to have gained a sense of security from realizing that she'd be back in Minnesota for the rest of the month.

As we began our sixteen-hour journey, I reached down and grabbed my iPhone. "Alright, lady, what would you like to rock out to first? We've got everything from Adele to Yeasayer. Not quite everything from A to Z, but close." I pulled out my adapter and plugged it into the cigarette lighter outlet. I quickly realized that it didn't light up. "Doesn't this work?" I asked, dismayed.

"No way, Jose!"

"Fuck, are you kidding me?" I asked as I fiddled with the outlet.

"No, I had it disconnected. I don't smoke, why would I need a cigarette lighter?" Janet said proudly. "Besides, I have my tape player and tapes with the songs from all my favorite Broadway musicals."

"Oh my God, are you kidding me?" It was going to be a *very* long trip.

"It won't be bad!" Janet chirped, patting my arm. "Plus, you need to hear all about my breakfast date."

"Alright, let's hear it," I said as I checked my email on my BlackBerry.

"Well, there isn't really much to tell," she started and continued without taking a breath. "I met him at Bistro Bis. It was fun. We had a nice time. He said we should start reading the same book for date two so we can compare thoughts."

"Wait a minute! Why are you leaving out all the good details? I mean, come on, you were gone all morning! Did you walk right up to him? 'Hello, Senator Jenkins, I'm Janet, I work for Senator McDermott and I've been following you around and stepping in front of your hard cane and running home to my computer to write you all night long.'"

"It wasn't like that at all. He made reservations so the hostess escorted him right to our table. I didn't tell him I worked for the boss. Duh. You think I'm stupid?" she asked.

"Stupid and love seem to go together," I replied.

"I think reading the same books would be romantic," she swooned as a smile washed over her face. "We need to think of a book so I can email him later tonight."

"We'll have plenty of time to think of a book on this drive," I said, trying to feign excitement. "Maybe you should suggest the Kama Sutra!"

"Oh my God, I forgot to tell you!" Janet said. "You'll never guess what I did at breakfast. I was so nervous that I literally started choking while drinking my orange juice. It was bad. The orange juice went down the wrong pipe, and I started choking and coughing all over the place. You know, coughing hard, the almost-ready-to-puke type of cough. I thought I'd never recover!"

"You literally choked?!"

"It was horrible. Jenkins asked if I was alright. But I couldn't talk and he couldn't see me," she answered. "It was absolutely horrible and completely embarrassing. The only redeeming factor was that he couldn't see how red my face was or the tears streaming down it."

"So what happened?" I asked as I continued to check my email.

"He came over and grabbed my boobs!" she laughed. "He couldn't see me so he felt his way down to my abdomen and started to do the Heimlich maneuver!"

"Wait, this happened right in the middle of the restaurant?" I asked, shocked. "Didn't anyone come over to help you? Or think it was odd that a blind man was groping a choking woman?"

"I don't know. I was too overwhelmed by him touching my boobs that I didn't notice or care. Plus, I couldn't breathe!" she answered.

"So how did this romantic morning end? When are you meeting at the library for your book report?"

"I paid the bill and we shook hands," she answered nonchalantly.

"Wait! What? You paid for breakfast?" I asked. "You had breakfast with a United States Senator you met online and you picked up the flippin' check?"

"Yeah. So what?"

"Don't you think that's weird? Do I have to remind you that you're flat broke? Plus, you know as well as I do that a gentleman should pay for a date—especially a first date," I said, appalled. Then I burst out in heavy laughter from the ridiculousness of the situation. "That is some funny shit."

"It was only, like, forty bucks," she said as she rolled her eyes.

"Still, it's the principle. I can't believe you paid." Janet was one of a kind. "'Excuse me, Senator. I only shop at grocery stores that offer ten items for ten bucks, and my best friend has to steal toilet paper and tampons from the Senate office building bathroom. But let me pick up our check. Times must be tough for you, Senator.'"

"It wasn't like that at all," she insisted.

We sat in silence for a long time.

"What was I supposed to do, he couldn't see the bill sitting there!" she shot back.

"You think he's never been to a restaurant before? Of course he knows there is a bill to be paid. He's blind, not a blind redneck."

"I think we would have sat there all day. He didn't even motion or feel for the bill," she told me.

"Well, how does he know where his food is on the plate?" I asked.

"Easy—everything is arranged as a clock. Eggs at one, toast at four, and, um, sausage at six," she said. "Get it?"

We both laughed, and soon I dozed off with my BlackBerry in hand.

I woke up to Janet swearing up a storm. "Holy shit! For Christ's sake, I can't see shit!" Then she yelled at me to wake up.

"Where are we and what are you doing?" I asked as Janet careened the car toward the side of the road.

"I think my trunk latch just broke!" she panicked.

I told her to settle down, and once she was safely pulled over on the shoulder, we got out to examine the situation. "What happened?"

"I was just driving and all of a sudden the trunk flew open and passing cars kept waving at me. So I panicked and pulled over."

"Okay," I said. "Well, there isn't much we can do about it here. I think we need to stop at a gas station to see if we can get it fixed."

"I don't think I can drive like this," Janet told me after we were under way again. "This is just way too much stress."

I encouraged her to calm down and she made it to the nearest exit, where we pulled into the closest gas station. We got out to examine the damage, and to our dismay, it seemed the trunk latch was really broken. We weren't going to be able to close it all of the way. "Ugh," I said in frustration, "I think your trunk is fucked."

"I know. People are staring at us," Janet said, trying one last time to close the trunk lid.

"You'd stare too! We look like idiots!" I said as I tried to help her slam the lid.

"We just need to get this damn trunk closed!" she bitched.

I went into the gas station and bought some bungee cords. "You can take the girl out of South Dakota, but you can't take South Dakota out of the girl," I said as I crawled underneath the back of the car to hook down the trunk lid.

"I think that's tight enough. God, I've got dirt and grease all over me," I said in frustration as I got back into the car.

Hours passed while we continued the journey to Minnesota, and I didn't feel the immense need to check my email. The time went by quickly, and Bessie was managing the trek with flying colors. We drove straight through the night without resting and we both cheered when we saw the "Welcome to Minnesota" sign at the Wisconsin border.

It was exactly 5:30 a.m. as we pulled into the senator's driveway. Janet parked her car right next to another car already there. We were both exhausted from the all-night drive.

"God, we look terrible," Janet said as she put on lipstick.

"It's to be expected. We literally packed our bags for a month and drove halfway across the country—all within twenty-four hours. They shouldn't expect to see beauty queens."

"All I want is a bed," she answered.

"I know, me too," I said as I pulled our bags from the trunk.

"This is sort of weird," Janet said as we walked up to the McDermotts' front door.

"Yeah, it is. I mean, what do we do? Ring the doorbell?"

"There aren't any lights on in the house," Janet said as she snooped in the windows.

"Rose told them we were coming. They should be expecting us."

"Go ahead and knock," she said.

"God. You are such a chicken," I said, and knocked nervously. We waited for a solid five minutes and nothing happened. "Should I call Margot?"

"You can, I'll just go wait until later in the morning. I can sleep in the car. I don't want to piss them off," Janet said.

"Yeah, this is useless. You're right. Lame, but always right. Let's wait until 7:00 a.m. and try again," I said as we both headed back to the car.

We reclined our seats as much as we could and immediately fell into an exhausted sleep. After what felt like minutes, I woke up to Janet poking me.

"Listen, did you just hear that!?"

"What the hell are you talking about?" I asked, pissed that she woke me up.

"Shut up and listen. I heard it again!" she said, looking around. "There's someone in that car," she said squinting at the windows.

"You're losing your mind," I told her, encouraging her to go back to sleep.

"No. Don't you hear that sound?"

"It's in your head!"

"No, I hear something. I'm getting out," she said, opening up the car door. In a matter of seconds, Janet was back in the front seat, slamming the car door behind her. She was white as a ghost.

"What?"

"I think I just saw McDermott's dad in the act," she said.

"What are you talking about?"

"Go look for yourself!" she yelled.

"I'm not looking! But, really, what did you see?"

"Do you need line-by-line details? I swear to you that McDermott's dad is having sex right now in that car," she said, pointing.

"Shut up, Colonel is eighty-eight years old," I laughed. "I bet he can't even get it up. Viagra can't be that effective, can it?"

"If you think I'm kidding, go look for yourself. It's been awhile since you've see a dick," she sniped.

"You should talk," I shot right back.

We both started to slide even farther down in our seats, so as not to be seen. Just as I was thinking about popping up to take a look, I saw Colonel and a hot young blonde get out of the car. McDermott's dad was pulling up his pants.

"Holy shit! That's Margot!" exclaimed Janet.

"Shhhhhh," I told her. I too was shocked to see Margot come sliding out of the car.

"Taking care of the kids... and the boss's dad," Janet laughed.

"That's what I call one full-service nanny!"

"Fuck, they see us!" I whispered as I saw both of them glance in our direction.

"Pretend you're sleeping," Janet whispered back.

We let them pound on the windows a few times before Janet rolled down her window after pretending to wake up.

"Oh, hi," she said.

"You guys should come inside," welcomed Margot.

"Oh, yes, you gals need to come inside and get settled in," Colonel

said as he looked my bare legs up and down. Colonel helped carry in our luggage, and I could see Janet's eyes wandering down his body in disgust.

"I can't believe you two are going to stay here for the month," shouted Margot.

"I can't believe it either," Janet murmured.

"We're pretty tired, Margot. Where can we unpack and get some rest?" I asked.

Margot gave me a puzzled look. "We don't have any spare bedrooms. Karma told me that you'll be sleeping on air mattresses in the main living room."

"That'll be just fine," answered Janet.

"Should we just go this way?" I asked, pointing.

"That's the living room, but we don't have any air mattresses yet. And per Karma's rules, we need to be 'house ready' at all times. You'll need to blow up your mattresses each night and put them away by 6:00 a.m. I also can't have you leaving anything in the living room," she instructed. "So make sure all your personal belongings aren't kept in the main living area."

Janet and I walked into the living room. We stared at each other and I whispered, "I can't sleep on an air mattress for a month and live out of your car's trunk."

"Shit, my trunk doesn't even close," she whispered back.

"I love you dearly, Janet. But sharing this little space with you and working together every day is going to drive me nuts."

"I know, but we have to make this work," she said.

"I think this is fucked up. Everyone else in that godforsaken office charges trip expenses up the wazoo like they aren't spending taxpayer dollars and we're stuck here!"

"It won't be that bad," Janet said as she turned on the TV. Her jaw dropped. I looked over and saw that it was tuned to pay-per-view porn. "Well. Speaking of sex..."

"Not now. They're right in the other room," I warned.

"Who in their right mind would find that octogenarian an appropriate hookup?" she asked.

"I know, it's just plain gross," I answered.

"Gross? I can think of better words than gross." Janet just wouldn't drop it. "I mean, do you think the senator knows his children's nanny is sleeping with his dad?" she asked.

"It is gross. And I have no idea if the senator knows. But you had to know his house was going to be weird," I said.

We tried to fall asleep in the living room chairs, but were woken up by the one and only Karma McDermott. "Hi, girls," she said loudly as she swooshed into the room, completely done up without so much as a hair out of place.

We greeted her as she went to hug each of us. It was uncomfortable, but she did seem welcoming. "We're very thankful you girls are working for Anders. I know he really appreciates you both coming to work at the Minnesota office," she said, staring at our luggage.

"Please make yourselves at home, our home is your home," she told us as she walked away.

"God, I have to admit, Karma was actually just nice," Janet said, her shock at the fact evident in her voice.

"This is just weird," I said, slowly sitting down again. "Maybe things won't be so bad after all."

Like a brewing storm, Margot came whirling into the living room with a bagel in one hand and a clipboard in the other. "I'm so glad you guys are here to help me out," she said, out of breath. Janet shot me a nervous sideways glance. "Janet, Karma was hoping you'd take the senator's father to the VA this morning for his regular checkup, and also to follow up on the senator's request regarding his father receiving the Purple Heart Medal badge," Margot ordered.

Janet shot me another nervous glance. "You want me to take the senator's father to the VA this morning?" Janet asked, clarifying that she heard correctly.

"Yes, that would be wonderful!" Margot shot back.

Capitol Hell

"I'll head over to the office this morning," I said quickly, before Margot had the chance to order me to do some random task.

"Excellent, I was hoping you could drop off Karma at her yoga appointment on your way," Margot told me.

"I don't have a car here. Janet has to cart me around."

"Janet, how about you drop Allison at the office, Karma at yoga, and then come back to pick up the senator's father for his appointment?" she asked.

Janet glared at me again and nodded her head. "I'd better go clean up Bessie."

"I think my favorite phrase this month is going to be, 'This is fucked up,'" I told Janet. I could tell she was exhausted from driving all night long. I felt bad for her and wondered how she was going to pull through the day, which included chaperoning the senator's father to the world's most bureaucratic medical office. We showered and got ready for our first day working in the Minnesota office.

Janet dropped me off. "I'll come into the office after the medical appointment and hopefully we can head home early tonight," she said as I slammed the car door.

"Good luck," I told her, knowing her day was likely to be longer than mine.

My stomach twisted into knots as I walked into the office. One might think that transitioning from the DC office to the Minnesota office was no big deal because we talked to our in-state counterparts on a daily basis. But that wasn't the case in the congressional world. Instead, while I had a great relationship with Trista, there was a distinct tension between the state office and the DC office. The staffers in the state office always seemed to believe the DC staff thought too highly of themselves and had a "DC mentality." The staffers in the DC office felt the state office personnel didn't understand the constant pressure of Capitol Hill. From the tight schedule to the huge workload, Washington's hectic pace simply wasn't understood by the folks in the state office.

As I stepped into the office, Trista offered a genuine smile and huge welcoming hug. I unloaded all my files and folders into an empty spare office. Thankfully, it was located next to Janet's temporary office. The morning went quickly, and I fended off endless yawns. Around noon, I started to worry about Janet and her adventure to the VA with Colonel.

Trista was anxious to meet with both of us about the August recess, the senator's upcoming presidential announcement, and the Iowa Straw Poll. Trista was thrilled to have the extra hands. Just as Trista and I were leaving to grab lunch—one of the luxuries of working in the state office—the receptionist told me that Rose was on the phone and needed to speak with me immediately.

I took a deep breath before I answered her call. "Hi, Rose!" I answered trying to be cheerful and alert. After some small talk about our trip and the McDermotts, Rose got to the heart of her call. "I'm afraid we can't talk Blair out of filing a hostile work environment complaint with the Senate Ethics Office against our office regarding you and Janet," she explained.

"Wow, I'm stunned. I don't think he has a leg to stand on," I told her.

"Yes, we were hoping this would blow over with time. But today Charles and I sat and listened to Blair, and he's very distraught," she reinforced.

There was an awkward silence. Finally I said, "Can you tell me or at least offer a clue about Blair's allegations?" I asked.

"Blair is concerned that both you and Janet don't allow him to perform his job duties without making him feel inadequate and that you don't include him in conversations," Rose said.

"Include him in conversations?" I asked, completely confused.

"Yes, Blair had three or four examples of how you two didn't include him in conversations. He says you sit with your backs to him at meetings and write notes on paper that he believed to be about him," she answered.

"You've got to be kidding me! I sit near Lindsay in meetings, and

any note I'm writing on paper is about scheduling questions! They have nothing to do with Blair. This is unbelievable!" I said, shocked at the ridiculousness of the situation.

"It's serious to Blair and our office. We're going to send a member of the Senate Counsel to Minnesota to do an internal investigation and make a decision regarding the complaint. In the meantime, Blair has asked to work from home. The two of you may not contact him directly. Please relay this information to Janet and make sure you send any emails to Charles or myself and we'll pass them along to Blair," Rose ended quickly.

I hung up the phone and stared at Trista in disbelief. I explained everything to her, and she couldn't believe it either. "You and Janet are the hardest working people in that office, and two of the friendliest," she said, perplexed.

I wondered what was going on. If Janet and I were the problem, why would Blair need to work from home? We were now more than a thousand miles away from him. Something didn't seem right.

Trista and I went to lunch. When we returned I found Janet slumped over her temporary computer pounding on the keyboard. "My damn password doesn't work," she said.

"That sucks. But you know what sucks even more?" I asked.

"Driving Miss Karma all morning and bringing the senator's father to have his blood drawn at the VA and being expected to bring the senator's teenagers to the Mall of America tonight after work in your personal car with gas prices skyrocketing?" Janet answered in a fiery tone.

"Ugh, that does all suck. But we've got a bigger problem," I said, shutting her door.

"That little bitch Blair is actually filing a hostile work environment complaint against us. Rose called to tell us they're sending a Senate lawyer to do an investigation and we can't talk to Blair by email or phone. We need to go through Rose or Charles," I reported.

"What? Isn't a hostile work environment when an employee

fears going to work because of intimidation or retaliation including harassment?" she asked.

"I don't know. I think so. Blair says we sit in our chairs with our backs to him, and we pass notes," I said with an incredulous smile on my face.

"We pass notes? We don't even have any meetings together or have time to scribble notes about Blair to each other," she said firmly.

"He's actually working from home until the investigation is complete because he says he's fearful of our work environment," I told her.

"We aren't even there. How could we be the problem?" she asked, just as perplexed as I was.

"Must be nice to roll out of bed and log into your email while watching daytime television," I suggested. "I'm sure he just doesn't want to miss the thrilling plot of *Days of Our Lives*."

"Shit—just having a bed would be nice right now," she shot back.

"Right. No shit. Maybe we should drum up a complaint against Rose for making us sleep on blow-up mattresses in the senator's living room. That's pretty hostile," I suggested, only half kidding.

"We have a solid case, especially after witnessing Colonel getting a piece of the nanny's ass last night." Janet laughed.

"So how bad was it today?" I asked.

"Unbelievable. After I dropped you off, Karma had the gall to complain that Bessie had a little rust on her and asked me to drop her off a block away from yoga so no one would see her getting out of such a piece of shit. Then I went all the way back to pick up Colonel, and can you believe that he didn't even have a frickin' appointment set up for today?" she said.

I didn't say a word, just let her continue to vent. Thankfully, the office door was still closed.

"We got to the VA and he asked me to bring him to the emergency room. Apparently, if you go there, you have to be seen right away, without the normal waiting times like everyone else. You don't even have to have an emergency. He said he needed his blood checked for

insulin. He also asked for his medical file. He told me I needed to make a copy of his damn medical file so I could get him the Purple Heart Medal honor. I've been over this a million times with the senator; his dad doesn't qualify for that award. I don't know what I'm going to do with the medical file," Janet steamed and threw down the file on her desk.

"Yeah, that all sucks."

"I just want to go someplace and sleep for five hours. We don't even have a place to go sleep," Janet said.

"Let's head to the McDermotts' and see what's going on," I suggested. "Maybe we could crash on their couch or something."

"Not worth it. I'm supposed to pick up the kids for the mall tonight. Remember?" she asked shaking her head.

"I think we need to talk to Charles and tell him what's going on, what we're being asked to do," I said. "It's only day one and things are already screwed up."

"I don't want to cause any havoc or piss off the senator," Janet replied.

"I just think Charles would help us," I told her. "I mean, really. Can you imagine this situation being any worse?"

We heard a knock on Janet's door and realized we'd been talking for the past hour. I opened the door to see Trista's smiling face.

"You gals ready to talk about this weekend?" she asked.

"I think right now we both need a bed and good night's sleep," I told her.

"It's only 3:00 p.m.! In this office, we work at least until 4:30 p.m.!" she added, as if we were trying to skip out early. I could see Janet thinking the same thing I was. In Minnesota, 4:30 p.m. is closing time. In DC, 4:30 p.m. sometimes is your earliest opportunity for lunch!

"It's just been a long day. We didn't get any sleep last night because we drove all day and night straight through from DC," I added.

"We need to figure out the senator's schedule and the announcement for Saturday," Trista added, seeming a bit nervous.

"Got it," I said, walking toward my office to grab a notebook.

Trista shut the door and we waited for her to take charge of the meeting. She just looked at both of us. Janet, annoyed with the silence, spoke up. "What do you have planned for the boss?"

"Rose told me you guys were in charge of the senator's announcement and would be taking the lead on the weekend planning, advance, and implementation," she said, delegating all duties to us.

"We haven't heard anything about it besides the hockey stick screw-up," I told her.

Trista looked shocked. "We'd better get Charles on the phone immediately." She left the office to make the call. Janet and I just stared at each other in disbelief. Really, how could this office be so dysfunctional?

"I can't plan a presidential announcement. I can't even hold up my head right now," whined Janet.

"It can't be that hard. We just need to get some volunteers together to wave signs and cheer, put McDermott on a stage, place some friendly faces behind him for the camera shot, write up a few talking points, throw in some red, white, and blue, get someone to do a press release, and call it a day," I said. "We can do this in our sleep."

"We might actually need to do this in our sleep."

"If anyone can pull this off, we can."

"We'll do the announcement in front of the Minnesota Capitol. On the steps. Easy peasy," Janet added.

"McDermott for President," I cheered.

"Right, maybe Mr. President will realize his two inept staffers who are terrible with attention to detail, but lifesavers for his wife and father and kids, need a place to sleep in the White House," Janet said.

"No shit, we better get good jobs out of all of this," I added.

"I wonder if the Secret Service would let Colonel have sex in the White House driveway."

"You won't have to worry about it. You'll be First Lady if you keep creeping on Jenkins," I teased.

"You'll be hired as chief of staff," Janet promised.

"Sounds good," I added, as Trista peeked in again.

"I talked with Charles. He's sending you guys an email right now. He said to check your personal email accounts. He's hoping you'll plan a fifteen-town bus tour across Minnesota for the senator's announcement Saturday. Let me know if you need anything!" Trista said as she walked away.

Janet tried to log on to her computer and was still locked out. I could feel her eyes brewing for a fight.

"Let's check my computer," I suggested. We walked to my office. I was able to log in to my computer. I saw the new email from Charles.

Hi Janet and Allison! I hope you guys survived the big drive and are well rested. Let's plan a fifteen-town tour across all ends of Minnesota for Anders's announcement. Pick out all the major media hubs and let's try to pack two or three motor coach buses with volunteers to ride along. Anders will need a separate car to ride in, and make sure you have staff doing the advance work at each stop before he arrives. I'm off to my son's school choir concert and then walking the dog. My BlackBerry is on though—let's do this, team!

And so the campaign began.

8

Advancing and Canvassing Minnesota

"**Y**ou have got to be kidding me! We need to plan a fifteen-town bus tour across the entire state of Minnesota for Saturday?" I asked Janet repeatedly as we battled to see who could scoop up the buffet's sweet-and-sour chicken the fastest.

"I just want to sleep," answered Janet.

"We have no hotel room, no real bed, no place to unpack our overloaded suitcases, and now we have to pull an all-nighter to plan this damn campaign announcement," I rattled off while eating fast.

"I hate our jobs and I'm really starting to hate our lack of social lives," Janet said, as she checked her bank balance online.

"I know but thank God we have each other. I can't imagine being stuck in this pressure cooker by myself," I stated as my BlackBerry began to go off. "Now what?" I yelled in exasperation. I had a new message from Lindsay and I couldn't quite comprehend it. I passed my BlackBerry over to Janet for her to read.

Hi! I hope you guys made it home safely and are enjoying Minnesota. I don't know how to break this terrible news to you, but the senator just called me. He's itching badly and has asked to be driven to the ER. I've got Cam driving him there now—in my car since Cam still hasn't gotten his back. The senator thinks his office furniture might have fleas and he's been exposed. He said his arms, legs, and back are covered with huge red bites. I'll keep you posted and I'll order him flowers. I'll send you the total amount so we can all pitch in.

"I don't have any extra money—let alone money for flowers because the boss has a slight itch," Janet stated as she munched on an egg roll.

"Plus, you know he doesn't give a shit about flowers," I continued.

"Yuck, fleas on his Senate furniture. That's disgusting," Janet cringed. "That's worse than lice!"

"God. I'm starting to itch just thinking about it," I said. "You don't think it's bedbugs, do you?! Can you imagine if McDermott ends up being responsible for infecting the entire Senate office building with bedbugs?"

"I'm itching now too…" said Janet, scratching her arms. Within seconds, there was another email from Lindsay. I read it out loud to Janet: "I'm very worried about the senator. It says online that cancer can start with your skin itching. I don't know how on earth his Senate office furniture could be infected. I wish you were here to help me! The sky is falling!"

"I just searched flea bites online," Janet told me. "I don't know what the hubbub is all about. He just needs to take an oatmeal bath and to use some calamine lotion."

"The senator is a smart guy. I mean, he can go buy a bottle of frickin' lotion and take a bath, right?" I asked her.

"God, I sure hope so," Janet said, smirking.

"What's so funny?"

"Jenkins is online and he just sent me a sweet message," she answered.

"Come on, read it to me. What does Senator Blind Date have to say now?" I asked. Then I caught myself. "No pun intended."

"Nothing important—he just wants to know if I want to go on a weekend hunting trip with him," Janet stated matter-of-factly.

"He's blind," I said. "How can he go hunting?"

"So is Lionel Richie."

"I think you mean Stevie Wonder," I said. Janet was terrible at keeping her celebrities straight, which was funny, because she loved gossip magazines. It was one of those things I'd never understand about her. We sat in an awkward silence.

"God. I can't believe McDermott has ticks," Janet said.

"Karma is going to freak out. I bet Lindsay will be washing all his bedding and scrubbing all his furniture." I was starting to feel bad for Lindsay.

"Don't you think they'd hire a professional service to come in and kill all the fleas?"

"PETA will be protesting our office! They'll demand that McDermott wear a flea collar and use some completely ineffective organic remedy!" I laughed.

"Can you imagine?" Janet exclaimed, cracking up.

"So the NRA is sponsoring the hunting trip. It's in three weeks! It sounds like a hoot," Janet gushed. "Jenkins said he'd fly me to Colorado to meet up with him," Janet whispered.

"Why are we whispering?" I asked.

"I don't know. You never know who might be around to hear us."

"Trust me, no one gives a shit about your doomed love affair with Jenkins," I replied snarkily. "Besides, are you forgetting that week is only one week before the Iowa Straw Poll? And let's face it, Charles will have us both working ninety-hour weeks. You can't run off with the senator's opposition and play GI Janet for the weekend," I said, trying to redirect her energies and focus.

"I've never held a gun before," she laughed. "Get it?"

"Oh trust me, doll-face, I get it," I said, laughing with her.

"I want to go with him. It'd be fun. Besides, a hunting trip paid for by the NRA. I bet the hunting shack could easily be revamped into, oh I dunno, a sweet lovers' den," Janet said with fire in her voice.

"Give it a rest. We have a fifteen-stop bus tour to plan for our boss—who, incidentally, has bites all over his body and is in the ER right now. Remember?"

"You're right," she said. "We'd better get going. I have about two hours before I turn into a pumpkin."

Janet took charge of managing the logistics of the bus tour while I mapped out our route, stops, and timing. We were pleased with our work; within two hours we had a viable tour agenda with fifteen stops throughout Minnesota in a nonstop twenty-four-hour period. We sent our drafts to Charles for approval and decided we'd continue working on the details in the morning.

"Are you ready to retire to Casa McDermott?" I asked as I packed up my bag to leave the office.

"I'll never be ready for Casa del Sex in the driveway," Janet answered.

"Don't knock it til you've tried it," I said, winking at Janet.

"God, what a long day," Janet said as we walked out of the office into the dark evening.

"We arrive when it's dark out and we leave when it's dark out. This isn't the August recess I'd anticipated," I complained.

"I'm not in the mood to entertain Colonel, Karma, or Margot, and there is no way I am bringing his brats to the mall tonight" Janet whined.

"Oh no, we're heading straight to our blow-up mattresses and tucking ourselves into bed. Hopefully they'll all be in bed by the time we get there."

"Perfect," exclaimed Janet.

We arrived at the McDermotts' and didn't know if we should knock or let ourselves in. As we were debating what to do, we both jumped as Colonel silently appeared from the garden. He insisted that we sit outside with him and enjoy his favorite drink, Jack and Coke on the rocks. As he poured the two strong drinks, I visualized Janet puking after her first swig. Being born and raised in South Dakota, I had an appreciation for hard liquor, but lemonade with sugar was about as heavy as Janet could take it. Colonel offered us two glasses with 90 percent booze and 10 percent Coke, then lit himself a cigar. Janet took a sip and instantly started coughing hysterically. I kicked her under the table to stop. Then I almost fell off my chair when Janet, without warning, downed the entire glass like it was a shot. Her eyes watered, and I looked around desperately for something for her to vomit in.

But instead of vomiting, Janet held her own and Colonel poured her another drink. Within minutes she downed that one, too. I didn't want to be last girl standing, so I decided to catch up with my drinking buddies and show off my tolerance. I downed three large glasses of Jack and Coke in short order. Colonel passed me a lit cigar and I sat back, loving the smell of cigar smoke. I instantly began to laugh when he passed Janet a lit cigar. Before I knew it, Janet inhaled deeply and after a beat, vomit began to flow from her mouth and nose. I rushed to help her as Colonel sat stunned. Janet rushed to the senator's makeshift garden and unloaded her entire night's worth of dinner, drinking, and smoking within a matter of minutes. She walked back to us and pretended nothing had happened. I was amazed at how fast she recovered.

Colonel asked about the office happenings and like two schoolgirls we downloaded all the office gossip. However, despite being a bit drunk, we censored the stories we told him. He didn't hear, for instance, that

Anders had flea bites and asked to go to the ER. He shared a few personal stories about the senator from his childhood and it made us both realize that Anders puts his pants on one leg at a time, just like the rest of us.

I checked my BlackBerry and saw that I'd missed a number of messages, including Charles asking Janet and me to set a budget for the proposed bus tour, and Rose ordering Lindsay to have the senator's office disinfected overnight, which she deemed an emergency. I was shocked to see that the senator also sent a staff-wide email that read: "I'm in the ER and very tired. Please hold all calls and meetings for tomorrow. I'm going to see the Senate doctor in the morning to find out how on earth I got fleas." I passed my BlackBerry over to Janet so she could read the message, and she couldn't hold in a contagious giggle.

"Yuck, the senator really has a case of the bugs!" she laughed.

Colonel didn't seem interested in the least and poured himself another drink. He definitely enjoyed entertaining two younger women. Fifteen minutes later, Karma came running out of the house into the garden. "We need this house disinfected immediately! How dare you leave my husband while he was hospitalized!" she exclaimed. Janet rolled her eyes.

"I'm sorry, Mrs. McDermott, we were asked to come to Minnesota by Charles. Rest assured Lindsay and Rose have the senator's best interests at heart. I'm certain the office will be cleaned tonight," I reassured her.

"If you think Lindsay and Rose have my husband's best interests at heart, you're kidding yourselves. The only two people in his office from the campaign who are loyal to Anders are sitting right in front of me. I can't believe you would sit here drinking while he's lying in a hospital bed!" she exclaimed. "I just hope you two don't have fleas too!"

"Can we do anything to help you?" Janet offered, ignoring her last comment.

"Yes, as a matter of fact, you can! Charles just called me about Saturday's bus trip. I refuse to ride a bus across Minnesota with volunteers. You can find me a car and driver, and I'll get on the bus at every stop to make an appearance. But I won't be riding on that bus!"

"I will run that by Charles," Janet told her.

"No, you don't understand. I will not ride the bus. Six simple words to learn: I will not ride the bus! You don't need Charles to approve anything. Charles is the senator's worst chief of staff. He doesn't understand that I need private time this Saturday to prepare for each tour spot. I can't be on the bus, bouncing around, trying to make small talk with a bunch of strangers who think they know me and my husband!" Karma told us.

Janet took a large gulp of her freshly poured drink. Karma stood up and started pacing around the garden. Janet kicked me under the table. "I need to practice my speech for Saturday. What am I supposed to say? America, please vote for my husband, he is kind, handsome, and has fleas?" she asked.

Janet laughed and I kicked her back after I noticed Karma wasn't joking around. She was serious. Karma's cell phone rang and we both eavesdropped on the conversation. "Don't they know who I am?" she asked, and then listened for a moment before she continued. "I'm an actress. I am not riding a bus with a bunch of volunteers who rarely shower and want to talk about pro-life issues the whole time. I eat vegan and require fresh vegetables at each stop. I can't be exposed to nonorganic vegetables. I might break out from the pesticides. Yes, I will get my hair blown out Friday afternoon. But I'm not riding that bus," she ended the phone conversation.

Without another word, Karma sat down at our table and drank all of Janet's drink in one gulp. "The three of you don't realize how important you are to Anders, how much he needs your love and support. But I will not ride that bus, and Janet I'd like you to accompany me for the entire tour Saturday. I'll need your assistance," Karma said in a nice manner.

"Yes, I'd be happy to travel with you, Mrs. McDermott, but I

do need to run it by Charles," Janet stated, trying to get out of the increasingly uncomfortable situation.

"You girls don't need to run anything by Charles. You are here with us now and Anders has complete trust in your work. He has no one better. I speak for Anders, and what will be will be," she commented. She rarely made sense.

"Speaking of Charles, we need to do a budget for the tour and send it to him tonight," I reminded Janet as I stood up, a bit woozy from the three whiskey drinks I'd consumed.

"You can tell Charles I said the budget should be limitless! This is Anders's big moment!" answered Karma.

"If it only was that easy," Janet said.

"Judging by how many fundraisers Anders is doing, and how we can count on his friends to deliver when asked, this Saturday shouldn't need a budget. You girls don't hold back. Make it spectacular!" added Colonel.

"Well, we have to do a budget, and I'm about ready to pass out," I told him.

"Oh, Allison, can you be sure I ride with Anders on the tour? I don't want to be stuck in any old bus, either. I need to be with my son. Front and center," added Colonel.

"Of course," I added, shooting Janet a look. I wondered how we were going to make all of this work.

Janet and I entered the McDermott house and prepared a quick budget that we both thought was simple and realistic.

Budget for 15-Stop Announcement Tour

3 motor coach buses (rental and mileage)	$7,500
signage at events	$2,000
sound equipment	$4,000
rental cars for entourage/family	$1,000
breakfast for volunteers	$250
lunch for volunteers	$500

dinner for volunteers	$1,000
snacks for volunteers	$250
meals for McDermott family	$500
hockey sticks and jerseys	$350
organic fresh vegetables	$250
Total:	**$17,600**

"I don't know if Charles is going to go for a $17,000 budget," I stated.

"That's peanuts according to Karma, and we really don't know what kind of money the campaign has raised. Let's just send Charles what we've estimated and see what he says," Janet suggested.

"Well, judging from the message Rose just copied me on, I don't think we should bat an eyelash. Get a load of this," I said as I passed my BlackBerry to Janet.

"Holy fuck," she said as she threw down my phone.

The message from Rose was directed to the senator and Charles. It asked for their permission to spend $52,000 to get the office disinfected overnight. "I guess the senator will be a little low on tea for a while," Janet quipped.

"That's double my salary," I added. "I'm going to send Charles our budget and then take a shower," I told Janet as she tucked herself into bed.

When I returned, I could see Janet lying on her air mattress with her BlackBerry in hand. "What are you doing?" I asked.

"Never mind. Don't you have to brush your hair a hundred times or something?"

"No, Cinderella, I don't. What are you doing?" I asked again.

"I just told Jenkins I could go on the hunting trip. I need to send in my personal information to the NRA lobbyist. We're staying at some all-star hunting ranch that has a spa. It sounds pretty ritzy," she added.

"I'm going to bed. But don't let this destined-to-fail love affair get you fired," I warned.

The next morning came too early. Janet and I rushed out the door, and on the way to the office I read my emails. Charles wasn't pleased with our budget proposal. He wrote, "I think we can spend the money for the buses, signage, and sound; our volunteers can pack a lunch. What is the 'organic fresh vegetables' line item?" I read the other messages and saw that Charles had approved the funds for disinfecting the office.

"Are you flippin' kidding me!" I said in response to Lindsay's message. Then I read it to Janet: "Hi, the senator was discharged and is heading to his apartment. He's asked that Cam stay with him all night in case of emergency and he'll be out of the office all day today. I've ordered him flowers to cheer him up. You owe $62.47. Can you send me the cash today? Just put it in the Minnesota mail envelope. Thanks much! Lindsay."

"Am I missing something here? Didn't the boss just have a little itch going on?" Janet asked.

"That's what I thought. I don't have $62.47 to waste on get-well flowers for flea bites. And can you believe Charles won't fork over a few grand to feed volunteers, but we can spend fifty thousand on bug spray?"

We walked into the office and were cornered by the office manager, who informed us that the office coffee pool was empty and everyone in the office was required to chip in $28 to replenish it. As neither of us drank coffee, we informed her that we'd pass on the pool and thanked her for making us feel a part of the team. That obviously wasn't the right move.

"I don't know how you ladies do things in DC, but here in Minnesota, we all work as part of a team. And being on a team means everyone pays their dues." I stared at her blankly as she continued. "Besides, our specially brewed Caribou Coffee isn't just for our staff members; it's for our constituents, too. Obviously you ladies have spent far too much time inside the Beltway and have forgotten your Minnesota manners."

We gave each other sideways glances and dutifully reached into our purses and handed over the $28.

"We've been at work for less than fifteen minutes and I'm already ninety bucks in the hole!" I said as I opened my office door.

"I guess today we're really working for the people," Janet said.

I wrote back to Charles about Karma's request for organic fresh vegetables at every bus tour stop and informed him that the previous night, she'd asked Janet to be her personal assistant for the trip. Seconds later, Charles called my personal cell phone.

"What in God's name is going on over there?" he asked without saying hello.

"I know. I know."

"Do whatever you need to do to keep her happy! Just don't tell me anymore about this nonsense. My hair is gray enough as it is! I don't want to know anything else about what Karma's up to. She's going to be the reason we lose this nomination, Allison. You just watch!"

"Will do," I said, unsure how to respond.

"What else is going on there? How's Janet?" asked Charles.

"We're both good. We got some much-needed sleep last night. We're going to work on the bus tour today."

"Sounds good. You two hold down the fort and try not to get caught up in any more hostile work environment lawsuits," Charles said, giving us a hard time.

"We don't have time to be hostile!" I kidded back.

Senator McDermott's Minnesota office primarily focused on constituent services, ensuring that the citizens of Minnesota got the help they needed when dealing with federal agencies and typical bureaucrat nonsense. While the busy staffers helped Minnesota seniors get their Medicaid and new immigrants obtain visas for their loved ones, Janet and I kept to ourselves. Casework, as it was called, wasn't our thing, though Janet had done casework in the past and was a pro at it. We kept our focus on the senator's scheduling priorities and made sure not to get entangled in constituent services affairs. After all,

the folks in the Minnesota office were supposed to be the experts, not us. But that morning was an exception, and somehow Janet ended up being the lead caseworker. All of the office's usual caseworkers were on vacation or out sick, and constituents kept calling and showing up at the office asking for assistance. Trista, unsure of how to deal with them, roped Janet into managing the situation. After a few hours, I could see Janet's patience was wearing thin. I could hear her meetings from my office.

"My soybean crop got flooded out this year, and I'm still waiting on my subsidies," a farmer complained.

"My son was admitted to the Air Force Academy, completed three years, and now he's getting kicked out because they said he had a precondition of asthma that he didn't disclose. They want him to pay back the full tuition scholarship they gave him!" a hysterical mother wailed.

"Where's my tax refund?" another constituent demanded.

"I can't take it anymore," Janet said as she plopped down into my office chair. "Honestly, how dumb do people think we are?" I could see the rage in her face as she continued. "This guy just had the balls to come sit across from me in a US Senate Office with a phony passport. It literally had a picture *pasted* on the passport, and he had the nerve to tell me it was real. It was pasted onto the passport, I could peel it off!" she yelled.

"Whoa, that's bad. What did you say?" I asked.

"I couldn't say anything, of course. But I took his information and told him I'd pass it along to the State Department. But who the fuck does he think he is? Coming to the country we both love and pulling this crap?" she asked.

I couldn't argue with her. It was disrespectful to our country and frustrating beyond belief. Her day didn't improve, and after a few of the more interesting constituent meetings, she'd stop in to give me an earful. During the course of the day, she had two separate constituent meetings in which she heard about non-US citizens being denied disability due to citizenship delays. "So our law requires refugees to wait seven years before applying for citizenship. They don't pay a dime into our social security system, yet still qualify for social security disability. Allison, guess what disability these two had?"

"Um, I dunno," I answered as I typed up the bus tour media release.

"Depression!" she yelled.

I stopped typing. "What?"

"Yes, they say they're depressed because they miss their family back home and therefore they can't work. They can't get out of bed in the morning because they're homesick."

"What a joke," I said.

"You have no idea how much I wanted to tell both of them to pack their bags and head back home if they didn't want to be a conscientious citizen of the best country on earth. Start packing and don't let our fence hit you on the way out," she said.

"What did you tell them you'd do?" I asked.

"Usual drill, I'll write a letter on behalf of the senator requesting that their citizenship be expedited. It's such a joke!" she said.

"Well, maybe if they become citizens and their families move here, they'll conquer their depression and get jobs," I said, not helping the situation.

Just as she was leaving my office, the office manager came with another drop-in constituent meeting. "This is going to be interesting," Janet said as she reviewed the intake form. "This one was denied social security disability because of her weight," Janet griped, heading toward the office lobby.

I couldn't hear Janet's meeting, but the strong scent of body odor and shit filled our office suite as she showed the constituent to her office. She's going to lose it, I thought.

The afternoon flew by for me, but I noticed that Janet's meeting was taking an unusually long time. Lindsay informed me that the senator was flea-free and ready for his announcement tour. Rose called to let us know that the hostile work environment investigation and

interviews would take place early next week. I felt caught up with all my work and had even solved the problem of feeding the volunteers on the bus. I arranged for additional volunteers in three of the planned locations to organize a Minnesota-themed potluck meal. After all, who doesn't like a hearty tater-tot hotdish? Not only did my plan cut down on expenses, but it would add to the wholesome quality of the tour overall.

Janet walked her constituent back out to the lobby and came immediately back to my office. She slammed the door behind her. "Did you smell her?" she asked.

"Is that the stench floating in here with you? It smells like bad gas."

"Yeah, bad gas is right. She had gastric bypass surgery three times and was working for the US Postal Service sorting mail. She overate once and ruined her first surgery. Her stapled stomach broke and they had to restaple it. It burst again, and they tried to restaple it, but apparently it's been stapled so many times that it can't be fully closed again. Her fellow employees couldn't bear the smell of gas coming from her opened intestine and stomach, so she quit. She's filed a social security disability case and was denied, because the social security office designated her weight-loss surgery as elective," Janet explained.

"That's awful, but she did elect to have the surgery," I replied. "Not to mention, she did choose to eat that much in the first place. I don't really think our tax dollars should be paying for her overindulgence."

"I don't even know where to start with her case," Janet said, "but she gave me an idea!"

"What are you talking about?" I asked.

"I looked at my timesheet and I have eighty hours of available sick time. I think I'm going to tell Charles that I'm having gastric bypass surgery and go with Jenkins on the hunting trip instead!"

"I think you've been exposed to too many gas fumes! Have you lost your mind? First, you don't need gastric bypass surgery, and second, you'd go hunting instead of having the surgery? Forgive me for being blunt but Jenkins is the one who's blind, not Charles! What happens when you don't lose any weight, you idiot?" I asked.

"I can lose weight. There's no other way. Charles will never let me go with Jenkins on the NRA hunting trip. This could be my answer," she said.

"Okay, I've had enough. You're not going to lie about having gastric bypass surgery and lose your job for not only lying to your boss, but also misusing sick time, to have a one-time hunt and hump with a US Senator—a relationship that won't even last past the trip," I lectured.

"I want to be alone with Jenkins in a remote hunting cabin," she answered, apparently unconcerned with any of the potential consequences.

"Did you hit your head today?" I asked. "Or did you just leave it back at the McDermotts'?"

"How's our bus tour coming along?" she asked, in an obvious change of subject.

"We're all set. Charles said to do whatever Karma wants, but we aren't to tell him anything she asks us about," I told her.

"Did you convince him to give us any more money to pay for food for the volunteers?" she asked.

"No, but I figured out a solution. Instead of begging Charles for more money, we're going to have volunteer hosts at three stops to organize potluck meals," I answered. "It'll be great!"

The rest of the day passed smoothly. We arrived home to an empty McDermott house and crashed in front of their downstairs TV. The house felt empty, not like a home. We both felt uncomfortable being alone there, but the solitude was a nice respite. The senator was set to arrive home that evening and we nervously anticipated his arrival. It was odd enough sleeping in the senator's house, but sleeping with him in a room nearby made it even weirder.

Janet and I fell asleep on separate couches with a bowl of microwave popcorn on the floor between us.

"What the hell was that?" Janet suddenly yelled. I opened my eyes to the sight of Janet swinging a broom in the air.

"What are you doing?" I asked, confused.

"There's a bird flying around in here," she said, flailing around with the broom.

All of a sudden the "bird" zoomed past our heads and we screeched. "I don't think that's a bird. I think that's a bat!" I said as I grabbed the broom from Janet.

As I swung the broom in the air, Karma walked into the basement. "What on earth are you doing?" she asked.

"There's a bat flying around in here," I told her as I tried to hit it.

"Don't be silly, we might have fleas but we certainly don't have rodents," Karma insisted, grabbing the broom out of my hands. As Karma waved it around, the bat flew past and landed on Janet's head. She froze. Karma dropped the broom and ran out of the room screaming.

"Hold still," I told Janet, picking up the broom. I swatted the bat hard and it fell to the ground.

The look on Janet's face was priceless. "First fleas and now bats!" she yelled.

Karma came dashing into the basement with Colonel following with a drink in one hand and a broom in the other. "You gals hit the floor and I'll take care of this," he yelled.

"We killed the bat," I reported, as Janet and I laid down on the floor.

"They travel in packs," said Karma.

"Really?" Janet asked. I rolled my eyes.

"We all need to hold still," encouraged the senator's father.

"But bats are blind," exclaimed Janet.

"And we know how you love blind, horny beasts," I laughed and winked at her.

"Girls, I need you to be serious," Colonel said. "Bats carry disease and while I was in the Army, I learned all about safety and precaution. Speaking of which, Janet, did you get my badge yet? Anders said you'll get it for me. I need that for my taxes. It's a good deduction."

Janet lay next to me in silence and whacked my elbow with hers. I could tell she was appalled that Colonel had just admitted that he wanted the military honor for tax purposes. For months Janet had been telling the senator that his father didn't qualify for the badge, and aside from making up history, the chances of him being awarded the honor were slim to none.

"I'm trying the best I can," answered Janet, trying to dodge the question yet again.

"Don't they know who I am?" he asked.

"Focus. We need to kill all the bats," Karma insisted.

"I really don't think they travel in packs," I said finally.

"Everyone, pull the cushions out of the furniture and help me look around," Karma said as she rummaged around, randomly looking for the bat's pack mates.

Thankfully, we didn't find any more bats in the house. Karma insisted that we bury the dead bat in their backyard. She was nervous that if we threw it in the garbage, Anders would make headlines in the morning paper and PETA would protest in front of their home.

Colonel, Janet, and I took the bat outside and buried it as deep as we could in the backyard. While we were gathered outside around the grave, Margot came home. She seemed distraught.

"We need to stay outside for a few hours," she told us nervously. Janet and I gave her a questioning look. "Anders is about five minutes out. Karma and Anders haven't seen each other for a while and they need free range of their home. They can't keep their hands off each other when he gets home. They head straight to the bedroom and it goes on for hours," Margot reported.

"I didn't just hear that, did I?" asked Janet.

"Sex is popular around here apparently. Too bad, I'm in a major drought," I added with a laugh, thinking about Cam.

Janet and I sat out in the garden and Margot and Colonel joined us, probably because they didn't have anywhere else to go. "Are you girls ready for Saturday's big tour?" Margot asked.

"Yes, I think we should be all set. Tomorrow we'll just wrap up all the final details and be on the road Saturday morning. It should be lots of fun!" I told her, actually excited for the adventure.

"I want to ride with my son. I don't want to be stuck on any bus. I want to be right next to him and the action," Colonel told us.

"We've got you covered," I reassured him.

The senator arrived home and came over to the garden area. He looked tired, but had no obvious bumps from the flea bites. "Hi gang, glad to see you all outside!" he said as he patted Janet's shoulder.

"How are you feeling?" asked Margot.

"I'm fine. Nothing a US Senator can't handle," he said as he flexed his muscles. We all laughed. "Oh, Janet, I need you to do me a favor tomorrow. I got a call on the ride home from Jack Fletcher. His personal massage therapist is having some immigration issues. Jack is a friend and we need to help him out," the senator added as he headed into his home.

"Right now it's 9:30 p.m. We need to stay out here until at least 11:30 p.m.," Margot told us, counting on her hand.

"Two hours," I gasped.

"They go at it like horny dogs," Colonel said.

"I really need to get online. I'm going to grab my laptop and be right back," Janet said, walking quickly into the house.

"I hope she doesn't interrupt them," Margot said ominously.

Janet returned with her laptop and whispered to me, "Karma and the senator aren't having sex. They are yelling at each other at the top of their lungs! I've never heard such cussing and fighting before."

I motioned to her to be quiet. As Margot suggested, we sat outside for two hours. While I played games on my iPhone, Janet chatted with Jenkins on her computer. Her occasional outbursts of laughter annoyed me, and I continued to worry that her heart would be crushed by Senator Blind Date.

The next day arrived and we had less than twenty-four hours before hitting the road for the fifteen-stop bus tour. My job for the day was to review the senator's advance folder, which included extremely detailed information about each stop and talking points. Each stop's advance information included names of important people and past friends of his campaigns. We drafted answers to every possible question he might receive and organized everyone's contact information to be readily available and clearly labeled.

Janet was frustrated because she spent the entire day trying to manipulate the immigration status of the so-called "massage therapist" who was in the county illegally. The senator's "friend" making the request was a bigwig car dealer who had maxed out in donations to the campaign. Somehow, by the end of the day, Janet was able to secure an interview at the US Embassy in Prague, and the massage therapist was granted special permission to exit the country to have her visa interview without threat of consequences for her immigration status. I had no idea how she managed it, but she spent the rest of the day whistling and singing, "I've got friends in high places… ," a play on a Garth Brooks song. It was growing increasingly annoying, and I was glad when we had everything almost ready for the following day.

With all the materials ready and the cars packed for the tour, Janet and I went to the McDermotts' home for a good night's sleep before our fifteen-stop adventure. We had no idea what awaited us.

9

The Political Wheels on the Bus

I woke up with a spring in my step and a zest for life. Over the next twenty-four hours, I would transform from a Senate staffer to someone working for a presidential candidate. I'd be on a fifteen-stop bus tour across Minnesota with Senator McDermott as he announced his foray into presidential politics. It was incomprehensible that the man I told where to go and what to do was positioning himself to be the leader of the free world. It was rewarding to work for a man who aspired to be President of the United States, the most powerful country in the world. And to think that I, a small-town girl from South Dakota, could have such an amazing

opportunity was almost beyond comprehension. It was easy to lose sight of that with all the nonsense and constant pressures of my job. But on days like today it was just as easy to be thankful. I couldn't help but feel excited, and I began to fantasize about working in the West Wing. From South Dakota to Pennsylvania Avenue, I thought.

As I pulled on my "McDermott for President" red, white, and blue T-shirt and matching baseball cap, I proudly looked at myself in the mirror. I was ready for the battle that a presidential election was sure to be. Despite everything, Senator McDermott put a lot of trust in me. I was honored, and I couldn't let him or my parents down.

I noticed that Janet was being unusually quiet for a morning of such importance. I went to wake her up and noticed that her air mattress was already deflated and put away. I went to the kitchen, expecting to find her downing a Diet Coke as a morning stress reliever, but she wasn't there. In fact, she didn't seem to be in the McDermott house anywhere.

"What in God's name are you doing?" I asked after I found her sprawled out in the McDermotts' garage. She had a crazed look in her eye and was surrounded by thousands of personalized water bottles that announced "McDermott for President" on their labels.

"What does it look like I'm doing?" she asked as she peeled off a manufacturer's label and replaced it with a campaign sticker.

"You did all of these bottles already?" I asked, stunned, looking at what had to be thousands of bottles surrounding her.

"All night long, while you snored away," she griped and passed me some stickers.

"Who asked you to do this and when?" I asked.

"Last night while you were getting your beauty sleep you didn't hear the pounding on the window? Trista was outside and I woke up. She said Charles was worried about us buying the wrong kind of bottled water and pissing off a few of the donors—some of whom are apparently in the water-bottling business. So Charles told us that we needed to get all these bottle labels off and replace them with 'McDermott for President' stickers," Janet said.

"Where's Trista?" I asked.

"No clue. I tried to wake you up, but you were out cold. I've been doing this since 11:00 p.m.," Janet answered.

"Oh my God, I'm so sorry! I can't believe you couldn't wake me up. I did take a few Tylenol PM that I stole out of the medicine cabinet last night to get a good night's sleep. I didn't realize it would knock me out like that. Usually I'm half-awake in case McDermott emails me," I explained as I grabbed a few bottles and stickers.

"I need to go shower. I think we can have the bus volunteers do the rest of these bottles on the bus as we travel," Janet said. She sounded exhausted.

I didn't have the heart to correct her. Charles had already ordered me to ask all the volunteers to bring their personal cell phones so they could make campaign calls as we traveled. Charles had me make up hundreds of pages of call sheets with suggested polling questions on budgets, earmarks, and amending the Constitution for marriage rights.

During Anders's Senate campaign, Janet and I ran the volunteer center. After the campaign ended, we were known for having one of the best volunteer organizations and grass roots campaigns in Minnesota history. Janet and I were naturally welcoming to volunteers, and we made sure that each volunteer was treated with respect. Many times Janet or Babs, an older campaign worker and friend, would even pony up personal money to buy volunteers refreshments to keep them excited about campaigning. As a result, we had an extensive list of willing and loyal volunteers. I knew many of the volunteers who would be joining us on the bus ride, and making phone calls to ask strangers to define marriage was uncomfortable for some of them.

During the McDermott Senate campaign we worked day and night for our volunteer center, making sure every person who volunteered for Anders did something. We tried our best to give the volunteers meaningful projects. We took personal responsibility for ensuring the volunteers were treated like paid members of the campaign team. Often campaign staffers would view themselves as more important than our

volunteers. They didn't realize that any successful campaign needs a solid bank of volunteers to succeed. During McDermott's Senate campaign it had become evident pretty quickly that our volunteers got stuck doing many of the shitty jobs and then some paid staffer would conveniently take credit for the work.

I distinctly remembered one time when Janet and I organized a pancake breakfast for the volunteers. We dreamed up a fun event titled Super Sign Saturday. It was our way of encouraging volunteers (whom we personally recruited) to attend this specific event to eat pancakes and get as many lawn signs hammered in across Minnesota as possible. We launched a volunteer sign-posting machine. Signs and pieces of rebar by the thousands were out of the campaign headquarters in hours. Not one paid campaign staffer helped with this effort, but during our weekly campaign team meeting with Anders and our campaign manager, they all magically and independently took credit for their involvement in Super Sign Saturday. Janet and I, who did all the work, along with our army of terrific volunteers, were infuriated. But we figured that McDermott and Charles had to know that we were responsible.

We ran the volunteer center like our second home, always ready for guests. We kept it clean (which is unheard of in a campaign headquarters), profanity-free (at least for the most part), and warm and welcoming.

Janet was adept at getting the volunteers to make phone calls on behalf of the campaign. I would almost pee my pants when I heard the bullshit she'd tell the volunteers to get them to redouble their efforts. "Political research and statistics show that for every successful call we make, five additional people go to the polls on Election Day. Viewing a campaign sign only generates two additional votes," she'd say.

Upon hearing this, the volunteers would make more calls than ever. I asked Janet where the hell she got a statistic like that, and she said, "Shut up. I totally made it up, but look, it's working." You couldn't argue with Janet. The volunteers would show up, stomping their feet and claiming they wouldn't make any phone calls. But within fifteen minutes they'd be dialing all afternoon without any whining or hesitation. Then they'd repeat Janet's statistics to all the new volunteers coming in that day. Every time I'd hear the "five votes per call" statistic, I'd giggle out loud.

We took all volunteers who showed up, young and old, single and married. A campaign headquarters can be a singles club for potential daters seeking someone of similar beliefs and values. Time and again the same single volunteer would show the same night of the week hoping the volunteer he or she had an eye on would be there again. We caught on to this and started having Singles Night. It may not have been speed dating exactly, but it attracted additional volunteers. Even if their main purpose for being there was to get some ass, as long as they helped get some asses to the polls, we really didn't care.

One of our favorite volunteers was a young twenty-year-old college student, who'd show up in a beat-up leather jacket. He would routinely go on a smoke break every hour. We didn't know his last name but we joked around, and I flirted with him occasionally. Janet and I were stunned to learn after the campaign that he was part of one of Minnesota's wealthiest families. As we sat in the Minneapolis Orpheum Theater for a Christmas concert, we watched him and his family prance into the theater dressed in black-tie attire to front-row seats. To us he'd been just like any other college student who loved politics and worked two jobs trying to pay tuition. We didn't show him any special attention and, frankly, I think he liked that we treated him just like everyone else. When I saw him at the theater, though, I cursed myself for not flirting with him more.

Life on the campaign trail was always crazy. Charles always warned us to be on the lookout for campaign spies and to be careful of volunteers asking too many questions. One might have called him paranoid. We had to hide maps of where the senator was campaigning, where he was going next, and where he'd been in Minnesota. We were secretive with projects relating to fundraising and made sure only our top volunteers were privy to donor prices and expenses. Our volunteer center became a well-oiled machine and began attracting so many volunteers that a few times we had to actually make up projects for volunteers to work on, not wanting to turn anyone away.

Ninety percent of the time, we did all we could to accommodate volunteers and use their expertise. Some days that was easier than others. One day we went above the call of duty when we spent an entire Saturday morning with a volunteer who was committed to making calls for Anders, "his guy." The volunteer was elderly, wheelchair-bound, and legally blind. He couldn't read print smaller than a seventy-two-point font. I had no idea how he'd made it to the campaign headquarters, let alone how I was going to deploy his skills. But I had to give him credit, he was determined to make calls for his candidate. I spent my morning enlarging phone numbers to a single number per page so that one telephone number occupied ten pages. And despite enlarging the numbers, he still had to pull out his magnifying glass! We went through a half a ream of paper that morning and got five calls made. My patience was tested, but I was encouraged by his drive for independence, and thought more people in America could learn a lesson from him.

I caught myself daydreaming down volunteer memory lane just as Janet came back outside to the garage. She was pulling on her campaign T-shirt. "Really? You brought me a frickin' kid's large!" she asked, trying to stretch knit around her large breasts.

I didn't have the heart to say that I'd actually grabbed her an adult large. The T-shirt not only looked uncomfortable and ridiculous, but it was borderline inappropriate. Her boobs were so big they caused the *McDermott* to become distorted as it stretched across her breasts.

"Jesus, this looks awful," she said miserably.

"You look fine," I replied, not looking her in the eye. I rarely lied to Janet, but we didn't have any other shirts with us, and I needed her to stop tugging at her boobs before we were in the company of the volunteers. I just hoped the shirt would stretch on its own.

We loaded the car and drove to the headquarters to meet the buses. On the way, we reviewed the list of items we needed: cell phone chargers, credit cards, call sheets, advance memos for Anders, advance memos and folders for Charles, directions to each stop, and most importantly, a contact person and telephone number for each of the fifteen stops. Even if everything started to go to hell, we'd be able to call each advance team member and delegate whatever duties and bizarre requests popped up.

I was pleased to see our tour buses parked beside the headquarters parking lot. While I started unloading coolers and our various supplies, Janet quickly reserved seats in the front of each bus for the McDermotts, Charles, and us. The television crews started to line up in front of the buses and asked when we anticipated the senator's arrival.

"He should be here at 6:35 a.m.," I answered. As his scheduler, I knew exactly when and where the senator would be at all times. It was great when reporters asked questions and I immediately knew the answer. Our schedule for this was down to the exact minute. I went over it repeatedly with Charles to ensure we could make all fifteen stops in twenty-four hours, as we'd promoted to the local and national press. At this location, our first event of the tour, Charles thought it would be best if we didn't have any flashy backdrops—just a podium directly in front of the buses with all the volunteers huddled behind Anders. Of course, Karma, Colonel, and the senator's kids would be placed on both sides of the senator.

As I talked to the volunteers and tried to connect names with faces, Charles leaned into my ear and said, "Where are the Somali and Asian volunteers?" I gave him a weird look, not understanding what he was asking me. "We need Somalis and Asians up in the front row, now," he ordered.

Janet came over to me and I told her, "Charles wants Somali and Asian volunteers up front before the senator gets here."

"Should I call my casework files?" she asked with a laugh.

"I don't know," I replied, already freaking out. "I don't think we have any. It didn't even cross my mind."

"Beggars can't be choosers," Janet replied. "I mean, we only had two flippin' days to pull this tour together, and we were pulling teeth to get enough volunteers to fill three buses," she added as her eyes scanned over the volunteer crowd.

"I don't think we even have a black person on the bus," I mumbled.

I started to panic as I saw the clock tick past 6:40 a.m. with no sign of the McDermotts. I heard them up this morning, and Margot had assured me she'd drop them off in time for the launch of the senator's presidential campaign. You wouldn't think you'd be late to your own major national announcement. Out of the corner of my eye, I saw Janet and Trista distributing the campaign shirts. I could see them looking at the sizes carefully and I wondered what was going on.

Trista came running. "Where are the adult T-shirts you ordered?" she asked, out of breath.

"All the shirts are in those two huge boxes. We only ordered adult small, medium, large, and extra large," I answered.

"Damn it. I knew I should have handled the shirt order. You two fuck everything up," she panicked.

She started kicking the dirt around with her shoes. "All those fucking shirts are for fucking kids!" she yelled to Charles.

The press all turned to look at her. "Trista, quiet down. You're like a bull in a china shop," ordered Charles as he came over to us.

"Janet and Allison only ordered youth T-shirts. Anders is going to be fucking floored," she hissed to Charles.

Charles gave me a look and didn't say a word. "I placed the order myself. I ordered adult sizes," I explained. "I don't know what happened."

"We've got what we've got. We'll have to make do," Charles replied, coming to my defense.

Janet came over and stood next to me. "Those are only youth T-shirts," I explained.

"Seriously? You just made my day! I thought I was pregnant or gaining weight!" she said happily.

"Have you lost your mind? You're still the virgin queen of online dating," I reminded her.

"Well, I was just worried that I'd gained weight overnight after I had to cram my gals into this flipping shirt. And I read online that rapid overnight weight gain is a sign of early pregnancy," she said.

"Whatever you say. But I think you need to actually have sex before you get pregnant. Maybe you should give up online self-diagnosis." I laughed.

The press started to disengage and asked again about the senator's ETA. Charles typed nervously on his BlackBerry, and I emailed Margot for any indication of when the senator and his family might arrive. Finally, after what seemed like hours, I saw their SUV pull into the parking lot. It was 7:00 a.m., and they were a half-hour late, but I was relieved they'd arrived. The senator, Karma, Colonel, and the kids piled out of the SUV like it was a circus car. They walked over to the podium and all the volunteers cheered waiving signs and "McDermott for President" hockey sticks (a corrected batch, of course).

Margot walked toward me. I had stationed myself at the back of the crowd. "Sorry we were late," she said. "Karma needed a large-double-soy latte, and the first Caribou Coffee we stopped at was out of soy milk. So we had to drive a few extra miles to find another," she explained.

"No problem. Just glad to see you all here," I said, annoyed.

"Where should I put Karma's luggage?" she asked.

"Luggage?"

"Yes, Karma packed a few bags and necessities for the big trip," she told me.

"Oh, I'll give them to Janet. She can keep an eye on them while she helps Karma today," I answered.

"It'll be so nice to have Janet's extra hands today with the kids, Colonel, and Karma," Margot added. "I can't take care of them all by myself."

Puzzled by that remark, I asked, "Are you joining us for the tour?"

"Fuck yeah, Allison! You think you're the only one heading to

Pennsylvania Avenue with the McDermotts? I'm coming along to live in the White House. I'll be attending all the parties and state dinners! I'll probably even end up being the First Lady's social secretary!" she said, smiling.

"Sounds great," I told her as I tried to contain my distaste. I could only imagine what would happen if crazy Margot was let loose in the White House. I started to wonder what bizarre things she'd do on our bus tour. Fifteen minutes was too much time to spend with Margot; a full twenty-four hours would put anyone over the edge.

"What's she doing here?" asked Charles.

"Who?" I responded.

"The wigged-out nanny!" he answered.

"Margot. She just told me she's coming on the tour to assist Karma, Colonel, and the kids," I told him.

"Oh good God, heaven help us all!" he answered. He turned back and added, "Remember, I don't want to know anything she or Karma does or asks for!"

"Got it!" I promised. That was Charles for you, always overreacting.

After the initial announcement was over, the volunteers quickly filled the buses and started to ask which bus the McDermotts were going to ride in. Janet and I dodged their questions; we didn't have the heart to tell them that the McDermotts were too good for the buses. As soon as the McDermott family got back into the SUV, though, the volunteers began to realize they wouldn't be riding in the buses with us.

Charles sat in the row in front of Janet's seat, while I was across the aisle from her. Charles pretended to do a crossword puzzle, but we both knew he had one ear on our conversation.

"Did you see Karma's makeup bag?" Janet asked me.

"No, but she does realize we're going to Wadena, Minnesota, right?" I asked.

"Who's in charge of our stop in Faribault?" asked Charles, shutting us both up.

Janet and I both started paging through our advance folders, and

I could tell Janet was thinking the same thing I was: Charles, you have this information. Dig it out yourself.

Janet found the answer first. "Nate and Pete," she told Charles.

"Oh great, did we title this stop Two Men and a Stop Not Working?" he asked. Janet and I exchanged eye rolls. We knew exactly what Charles was referring to. Nate and Pete looked great on paper but couldn't sell mini donuts at a county fair.

"You gals called the local legislators and mayors from around each stop and invited them to join Anders today, right?" Charles asked.

"We called them all," I said.

I could see Janet getting nervous about our first stop, which was now only five miles away. She started rummaging through her advance folder.

"We got this," I said, winking at her.

When we pulled into Faribault, the designated location looked as empty as a ghost town. Then we saw a small group of people huddled around a picnic table waving at the buses. "Oh shit," I said, as Janet and Charles came over to my side of the bus to look out the window. "Where is everyone?" I asked.

"The boss is not going to be happy," Charles added.

"I don't know what else we could have done. We called list after list of supporters to come out and cheer on Anders's presidential campaign," I said, looking at Janet desperately.

"We make this as great as it can be and get out as fast as we can," Charles ordered.

The volunteers quickly filed off the buses and gathered around the modest crowd of a dozen supporters. There were two newspaper cameras and the national press corps that was following the buses. I noticed that Karma wasn't standing next to the senator as he marched in, shaking hands and moving to the front of the group. In fact, Karma was nowhere to be seen.

"It's so good to see everyone here in Fairmont," McDermott said incorrectly.

Faribault. Couldn't he at least get the name of the town right?

Janet gave me a nudge and muttered, "This ought to be good," as Margot walked toward us.

"Karma isn't going to get out at a tour spot unless there are at least a hundred people waiting when we arrive," she informed us.

"That sounds supportive," Janet said.

"I'm sorry. Did you say something, Janet?" Margot asked.

"Yes, I said that sounds very supportive of her husband," Janet answered, not backing off.

I was shocked that Janet actually confronted Margot about the McDermotts, and I tried to change the subject. "Our next stop is Rochester. That should garner a big turnout and lots of media attention since it's a regional hub," I said cheerfully.

"Let me guess, Karma will need to stop curbside to reapply her makeup before Rochester," Charles said as he greeted Margot.

"Very funny, Charles," Margot laughed as she hit his back.

"I wasn't kidding," he told her. "Girls, I want to know nothing. Nothing!"

"We got it," I said.

Then I saw the volunteers quickly return to the buses, and I heard Anders yell at Colonel to hurry up so we stayed on schedule. Colonel was making friends with the older volunteers, many of whom, conveniently, were single and widowed. Even at his advanced age, Colonel still had a way with the ladies. I saw where Anders got it.

"Next stop, Rochester, Minnesota, home of Mayo Clinic!" yelled the senator as he stepped foot onto our bus. Then he bent over and instructed Charles, "Need more supporters at each stop. This was pitiful!"

The bus of volunteers cheered and quickly snapped pictures of Anders. Charles seemed uptight and started pounding away faster and faster on his BlackBerry. Janet and I ignored his nervous energy.

The ride from Faribault to Rochester seemed fast and uneventful. We arrived at our tour stop and hundreds of supporters lined the parking lot. They were waving campaign signs, hockey sticks, and homemade signs. It looked and felt more like a presidential campaign rally than the stop in Faribault.

As we got off of the bus, I noticed the senator's SUV hadn't arrived. I texted Margot for an ETA. When I didn't get a response, I started to worry. The bus tour was timed down to the minute, and each stop needed to proceed without a hitch. We were already running thirty minutes behind, and every additional minute meant volunteers were left waiting outside in the sticky heat of August in Minnesota.

After several minutes, the senator, Karma, Colonel, and the kids arrived carrying and eating bagels. "Where did you get the bagels?" I asked Margot, who took a large bite of hers.

"Oh, these? Karma knows this great bagel café here in Rochester and she insisted we go," she said. "They even serve vegan bagels!"

"Margot, we don't have time for unscheduled stops. You need to put your foot down. There's plenty of food stocked in your car," I snapped. Just as I finished chewing out the nanny over bagels, I realized an uneasy silence had descended on the cheerful crowd. My BlackBerry started vibrating endlessly to indicate a series of emails—clearly something was not right.

I was beginning to piece together what had just happened and quickly realized that the senator was standing on the stage next to Mayor John Marvin. The mayor introduced Anders to the Rochester crowd. Unfortunately, the senator's mic was still on when he asked the mayor why the name Marvin is everywhere in town—Marvin bank, Marvin candy store, Marvin wind turbines, and Marvin grocery. The local crowd heard the bizarre question and was stunned into silence with the realization that the senator didn't know that the man standing next to him, who had proudly proclaimed him a close personal friend during his introduction, was in fact Mayor *Marvin*.

"You've got to be kidding me," Janet proclaimed, walking over to me.

"Doesn't he read the advance we write up? Why would you ask Mayor Marvin why his name is all over everything?" I said.

"Duh, I mean, like, why do you own all of Rochester?" Janet questioned sarcastically.

"Right. I mean, come on. Any moron should be able to figure out Marvin is *Marvin*," I answered.

That awkward mistake was the sole error of the Rochester stop (if you didn't count their tardiness due to the bagel stop), though. Rochester turned out to be a nice rally, and the senator seemed pleased. Our next two stops took us across Interstate 90 from the southeastern corner to the southwestern corner of Minnesota. Both stops were nicely attended, and the senator did an excellent job. It seemed the slip-ups were behind us. In fact, thanks to our excellent bus drivers, we were able to make up thirty of the forty-five minutes we'd lost, and now were only fifteen minutes behind schedule.

It was time for our first meal stop, and Trista and I had arranged to have the Minnesota Pork Producers host a quick on-the-road barbecue picnic for the volunteers and the tour entourage. The lunch stop was in Tyler, a tiny rural Minnesota town just fifteen minutes from our previous tour stop. Tyler had one stop sign and no stoplights, so it was easy to find the city park. The Pork Producers had gathered by the dozens and were waiting with grills blazing. It smelled amazing, and my mouth began to water.

"Now this is living," yelled Charles, stretching out of the bus and smelling the aroma of barbecued pork mixed with manure.

"Oh my, I can smell the barbecue and corn on the cob," I said, almost passing out from hunger.

The volunteers quickly lined up and were extremely vocal in their thanks to the Pork Producers for their grilled chops, pulled pork sandwiches, and the array of other goodies they'd provided for lunch. (All in-kind contributions, of course.) I noticed Anders shaking hands and rubbing elbows with the farmers, but he was not eating any pork chops.

"Ah, shit," I hit Janet with a good solid whack.

"What was that for?" she asked, licking her fingers.

"Why didn't you remind me that Jews don't eat pork?" I asked.

"Who is Jewish?" she asked, looking toward the volunteers.

After Allison, replies, "the Senator you idiot."

"He doesn't even have a Jewish last name." Janet remarked.

"His mom was Jewish," I replied. "He wouldn't eat anyway," Janet said, taking a bit of her corn on the cob. "Besides, he's only Jewish half the time. He may not eat pork, but he can eat the corn on the cob, potato salad, and beans."

"Where the hell are Margot and Karma?" Charles asked, rushing up to us with his second pork chop in hand.

"I haven't seen them," Janet told him.

"Neither have I. They aren't Jewish, so they should be able to eat pork," I answered.

"Oh, don't worry about Anders and pork. He eats it all the time," Charles said, killing my theory.

"Told ya," Janet chimed in.

"Oh, Margot is calling my phone," I said, answering it.

"Allison, I need your help," Margot said.

"What is it?" I asked.

"Can you please come to the park's bathroom? And don't bring anyone with you," she ordered.

"I don't want to know anything," Charles reminded me as I went off to find the park's remote bathroom.

When I arrived I found Karma's hand stuck in the condom vending machine. "Oh my gosh, how can I help you?" I asked, trying not to laugh.

"We were trying to get these," Margot pointed at the machine. I noticed the machine was advertising neon twisted and ribbed fire-and-ice condoms for female pleasure.

"We put our quarters in the machine, twisted the knob, and nothing came out," Karma explained.

"I gave the machine a smack and an alarm started to buzz very loudly," Margot said. "Karma put her arm up into the machine to stop the buzzing sound, so we didn't cause a scene in the park bathroom."

Capitol Hell

After surveying the limited options, I grabbed Karma's arm and pulled as hard as I could. Her hand came loose, she lost her balance, and fell onto the wet, dirty bathroom floor. "I think you just dislocated my shoulder," she complained. "And now I need to change. My clothes are dirty from this nasty floor. What were you thinking?"

"I was just trying to help," I answered as I attempted to wipe the dirt and grime off the ass of her dress. She gave me a dirty look. I didn't say another word to either of them, I just walked out of the restroom.

"I don't want to hear anything," whispered Charles when I got back to the rally.

"I got it," I said, unable to contain my laughter over the absurdity of what had just happened.

The volunteers piled back on the buses, and Janet and I swapped stories from the meal stop. "I wonder how fire-and-ice condoms work," she asked.

"For someone who hasn't had sex, your mind sure is focused on it," I said.

We were off to our next stop on the tour, Hutchinson, a midsized tourist town in the central part of the state. As we arrived into town, a city police car pulled in front of our tour bus. Without warning, the patrol car turned on its lights and sirens. It appeared that we were to have a police escort to our campaign stop. It was unplanned, but turned out nicely. Besides the escort, the stop went off without any surprises, and the senator seemed pleased. Karma decided to play nice at this stop and started to look like a presidential candidate's wife. Aside from her wardrobe changes for every stop, Karma seemed to be getting better at behaving herself.

After the stop in Hutchinson, the senator and Karma boarded our bus and I thought they would simply stay on for a few minutes. But they decided to ride the next leg of the trip on the bus with the volunteers. It was fantastic. The volunteers were excited and would randomly approach the senator with personal questions and requests. Karma ignored the volunteers for the most part, but at least didn't say anything offensive to any of them. Having them both on the bus made for increased tension, and it was interesting to watch their interactions. They sat in separate sets of seats and barely talked to each other. As we rode, Janet and I nervously waited to arrive at our next stop in Fergus Falls. Suddenly Janet swooped into my seat with her phone in hand. I saw it buzzing and asked her who it was.

"Jenkins, you idiot," she exclaimed.

"Silly me, I don't know Senator—I mean Chairman—Jenkins's telephone number by heart," I snapped at her.

I could feel Charles and the senator staring at us. I didn't know if it was my imagination, or if they'd overheard us. "Keep it down, Charles and the boss are looking our way. They'd die to know you're online dating and co-senate-mingling with Jenkins," I whispered to Janet.

"I can't answer his call right now," Janet said, staring at her vibrating phone.

"Um, no shit you can't. But why isn't his call going to voice mail?" I asked as her phone vibrated for what felt like three straight minutes.

"I do have voice mail. But he keeps calling me repeatedly. He must need me," Janet mumbled.

"Now you think he needs you?" I questioned. "We're sitting a seat away from the boss. Take off your naïve panties and get real for once. You're starting to really annoy me. You're playing with fire. You know Jenkins is the boss's main competition in the presidential primaries. What do you think he and Charles would do if they found you out?"

Janet gave me a look of disbelief and moved back to her seat. Her phone was still on, and I could see her texting like a teenager in heat. Truth be told, I was sort of happy for her but was also worried that Jenkins had only one or possibly two interests in mind: 1.) to get laid 2.) to get inside information on McDermott. Unfortunately, Janet was going to be his victim, and I wanted to protect her. But I also knew she was a grown-up, and maybe a broken heart is what she needed to get her common sense back. I just hoped she didn't sink the campaign in the process.

Janet began texting me from across the bus aisle: "He wants me to call him ASAP."

I wrote back: "Don't call him from this campaign bus. He's running for the party endorsement against your boss!!! Wake up!!!"

She texted back: "Whatever."

I knew trouble was brewing behind the "whatever" comment, and I thought I might have to hold an intervention. When Janet set her mind to something, it was full steam ahead. Thankfully, we soon arrived in Fergus Falls, and there was a crowd of hundreds waiting for Senator McDermott. I waited for all the volunteers to empty out of the bus and noticed that Karma wasn't moving out of her front-row seat. "Is everything alright, Mrs. McDermott?" I asked before exiting the bus.

"Yes, Amy, I'm just going to change my clothes on the bus before the rally," she answered.

I didn't know if I'd heard her correctly. You would think she'd be able to remember my name after staying at her home for a week and working for her husband for the past year as his personal scheduler and campaign assistant. Karma never ceased to amaze me.

The Fergus Falls rally was full of energy, and I enjoyed seeing Anders campaigning again. He was a natural and the hard-working folks of rural Minnesota loved him. I didn't see Janet for the entire rally and wondered if Margot or Charles had put her on an emergency task. Then I looked across the street and saw Janet crammed into an old telephone booth. I couldn't believe she was standing inside the booth, and it appeared she was actually using the pay phone instead of her cell phone. All of the sudden, Janet came running across the street, panting heavily. She said, "I need a few quarters or other change."

"Jesus, I assume these aren't for a tampon emergency," I said, handing her my last few quarters. She ran back across the street and slammed the door of the phone booth, drawing the attention of half the rally crowd, including Charles.

"What the hell is she doing?" he asked me.

"I think she's calling her parents about the dinner stop at their home," I lied.

"Why in the phone booth?" he wondered out loud.

"Oh, I think just because it's loud out here with the rally, and you know Janet. She's a bit weird, now and then." I laughed, hoping Charles would change the subject.

"I grew up here in Fergus," Charles said.

"I didn't know that," I said. "I always assumed you were a big-city guy."

"Big city? No, Allison, I much prefer this lifestyle to city life," he replied. "You don't realize what you've given up sometimes until it's all gone."

Janet joined us, out of breath. "Everything okay with your parents?" Charles asked her.

She looked dumbfounded by the question and said, "Of course, they're excited and my mom even has cheese cut in the shape of the letter M for McDermott."

"The two of you were raised right in towns like this. This is what America is all about, being able to know your neighbors and who's teaching your kids," Charles said in a soft tone.

"I think he's bipolar," Janet whispered to me.

"No, give him a break," I said. "Charles is a good guy. I think he knows right from wrong. He realizes Anders is high maintenance." We watched Anders grab the elbows of all the women crowding around him, and we both noticed Karma becoming more and more uncomfortable as supporters put their arms around her for photographs.

"She'd better get used to it or this is going to be one helluva long campaign," Margot said, appearing out of nowhere.

"You'll have to start bringing cases of disinfectant with you," I laughed, only half joking.

"Who were you calling from the phone booth, Janet? Were you ordering candy?" Margot asked.

"Candy?" Janet questioned.

"Oh, I just saw you in the phone booth across the street. That's where we order our candy," Margot insisted.

"I think we have some candy on the bus," Janet replied.

"Really?" Margot asked.

"Sure, just check the coolers. I think we bought quite a bit," Janet told her.

Margot walked away and I corrected Janet right away, "She's not talking about candy, like chocolate bars. She's talking about nose candy!"

"Nose candy?" she asked.

"Cocaine!" I answered.

"Oh, I wasn't calling about buying drugs," she replied quickly.

"No shit. Instead, you were calling Senator Blind Date from your boss's campaign against him," I snarled back at her.

"Easy does it. I just wanted to call him back," she whispered.

"And you couldn't wait until we got home in the morning?" I asked. "Let me guess, he *needed* you?"

"No, it was a little worse than that. He wanted to have phone sex this afternoon," she reported matter-of-factly.

"What?" I asked.

"Lay off. He was just wanting to hear my voice. He asked me to say a few things to him while he jacked off. I think," she answered.

"Holy shit, you were just having phone sex in a phone booth across the street from Anders's campaign rally with his main opposition?" I asked.

"Yes, and who cares. You've had real sex with tons of guys. This is harmless," she answered.

"You are so in over your head that you don't even recognize reality anymore," I replied.

As we continued our heated conversation, the volunteers filed back on the buses without needing any direction from us. Janet and I were the last two back on the bus and were greeted by Charles with, "It's about time, you two. Everything alright?"

We both put on fake smiles and said, "Fine," in unison, opting to sit away from one another.

We had only one stop before our evening meal at Janet's childhood home, and we had successfully survived half of Anders's big announcement tour. So far the tour was eventful, fun, and surprising. We were scheduled to arrive at Janet's home at midnight, and then we had seven more stops before arriving back at the campaign headquarters. The final stops were planned for the wee hours of the morning and the volunteers, while still fired up, were starting to get tired and hungry. They were also beginning to see Anders's and Karma's true colors.

Our new campaign slogan: "Perception isn't always reality."

10

Are We There Yet?

"I'm excited to show Anders my childhood home," Janet said as we sat on the volunteer bus halfway through our announcement tour.

Our next stop on the tour was dinner at Janet's home in Detroit Lakes. Her parents had worked all day on the logistics and anticipated our arrival at 11:30 p.m. "What is your mom making again?" Charles asked.

"She's making tater-tot hotdish with venison, and she has sandwich fixings for those who prefer just a little nibble," Janet told him proudly. "I grew up on the stuff. Trust me, it's delicious!"

I glanced at Karma and noticed her whispering over the seat into the senator's ear. The McDermotts and Margot had decided to ride the volunteer bus again for this leg of the tour. I hoped Karma didn't pull any nonsense at Janet's home.

"It takes a helluva lot of hotdish to feed buses of volunteers," Charles pointed out.

"They have it under control. They'd do anything for Anders," Janet said with excitement.

"Your parents are awesome," Anders said, jumping into the conversation.

"I will not eat Bambi," Karma yelled out of the blue. Charles rolled his eyes at me.

"You can't tell the difference between venison and beef. Besides, venison is healthier for you," I told her, trying to protect Janet and her parents from Karma's continual tantrums. "It's lower in fat," I added trying to mitigate the situation.

"She'll have sandwiches," Janet said again.

"I don't eat homemade food from strangers, and eating Bambi smashed between frozen potatoes dripping in cream of mushroom soup is not healthy, Allison," Margot asserted in Karma's defense.

"Funny, I didn't know nose candy was healthy," piped in Janet.

Both Charles and I shot her a look to shut her up.

"Venison has lead," Karma stated.

"I don't think you should say that on the campaign trail. Minnesota, and the Midwest overall, is full of hunters who supply food for their families. I'd guess that 95 percent of it is venison," corrected Charles.

"Charles, you're wrong. Hunters use lead bullets to kill the deer. Therefore, the deer meat is called venison. This is extremely important, and I fear for all those who are eating lead bullet meat. They'll be poisoned," Karma stated defensively.

"Are we against hunters now?" Charles asked Anders, ignoring the absurdity of her comments. "Should I have our team modify our messaging to focus on non-hunters, non-game folk? Sounds like a losing campaign to me! We don't need to run afoul of the NRA right off the bat."

"This conversation doesn't need to leave the bus. But I do agree with Karma and Margot. I prefer we stop at a fast-food place before our dinner stop," Anders said.

"We can't afford to buy meals for all the volunteers," argued Charles.

"I'll pay for it personally. I want to stop at a fast-food restaurant," Anders said, determined. Charles asked the bus driver to stop at the next exit.

The senator stood up and the volunteers, who expected a campaign rally speech, started to cheer, holler, and clap. The senator told them, "Karma and I will be buying you dinner tonight. Our treat! We'll find a place soon." He sat down without saying another word.

I was upset that Janet's parents had volunteered, planned, and donated dinner at their home. It would be devastating for them to see their many pans of tater-tot hotdish barely touched.

As the bus pulled into a McDonald's, Janet, Charles, and I stayed on the bus, and didn't follow the volunteers. "Let's go, you guys," the senator shouted as he waved to encourage us to get up.

We all shook our heads no, and I said, "Thank you, Senator. But I think we'll all wait for some homemade hotdish!"

"I've never been to one of these damn places before. I don't know how to order, what the fuck to order, what's good, or how to pay for everyone. And my staff are going to keep their asses on this bus?" the senator said in a childish rant.

Obviously annoyed, Charles answered aggressively, "It's easy, just sing the jingle, 'Two all-beef patties, special sauce, lettuce, cheese, pickles, onions on a sesame seed bun.'"

"I try to do something nice for our volunteers and our supporters, and this is the thanks I get," the senator muttered as he exited the bus by himself.

"You've got ten minutes," Charles shouted after him.

After he was gone, the three of us roared with laughter. "Oh, good God," Charles heaved.

"I can't believe he's never been to a fast-food place," Janet said.

"I mean, come on, he can vote on legislation that will revamp our healthcare system. But he doesn't know where chicken nuggets come from?" I laughed.

The volunteers came back on the bus quickly with bags of food and grins on their faces. Soon the bus smelled like french fries and hamburgers. Twenty minutes later, the senator and Karma came back laughing and carrying bags of food. Apparently, Karma was off her vegan/organic kick for this leg of the trip. The senator handed me the receipt and told me, "I charged this to the campaign. Make sure Trista gets this receipt."

"Anyone want an extra burger? We got a few extras. Charles?" asked the senator.

"No, I'm waiting to be killed by venison drowned in soup and smashed with tater tots," Charles told him.

"And now we're off to Janet's before the final half of our tour," announced the senator in an unnatural, overly excited mood. All that grease must have gone to his head.

I glanced down at the receipt and mouthed to Janet, "$625!" I was annoyed that the senator had announced to the volunteers that he'd be buying their meals personally and instead used campaign donations to pay for them. It would have been nice to actually have a real budget for this tour instead of Janet and I cobbling it together on a shoestring.

As we drove to Janet's, I was surprised but pleased to see an email from Cam on my BlackBerry: "Hey you, I just wanted to check in and see how Minnesota was treating you! Sure would love to be back home with you. The office is dull without you. Hope you have a great tour! Cam."

I read his message three times before I forwarded it to Janet. Apparently, Janet was also online. "That's nice—he's a good friend," Janet said as she scrolled through messages. That's all, I thought. He's a good friend. Within the past three months, my best friend (i.e., the virgin) had suddenly become an expert on relationships and I was starting to get annoyed. After weighing the decision of whether or not to write back to Cam now or wait, I decided to respond. I was never good at playing hard to get. I sent Janet a draft of my message and asked for her input: "Hi Cam! GREAT to hear from you! Minnesota in the summer is always the best, but I do miss DC. We're on the tour right now and Anders is doing awesome! It's fun to be campaigning again! You should ask Charles about joining us next month for the Iowa Straw Poll. It would be so fun to hit the after-parties with you!!! Talk soon, Allison."

"Are you sure he isn't gay?" asked Janet.

"No, he's not gay. He's into girls," I answered.

"Who is gay?" asked Margot.

"Man, nose candy must work miracles on hearing," Janet mumbled. I could feel the tension brewing between Janet and Margot. They were polar opposites. I gestured to Janet to back off.

"No one is gay, and if they were, who cares?" I asked.

"I think he is," Janet replied.

"He isn't," I answered, annoyed. "That message was sweet and unexpected!"

"How much longer until your folks' place?" the senator asked Janet.

"Ten more miles," Janet told him.

I looked at my watch and realized we were now forty-five minutes behind schedule. "We need to get back on schedule," ordered the senator. I rolled my eyes. If we hadn't stopped for fast-food, we'd have been on time.

The senator and Karma scarfed down their cheeseburgers and large containers of french fries like they hadn't eaten in weeks. And, Karma suddenly became vegan free!

"Welcome to Detroit Lakes," Janet exclaimed as we drove past a big welcome sign. She directed the driver to her home, and the volunteers quickly exited the bus in excitement. Charles gave Janet's parents warm hugs. I loved seeing the effort and creativity her mom

put into this stop. Their home was decorated in red, white, and blue and pictures of Anders from prior campaigns were strategically placed throughout. I was amazed that three buses of volunteers were able to fit into their cozy home. Janet's parents were the perfect hosts. They encouraged lots of eating and drinking. The tater-tot hotdish hit the spot, and I was relieved to see that the volunteers were gobbling it all up, despite the $600 worth of cheeseburgers they had eaten.

I came downstairs, and the senator called me over. He sat in a chair and looked a little pale. "Do you have any stomach medicine?" he asked.

"I'll check with Janet's mom," I answered.

"I think I got food poisoning from that hellish restaurant," he added.

"Oh no," I answered, knowing you don't eat multiple cheeseburgers and expect to feel great. I didn't feel sorry for him.

"Can you check on Karma, please?" he asked.

"Of course. Where is she?"

"Either still on the bus or back in the SUV. Ooohh, the pain is killing me," he moaned.

"What's wrong with the boss?" Janet asked.

"Fast-food!" I told her. "He needs some stomach medicine and I need to check on Karma."

"Would venison help?" she laughed, not feeling much sympathy for him either.

A few minutes later Charles announced, "Thank you for the incredible hotdish and hospitality. But we've got a presidential campaign to win! Let's get moving again, friends!"

The senator walked out of Janet's parents' house without saying good-bye or showing any appreciation. Before we left, Janet had found some generic medicine and gave it to him. Apparently, McDermott preferred nongeneric drugs, however, and chose to skip the generic medicine. I thought it was odd that he could rail against the high cost of medicines on the Senate floor and encourage generic medications for senior citizens, but then not use them himself. But he was the one who was going to suffer because of it.

As Charles rushed back onto the campaign trail, Janet and I hugged her parents and thanked them. Karma, Margot, and the senator choose to ride in the SUV for the next leg of the trip. It was just after midnight and we were leaving their driveway, heading toward a tiny Minnesota town of a few thousand called Wadena. As we began to pull out, the mother of a six-year-old came to the front of the bus in desperation. "Can we have silence on this bus, please?" she asked.

No one said a word. "That might be hard," Charles finally responded.

"My son needs to get some sleep," she answered.

"This is a campaign tour, and I need our volunteers fired up, not sleeping," Charles stated.

"Can you pull over the senator's SUV, please?" insisted the volunteer.

"Ma'am, we're almost an hour behind schedule, and I'm the senator's chief of staff. What can I help you with?" Charles asked, his patience being tested.

"I need to speak with Karma," the mother answered and started to cry.

Charles had never been good at dealing with tears. "Oh good God," Charles mumbled as he asked the bus driver and the SUV's driver to pull over. They slowly stopped and the mother got off the bus without her child. She ran to the SUV and we could see a window was down. The woman was talking to Karma.

The mother ran back to the bus and rushed down the center aisle. She grabbed her crying six-year-old son and raced him out to the SUV.

"What in God's name is going on?" Charles asked.

I was intrigued and was surprised that Janet wasn't watching this real-life soap opera unfold before us. Instead, she was engulfed in her

BlackBerry, no doubt emailing Jenkins.

It appeared from a distance that the mother handed her child over to Karma. The mother came back onto the bus and didn't say a word. She wandered back to her seat. I was flabbergasted. I couldn't believe she'd just talked Karma, Margot, and the senator into babysitting for this leg of the trip. Then again, I thought, a six-year-old was probably easier to manage than any one of them. We arrived in Wadena forty-five miles later. The town was dark and motionless. We pulled into our rally spot and I couldn't believe my eyes. Supporters lined the lot and anxiously awaited the senator's late arrival. Signs and flashlights were numerous, along with flags and banners. It was one of our best-attended rallies, and I was shocked that supporters at such a late hour were engaged and excited.

As we poured out of the buses, a strong gas odor spread throughout the rally. "What is that stench?" Janet asked as she plugged her nose.

"I have no idea but it reeks," I answered, almost gagging.

"I know shit and this town smells like shit," Charles stated.

"I don't remember Wadena smelling so bad before," Janet said. The smell was nauseating, and it seemed to be coming from the senator's SUV.

Margot and Karma came over to where we were standing and looked mortified. "Charles, we need our van cleaned out immediately!" Karma ordered.

"Is there a problem?" Charles asked. "That damn kid started having fart competitions with Anders," Karma stated with a straight face.

"Unfortunately, that kid is a little shit. It was dark in the van and I didn't realize that he took off his pants and underwear. The fart competition started and it was contagious," Margot told us.

"It was awesome. Anders was ripping and roaring with the young lad," joked Colonel.

"It was unbearable and not presidential at all. Why would you suggest that little snot ride in our van?" asked Karma.

"We had nothing to do with the kid. The mother approached you,

you caved in, and apparently got gassed," laughed Charles.

Margot and Karma stormed off and joined the senator front and center. I couldn't stop laughing.

Colonel stayed back with us during the Wadena rally. I could tell that, at his age, being up all night traveling was taking a toll.

"You got any smokes?" he asked Janet.

"Me? I've never smoked anything in my life," Janet asserted proudly. She must have repressed her drunken cigar-smoking incident.

"You're missing out, kid. No sex. No booze. No smokes. What the hell do you do for fun?" he asked her. Janet ignored his question and he turned to me next.

"How about you, Allison? I know a girl with long legs like yours can live a little and party," he said as he stared at my legs. I suddenly wished I'd worn jeans instead of shorts.

"Good, clean fun, sir. Good, clean fun," I laughed.

If only he knew that his son's demanding personality was killing my dating and sex life. I started to daydream again about what my life would be like with Cam. It was easy to dream and at the late hour, I was exhausted. I was sick of fantasy, though—I wanted reality. I thought about how much more fun it would have been to have Cam along. He was always a calm voice amidst all of the madness.

I felt a tug on my shirt. "Excuse me?" asked a woman. Her face was painted in Anders's blue. Janet and I both looked at her.

"Yes, can we help you with something?" Janet asked, startled.

"Are you Janet?" she asked.

"Yes, I am," she answered, reaching out to shake her hand.

"Can I hug you?" she asked. She didn't waste any time and grabbed Janet tightly. Her tears dripped onto Janet's shirt, and I was confused. Is this lady nuts?

"I'm Jackie from Brainerd. You got me my twin boys from Liberia when the Embassy was closed. I can't believe I'm actually meeting you. You got me my family," she said with the biggest smile I had ever seen.

"Oh my gosh, Jackie. It's a pleasure to meet you," Janet replied.

"You saved my boys' lives. Can I meet the senator to say thank you?" she asked.

"Of course you can! He'd love to meet you. Let's go over here and I'll try to pull him aside," Janet told her.

We walked over and placed ourselves strategically in an attempt to get the senator's attention. Karma and he were shaking hands, and trying to quickly move along to our next rally stop. I was able to make eye contact with him, and he came over to us.

"Senator, this is Jackie. We were able to secure adoption pink slips for her twin boys from Liberia," I said proudly.

"I need hand sanitizer right now," he snapped.

"Charles has new bottles. I'll grab some before we leave Wadena," I answered.

"Senator, I just wanted to say thank you for Janet's terrific work and your help in securing visas for my boys. I'm incredibly thankful for you and your office," Jackie told him while trying desperately to hold back tears. "Because of you, we're a family."

"Great—great—just great," the senator answered, hugging Jackie. Seeing the senator in a bear hug with Jackie, Karma walked over to us. She asked me, "Is this a donor I should recognize?"

"No, Mrs. McDermott, we were able to help secure visas for her twin sons from Liberia, and she just wanted to say thank you," I answered.

"She's not a donor?" she asked.

"I have no idea who are donors and who aren't. We just help any Minnesotan who needs extra help with federal agencies," I answered.

"Why wouldn't she be a donor?" she questioned. "All that work and all he gets is a hug. We got her two children," she commented. I ignored her, and then was surprised to see Karma actually hug Jackie. The senator called Charles over to share the great news and to get hand sanitizer more quickly.

On the way back to the SUV and buses, I overhead Karma ask

the senator about soliciting donations from people like Jackie. I was proud that he didn't seem interested and said there was a fine line between the campaign and public office.

Charles must have overhead her questioning and said loudly, "Hell, if we got $500 for every kid Janet has helped through the foreign adoption process, we'd be flying instead of riding on a rental bus right now!" Janet and I smiled knowingly to one another.

The sky was dark and the volunteers returned to their buses quickly.

Now, with only three more stops to go, the end was in sight. In the wee hours of the morning, we had successful stops and rallies in Little Falls, St. Cloud, and Anoka before we returned to our campaign headquarters in St. Paul at 6:00 a.m. Charles was determined that we arrive at our final destination on time. He had morning news crews scheduled to tape the senator (and now presidential candidate) as he showed off his campaign parade vehicle, the Zamboni.

The announcement tour was a success, and I was anxious to get home. Janet and I looked terrible, and we had zero interest in being on the morning national news shows. We positioned ourselves toward the very back of the rally.

"I think someone is taking our picture," Janet said.

"You are imagining it," I told her.

"No, didn't you see that flash?" she asked. I turned around and saw a reporter and photographer snapping pictures of our backs.

"Are you fucking kidding me? I don't want my ass on the front of any newspaper!" exclaimed Janet. I couldn't agree more. We both pulled our shirts lower to cover our asses, and I saw Janet snarl at the reporter and photographer.

"I think we're too late," I said as the reporter pulled out her notepad to record our names.

The media now watched and recorded every move of both the senator and Karma. I got the impression that Karma was enjoying the sudden attention and fame.

Charles did a nice job unveiling McDermott's Zamboni, which was decorated in red, white, and blue. The Zamboni was decked out with life-size pictures of the senator doing Minnesota's iconic hobbies of fishing, playing hockey, and curling. The Zamboni had a horn that played the Minnesota Wild's theme song, which loudly alluded to the fact that the senator brought hockey back to Minnesota. Now, he was ready to take the Zamboni across the nation as he cross-checked his opponents and attempted a hat trick by fixing our nation's economy, curbing unemployment, and reducing the national debt.

The Zamboni would be housed at the Minnesota State Fair, which opened in less than two weeks and is the second largest state fair in the country. The Minnesota State Fair is like no other event on earth. It's the home of fried pickles, anything and everything deep-fried on a stick, and politics, politics, and politics on every corner. With millions of possible voters coming through the gates, the fair was an opportunity for a politician to milk a cow, debate on the radio, and connect with Minnesota's average Joes while consuming an ungodly amount of calories.

The McDermott fair booth would have a hockey theme complete with pictures on the Zamboni, a cutout of Anders in hockey gear and Karma in a cheerleading uniform, and miniature hockey sticks for kids. In the past, I would have run the senator's campaign booth at the fair. But because of the announcement tour assignment, Charles pulled the fair booth from my list of duties and I was grateful.

When all the volunteers headed home after the Zamboni unveiling, Charles told Janet and me to take the day off to sleep. As a reward for our hard work, he asked us to come for dinner at his house that evening. We headed to the McDermotts' to get some sleep. We had been up for over twenty-four hours and were utterly exhausted. But of course, sleeping during the day wasn't on the agenda for Margot or Colonel. I had no idea how they were still awake, but figured they must have slept in the van.

After we arrived back at the McDermotts' home, I could sense something wasn't right. Janet was extremely tired, and when she reached the point of either being extremely tired or incredibly hungry, she turned into another person. It was sort of a Dr. Jekyl and Mr. Hyde thing.

As soon as we stepped in the door, Margot bounded up to us, all amped up. "You girls want to go shopping for fair outfits?" she asked.

"I think I'll stick to McDermott blue," Janet said. "The last thing on earth I want to do is go shopping."

"Oh come on. We could go to the mall, try on clothes, and model them for each other, pick out terrible Minnesota outfits, and then we can just return the clothes," she said.

"We can't return clothes we wear," I answered.

"I do it all the time! No one asks!" Margot answered.

"I have no interest in shoplifting," Janet told her as she headed to the living room.

"And neither do I," I said, following her.

I was almost asleep when Margot entered the room with a high-pitched whistle.

"What the fuck are you doing?" Janet asked as she woke up.

"Time to go shopping," Margot exclaimed.

"Margot, we told you we're not going shopping," I yelled.

"At least give me a ride," she begged.

"Oh for Christ's sake, why can't we just get a full eight hours of sleep?" Janet snapped.

I agreed. We had earned eight hours of sleep at the very least. I figured Margot must have had some "candy" to have so much energy after the bus tour.

"We'll give you a ride," I said, hoping to get rid of her for the day. We dropped Margot off at the Mall of America and figured that would keep her busy for a while. After we dropped her off, Janet pulled into a hotel parking lot across the street.

"What are you doing?" I asked.

"I'm done," she snapped. "I'm sick and tired of sleeping on an

air mattress. I'm done. We're going to sleep here until dinner at Charles's. We'll talk him into reimbursing us, trust me," she said. "You know there's no way we can get any peace and quiet in that mad house."

"Okay, you're the driver," I said as I got out of the car.

We walked into the hotel and Janet explained that we'd only need a room for a few hours. The hotel had only one room available that early in the day. Janet took it without hesitation. It was a suite with a king-size bed. We both crashed on the bed and slept like rocks. We set the alarm to allow both of us enough time to get ready for dinner at Charles's. We both desperately needed to shower, but at that point valued sleep more than cleanliness.

The next thing we knew, the alarm clock went off. We both could have easily slept through the entire night.

"Did you see how that desk clerk looked at us?" Janet asked me as she sat up on the bed.

"It was weird. The clerk was weird," I answered.

"I think he thought we were lesbians," Janet laughed.

"Oh, I bet you're right," I laughed loudly.

"I wonder which one of us he thought was the butch?" Janet asked.

"You're crazy. You, for sure! You have short hair and you're more dominant," I teased. Janet just rolled her eyes at me.

We got ready to leave for dinner. The shower felt wonderful. Janet checked us out and gave me the hotel receipt. "Holy shit, Charles is going to freak!" I yelped.

"He is not, how much was it?" Janet asked.

"It was $275, and it says we stayed in the honeymoon suite," I added.

"$275 is a lot for a few hours! But he spends double that on weekly flights back and forth to DC, and his hotel room in DC is triple that price," Janet argued.

"You're in charge. I'm just glad it's on your credit card and not mine," I responded.

We pulled up to Charles's house and went inside. The entryway was lined with his children's artwork. "Charles is a good boss," Janet said.

"You won't be saying that in two hours when we leave with an unpaid honeymoon suite bill," I answered.

"I never thought you'd be the person I spent my first honeymoon night with," Janet laughed.

"How was it for you, darling?" I asked.

"Funny, I don't remember a thing," she answered.

We could see Charles's kids staring at us from above. Charles motioned for us to come upstairs and I said, "They're well trained, they don't talk to strangers!

"You two look mighty frightening!" Charles laughed as he motioned for us to sit down.

Despite that crack we enjoyed a fabulous Italian dinner with Charles and his kids. His wife, Maralee, was gone on a ladies' night out. After twenty-four hours alone with the little ones, she needed it. Regardless, Charles had gone all out. Best of all, he informed us that he'd talked to Anders about a pay raise for both of us. He praised our work and told us that he and Anders understood the long, hard hours we put into our jobs. He knew we were loyal employees.

"On Monday, please check in with the others about the fair booth and stuff," Charles instructed.

"I can't even think about the fair until Monday. We really need a break," Janet added.

"How's life at the McDermotts'?" Charles asked. We both paused and didn't respond right away.

Out of nowhere Janet blurted, "We couldn't stay there today. I think they have mice all over, and Allison is sneezing from a rodent allergy. So we got ourselves a hotel room this afternoon. We wanted to run it by you first, but we couldn't reach you."

"Mice. Really? You gals stay at the hotel through the weekend, and we'll think of plan B on Monday," he concluded. We thanked Charles,

and Janet sang a good-bye song to his kids. They ate it up.

"Nice work, sister," I applauded Janet.

"You just need to know how to work him," she added with a wink. She had told a little white lie, but I didn't care. If I had to fake a mice allergy for the rest of my life, I'd do it to get out of that godforsaken house. We went to the McDermotts' and packed up our belongings. We found a different hotel with two double beds and spent the entire weekend ordering room service, relaxing in the hot tub, and charging spa treatments to our room bill. Expenses be damned! We figured we deserved a little pampering after the week we had. I called Veronica to update her on our latest adventures. She couldn't believe her ears and told me all about her "normal" Senate office and Senator Thomas.

Monday came too quickly. The Minnesota State Fair, debates across the nation, and primary elections would all culminate in the Republican National Convention the following summer.

But first, I was focused on getting Cam to visit Minnesota for the fair.

11

Politics on a Stick:
The Minnesota State Fair

As we entered the state office on Monday, I could tell that we still n eeded a few days to recuperate before wading into full campaign mode with both high heels again.

It was clear that we were missing out on the fun of August recess. It seemed that almost everyone was on vacation, even though the senator had just announced he was running for president. We kept receiving annoying automatic reply emails from our DC colleagues. The best one was Lindsay's: "I'm out of the office from August 10 to

August 30. If you need to reach the senator, please call Allison." Not only did she forget to leave my last name, but she also failed to provide any of my contact information. Her message was worthless.

Janet also noticed the pattern of out-of-office bounce backs. "Doesn't anyone talk to each other in that office? I just got a message from Heidi that said if you need help, call Lindsay," Janet laughed.

"She's out, so call me. No big deal, I can jet back and forth to DC nightly," I laughed.

I could hear Janet moaning out loud as she went through the stack of constituent requests. They had piled up over the past few days.

Just then Trista flew into my office, "Charles is on the phone and needs to talk with both of you immediately." Janet moaned again as I answered his call on speaker.

"Hey Charles! Thanks again for the hotel this weekend!" I answered.

"You're welcome. Just give Trista the bill. Why don't you guys stay at a hotel all week?" he answered. Janet almost started choking in surprise. I quickly motioned for her to knock it off.

"Look, I need you guys to focus on the state fair booth. I need your leadership. We've got our hockey theme, get it staffed with volunteers, and make it cool," Charles said.

"Sounds great," Janet replied.

"Let's keep this simple. I need you guys to take over and get it done. We need to be ready to roll for the fair," he added.

"Okay, will do," I told him as I looked at Janet with despair. She gave me a reassuring look.

"Just keep me updated and thank you, guys," Charles said and hung up.

"Fuck, really?!" I stated.

"We knew this was coming. It'll be easy," Janet reassured me.

"The state fair is a big deal and we have less than two weeks. The senator will expect professionalism. We have an opportunity to reach out to millions of people each day," I said, almost in a panic.

"They've been working on the booth for months. They've been building Anders's warming house. Really, all we need to do is find volunteers for shifts each day, figure out some cool swag, and come up with some catchy campaign phrases," Janet said, blowing off my concerns.

"Okay, well first things first. Let's go look at the booth," I suggested.

Trista gave us the contact information of the volunteer who was building the booth and within a few minutes we were off. When we got to Handyman Phil's house we stared in shock at what was supposed to be a warming house.

"Phil, what is that?" I asked, referring to the building before us.

"It's a fishing shack! Just like you asked for," he said proudly.

Neither one of us was sure about how to proceed. "Phil, it was supposed to be a hockey-themed booth, not fishing-themed," I stated firmly.

"And it looks unfinished," added Janet.

"Well, it's too late now. But by fair time you'll have yourselves one helluva fishing shack," Phil told us. We were silent. "Besides, I like fishing," he concluded.

Janet and I thanked him for his hard work. "Charles will fix this," Janet said, and we started back to the office.

"He'll be fine. We can change our theme from hockey to fishing," I added. "Maybe the Zamboni can tow a boat."

Janet just laughed.

"We need to get pictures of Anders and Karma fishing," I said, trying to get her to focus on the problem.

"He loves to fish. They must have old pictures we can just blow up. Remember—gosh, wasn't it just last year that he spent a week fishing with that morning anchor from CNN up north?" Janet asked.

"You think they were fishing all week?"

"Yes, I do. What do you think they were doing in International Falls, Minnesota, for a week?" Janet asked innocently.

"Stop being so damn naïve! She's a big time city anchor. Do you

think she really wants to come to Boondock, Minnesota, to fish for a week?" I responded.

"I like I-Falls," Janet said.

"You would like I-Falls. But I don't think fishing would be at the top of your to-do list if Jenkins took you there," I pointed out.

"Oh, you don't think—?" Janet said, looking shocked.

"Hook, line, and sinker."

"But the senator does love to fish. Last summer he went to Alaska to fish," Janet added.

"God. Stop being so naïve. He went because it was a free trip to Alaska, and he was trying to butter-up to Starr as Chair of the Appropriations Committee," I argued back.

"What's up with you today?" she finally asked.

"I'm just sick of this shit. I have no money, no life, and we're constantly doing special projects to save the fucking day," I complained.

"This is an easy one. Let's just break it down into tasks. First, we need to come up with some swag ideas. This afternoon let's sit in the conference room and dream up campaign slogans and themes. We'll order up the swag to match the theme, find us some volunteers, and call it a day," Janet said in a no-nonsense manner.

"Okay, you're making the state fair sound way too easy," I added.

"Really? I think this will be pretty fun," Janet said as she walked out of my office.

I sat there motionless. I didn't know where to begin. I felt overwhelmed and was restless, and the hot August sun beating through my window wasn't helping. Instead of coming up with slogans, I found myself staring at my checking account balance online and calculating the total of my earned vacation hours and comp time. I had accumulated more than ninety-two hours and had no plans to use even an hour of it before Christmas. It was rare that I let an entire morning go to waste, but today I needed a break. So I blew off the senator's scheduling and personal requests.

After wasting most of the morning, I noticed unread messages from Rose. I was nervous about the hostile work environment investigation that was about to begin. I knew we hadn't done anything wrong, but an investigation was still scary enough to make me sick to my stomach. Rose's messages were polite and innocuous. She informed Janet and me that we'd be interviewed tomorrow about our interactions with Blair. He didn't have a leg to stand on and his silver spoon wasn't going to help him this time. He didn't know how to work successfully with anyone, and I thought any interviewer worth her salt would pick up on that immediately.

I was curious to know if anyone else in the DC office knew about Blair's complaint. I hoped it wasn't the office gossip of the week. I figured if there was talk, Cam would spill the beans. Plus, a random message to Cam couldn't hurt anything. I wrote and rewrote a message to Cam until it was perfect:

> *Hey Cam! Greetings from a hot sizzling day in Minnesota! I hope you're having a great recess. How is everyone there? Anything happening? Janet and I just found out we are in charge of the state fair booth. We've picked a fishing theme. Drop me a line (no pun intended). Let's catch up (no pun intended). Allison.*

I had another pun about having walleyes for him, but I deleted that one. Within seconds, Cam wrote back:

> *Hey you. Good to hear from you. Not much here happening at all. The office is empty. It's pretty much just Morgan and I. He wants to take me to Virginia Beach this weekend. Sort of weird, don't you think? I'd rather be there—I love me a good Minnesota summer day. Tell Janet hello and keep in touch!*

I didn't wait to respond:

> *You should come here and help us with the fair! Virginia Beach with your boss for the weekend. Odd. Let me know if you want*

*to come help us. I'll ask Charles for you!!! We seriously could use
the help!*

I walked into Janet's office with a skip in my step.

"You have that look," she said.

"Cam just emailed me," I answered.

"Nice," Janet said as she typed.

"What are you doing?" I asked. I was annoyed that she didn't
seem to care at all about Cam's message.

"Oh, nothing," she answered.

"I call bullshit. What are you doing?" I asked as I leaned over her
computer.

"Nothing," she answered and pushed me away.

"Are you kidding me?" I asked.

"What?" she answered.

"Since when do you book hotel rooms in Charleston, South
Carolina, for $550 a night?" I asked.

"Oh, this isn't for me," she answered. "Jenkins just needed me to
book him a few rooms for one of the debates coming up."

"What?" I asked.

"Really, it's no big deal. Don't be such a drama queen. I'm helping
out a blind friend who needs a hotel reservation," she added.

"On your credit card!" I asked.

"He'll pay me back. He's a United States Senator," she answered.

"This is getting weird," I told her. "Why are you reserving the
rooms? Doesn't he have bitches like us?"

"I didn't ask. I just want to help him. You're reading way too much
into this," Janet answered as she entered her credit card information.

"I hope we don't need that credit card. It'll be maxed out quick at
550 bones a night," I added.

"That was gross," Janet said.

"What was gross?"

"'550 bones a night,'" she answered.

"Oh my God, you are such a pervert," I told her. "That's not what I meant."

"I don't think they charge anything for the room, they just use the card to reserve it," she told me.

"I'm going to call Karma about fishing pictures and then do you want to grab lunch before coming up with fair slogans?" I asked.

"Sure. Sounds good," Janet said without even looking up at me. I left, frustrated with Janet but pumped that Cam had written back to me already.

He wrote: "I don't want to go with Morgan to VB. Can you ask Charles about MN for me? He seems to really like you a lot."

I wrote back instantly: "Of course, will do that right now!"

I decided to email Charles instead of calling him:

Hey Charles: We're starting on the state fair booth. It has been changed to a fishing theme so scrap the Zamboni. I'm going to call Karma to see if she might have some good fishing pictures of Anders. I think I remember him fishing last summer with a reporter from NYC? Also, we were thinking it might be helpful to have Cam fly to Minnesota to help staff the booth. Given the fact that so many farmers and ranchers come to the fair, it would probably be helpful to have someone with his expertise on board. Thanks much! Allison.

There was a nearly immediate phone call from Charles.

"That's fine about Cam. Don't call Karma about the pictures. I'll find you some," Charles said, straight to the point as usual.

"Great," I told him, and ended the call.

I walked into Janet's office. "That was odd. I just talked to Charles and he said he'll get us fishing pictures of Anders," I told her. "You ready for lunch?"

"Nice," said Janet, continuing to type.

"Now what the heck are you doing?" I asked.

"Nothing!" she answered.

"Seriously, what the hell are you doing?" I insisted.

"I'm applying for a new credit card, if you must know."

"Oh my God. You're out of control!"

"Let's go," Janet said as she got up from her computer.

"Oh, yeah. And Charles said Cam can come help us with the state fair!" I told Janet happily.

"Smooth move," she said. "And you think I'm playing with fire. You get the chief of staff to send your wanna-be lover to work a campaign fair booth when we have volunteers chomping at the bit to help." Janet laughed.

"Oh my God, you can't even compare our situations. You're online dating the senator who is running against our boss for the party's endorsement and nomination for president while paying for his hotel rooms on your personal credit card," I said. "I'm just looking for a little intra-office fling, that's all."

"All harmless and fun," she added as we walked outside.

"It sure is super nice out today," I stated as I put on my sunglasses.

"Maybe we should go find a hotel and have our meeting outside?" Janet suggested.

"We do our best work while floating in a pool soaking up the sun," I added.

"Should we?" Janet asked.

"Why not? We both have our BlackBerrys, and we've been working nonstop. Charles did tell us to find a hotel, and it's work related," I added.

"Sold!" Janet answered.

"I like it. I like it." I laughed.

We agreed on a hotel in downtown St. Paul that had a rooftop pool and sun deck. We checked ourselves in and unpacked our clothes. "It is going to feel awesome to have a dresser and our own beds this week," Janet stated.

"I know. Our own beds, unpacked suitcases, and a rooftop sundeck!" I added.

"I sure hope the hotel has free Wi-Fi," Janet added.

"Oh my God, if you are up all night emailing and sexting with Jenkins, I'm going to kill you. I am seriously almost ready to confiscate your BlackBerry."

We decided to order room service on the sundeck. We had our swimsuits on and pads of paper ready for our meeting. We were set.

"These margaritas are going down way too easy under this sun," Janet laughed.

"Easy does it, lush!" I laughed.

"So we have the fishing shack. Charles is working on photos of Anders fishing. What else do we need?" Janet asked.

"We need to give stuff out for sure. Everyone comes to the fair for the free shit."

"What could we give out that's related to fishing?" she asked.

"God, I have no clue. Everyone always wants a bag for all the free shit they collect. Maybe that," I proposed.

"I think we've done Anders's bags in the past, though," Janet answered. "How about a fishing hook: Get hooked on McDermott!"

"Lame. You can't see a hook. They're too small. Plus can you imagine if some fair-goer got 'hooked' on a hook? We would never hear the end of it. McDermott would probably get sued!" I said. "I think we need stickers so people walk around with McDermott shit on."

"Oh, you're right," Janet sighed. "We can't do stickers, though. The fair rules ban them. We could do huge buttons?"

"A funny button would be good. People love buttons," I added.

We began making a list of button suggestions to run by Charles:

1. Get hooked on Anders—McDermott for President.
2. Catch of the Day—McDermott for President.
3. Anders Knows Fishing.
4. No Bass about It. McDermott for President.

5. He's Fishing for You.
6. Bobbing for Anders.
7. Get Hooked by McDermott—America's Best Catch.
8. One Fish. Two Fish. Three Fish. Karma's a Bitch.
9. Little Pole. Big Net.
10. Anders for President—He's Got Your Line.
11. No Crappies. Just Walleyes. McDermott for President.
12. No New Taxes. Just Reeling and Dealing. Anders.
13. Bringing Minnesota's Fishing to All of America.

"Our list is pretty good, but we need to delete the Karma one," Janet said.

"Totally. I like the simple one about getting hooked," I told her.

"We still need something cool to hand out. How about Anders bobbers?" asked Janet.

"That would be good, bobbers and buttons. Cheap, and easy to bring to the booth every day," I answered. "Plus they will even have some utility value."

"God, remember the last campaign when we had the great idea of handing out campaign signs from the booth?" Janet stated.

"I actually had red marks and bruises along my arms that year from hauling those damn signs and posts," I recalled.

"Yeah, it was a good idea but we didn't think about not being able to keep stuff in the booth overnight," Janet added.

"I love the state fair. Where else do you have millions of people walking around eating crap on a stick and loving Minnesota?"

"I hate it. It's so dirty and all people do is walk up and down the streets," Janet complained.

"Oh, come on—it'll be fun. I like our fishing booth," I added.

"I just hope Anders shows up every day to shake some hands," Janet added.

"I have him scheduled to do a fair appearance every day for a few hours," I added.

"Let's just hope he does it," Janet answered.

"He'll need a case of hand sanitizer!"

"Shit, he's going to need a case of Tums. If he can't swallow a McDonald's cheeseburger, I don't think he can handle a Pronto Pup," Janet laughed.

"I'm so excited for the Sweet Martha's chocolate chip cookies, fried cheese on a stick, pork chop on a stick, and fried Snickers and Oreos!" I exclaimed.

"I'm out this year," Janet told me.

"What? Oh, come on! We can split everything!" I proposed.

"No, I'm out," she insisted.

"When you see that butter-dipped corn on the cob and a carton full of cheese curds, you'll be game," I reassured her.

"I'm telling you, I'm out this year. Maybe just an ice cream cone," she answered.

"Whatever. Speaking of food, we've been out here all afternoon and it's almost seven. I think we should find some dinner," I added.

"Yeah, I think I may have fried my skin. I'm feeling a bit red," Janet said as she dabbed at her sunburned face.

"We can find some aloe."

"I want one last good dinner before my big diet," she announced.

"Where have I been? I didn't know we were breaking in a new diet tomorrow," I said.

"Yep, tomorrow. All protein and no carbs. I need Charles to think I've had a gastric bypass so I can swing the hunting trip!" she added.

I rolled my eyes. "Okay, I'll do it with you. It'll be better if we do it together," I reassured her. I figured a little weight loss couldn't hurt.

"You look like a starving model. You can't afford to lose two pounds," Janet stated.

"Shut up—I can lose some weight, too. Plus, protein diets are good with a buddy. Maybe we can work out every night, too!" I suggested.

"This all starts tomorrow," Janet was quick to add.

"Got it. So what do you want for the last supper?" I asked.

"Bag of chips and dip?" she joked.

"No, let's go eat dinner and come back early to watch some trashy cable TV," I said. "I've been going through withdrawal since staying at the McDermotts' house."

We had a nice last supper, complete with bacon cheeseburgers, fries, and, of course, a huge chocolate milkshake for dessert. When we finished, I could see Janet was anxious to get back to our hotel. Her obsession with Jenkins was starting to affect her interest in doing anything but communicate with him online. It was annoying, and it was consuming her. Back in the room she was online and typing rapidly before I could even turn on the TV.

"Don't you guys ever run out of things to say to each other?" I asked.

"No. Right now we're playing a little question-and-answer game," she told me as she stared intently at her computer screen.

"You do what?" I asked.

"Just send each other questions. Like, how many people can you say with confidence have your back? Which season do you like better, fall or spring? Do you sleep in the nude?" she continued.

"Oh my God, you asked a United States Senator if he slept in the nude online!?"

"Yes! And yes, just so you know," she answered.

"Excuse me while I go throw up," I replied. "The last thing I want to picture is Senator Jenkins in the nude."

I also went online and sent Cam the news about him being able to travel back to Minnesota for the fair. The idea of having Cam with us at the fair excited me. I counted the number of days until he'd arrive. Then I researched "hostile work environment" online. "I'm a little nervous about our interviews tomorrow," I told Janet.

"We have nothing to worry about. We haven't done anything wrong," she answered.

"Get a load of this," I said, then read aloud, "'A hostile work environment is primarily a legal term used to describe a workplace situation where an employee cannot reasonably perform his work, due to certain behaviors by management or coworkers that are deemed hostile. Hostility in this form is not only a boss being rude, yelling, or annoying. It is very specific, especially in the legal setting when one is suing an employer for either wrongful termination or for creating an environment that causes severe stress to the employee.'"

"Which part of that definition does Blair have anything close to a claim about?" Janet asked.

"I know. We haven't done anything to that little pussy," I added. "I'm still nervous, though."

"If anything, we can list example after example of Blair, Heidi, and Lindsay's behaviors toward us. But I don't think we should be tattletales," Janet added.

"I mean, what do we say tomorrow? Blair is a little pussy?" I questioned.

"No, I think we just answer any questions they have for us and be truthful. We have nothing to hide," she answered.

"We haven't done anything wrong. I can't believe he's wasting Senate money on such a joke of a complaint. Do you think this goes into our personnel files?" I asked.

"I hope so. I think it'd be good for us to have an official record to show that we're not guilty of anything. I just think it's crazy that we have to do interviews and that they're doing a full-blown investigation. Didn't Rose say he complained about how we sat in our chairs during a meeting, and that we took notes?" she asked.

"Yup, he said we sat in our chairs with our backs turned and we wrote each other notes about him all the time." I laughed.

"Funny, I didn't know I sat weird in a chair. And, trust me, if I was going to write notes during office meetings I'd be writing Jenkins a love letter, not catty notes about Blair."

"So now you know braille?" I asked.

"Not yet, but he can work his hand across my bumps any day," she said, laughing.

"Excuse me, Senator, would you like to read my breasts—I mean mind?" I cracked.

"Excuse me, oh sexy, handsome love machine, come read my body," she retorted.

"Excuse me, Senator, did you just point your penis at me?" I continued.

"Holy shit!" Janet yelled abruptly.

"What?" I asked.

"I think Blair filed a hostile work environment complaint in his last job with the congressman," she said, focused on her laptop.

"What are you talking about?" I asked.

"I literally just searched his name and *hostile work environment* and look what I pulled up. It looks like the congressman's office paid him a cash settlement!" she stated.

"That little bitch," I said as I lay down next to her on the bed to see her search results.

"Yes, look at this. He got about $50,000 from the office," she said.

"That little bitch," I repeated. "So he's just looking for a big payoff!"

"That *little bitch* sure seems to know how to work a hostile work environment complaint through the system so he can cash in," Janet stated.

"It makes me sick to my stomach," I added.

"What do we do with this?" she asked.

"We need to tell Charles or Rose ASAP!" I answered.

"You can tell them," she answered.

"How do I explain why we were doing an Internet search for *Blair Bloomberg* and *hostile work environment*?" I asked.

"They won't ask. I wonder if they know about his track record?" she asked.

"What a little bitch," I said again, as I emailed the link to Charles and Rose.

"Doesn't it make you sick? $50,000 in a settlement! I wonder what happened. Someone made fun of his sweater vests or that he spritzes Evian on his face?" Janet said sarcastically.

"I hope they don't cave in to this stupid, zero-credibility complaint against us," I replied.

"How does anyone expect us to work with him after this is over?" she asked.

"I guess we should just be normal. Or at least treat him like everything is normal," I added.

"Odd," she said.

"Yes, that's the motto of our office, remember."

"No, I'm not talking about the office anymore. Check out Jenkins's answer to my last question," she said, showing me on her screen.

"No, he didn't just ask you that!" I stated.

"How do I answer?" she asked.

"I can't believe he'd actually write a question like that. Aren't all his emails public information?"

"No, he's using his personal email account," she answered.

"Not to rain on your parade, darling, but how do we know this is really Jenkins?" I asked. "I don't care how horny a person might be, a senator should have more common sense than to ask you, a virtual stranger, if 'withholding ejaculations using the Pubococcygeal (pc) muscle is dangerous or harmful?'"

"I'm not a stranger!" she argued back.

"Pretty sure he's going to pull an Anthony Weiner and send you some dick pics," I said. "Let's bring this back to reality for a minute. How many times have you been with Jenkins face-to-face. One, right? Then, all of the sudden, he's your Mr. Everything and you've become his side do-it-all-for-him bitch."

"But it's really not like that," she argued.

I knew I wasn't going to win the argument but thought maybe a reality check would be good for her. "Are you still going with him on that weekend retreat?" I asked.

"I hope so. I need to figure out how to pay for my airline ticket," she answered.

"Wait. What?"

"What?" she asked.

"You have to pay for your airline ticket to meet up with him? I thought you said it was all expenses paid?" I asked.

"Yeah, so what?" Janet answered.

"Oh no, you are not going," I said firmly.

"What?" she questioned.

"No. I'm done with you playing this lovers' game that's missing the key word: *love*. I can't sit back and watch you throw away any more time and money on this."

"Whatever. You don't understand," she whined. She started to type even faster, dismissing me. I shook my head at her and turned away.

I went through my work emails and, surprisingly, didn't have any work or requests from the senator or Karma. I flipped through the TV channels and decided some E! reality TV was just what I needed.

An hour later, we both were taken aback by breaking news about the Republican presidential race. All the major news channels began to report that Minnesota Congresswoman Nancy O'Connor would be announcing her presidential candidacy the following morning via an online announcement.

"O'Connor doesn't have a chance," Janet stated.

"She's so far to the right that I think her nipples even slant that direction," I laughed.

"Not only far to the right, but she's just plain goofy and weird," Janet laughed.

"She's the definition of a right-winger!" I responded.

"Remember when we asked her about how she became a patent attorney?" I asked.

"Oh, I remember. Didn't she tell us she wasn't sure what profession she should enter, so she asked her husband for guidance, as the Bible directs?" Janet answered.

"Yes. Can you imagine: 'Oh, dear husband, you are head of my household and my life. What profession would you like me to have?'" I laughed at the idea.

"'My life is controlled by you, and you want me to be a patent attorney. Yes, I'll be a patent attorney,'" Janet continued. "'You'd like my hair short? Yes, my master. You'd like me to have fifteen children? Yes, my womb is ready, my master.'"

"No wonder we're both single," I said.

"I have no desire to have some guy tell me what I can and can't do," Janet stated.

"Remember that time we were early for Anders's town hall in St. Cloud, and O'Connor came in without any staff or help for her tax rally? We ended up making signs at the last minute and running her entire event."

"Did she even say thank you?" Janet questioned.

"She was too busy putting lipstick on the pit bull."

"I respect that she's entering the presidential race. But really, O'Connor? She isn't ready and we both know she makes shit up all the time. She invents history to back her old-school conservative mojo," Janet stated.

"She's awful," I responded.

"The media is going to love this race. We've got the blind chairman with deep pockets and the support of the party's core; Anders, The Senate Flavor of the Month Jewish guy who hasn't served more than a year in office; and now O'Connor, the Tea Party's cheerleader who cares more about her high heels and matching purses than getting results," I summarized grimly.

"I don't think O'Connor has passed one amendment or piece of legislation since she's taken office," Janet said.

"She's the most partisan woman on the Hill," I added.

Janet started to sing, "I am woman hear me roar through this race I will not bore!"

"Is this race big enough for two Minnesotans?" I asked.

"O'Connor will be out. She'll be out by next week after some ridiculous gaffe," Janet added.

"You should email Jenkins about O'Connor and see what he writes back," I suggested, interested to hear his response.

"Good idea, I'll do it right now. How about this: 'Hi—O'Connor's in. What do you think?'"

"Very personal," I laughed.

"What do you want me to say? 'Hi, my sexy, blind love machine. When are we moving to Pennsylvania Avenue? And since you'll cream over O'Connor, can she be our Secretary of Kinky Activities at the Department of Internet Relations?'" Janet asked playfully.

"I like it, I like it." I laughed.

Charles wrote back to thank us for the information about Blair. I got ready for bed. Janet was still mesmerized by her laptop. "Holy shit!" she yelled as I brushed my teeth.

"What?" I mumbled around a mouthful of toothpaste.

"Jenkins is calling me," she screeched.

"Holy fuck!" I yelled. "Answer it!"

"I'm scared," she said, shoving the phone at me.

"What? You want me to answer it?" I asked.

"YES!" she yelled.

"Oh my God, you frickin' pansy," I said before I answered the phone. "Hello."

There was a long silence and then I could barely hear Jenkins ask, "Janet, is that you?"

"Um, yes, sir, this is Janet," I lied, looking at Janet who was perched on the bed, white as a ghost.

"Don't call me sir, my love kitten," he said.

I felt sick. "Purrrrr."

"That sounds like you, my love kitten. Are you ready to get frisky?" he asked, laughing.

"How are you?" I asked.

"Missing you and wondering what you're wearing tonight, my little pet," he said.

I could barely control my laughter and felt nauseous. "Don't be silly, Senator," I responded as I stared at Janet.

"You heard about Nancy tonight?" he asked.

"Yes, we just saw the news and I wondered what you thought," I asked as I tried to disguise my voice.

"It sounds like my love kitty has a cold and needs some warm milk to smooth her throat," he said.

I almost gagged out loud. The thought of Jenkins referring to his cum as warm milk disgusted me. I never knew Jenkins was so kinky. I was disturbed by his direct conversation. Janet was definitely in over her head with this pervert. "What do you think about her chances?" I asked, changing the subject.

"Nancy is an idiot. She has no friends in Congress and only cares about getting interviews. She'll be in the race until a lucrative contract comes her way," he spoke freely.

"She's a media queen," I added and looked at Janet for what else to say.

"And you are my queen, my love kitten," he answered.

There was an awkward silence and I motioned for Janet to help me with the call. She scribbled on a piece of paper: "Ask him about the retreat?"

"So, how about the retreat?" I asked as I rolled my eyes.

"I don't think you should come, my love kitten. Airfares are high and I want our first night of lovemaking to be secluded, away from any press cameras or staff. I hope you understand," he answered, surprising me.

"Yes, our first night will be memorable. Life-changing," I said as Janet threw a pillow at me.

"Life-changing?" he asked.

"I meant to say, our first time together will be magical," I corrected myself. "I have another call coming in that I must take," I said, trying to end the worst conversation of my life.

"Oh, my love kitten, purrrr for me all night," he said.

"Oh, I'll purr alright," I said, glaring at Janet.

"I miss you, my love kitty," he said before he hung up.

"I love you, Janet, but I will never, ever do that for you again! Have you lost your mind? Do you realize that I just purred for the United States Senator who is running against our boss for the Republican presidential nomination while you sat and stared at me?" I yelled.

"What did he say about the retreat?" she asked anxiously.

"You'll have to wait to get laid until you're grown-up enough to answer his calls," I yelled again.

"The retreat—what did he say?" she pressured.

"He basically blew me off about the retreat. You are not going. You're playing with fire. And since when does he call you his love kitty? That is weird," I insisted.

"I'm sure he didn't blow you off about the retreat. You seem jealous. It's all harmless," she added.

"Aren't you deathly allergic to cats?" I asked, not taking the bait.

"He really blew off O'Connor, huh?" Janet said, changing the subject.

"He didn't even seem to care at all. He was almost arrogant about it."

"I think if you're running for president, you have to have a lot of confidence. You've seen the attack ads during presidential campaigns. You have to think of yourself as the only one who can win," Janet argued.

"It does take quite an ego, I guess," I conceded, not wanting to get into a fight about it.

"How weird is it that we, two small-town girls, know three people running for President of the United States?" Janet added.

"When you say it like that, it sounds crazy. And they're all weird. Is anyone normal in public office?"

"That's a good question," she answered as she tucked herself into her bed. "Jenkins may be a little weird, but he's my kind of weird!"

After a long silence, I said, "Senator Thomas seems normal. Veronica really likes him."

A few moments passed. "There's no one I'd rather do this job with than you, Janet," I told her as I drifted to sleep.

"Same here, my love kitten," she laughed.
"Gross," I said and fell asleep.

＊　　　＊　　　＊　　　＊　　　＊　　　＊

The week flew by. We were busy dealing with the investigator's interviews, tracking the progress of the fair booth, and sticking to our protein-only diets. We also worked hard to ensure the fair's success with volunteers, giveaways, and themed campaign materials.

Charles was on board with "I got hooked by McDermott: America's Best Catch" for our state fair slogan. He asked us to order buttons, bags, and bobbers. Handyman Phil told me the booth was finished, and it looked like it was Anders's fishing shack. In the evenings, Janet and I created handouts in the style of fishing regulation cards that detailed Anders's positions on key national issues.

Blair's ridiculous hostile work environment complaint also proceeded. The interviewer conducted unscheduled interviews with everyone in the Minnesota and DC offices throughout the week. He questioned Janet and me twice and was shocked to learn about the prior similar complaint and settlement awarded to Blair.

He asked both of us to physically demonstrate how we sat in our chairs during meetings, and he questioned Janet about slamming her office door. He was perplexed when Janet explained she didn't have an office door, and wondered (as we did) how she could slam an absent door. The interviewer asked a few follow-up questions about our relationship with Charles, inquiring whether or not we believed we were treated more favorably than other staff members by Charles or the senator. I explained that we worked around the clock to meet higher expectations than other staffers, and that we were extremely underpaid, overworked, and frequently reprimanded. The interviewer left without giving us any hint of where the complaint or investigation stood.

Our Atkins diets began to take a toll. When Janet went on a diet, there was no messing around. We both followed the horrible diet to

the letter. We survived the entire first week eating only eggs, meat, and cheese. I didn't see any results, but we were sticking to it. We started power walking every day before and after work. She had it bad for Jenkins to go to such extremes. I think part of her hoped he'd change his mind about the hunting trip.

Anders, Karma, and Charles all seemed happy with our work—and our ATD. We took that to heart. Anders was focused on the state fair, the Charleston debate, the Iowa Straw Poll and the Republican National Convention. Karma was accompanying Anders across the nation to fundraise all week, and she stayed out of our hair for the most part. She was one of the few individuals on earth who seemed to actually enjoy hobnobbing with donors. I suspected it was mainly because the male donors gave her so much attention.

Cam was scheduled to arrive in Minnesota the following week to help with the final details of the state fair, and I continued to look forward to his arrival. I purposely scheduled us together at the booth. I chose the closing shifts, thinking we could walk around the fair or hang out afterward. Janet continued to talk to Jenkins two or three times a day and was still on cloud nine. All in all, things seemed to be going swimmingly.

✳   ✳   ✳   ✳   ✳   ✳

"I never get sick," I insisted to Janet as I lay buried under the covers of my hotel bed.

"I think you should just chill out today and stay here," Janet insisted as she got ready for the heavy workweek and the start of the state fair.

"I'm not going anywhere. I feel like I got hit by a bus," I said, aching all over.

"I'll check on you later today to see if you need anything," Janet said before she headed out the door to the office.

I felt like I was on my deathbed. I was frustrated to be stuck in bed while Cam arrived in Minnesota over the weekend. The Great Minnesota Get Together, as the Minnesota State Fair is often called, was set to open later in the week. We still hadn't really seen Anders's fishing-shack fair booth, but our campaign handouts and swag had all arrived, and without any spelling mistakes! Success! Charles found some great pictures of Anders fishing and we had them blown up to life-size figures. He actually looked like a fisherman. Everything seemed right on track.

I scheduled the senator to appear at the booth for a three-hour period each day. Press interviews were arranged for before and after each fair appearance. Trista bought the senator three new pairs of blue jeans and light blue plaid shirts to wear. The new casual clothes allowed him to fit in with the blue-collar folks who were expected to attend the fair. And while the last preparations were happening, I was stuck in bed with a fever, aches, and multiple pains. Worst of all, I could not stop throwing up.

I woke up to a phone call from Janet. "How are you feeling?" she asked.

"Shitty," I answered.

"That's not good. You need anything?" she asked.

"A case of medicine,"

"Get some more sleep," she instructed.

"What's going on?" I asked.

"I just went to look at the fair booth with Cam. The volunteers delivered it to the fairgrounds today. I'm embarrassed," she told me.

"What do you mean, embarrassed?" I asked.

"I've never seen anything so ugly. Cam just stared at it and didn't say anything," she said.

"Really? That's not good. I mean, it's a booth, right?" I asked.

"It's a shack. I don't think Handyman Phil has touched it since we saw it last!" she explained.

"What are you going to do?" I asked.

"The best we can. I hope with the pictures it'll be okay."

"It will be. Just cover everything up with posters and pictures," I reassured her.

"Oh, did you hear that the investigator dismissed Blair's complaint without merit?" she asked.

"No, I haven't read any messages or even gotten out of bed. But really—that's great news."

"Serves the little bitch right," she remarked.

"Uh oh, I'm really not feeling very well. Can you call me later?" I asked before I hung up the phone. Then I leaned over to vomit one more time. I kept a trash can next to the bed for this very purpose. I couldn't understand how there was anything left to throw up. All I'd eaten over the past day was soda crackers and water. I felt miserable.

At some point, I dozed off again. I woke up in sweat-soaked sheets. I went to take a shower and almost passed out in the bathroom. I crawled back to my BlackBerry and dialed Janet. "Can you come get me? I'm sick."

I felt weak. Janet and Cam showed up together. I felt so terrible that I didn't even care that Cam saw me half naked and in such a terrible condition. "I think you'd better go to urgent care," Janet insisted.

"I think you might be right," I muttered. Cam helped me out of bed and into the car.

I was only in urgent care for an hour before I was admitted to the hospital for an unknown illness and a kidney infection. Janet and Cam took care of my every need. Janet informed the senator, Charles, and Rose that I'd been admitted. I didn't hear anything from the senator or Karma, but Charles came to the hospital within hours. I still felt miserable, but the IV fluids they pumped into me helped with the dehydration.

Charles sat with Janet, Cam, and I as we waited for a multitude of test results.

"You'll do anything to get out of working the fair!" Charles teased as he gave me a wink.

"I'd much rather be eating cheese on a stick than having needles shoved in my arms," I said, not seeing any humor in the situation at the time.

"Speaking of the state fair, you need to warn Anders about the condition of the booth," Janet said to Charles.

"What do you mean?" he asked.

"It's ugly. It looks like it's made of plywood," Cam described.

"Plywood?" Charles asked.

"It's not finished. It's a plywood box," Janet insisted. "Something needs to be done. It wasn't even painted."

"Oh great, just what I need—Anders pissed about his fair booth. Add that to the shit list that keeps getting longer and longer," Charles said as he began to type furiously into his BlackBerry.

One of my treating physicians walked into my hospital room and asked if everyone present could hear the details of my results.

"Why not? They're like family to me," I answered.

The physician said they ran a bunch of tests and couldn't determine a diagnosis. He repeatedly asked me if I was using drugs or had used drugs in the past. Charles took on the father role and reassured the physician that I wasn't a past or current user.

"Maybe you have Lyme disease," Janet stated as she scoped out diseases online.

"It's not Lyme disease," the physician assured and asked again, "Are you sure you aren't using drugs, Allison? We can ask your friends to leave."

"I've never used drugs in my life, doctor," I answered.

"Any changes in your diet?" he asked.

"No, not really," I answered, not wanting to get into the details of our crazy diet.

"Yes!" yelled Janet. "We just started the Atkins diets. We've been on it for the past three weeks."

"That explains the kidney failure," the doctor explained. "You are not a candidate for protein-only diets. You'll need to stay here overnight. It's possible you could be discharged tomorrow."

"Great, I try to lose a few pounds and I land myself in the hospital," I said wryly.

"Well, now that we know you're going to live, I'm going to head home to figure out how to lower Anders's expectations about the booth," Charles said, squeezing my arm as he left.

"Shit, I'm sorry. I feel like I made you sick," Janet said.

"Don't be silly. Who knew I wasn't a candidate for a protein-only diet?"

"You get better, kid. We need you at the fair by the end of the week," Cam told me.

"Will do. Thanks, you guys," I said. "It's great to know I have such good friends."

Thankfully, I slept through the entire night. The next morning I was told that if my blood results improved I'd be discharged by early that evening. I called to tell Janet.

"Hey, I should be out of here later today," I said excitedly.

"Awesome news," she said, sounding distracted.

"What's going on?" I asked.

"I think we've been busted by the fair booth police," she replied quietly.

"What do you mean?" I asked.

"Trista is on the phone with the state fair organizers right now. I think they're saying our booth is an eyesore and it needs to be improved within twenty-four hours, or they'll pull it out," she whispered.

"Oh shit, really?" I asked. "It is really that bad? I thought you guys were exaggerating."

"I gotta go. Let me know when I can pick you up," she said quickly.

I had more tests throughout the day, and the friendly nurses kept me hydrated. I was feeling much better. I called Janet to inform her that I could be discharged anytime after 6:00 p.m.

When Janet and Cam arrived for my discharge the hospital staff demanded that I be taken out to the main hospital lobby in a wheelchair.

"If I never see this place again, it'll be too soon," I said as I got into Janet's car.

"You look much better," Cam said.

"Thank you," I said, as I tried to fix my greasy, unwashed hair in Janet's little mirror. It was only then that I realized just how bad I looked. I immediately felt uncomfortable knowing Cam was seeing me in this state. Not only had I not taken a shower in days, but because my kidneys couldn't process all of the toxins in my system, I had a serious breakout. My face looked like a pepperoni pizza, my legs were unshaved, and I had not a drop of makeup on. Not exactly the look you want the man of your dreams to see.

"We need to make a quick pit stop at the fairgrounds to check on the booth," Janet announced.

"Did you hear? We're officially an eyesore," Cam laughed.

"Not good," I answered.

"We need to drop off some paint. We have volunteers ready to paint all night long," Janet said.

"Oh my gosh, that's crazy." I laughed.

"Nothing like asking volunteers to have an all-night paint-a-thon for Anders," said Cam.

"Welcome to our world," I replied.

We arrived at the fair booth and stared at Handyman Phil's handiwork. "That is one ugly fishing shack," Janet said, stating the obvious.

"It looks like it was made by a kindergartener." Cam laughed.

"Anders is going to be one pissed-off candidate," I predicted.

We unloaded the paint and Cam took charge and delegated duties. It was nice to see his leadership, and I had no idea he was so handy. As I stood there admiring him, I noticed Janet was walking oddly.

"Are you alright?" I asked her.

"Yes, why?" she replied.

"You have a weird bowlegged limp," I said. "What's going on?"

"Phone sex all night with Jenkins."

"What?!" I asked.

She didn't answer, but I was pretty sure she was alluding to playing with herself all night while talking dirty. Either that, or Jenkins had taken his phone sex up a notch. Maybe he'd asked her to gallop around the hotel room or something. Perhaps now she was his sex pony instead of sex kitten. I didn't want to know. Some things were best left unspoken. I pushed the possible explanations for Janet's morning-after limp out of my mind and walked back to the fishing shack. Cam was finishing up his instructions. We left the volunteers with the paint and supplies and hoped for the best.

"You gals want to grab a pizza?" Cam asked.

"Sure," I insisted. I wanted to spend as much time with him as possible, even though I looked like hell.

Janet stated, "Are you sure you're up to it? I mean, you were just in the hospital."

"I'm hungry and if that diet didn't kill me, a quick stop for a pizza won't," I joked. "I've been on a liquid diet for the past two days, and all protein before that. I need carbs!"

We ate an entire extra-large pizza between the three of us. Janet didn't fidget a bit at grabbing slice after slice and forgetting about her diet for the evening. For a short time I didn't even mind that I hadn't showered, had no makeup on, and had frizzled hair. At least I was staring into Cam's eyes. Somehow, that and the pizza made everything better.

When we arrived back at our hotel room I was shocked to see that Janet had picked up some bedroom toys while I was away. I didn't say anything to her about them. But clearly my virgin roommate had in fact played while I was away. Now I understood why she was walking funny. It seemed this virgin had popped her own cherry.

*　　　*　　　*　　　*　　　*　　　*

The volunteers came through for Anders and painted the booth to the satisfaction of the state fair organizers. For the next ten straight days, we worked at the Minnesota State Fair. It was exhausting, exciting, entertaining, and, of course, eventful. We quickly concluded that there were parts of this state fair we'd never want to forget, so we began a list of our favorite memories.

Top Ten Fondest State Fair Memories of Anders McDermott for President

10. Anders suffering from diarrhea every day after eating anything on a stick.

9. Janet having the gall to ask the State Fair Police Officers if they were "rent-a-cops or real cops."

8. Anders and Karma taking part in the fair's cow-milking competition. Karma got shit on.

7. Nancy O'Connor asking Anders in a live interview if he'd be her VP. To which he answered, "You want me to be your VP, honey? Not a chance, sweetheart," alienating the feminists.

6. Cam arguing daily with war protestors.

5. The breast-feeding mothers who planted themselves in front of our booth with their big boobs hanging out. They fed their babies and overgrown toddlers to assert their feminist rights and views. Thanks, Anders.

4. Charles and his kids showing up every day making sure the booth wasn't an eyesore.

3. Janet doing a daily tally of the number of O'Connor, Jenkins, and McDermott buttons she saw. Conveniently, Jenkins won her count hands down every day.

2. Karma and Margot showing up each day to work the booth wearing high heels and short skirts. Margot wiped her nose constantly during each shift.

1. Anders signing on to the no-new-taxes pledge with his fingers crossed behind his back.

We survived the various, often humorous, adventures until the state fair's traditional end date, Labor Day. And even then, no rest was in sight. Five days later the senator would headline the first Presidential primary debate in Charleston, South Carolina, with Jenkins and O'Connor as his challengers. After that was the Iowa Straw Poll, and by this time next year the Republican National Convention would convene in New York City, marking the party's official endorsement for the presidential election. We quickly learned that every minute mattered.

12
Watch What You Say:
The Great Debate

We were due to arrive back in DC in less than two weeks. It was going to be an exciting time for Anders's presidential campaign. Charles had assembled a team of staff that included Janet, Cam, Rose, Heidi, Trista, Morgan, and me. Charles had filed the appropriate paperwork for the entourage, and they joined us as dual Senate staffers and campaign workers. We kept track of how much time we spent on official versus campaign duties to ensure not campaign-finance laws, or senate ethics rules were violated. Our task: cover two major campaign events.

First up was the first national debate in Charleston, South Carolina. During presidential elections, it has become customary for primary candidates to engage in a series of debates. They're important because they allow the candidates to address the most controversial issues of the election. This first debate was a chance for the voters to get their initial glimpses of the presidential candidates. The debate was only a week away, and Anders had a lot of preparing to do.

The week following the debate, the first national straw poll would take place in Ames, Iowa. The Iowa Straw Poll is nationally known. It occurs every presidential election cycle in which there is not an incumbent Republican candidate. It takes place on the campus of Iowa State University and is by far the most prominent of many straw polls. The results are not binding, but it gives the candidates a sense of the strength of their campaigns early in the election process.

The Iowa Straw Poll was the first chance for the candidates to build momentum for their campaigns. It gives the winner a head start in what is bound to be a long election process. Since its inception, the Iowa Straw Poll has determined the Republican nominee for president three out of five times. We knew it was imperative that Anders not only perform well at the debate in Charleston but also that he win the Iowa Straw Poll. The competition was tough with Jenkins and O'Connor throwing their hats in the ring.

The Iowa event would also be an opportunity for Anders to shake hands and meet with potential national delegates. His presence and a certain amount of grandstanding, which would prompt him to be seen as a contender, were imperative. Charles was adept at delegating roles and assigning responsibilities for the two events, and he made sure all the bases were covered. But we knew we had a lot of work ahead of us. The assignments were:

Allison	Anders's scheduling and advance preparation
Janet	Karma's assistant

Cam	Anders's driver and body person
Rose	gofer/runner for team
Heidi	policy-issue preparation and family assistant
Trista	remain in office/responsible for anything needed
Morgan	debate preparation
Charles	chief of staff/campaign manager

I had to give Charles credit—he put together a reliable team of hard workers. When Heidi resisted the urge to binge drink, staving off diabetic reactions, she proved to be a policy whiz. She was actually smart and was able to craft solid talking points on almost any issue. She was also incredibly efficient, seemingly able to pull facts and figures out of thin air. Though she could be incredibly annoying, I had to hand it to her—she knew her stuff.

One position that remained conspicuously unfilled was press secretary. I hated to admit it, but the campaign was likely to suffer without Blair. I wondered who would handle the senator's campaign press releases, formal announcements, and, most importantly, his national interviews. After the investigator dismissed Blair's hostile work environment complaint, he went off the deep end. He informed the office (through his father) that he wouldn't be returning. Blair alleged that he'd been permanently scarred from the hostile environment created by the actions of Janet, Charles, and me. His father informed us that Blair was seeking professional outpatient psychological help for acute post-traumatic stress disorder. I was glad to be rid of that nut job. With or without Blair, the campaign must go on. Though he was quite press savvy, the campaign was probably better off without him. It was going to be tough, keeping the Senate Office running with a skeletal staff as we pushed forward in a presidential campaign, and we didn't need any distractions.

Both Janet's role and my role in the Charleston debate would be minimal. Charles, Heidi, and Morgan would take the lead. They had

already begun debate prep, springing random policy questions on the senator whenever they got the chance. They were scheduled to do their final prep with the senator on Wednesday, Thursday, and Friday, and the debate was planned for a live national television broadcast on Saturday evening. I was grateful for that timing. I worried that if the debate was held on Friday, it would provide too much tempting fodder for the cast of *Saturday Night Live*. I worried most that Anders would be the main target of the SNL parodies. While he could be well spoken and charming, every once in a while he had a tendency to place his foot firmly in his mouth.

"Good morning, Ali," the senator said.

"Good morning, Senator," I replied.

"Are you ready for Charleston and Iowa?" he asked.

"Yes, sir, I'm anxious and excited for you," I answered, unsure of what he wanted from me.

"Excited for me? You need to be excited for yourself, Ali. Your life is about to change! You won't have to worry about paying back your payday loans or heading back to that godforsaken home you call South Dakota," he said.

I faked a laugh and felt a tug on my heart. I believed South Dakota was a great state with hardworking folks who love nature, God, their families and neighbors, and their country. They'd take the shirts off their backs for someone in need. I didn't understand why he always acted as though Minnesota and DC were superior to my home state.

"Is my schedule for Iowa all set?" the senator asked.

"I'm working on it today, Senator. By the end of the day you'll have a binder with all the invitations, advances for the hundreds of events, and detailed notes about the concerns of all the local politicians, union organizers, and party nuts—and their personal information—all organized from A to Z. We've got you covered," I said cheerfully.

"You're the best, Ali. You really are the greatest," he said without the slightest bit of conviction. "Are we going to sit down with all the invitations and events so Karma and I can pick which we'll attend? Karma won't want to be stuck with the farmers all day." He winked.

"I'll schedule time on your calendar for Wednesday and include Karma, Margot, Janet, Charles, Cam, and Trista," I suggested.

"Wednesday is too late. I need to be laser focused on the debate by Wednesday. Let's do it tonight at our house," he instructed.

"Okay, I'll let Karma and Margot know we'll be there tonight."

Janet, without knowing the senator was in my office, came bouncing in and then came to a sudden stop. "Oh, I'm sorry. I didn't realize, Senator."

"You seem mighty happy today, Janet," the senator said as he kissed her on her cheek.

"I just scored immigration visas for a family of four children from Kenya. They've been waiting to be reunited with their parents for over five years. They'll be coming to Minnesota by the end of the week!" Janet exclaimed.

"Make sure you tell Blair about this. That's good news. I've been trying to befriend the African community," the senator said as he left my office to greet the interns.

"Doesn't he know that Blair quit?" Janet asked in a hushed tone.

"I dunno. Sure sounds like he doesn't know. I need your help big time. He wants to do the Iowa scheduling meeting tonight, and I don't have these invitations in any sort of order—and I don't know what any of these events is about."

"Let's get Cam to help us. We'll start organizing them by date and time," she said as she began to rifle through the invitations strewn across my desk. "There are hundreds of invitations here! There's no way he's going to make it to all of these!"

"I know," I agreed. "Look at this pile. There's everything from an ice cream social with veterans to breakfast with the egg producers. These events cover every bit of the day—breakfast, lunch, dinner, dessert, happy hour, and late night for three days straight. I think we need to pick out the best events and tell him about those tonight," I concluded. "He'll be overwhelmed if we show him all of these."

"Sounds great. We'll get this done by tonight," Janet assured me.

"I'll call Margot and tell her Anders scheduled a meeting for their place tonight," I told Janet. "Hopefully that will prevent us from walking in on anything inappropriate."

"This will be fun!" Janet responded.

"I think so too!" I said as I dialed Margot's number.

"Hi, Allison," she answered the phone.

"Hi, Margot. I just talked with the senator and he asked that I call you and Karma. He'd like to do the pre-Iowa scheduling meeting at the house tonight," I told her.

"Tonight? Here!?" she asked.

"Yes, the senator believes we're running out of time," I said. "The entire meeting shouldn't take more than an hour and it will only be me, Janet, Charles, Trista, Cam, you, and Karma."

"What do I need to do?" she asked. I could tell by her voice that her anxiety was rising. Margot wasn't good with change, or, for that matter, any real responsibility.

I tried to calm her down. "I don't think you need to do anything but let Karma know so she's there and prepared with her calendar. I want to make sure this trip goes smoothly for both of them."

"Colonel needs to attend too!" Margot instructed.

"Sounds fine to me," I told her.

"Can we have margaritas and chips and salsa?" she asked.

"Well, we aren't coming over for happy hour," I replied, frustrated. "The scheduling meeting is always down to business."

"Karma will want to host and have something," she answered.

"I'll leave those details to you, but I'll inform everyone to arrive by 6:30 p.m.," I stated and closed the conversation.

Cam, Janet, and I spent the entire day plowing through more than three hundred fifty Iowa-related invitations. We arranged them into piles of *should attend, possibly attend,* and *not attend.* Then we put the should-attend pile into a spreadsheet and organized it by date, time, and location. We made a copy of each invitation and announcement and complied seven huge binders for the meeting.

"After tonight's meeting, we should spend the week writing detailed advance memos for each event on the senator's final schedule," I said to Janet and Cam, feeling proud of all we'd accomplished that day.

We arrived at the McDermotts' at 6:15 p.m. and were greeted at the door by Colonel. "I want to ride with the senator to the debate," he told Janet before we'd even come inside.

"I'm sorry, Colonel. What was that?" Janet asked, looking confused.

"For the debate. I'm going with Anders. I want to ride with Anders!" he ordered.

"I'm not sure how we'll all get to the debate on Saturday, sir. But we'll be certain everyone arrives on time," assured Cam.

"You don't get it, kid. I'm riding with Anders," snapped Colonel.

I motioned to Cam to drop it, and we walked into the smoky kitchen. "What's cooking?" Janet asked, coughing.

"I'm making my own tortilla chips for the meeting," Karma told us. She was wearing a brand-new apron.

"Wow, that sounds impressive," Janet said as she looked into the oven.

"I don't like all the preservatives in nonorganic chips," Karma informed.

"Gotcha," Janet said, nodding her understanding to Karma and then rolling her eyes at Cam.

"I also made us fresh salsa from the neighbor's garden!" Karma exclaimed.

"The same neighbors who have the eight-by-ten-foot O'Connor sign?" asked Janet.

"I took all the tomatoes, peppers, and onions from their garden today while they were at work. I wiped them clean." Karma giggled.

"Blame it on rabbits," Margot replied.

Cam seemed nervous and out of place so I asked him to come help me distribute the binders for the meeting.

"Do I get one of those binders?" asked the senator's father.

"You can share with me," Janet said.

"I want my own binder, and I'm riding with Anders," he repeated as he kissed Janet on the cheek.

"Those are big binders," Margot observed as she showed one to Karma.

"Oh my, you elves have been busy today," Karma said, fanning away the smoke coming out of the stove. I leaned over stealthily and cracked open the nearest window.

Margot opened a binder and pointed out invitations to Karma. "I'm not going to the typical politician events," Karma announced. "They're boring and they make the wives do ceramics and crap. I don't do wives' events either. Isn't there something glamorous I can attend? I just bought five new designer gowns today."

"Maybe there'll be a cooking class," Janet whispered as she walked past Cam and me.

"Or a till-your-own-garden class," Cam responded under his breath.

Colonel was quickly paging through a binder, and he began showing Margot all the concert events. "I'm going to be with Anders the entire time in Iowa," he said.

Charles arrived and asked if there was something burning. I told him Karma was baking homemade tortilla chips for our meeting. He started coughing and gave me a wink.

"Charles, I'm riding with Anders to South Carolina and Iowa," Colonel announced loudly.

"That's between you and Anders, sir," Charles told him as he looked around the senator's home.

"Charles, what should I wear for the debate?" Karma asked.

"Clothes," he replied.

"Very funny," Margot inserted, and then continued, "Charles, are you ever going to trust Karma and me again? I don't think you should still hold last year's incident against us."

"Incident?" Charles said. Then he went off. "I don't think *incident* is the correct term to refer to a senator's wife posing for sexy photographs in a skimpy red nightie on a hotel rooftop."

"Anders knew all about it and agreed to the pictures, Charles. They were harmless. Loosen your tie and learn to trust me," Karma whispered as she rubbed Charles's shoulder.

"Do what you do, Mrs. McDermott, but my job is to protect the senator," Charles stated in a fierce tone. "And those kinds of antics put his job and mine at risk."

Clearly there was a history of tension between Karma, Margot, and Charles that Janet, Cam, and I were unaware of. The silence in the room was palpable. Thankfully, Trista and the senator soon arrived and it was down to business.

Charles opened the meeting by thanking everyone for their patience and hard work preparing for the Iowa Straw Poll. He informed the senator that we'd compiled binders with all the events, invitations, and a tentative schedule. We'd do detailed advance memos for all the selected events so he'd be prepared.

"Who picked the events on this schedule?" questioned the senator. We all exchanged looks, and no one answered right away.

"Well, Senator, we thought these events seemed like the best fit for you," I told him as I nervously grabbed one of Karma's burnt chips and dipped it into her homemade salsa.

"I don't like this Jewish group," the senator said as he quickly paged through the binder.

"I noticed a few concerts I'd like to attend," Karma chimed in.

"Concerts?" asked the senator as he continued. "I don't see any concerts on my schedule. We definitely want to do all the concerts and late-night parties!" Everyone started paging through the invitations, disregarding the tentative schedule.

"I don't want anything ever scheduled before 11:00 a.m.," Karma told the room.

"Got it," answered Janet.

"I'm going everywhere with you, Anders," Colonel stated.

"Sounds great, Dad," answered the senator. I noticed Charles rolling his eyes at Trista.

"Anders, I want to ride with you to the debate," Colonel continued. The senator didn't answer, and we all took note. "I'm not riding with the staff. They're always up to shenanigans, and it stresses me out. My heart can't handle it."

"Your blood pressure is our top concern," Margot reassured him.

"Let's refocus on Iowa and the schedule," instructed Charles.

"Who will be helping me?" asked Karma.

"I've asked Janet to staff you, Karma. And Heidi will assist Colonel. Additionally, Allison and Cam will be available for anything you need," Charles replied.

"I don't think these are the best events," the senator stated.

"Okay," replied Charles, looking at me.

"What do you suggest, Senator?" I asked.

"I don't know. I don't have time to page through this huge binder and decide. I'm running for president, for Christ's sake. Don't we know what events I need to attend? I want to be with donors—and not just ten-dollar donors. I want to be with good friends and the donors who matter. I have one opportunity to get this right, and I can't be looking like a fool going to a breakfast with midwestern farmers," the senator yelled as he got up to try Karma's salsa.

He spit it out onto the floor. "What the hell is that?" he asked.

"Anders McDermott, don't you ever spit on our floor again!" yelled Karma.

"Karma, not now. You sit and look pretty, honey," he scolded.

"Okay, gang, let's do this," Charles interjected, trying to prevent a massive fight. "I'll make some calls and see what the popular events are. But for now let's just RSVP *yes* for Anders and Karma to attend all the events they're invited to."

I immediately felt uneasy. "I just want to be clear: I'm supposed to accept all of these invitations? There are over three hundred and fifty of them. There's no way Karma and the senator can attend them all."

"You got it," Charles said. "Just RSVP *yes* for everything."

"But won't people be upset when he doesn't show?" I continued.

Charles cut me off. "Just do what I say."

I was about to reply when Colonel joined in, "I want to go with Anders! To EVERYTHING!"

"RSVP *yes* for three attendees for all the events. I want an advance prepared with exactly what the event is, who will be there, and who I should meet and talk to," ordered the senator.

"You're the boss," Charles told him.

I had an instant stomachache at the thought of all the work that was just dumped into my lap. How had a straightforward scheduling meeting gotten so far out of hand? The senator appeared more interested in attending concerts than connecting with the folks whose support he'd need to get elected.

During the car ride back to the hotel, Janet and Cam promised they'd help me every day and night until we had it finished. I was thankful to have them on my team.

"Has everyone gone crazy? RSVP *yes* to all three hundred and fifty events?" I asked Janet, who was online and typing within five minutes of returning to our hotel room.

"Jenkins just asked if we were going to South Carolina with the boss," she told me.

"Did you tell him yes, but our campaign pays for the hotel and we don't stay in rooms that are over $200 a night?" I asked.

"I just reserved him a room, that's all," Janet insisted.

"Don't you find it odd that his staff didn't do that for him? You put his Charleston room on your credit card?" I asked.

"He's blind."

"Funny, last time I checked blind people could make their own hotel reservations—or hire a campaign staff to do it for them," I said pointedly. She rolled her eyes and turned away. I knew it was time to drop the subject if I didn't want a fight.

"Did you try Karma's salsa?" I asked her.

"No, it scared me. I don't trust any cook with a clean apron!" answered Janet.

"Oh my God, it was the worst taste I've ever encountered," I said as I brushed my teeth. "I don't know how you screw up salsa, but somehow she managed."

"I'm surprised she would even attempt to cook," Janet laughed.

We both spent the evening online. Janet chatted with her cyber-lover Jenkins, and I began the RSVP process. The next morning came too early.

Charles was in the office before we arrived, and he had donuts sprinkled with bacon waiting for us.

"Oh my God, these taste amazing!" exclaimed Janet as she stuffed her face.

"I thought you two would like these," Charles said as he passed me one.

"This sure beats Karma's organic homemade chips and salsa." I laughed.

"That was salsa?" he asked.

"Tomatoes, pepper, and onions freshly stolen from the neighbor's garden," Janet shared.

"I don't want to hear anymore," Charles complained.

"Will you two write up a press release announcing that the boss will host a pre-debate rally, open to the public two hours before the debate?" Charles asked.

"Will do," Janet agreed.

"We're going to finish RSVPing for all the events and doing all the advances today," I said, wanting Charles to hear that we'd be pulling yet another all-nighter.

"Sounds good. Send me the release draft when you have it," he directed as he walked away whistling something his son had probably sung to him the night before.

"Add *press secretary* to our resumes," laughed Janet.

"Blair would be foaming at the mouth if he knew we were writing up the pre-debate rally release."

"Let's make it fun and anti-establishment," Janet suggested.

"You write it and I'll edit it," I suggested as I took another bite of my bacon-topped donut. "You're more creative than I am."

We went into our offices, and I could hear Janet typing loudly. "Can you 'type' any louder?" I asked sarcastically.

"Oh my gosh, I'm typing!" she said, sounding indignant.

"You only type like that when you're talking to Senator Blind Date," I yelled.

"Who is Senator Blind Date?" Cam asked as he walked into my office.

"Janet's made-up romance. She met him on one of those online dating sites." Trying to make the Janet-Jenkins cover more convincing, I threw in, "I don't think I could ever meet someone online. I prefer to meet people the old-fashioned way, you know, like through friends, or at work." I smiled.

He didn't take the bait, just responded with a broad smile. "He must be a real charmer to land you, Janet."

"Focus on work, guys," Janet ordered.

"Exactly, let's start on the advances," Cam said, getting down to business.

Cam took the binder of invitations and started doing the detailed advance work while I started calling to RSVP for the events that weren't up-to-date enough to have an e-RSVP. Cam had his work cut out for him. Advance work is a critical part of any campaign. It involves not only going to the scene ahead of time so the layout of the event is clear, but also requires figuring out how many guests will attend, how many speakers or VIPs are expected, what the topics of discussion will be, and—most importantly for Senator High Maintenance McDermott— where all the nearest bathrooms and exits would be. Cam wouldn't have time to physically go to all the locations ahead of time, but he was doing his damnedest to get the rest of the information distilled into an easy-to-read summary. That way the senator would know exactly what he was getting himself into when he arrived at each event.

I also explained to each of the event planners that the senator's

father would be attending with the senator and his wife. We had a mountain of work ahead of us, but after some quick organization, we felt we were making headway.

"I just sent you both the release draft," Janet hollered.

I opened my email and found her release. "Looks good to me, simple and informative," I yelled back.

"And Blair thought this job was difficult," she said.

"I think it's good, too," Cam chimed in.

"That took five minutes. No wonder Blair had all of that extra time to spritz water on his face," laughed Janet.

"Make sure you send it to Charles," I reminded her.

"Already done."

"Come help with these advances, fast fingers," Cam teased, referring to Janet's typing ability.

"That's the only thing she's fast at," I said laughing.

"Whatever," Janet rolled her eyes as she walked into our room.

"Release looks good," Charles yelled from his office down the hall.

"Now, what do I do with it?" she asked.

"Blair had national press lists on his computer," Cam said. "I'll try to find them for you. Maybe he put them on the shared drive. If not I'll reach out to the DC office. Our tech guy should be able to lift it off his hard drive."

"Alright, sounds good! Thanks Cam! We're quite the political machine," Janet said.

Within minutes Cam found what we needed, and we were back to work on the RSVPs and advance memos. While Cam and I worked on those, Janet spent the afternoon sending the press release to every possible press contact.

"This job is too easy," Janet laughed. "All I'm doing is hitting the *send* button. A monkey could do this!"

"Enough with the monkey comments!" I groaned. "Remember Karma's monkey- president gibe? We don't need another bad story to kill!"

"Blair wanted to make his job seem harder than it was. It was important to him to be 'indispensable.' And he had it out for you two," Cam told us.

"You're probably right," I replied.

"Of course I am. You guys outperform everyone in the DC office. You make their output and capabilities look less impressive by comparison. People naturally get defensive when you guys are around. Plus, you're both favorites of Charles," Cam said.

"Favorites," I laughed.

"I could think of a million other words than favorites," Janet said wryly.

"All kidding aside, you guys are smart and fun to be with," Cam told us.

I wanted to jump up and give him a big kiss on the lips. But I thought I didn't need to add a sexual harassment complaint to my personnel file. The more I hung out with him, the more I liked him, and I wondered if he felt the same. He was always so reserved. But I enjoyed spending time with him nonetheless.

"Janet, get in here," yelled Charles. He didn't sound happy.

Janet jumped up from the fax machine and nervously ran to Charles's office. I could hear him yell at her. "Read this sentence out loud!"

"'Senator Anders McDermott and Mrs. McDermott invite the citizens of South Carolina to join them for a public rally just prior to the debate,'" Janet read.

"Read it again and think," yelled Charles.

"'Senator Anders McDermott and Mrs. McDermott invite the citizens of South Carolina to join them for a public rally just prior to the debate,'" Janet read again slowly.

"The last time I spelled *public*, it was p-u-b-L-i-c," yelled Charles. Cam and I stared at each other, paralyzed.

Charles went on, "You didn't write *public*, you wrote *pubic*. As in sexual organs. The media is already having a field day with this! You just invited everyone to a pubic rally! What the hell is a pubic rally? It sounds like we're running a sex shop!"

"I'm so sorry. It was a typo," Janet said and continued hopefully, "Maybe no one will notice?"

"Your *typos* are getting us into trouble," Charles yelled. "The next spelling error you make, you're fired."

Cam and I stared at each other in disbelief. Janet came out of Charles's office and he slammed his door, startling us all. I could see Janet's face turning red, and I knew what was coming. Sure enough, her little pale face turned bright red, and her eyes began to stream tears.

"He's overreacting," I assured her in a quiet tone. She just looked at the ground and sniffled.

"We all read it, and none of us noticed it," Cam said. "It's not your fault."

"Don't let it get to you," I told her. "Let's bring all this advance work back to the hotel, grab some drinks and dinner, and forget all about this. We have other things to worry about."

Janet was quiet all night, and Cam and I kept running across Internet articles lampooning the press announcement. The national press was having a field day with McDermott's "Pubic Rally" announcement. We kept Janet away from the hotel televisions, afraid she might have a nervous breakdown if she heard the broad array of jokes from the political pundits on Fox News, CNN, MSNBC, and CNBC.

When Cam left for the evening I reassured Janet that everything would be fine in the morning. "Let's just get a good night's sleep and have a fresh start tomorrow."

"I feel like crap," Janet said.

"I know. And I'm sure the senator and Charles both know you're taking this one hard too. But it'll blow over. Everyone makes mistakes," I reminded her as we prepared for bed.

But I was worried about what would happen the next day. While the senator loved being in the spotlight, he hated being embarrassed. I knew he'd have to deal with the media head on, and I feared that he'd get so beat up by the press that he'd have no choice but to let Janet go. I tried not to cry myself, just thinking about the possibility of continuing the campaign without her. She and Cam were the only ones keeping me sane. My restless thoughts were interrupted by a buzzing sound.

"What the hell is that?" I asked, startled.

"I don't know," Janet said, talking in her sleep.

"I think it's your phone."

Janet popped out of bed to check the phone and said, "Oh shit, it's the senator!"

"You'd better answer," I insisted.

"Hello, Senator," Janet answered flatly as she stared at me. Her face was paper white.

"You're the worst press secretary I've ever had." He yelled loud enough for me to hear him across the room.

"I'm sorry, Senator," Janet answered.

"You are a terrible press secretary," he yelled again.

"Senator," Janet replied calmly, "that might be part of the problem. I'm not your press secretary, I'm a legislative assistant."

"You're terrible—no good for anything," he yelled.

"I'm sorry you feel that way, Senator," answered Janet.

"Have a good night, Janet. You've ruined mine. Terrible press secretary," the senator repeated before he hung up on her.

Her eyes welled with tears again. "Could you hear him?" she asked timidly.

"Yes, I think he was drunk," I answered.

"Terrible press secretary," she mumbled through her tears. "I'm not his press secretary! I was just trying to help out," she sobbed. "I ran the volunteer center on the last campaign, then did some casework, and then became a legislative assistant. Never once have I done anything remotely related to the press. And no one has even told me what my flipping title is on this campaign. How am I supposed to know what to do?" she asked, her anger growing. "All I was told was to help you and Karma. Since when is 'press secretary' part of that job description?"

"I know. He knows that too. He's a politician, he needs to blame someone," I replied. "Right now you're his punching bag. It will blow over. Trust me. I've been his punching bag enough to know. He once called me 'the worst travel agent ever.' This is no worse."

"What an ass," she stated.

"Let's just try to get some sleep," I suggested.

I heard Janet sniffling all night long, and when we got up her eyes were swollen from crying so much. We arrived at the office later than usual, and Janet was noticeably quiet. I felt caught up on the Iowa events, and Cam was helping me complete all the advance information. In addition to the expected particulars, I almost started asking each event coordinator for a date of birth, social security number, and their relationship status so the senator would have the information at his fingertips. It seemed to be an endless task.

Meanwhile my email account filled up fast with news alerts and with emails from random old friends and acquaintances who were sending me links and articles about Anders's receiving a fitting endorsement from CROTCH. I researched CROTCH and discovered it's a sex group devoted to Republican politics. According to online research, Creative Republicans Open To Careful Homo/ Heterosexual Sex was dedicated to encouraging spouses and significant others to take their lover to kinky clubs where they'd have sex in front of other people, but monogamously. They also were supporters of repealing the Defense of Marriage Act and supporters of gay rights.

I emailed Cam and told him to come to my office and shut the door so Janet wouldn't hear us.

"Did you see this?" I asked him.

"See what?" he asked as he read my computer screen. "Who the heck is CROTCH?"

"Apparently some kinky group of Republicans who just endorsed our boss for president," I answered.

"All because of the 'Pubic Rally' announcement?" he asked.

"Well, I don't think it hurt that Karma posed almost nude on a hotel rooftop last year," I answered.

"So what's their platform?" he asked.

"It looks like they're big supporters of gay marriage and exhibitionist sex!" I said.

"Oh, I'm just a Catholic boy from Minnesota," he laughed. "We don't talk about this stuff up north."

All this talk about sex made me want to jump him right then and there.

"You learn something every day working in the US Senate," I said.

"You can say that again. Though I never thought CROTCH would be part of my Senate learning curve." Cam laughed.

Janet knocked on my door, and we tried to stop our giggling. "What's going on in here?" she asked as she entered the room.

"Oh, we were just messing around," Cam told her.

"Oh really?" Janet smirked and gave me a wink.

"Well, not like that." I laughed. I could see out of the corner of my eye that Cam's face had turned bright red. I wanted to crawl under my desk.

"That's too bad," Janet said.

"You really are messing around! Why do you have the word *crotch* plastered all over your computer screen?" she asked in shock. I clicked to close the browser window on my computer screen.

Janet asked, "Seriously, what are you guys up to?"

Cam and I exchanged awkward glances. "It's good to hear your giggle is back," I told her.

"I'm on the shit list for the week, but I think this will blow over," she answered.

"It's going to blow for sure," Cam replied.

"What's that supposed to mean?" she asked, giving Cam a hard time. He turned red again, and I decided to rescue him.

"It's going to be hard at first, but the senator will soften over time," I said.

Janet jumped in. "That's what she said!"

We all burst out laughing. It seemed Janet was recovering from the whole debacle better than expected. I decided it was a good time to let her know how bad the damage really was.

"You're going to see this sooner or later," I told her as I pulled up the news stories. Janet sobered as she began clicking through the new articles.

"I feel sick to my stomach. All of this because I left the 'L' out of *public*," she groaned, burying her head in her hands.

"Look at it this way. Things have already climaxed," I said as I patted her head.

"Can we stop with the innuendos?"

"Fair enough," Cam said.

"Well, I wonder if anyone from CROTCH brings credibility to Anders's campaign—or money," I asked, hoping she'd see a brighter side to the situation.

"I've never heard of CROTCH before," Janet said as she navigated through their web site.

"Neither have we," I told her.

"Does the site list any of their members? I mean, heck, we might recognize a name," I said as we gathered around my computer.

We were stunned to read the name of the Midwest region's deputy chair. "No fuckin' way," I laughed.

"Blair Bloomberg II?" Cam questioned.

"How many Blair Bloombergs from the Midwest do you know?" Janet asked.

"Trust me, knowing one is more than enough," I answered.

"That kinky son of a gun," Cam said in disbelief.

"I never saw this one coming," Janet replied.

"Who knew uptight Blair was into adventurous sex?" I asked, stunned.

"The visuals are killing me," Janet said. "I thought he was asexual."

And Cam added, "It'll be fun to see how Charles spins this one."

"I think I'm going to be sick." Janet was obviously starting worry even more.

"It'll be fine," I told her, even though I doubted that myself.

"You gals packed for Charleston?" Cam asked.

"We're living out of suitcases," I reminded him. "We're always packed."

"Good point. I'm going to head out and get ready for Charleston and Iowa. I'll see you gals tomorrow at the airport. Don't worry, I'll be your security detail in case the media swarms you."

"I think I'm going to be sick," Janet repeated.

"He was kidding. Let's head out and get ready for Charleston and Iowa," I suggested as I packed up my things.

We had a mellow evening. Janet typed furiously on her laptop all night conversing with Jenkins. I charged pay-per-view videos to our room, the regular kind of movies. I'd had enough sexual stimulation for one day.

I was excited for the pre-debate rally, the debate itself, and to see how Janet would comingle with Jenkins. And the prospect of being with Cam in a new city was enticing, too.

The following morning Janet and I headed to the airport. The morning news shows all included brief mentions of the upcoming Charleston debate, but mostly focused their gotcha-style reporting on McDermott's accidentally scandalous pre-debate rally. We were surprised to find Cam, Trista, Charles, and the entire McDermott family sitting at our gate. It appeared they'd been bounced from their earlier flights to ours. I was amazed that I hadn't been called to deal with the situation, but then figured Trista had probably handled things firsthand.

"Good morning," I announced as we walked toward them. No one responded.

Janet found a place to sit away from everyone else and brought our bags with her. I could only imagine how uncomfortable she was.

"You want to grab a cup of coffee?" asked Cam, breaking the uncomfortable silence.

"I'd love to," I answered.

"Rough crowd," I said to Cam as we walked away.

"They're just nervous about O'Connor being on the same flight," he told me.

"Two presidential candidates from Minnesota taking the same flight to the same event, breaking news at gate A-7." I laughed.

"I can see their point. Both of them will be upgraded and could be just seats away from each other," Cam said. "You know the senator doesn't deal well with stress, and O'Connor is a nut job."

"There are so many different airlines flying to Charleston out of this airport. I don't think she'll be on our flight," I said as I sipped my coffee.

"Good thing you're not headed to Vegas today," Cam said as he pointed to Congresswoman O'Connor and her entourage approaching toward gate A-7.

"This is going to be interesting," I stated.

We stood back and watched the clearly nervous senator greet the congresswoman. It's always fun watching two competing politicians engage in small talk. They were asked to board first, and the senator's father followed Anders onto the airplane early.

"I hope to God I'm not sitting between Colonel and Charles," Janet stated.

"No worries. I booked us the last row in coach, and we know they don't sit back there." I laughed.

When we boarded the plane, we saw that Karma was sitting in the first row, the congresswoman and Charles were shoulder to shoulder in the second row, and the senator and his father sat next to each other in the third.

"That's quite the lineup," laughed Cam.

"I feel for that flight attendant," I told them.

"Oh my, can you imagine the random requests she's going to have to handle on this flight?" laughed Janet.

"We should warn her," hooted Cam.

"Excuse me, madam, but make sure you put one teaspoon of honey in the senator's tea in row three—but watch out for the old guy in that row, he'll put his hand up your skirt. Liquor up the woman in row one, and just stay clear of row two," laughed Janet.

"Ah, there's our old Janet coming back," I said.

"Do you think there are any Secret Service agents on this plane with two presidential candidates?" questioned Cam, looking around the plane.

"Secret Service agents aren't typically assigned until after the national convention," I told him. "But in today's day and age, you can bet there might be an extra air marshal or two."

The flight went quickly, and soon we felt Charleston's late summer heat in the Jetway. "I'm going to melt," warned Janet.

Karma and the senator's father were waiting by the taxicab line.

"Where is everyone else?" Janet asked.

"Morgan and Heidi are already here so they went to meet them for debate prep and asked that we take a cab to our hotel," Karma answered.

"Maybe the five of us could catch a cab together?" asked Cam. The airport cab dispatcher informed us that cabs only fit three adults.

"We'll get the second cab," I said grabbing Cam's arm.

"Okay," Janet agreed and shot me a nasty glare.

Janet, Colonel, and Karma climbed into the backseat of the first cab and drove off to the hotel. Our cab was only twenty seconds behind them, but it was semi-romantic riding with Cam to our hotel. If only we were staying in the same room.

When we arrived at the hotel I didn't see Janet and her charges. I began to wonder where everyone was. I BlackBerried her, but didn't get a response. I decided to wait in the hotel lobby for her instead of checking in on my own. Almost thirty minutes later the cranky threesome arrived at the hotel. Janet gave me a look that said, "Don't talk to me right now," as she helped Karma and the senator's father check in to their rooms. I could tell she was frustrated.

"Great, you'll be right next door to Senator and Mrs. McDermott," Janet said to Colonel.

"Where are you staying, Janet?" asked Karma.

"Well, it looks like Allison and I will be directly across the hall from you all," Janet said as she looked at our hotel key.

"Terrific! I'll need your help Saturday before the rally. My hair needs to be blown out," Karma told her.

"Ohhh," Janet said.

"I'll be able to assist also," I said, purposefully interrupting the conversation.

We all walked up to our rooms. In our room Janet dropped flat onto the bed and said, "You wouldn't believe it, even if I told you."

"Believe what?"

"What I just went through driving Mrs. McDermott and Mr. Daisy here," she said.

"What are you talking about?" I asked.

"Your friends across the hall, that's who." Janet continued, "Karma pissed off our cab driver so much that he circled around the entire Charleston area before bringing us here. Then Colonel went into some weird funk, and we had to pull over twice so he could smoke. To make matters worse, Karma got on her cell phone and called her agent to complain about our driver—while we were in the car! And of course, I was stuck between them in the backseat! It was bad, Allison! Karma kept screaming about the driver not knowing who she is!"

"No wonder you smell like a bad night at the bar," I replied.

"I wonder if Jenkins is in town yet," Janet pondered.

"We should grab dinner somewhere fun tonight with Cam," I proposed.

"Let's go spy on Jenkins at his hotel," Janet countered.

"You are ridiculous," I answered.

"It'll be fun. Plus he can't see us, and no one else knows I'm his secret lover," she responded.

"Secret lover? Don't you mean his personal credit card?"

"Get over it," she complained as she hopped into the shower.

"I'll go if you get Cam to go with us," I yelled.

"Of course you will," she yelled back at me over the shower. "Send him a message from my BlackBerry."

I threw on a very short skirt and high heels for our night on the town in Charleston. "Your phone is ringing," I yelled at Janet, who was blow-drying her hair.

"Oh, it's Jenkins," she said as she stared at the ringing phone.

"Answer him," I told her.

"Hi, handsome," she answered the phone. Gross. I couldn't hear the conversation but I could tell something was seriously wrong. "Oh, I'll come right there and check in for you." The conversation was over in less than a minute. "We need to go now," she told me as she grabbed her things and dressed quickly.

"What's up?" I asked cluelessly.

"I need to check in for Jenkins at the hotel," she stated.

"What?" I asked.

"Don't ask any questions, I just need to go and check in for him. There's something wrong with the reservation," she added as we quickly walked out to the hotel lobby.

"There is something wrong with you if you think this is at all normal," I added. "Where is his staff?"

We went to Jenkins's hotel where Janet checked in under her name and with her credit card. Then she called Jenkins, who asked her to deliver the keys to a woman sitting at the hotel bar. I could tell Janet was hurt by that strange direction.

"Maybe it's his executive assistant," I suggested.

"He said she's about thirty and a friend," Janet added.

"Well, this will be tricky," I said, looking around the bar.

"I have no idea," Janet said. She looked around, checking out every woman's ring finger.

Then, a sketchy-looking slender woman with a tattoo the full length of her right arm approached us.

"Are you Jenkins's assistant?" she asked.

Startled by that question Janet responded, "Yes, hi. I'm Janet. You are?"

The woman took the key and replied, "I'm old friends with the chairman. Thank you for getting me the key to our room. I can't wait to see him."

I thought Janet was going to pass out. We both walked away from the woman. Janet slumped into a chair at a nearby bar table. She didn't say anything for nearly fifteen minutes, a record for her. "I guess when it rains, it pours," she finally said as she guzzled the vodka tonic I'd ordered for her like a glass of ice water.

"Who knows, maybe they are just friends," I said as I welcomed Cam to our table.

"They are not friends," stated Janet.

Cam looked confused and asked, "Who are we talking about?"

"No one that matters," Janet told him.

Over the course of an hour Janet and I drank five vodka tonics. Cam was shocked by our ability to pound them.

"You girls are thirsty tonight," he said, clearing our glasses.

"It's been a rough week," I answered.

"It's been a pubic publicity helluva week," Janet slurred.

"You guys better slow down, or I'll be holding your hair tonight when you puke," Cam warned.

"Allison would love for you to hold her pubic hair," Janet laughed.

"On that note, we better sit a few rounds out," I declared.

"I think I'm going to find Chairman Jenkins," Janet announced loudly.

"What?" asked Cam.

"Allison, let's go. I've been through thick and thin with you—and tonight, you and I are finding Jenkins and doing some investigative work," Janet proclaimed as she stood, visibly drunk.

"Are we talking about Chairman Jenkins as in Senator Jenkins?" asked Cam.

"Oh yes, we are talking about that Jenkins. I'm his lover," announced Janet.

"You're his *what?*" Cam choked on his ice.

"Too much information," I told Janet.

"Come on, Allison, now or never," Janet declared, almost falling over.

"I think we'll take a rain check on dinner tonight," I told Cam.

"Oh, I'm not letting you two leave this drunk," he answered and continued, "I'll be your wingman. Someone needs to keep track of you two."

For the next four hours, Janet, Cam, and I spied on Jenkins at dinner with Ms. Tattoo. Janet was beside herself with disbelief. It was clear that Jenkins had a romantic interest in the sketchy woman. It appeared they were on a date and planning to spend the night together in the room Janet had paid for. Finally Janet had watched long enough, and we left.

"I hate to say it, but I told you so," I told her as I put her to bed. I looked over and noticed Cam had plopped down on my bed. We had worn him out.

"I still don't understand how you know Jenkins so well," Cam asked as he began to fall asleep. Rather than disturb him, I stayed quiet and lay down next to him. We all passed out. An unknown amount of time later, we woke up to Janet's phone, which was going off like crazy.

"It's your damn phone again," I yelled at her as I peered at the clock.

"Who is it?" she asked.

"I don't know, but it's 6:00 a.m.," I pleaded.

"Hello," she answered, grunted a few times, and then quickly hung up and started getting out of bed.

"Who was that?" I asked.

"Karma. She needs a phone charger right now and guess who has to go find one," Janet stated.

Cam rolled over and Janet looked shocked. "Nothing happened,"

I told her. "I can come with you for the charger. We can grab some breakfast." My head was pounding and I needed some greasy food.

"I'm going to worry about the boss today. I'll catch up with you gals later. Just please promise me you'll stay away from Chairman Jenkins," Cam pleaded.

"No worries there," I answered.

"It's just so weird. Why would he play this love-kitten game and talk to me all the time, then manipulate me into getting him a hotel room to entertain some floozy! I don't get it."

"Weird is an understatement. But all politicians are whores," I pronounced. "You're better off."

"I'm just going to ignore him all weekend," Janet said.

"Yeah, that will really get to him. He's running for president and doing a national debate tonight. You really think he's going to give two shits that some virgin from Minnesota isn't talking to him? You need to drop him!"

"Virgin?" Cam asked, as I gave him a wink.

Then he left to start his day and Janet and I went to find the urgent phone charger. But since we figured no retail stores would be open yet, we stopped for a greasy-spoon breakfast. After all the booze the night before, it tasted better than sex feels. After breakfast we hit the nearest Best Buy, one of our favorite Minnesota companies, for the charger. When we returned, we tried to grab a few more hours of sleep before the pre-debate rally and debate.

Charles had asked us to accompany the senator's father to the rally and the debate. We knew we'd need our energy to deal with his antics. Senator and Mrs. McDermott would be busy attending the candidates-only luncheon, which we thought might cause an issue with Colonel. We both fell asleep and awoke some time later to a loud knocking at our door.

I peeked through the security peephole and saw Karma standing in the hallway in her robe, holding a white shirt. I quickly opened the door.

"Where's Janet?" she asked without greeting me.

"I'm right here, Mrs. McDermott," Janet answered as she crawled out of bed.

"Bed? You ladies are in bed?!" she yelled.

"We were just taking a little rest before the day's activities," I told her.

"We aren't here for rest and games," Karma scolded.

"No, ma'am, we know that," I answered.

"Janet, you should be helping me!" she exclaimed.

"Of course, Mrs. McDermott. How can I help you?" Janet asked. She looked hungover.

"For starters, I need my blouse ironed and then my hair needs to be blown out," Karma ordered.

"I can do your hair," I interjected.

"I can't promise perfect ironing, but I'll give it my best shot," warned Janet.

Karma gave us both a look and then said to me, "Just make sure you do a better job on my hair than on your own." I ignored that comment. Then Karma came farther into our room and disrobed. She was naked.

"Let's do my hair," she said as she pointed to the rat's nest of blonde hair swirling about her head. I quickly grabbed a towel to cover her as she sat on the edge of my bed. As I tried to blow out her hair and make it look semiprofessionally done, Janet nervously ironed her white blouse.

"I don't know what I'm supposed to say or do today," she admitted.

"I think if you're just yourself today everything will be fine," I answered.

"Charles would disagree with you, Allison. I always screw something up," she said.

"You'll be just fine today," Janet said confidently as she showed Karma the freshly pressed blouse.

"I can't believe I'm wearing that blouse tonight. Charles is making me. It's so drab," she complained.

"It is a bit toned down and boring," Janet agreed. I was surprised she was so direct about it.

"You're right, Janet," Karma answered. "Allison, do you have anything I could borrow for tonight? Charles has locked me out of my closet."

I was stunned that Karma would even consider wearing something of mine. She only showed up to events in high fashion. The labels in her closet were Gucci, Prada, and Yves St. Laurent. The labels in my closet came from the sale racks at Ann Taylor Loft, Marshalls, and Nordstrom Rack—and the majority of my clothes came from Target.

"Let me think," I answered. I hoped she'd forget this crazy notion quickly. I was embarrassed for a presidential candidate's wife to wear my low-budget semi-trendy outfits.

"Both of you are always so stylish and funky," Karma complimented. I was shocked.

"We both definitely like to mix it up a bit. I guess you could consider us fashion forward in a politically drab culture," I laughed. "But it's nothing compared to your wardrobe," I gushed. Karma knew her way around the runway. As a former fashion model, she had impeccable taste.

"Well, Charles has denied me my closet, and I want to look fresh and fun. Please don't make me wear this dowdy blouse," she pleaded.

"Well, let's see what we've got," I answered. This could be fun.

After checking out a few items, Karma asked if she could borrow my very form-fitting bright yellow dress that was short in length and cut low in front. A Target original. The dress was smashing with her pale skin and blonde blown-out hair.

"I think you look great," I told her emphatically as I pushed her out the door in time for the luncheon. She looked like a bombshell, a million times better in that dress than me. Charles is going to die. But hey, what the senator's wife wants the senator's wife gets. Plus, it couldn't hurt to have an ally in Karma, even if the bond was forged over fashion instead of politics.

"Who knew a clearance dress that cost less than twenty dollars would be nationally showcased on Mrs. McDermott tonight?" I laughed.

"I like it, I like it," laughed Janet.

She went into the bathroom, and I noticed that she kept the lights off. "Did you just pee in the dark?" I asked.

"Yes, I was trying to see what it's like to be Jenkins," she answered without hesitation.

"You were what?" I asked.

"Just trying to see how hard life can be without vision," she stated.

"You are weird," I replied.

"It just makes me realize that Jenkins doesn't know the floozy looks like a floozy with that huge tattoo on her arm," she told me.

"Oh, I see where this is leading. You're trying to come up with some explanation for the fact that you were used by a US Senator."

"I wasn't used. I just don't understand what went wrong," she claimed.

"He took advantage of your trust and inexperience and used you," I answered.

"It just felt different," she told me.

"Again, why does a US Senator running for president need to use your credit card?" I demanded.

"I don't know," she yelled back.

"I'll tell you why. It's all a cover-up and he used you as part of it. Trust me; he's not playing cribbage with the floozy. They are fucking! You need to move on!"

Rarely did Janet and I get into heated discussions, but I was sick and tired of her not seeing the reality of the Jenkins situation. She had fallen head over heels for a scumbag who was taking advantage of her innocence. "Look, I know you think Jenkins was falling for you. And someday you will fall in love with Mr. Right. And it won't be that dope Jenkins," I said, trying to clear the air.

"I know you're right. But it stings a bit. I mean, look at me. Who

in their right mind would find me slightly attractive?" Janet asked as she stared at herself the mirror.

"Okay, Ms. Pity Party, enough with the bullshit. You know you're cute, intelligent, and wickedly funny. Most importantly, you have a great heart," I replied.

"Whatever," she said, and then finished getting ready. She was in a noticeable funk.

"We'd better check on Colonel and make sure he's getting ready so we can be on time," I suggested. "You never know what he is up to."

I walked across the hallway and knocked on Colonel's door. He answered the door wearing only his boxer shorts. I told him that we'd be leaving for the pre-debate rally and debate in fifteen minutes. I suggested that he meet us in the hotel lobby, and we'd hail a cab.

"I wanted to go with Anders. Whenever I go without him, it's always a headache," he complained. I assured him everything would be fine. After he looked me up and down, he agreed to meet us in the lobby. Then I noticed that he had a boner. Disgusted, I turned and hurried back to our room.

We waited for Colonel and hailed a cab. I told Janet about my earlier encounter, and she couldn't resist teasing me. "Maybe Colonel thought you were Margot," she joked. I told her to knock it off, and after a few more quips she finally silenced. At least it had put her in a better mood.

The rally was to be held two hours before the actual debate, which would take place in the Sottile Theater at the College of Charleston. The concierge told us it would be a quick ten-minute cab ride from our hotel to the campus. The senator's father sat in the front with the cab driver while Cam, Janet, and I shared the backseat. We left thirty minutes early just to be sure we'd be on time.

"I'm going to see my son debate for President of the United States tonight for the first time!" Colonel told our cab driver, glowing with pride.

"Oh, that's wonderful," the cabbie commented.

"You follow politics?" Colonel asked him.

"I listen to public radio all day driving."

"You heard of Anders McDermott?" Colonel asked.

"Oh yes, the senator from North Dakota who likes sex," laughed the cabbie.

"He's from Minnesota," I interjected.

Colonel lightly punched the cabbie's arm. "Like father, like son!"

"Holy smokes, look at this traffic," the cabbie said. We had just turned off the exit from the interstate and traffic was backed up bumper-to-bumper as far as we could see.

"What is this?" the cabbie asked, pointing at the one-way traffic.

"It looks like they turned the street into one way only for the debate and closed the other lane completely," Cam inferred. We weren't moving at all. The cab's meter total kept rising, and I asked Janet if she had enough cash on her to pay for it.

"I can't believe they only have one entrance to the campus for the debate, and they closed this other lane," Cam said.

"This is terrible. I guess they don't know how to run such a big event in Charleston," the cabbie said, sounding frustrated.

"I get to sit in the front row for the debate and Anders said I can join him on stage for the rally," Colonel told us.

"It'll be a great night," Janet exclaimed.

The cabbie started to get visibly upset about the terrible traffic and logistical failures of the event planners. We sat for twenty minutes and didn't move more than a few hundred feet at best.

"Anders says I get to sit in the front row," Colonel reminded us. Janet rolled her eyes at me and looked at my watch.

"This is insane," I said.

"We are not moving," the cabbie stated.

"Any other options to get there?" Cam asked him.

"This is it. This is the only road," he said as he blasted the horn. I began to get incredibly nervous that we wouldn't make the debate. I hoped the senator's transportation had proved more reliable than ours.

We waited another ten minutes and then the cabbie told us that he needed to take a piss. Without another word, he just got out of the car. Apparently he was going to find a place to pee. We sat there in disbelief, and with no one in the driver's seat. In less than a minute, the traffic began to slowly move forward, and clearly we had to move with it. Cam and I both tried to get out of the backseat fast, but the cabbie had locked our doors. We were stuck. Before we realized what was happening, Colonel hopped out, ran around the front of the cab, and jumped into the driver's seat. I had never seen him move so fast.

"Oh, I can drive," offered Cam.

"I got this, Cam," Colonel announced. "I used to drive all of the time in the war!"

We looked at each other nervously. I wasn't sure if Colonel even still had a driver's license. But he drove us forward, inching closer and closer to our destination. Finally the cabbie came running back to his car. Instead of taking the wheel, though, he got into the passenger seat, leaving the senator's father to drive. The traffic delay seemed to improve, and we began moving at a slightly faster speed.

"Wow, it's been almost an hour," Janet announced.

"We still have a few miles to go," the cabbie told us.

"I can't believe all this traffic is for the debate," I said.

"Whoever planned this one-way street should be fired," Cam agreed.

"Who is that coming up in the left lane?" asked the senator's father as he glanced in the rearview mirror.

"It looks like a motorcade," I said, looking behind me.

"Why would there be a motorcade?" Janet asked.

"I heard all first presidential debates are treated like presidential affairs. In advance of the event all the candidates receive a Secret Service detail if they elect it," Cam informed us.

"I thought they didn't get protection until after the national convention," I responded. "I think it must be the press corps motorcade covering the president's competition."

"That's interesting. So if Anders elects to have a protection detail we'll have agents working with us in the office," Janet said excitedly, ignoring my comment.

"Hold on to your shorts," Colonel yelled as he purposefully steered the cab into the left lane, positioning us between the two press corps motor coaches.

"Holy shit! Are we supposed to be doing this?" Janet asked.

"Careful with my cab, old guy!" the cabbie warned.

"Don't look right now, but there are two agents in the front of that bus armed with huge guns staring at us," I told Janet and Cam.

"What?!" said Janet as she turned her head.

"I said don't look!"

"Oh my God, this isn't good," Janet started to whine.

"Who are you people?" the cabbie exclaimed.

"I'm the senator's father and I need to be in the front row," Colonel said as he accelerated to seventy-five miles per hour to keep up with the buses. We cruised past all the stalled traffic. As we zoomed along I looked back at the agents, who were talking on their headsets and pointing their assault rifles and machine guns at us.

"When are we going to be at the campus?" Cam asked nervously as he looked behind us.

"Campus is about a mile up," the cabbie reported.

"I can't believe this turnout," Janet said as we passed hundreds of cars stalled on the one-way street.

I just prayed we wouldn't be shot immediately upon arrival.

As we neared the debate site we noticed supporters lined up along the side of the campus entrance waving signs that read, "CROTCH for Anders!" "Real Men for Anders!" and "McDermott Understands Us!"

"Look at all these people," Janet said, sounding amazed.

"I think they're all members of CROTCH," I guessed.

"Oh man, I'm in trouble," she said.

"Don't be silly, Anders loves attention," Colonel said, dismissing her worry. "And anyway, MaryAnn and I were members of CROTCH,"

he continued, referring to the senator's deceased mother. You had to hand it to the old kook, he never ceased to surprise.

As we rolled past hundreds of people waving CROTCH signs, we were startled by three hidden agents jumping out from the side of the street in front of our cab. They yelled and directed us to pull over immediately.

"Don't look now, but there are three huge machine guns pointed at our car," Janet stated.

The cabbie began to cry.

"Shush," I told him. Cam and I tried to roll down our windows but they were locked. The senator's father rolled down his window and announced, "I'm Colonel Anders McDermott, and we are here to see my son. I'm to be seated in the first row."

"Who?" asked the agent pointing his gun at Colonel.

"Colonel Anders McDermott, father of Senator," Colonel answered.

"Who?" the other agents asked, and directed us to remain seated.

"Roll down your window," Janet said urgently.

"I can't," I told her. The cabbie finally unfroze and helped by releasing the childproof locks. I rolled down my window immediately, and Janet yelled out to the agents, "We work for Senator McDermott, and we're just trying to get to the rally and debate quickly."

"You do realize that your car just interfered with an official motorcade, which is a federal offense," one of the agents said in a stern voice.

"We're just trying to get the senator's father to the event on time," I told them.

The agents made us sit still for another ten minutes, without telling us anything. Colonel started in about how things like this never happen when he travels with Anders. I was convinced we were going to end up in some holding cell somewhere.

"It will be fun explaining this one to Charles," whined Janet.

"We didn't do anything wrong," I said.

"We shouldn't have let an eighty-nine-year-old man drive," Janet said.

"We didn't have a choice!" I responded. "We were locked in the backseat, and he just hopped up there. What were we supposed to do?"

The agents finally allowed us to drive forward and suggested in very strong terms that we never follow a motorcade again.

"Advice well taken," I said as I rolled up my window.

Janet was sinking lower into the backseat beside me. "Charles is going to freak out," she worried.

"He'll be fine," Cam insisted.

"Maybe he won't find out," I added hopefully as we emerged from the cab.

Everywhere we looked we saw more CROTCH supporters lined up to get a glimpse of Senator and Mrs. McDermott.

"I've never seen anything like this," Janet commented.

"I'm supposed to be on stage with Anders," Colonel insisted and started walking toward the stage.

"We'll come with you," I shouted, grabbing Janet and Cam.

The rally crowd was already packed in, and we tried to jam ourselves through it.

"I have a bad hip," yelled the senator's father.

"We need to go just a little bit farther," Janet encouraged him.

"It's never like this with Anders," he mumbled.

"Look, goddammit, if I hear it's never like this with Anders one more time I'm going to take your cane and snap it over my knee," I blew up at the senator's father.

"Why don't you two go and grab some corner seats, and I'll take the senator's father to the stage," Janet said as she shot me a glance that told me to cool it.

Cam and I took her suggestion, and I could see her as she tried to weave herself and the senator's father through the crowd and onto the rally stage. Finally, I saw Charles help them onto the stage. The late summer heat in Charleston was overpowering, and I drank three full

bottles of water.

"Colonel has a full suit on, and no water to drink. This isn't the place for an elderly man," I said to Cam. Charles placed both Janet and Colonel front and center on the stage. I could tell Janet was pissed. If there was one thing she hated, it was being in front of a million cameras.

The rally began and when Senator and Mrs. McDermott took the stage, the crowd roared and started chanting, "Anders! Anders! Anders!"

The senator introduced Karma as his smoking-hot, sexy wife and the crowd roared even louder. It was clear to everyone at the rally that CROTCH supporters came out full throttle and that they were invested in the new champions on their team—Anders and Karma McDermott.

"I'm ready for a night full of action," joked the senator as the crowd cheered.

Karma yelled, "Tonight we're going to send a message across this nation. Anders and Karma McDermott don't want to regulate folks in the bedroom."

And the senator continued, "When we move into the White House, our agenda will be the people's agenda. We'll work hard to get things done, and we won't stop 'til the trail hardens up and those taxin'-and-spendin' whores are defeated! We believe in spurring the economy and stifling taxes, not your sex lives! Gone are the days when social conservatives rule. We're here to bring back the old-school conservative principles of limited government and states' rights." The crowd went nuts for Anders.

"Boy, he's really flexing his muscles," Cam stated.

"You meant to say, 'Boy, he's really thrusting his muscle,'" I laughed. Janet stared at me from the stage. I couldn't tell if the senator's father was enjoying the climactic moment or was about to collapse from the heat. The rally concluded and Anders and Karma walked in front of the stage and shook everyone's hands. Music pumped around the outdoor stage area and the excitement increased even more. Everything from "Jesus, Take the Wheel" to "Call Me Maybe" and "Don't Stop Believing" was played. The crowd went exceptionally nuts when "I'm Sexy and I Know It" played.

"'Jesus, Take the Wheel'? Anders is Jewish!" Janet screamed over the noise after she made her way over to me and Cam.

"I don't think Jesus would approve of the CROTCH platform," Cam added. We all laughed.

Colonel joined us and said proudly, "They love my son."

We waited for the crowd to settle, and the senator's father begged us to find him a lighter so he could light up. We relented and Colonel smoked nearly an entire pack of cigarettes before we entered the auditorium.

"I need to find my front row seat," Colonel told us as we walked into the debate.

"Lord help the ushers if he doesn't have a reserved front row seat," Janet stated.

Cam corrected her, "You mean, Lord help us."

"I think he should be in the front row. His son is campaigning for president, and this is the first major event. Let him sit in front and glow with pride," I said. We watched the senator's father struggle to find his seat until Charles showed him to his reserved seat in the second row. I could see the frustration on his face and empathized with him.

"I'm getting nervous for Jenkins," Janet claimed.

I raised an eyebrow and said, "That's strange. I hoped you'd be nervous for Anders."

Then the debate started as the three candidates walked onto the stage. Janet kicked me when Jenkins appeared first. Then she kicked me even harder when O'Connor appeared. I gasped. The congresswoman appeared to have just gotten a new dye job, and she looked like a skunk. Senator McDermott was the last to step on the stage and the crowd starting howling, "Anders!" The audience drew to an instant silence, though, as the university's show choir sang our national anthem.

Each candidate was invited to make an introductory opening statement, and the crowd was asked to remain quiet until all three candidates had finished. Congresswoman O'Connor went first and all I could remember her saying was that she was a soccer mom who didn't play well with others. Chairman Jenkins was next and he seemed confused. As he spoke, he was turned at an odd angle, not directly facing the audience. Jenkins's opening statement was, "Marriage belongs between a man and a woman," and then he began to pander to the religious right by rallying against gay rights and abortion.

"Damn it, he doesn't know where to look," Janet whispered.

When Senator McDermott stood for his opening statement, he accidentally spilled his water glass and it splashed onto Jenkins's suit jacket.

"Excuse me, Chairman. I'm overflowing with joy tonight," he proclaimed, inciting the audience full of CROTCH supporters to hoot and holler. Then he touted limited government, lower taxes, and states' rights. He nailed the opening statement and despite the instruction for the audience to hold their applause, they spontaneously burst into applause for him a number of times.

I daydreamed through the debate until Janet and Cam elbowed me from each side. "What, wait, what did I just miss?" I whispered snapping back into the moment.

"You didn't hear that?!" Cam asked.

"Holy shit, things just got hot in here," Janet whispered back.

"I can't believe he said that," Cam replied.

"Said what?" I whispered.

"Not now, we need to listen," Janet hushed.

The debate and all the excitement ended within the hour. I missed the major fireworks and was anxious to hear about what had happened.

After the debate Anders and Karma greeted more supporters on the stage, with the cameras following their every move.

Janet kept a close eye on Jenkins. "Are you going to go talk to him?" I asked.

"No, he thinks I went back to DC yesterday."

"What?" I asked.

"The hurt was too much to handle so I told myself that if he thinks I'm not here, then when he doesn't call or ask me to do something it's because he thinks I'm not here, not because he doesn't want to," she replied. I didn't know what she was talking about.

"What was the big brouhaha about during the debate?" I asked her and Cam, changing the subject.

Anders stooped pretty low by taking a swipe at O'Connor's immigration stance. He called her Mrs. Immigration Amnesty USA due to her lax policies and suggested that instead of a beauty pageant sash, she should wear a hijab.

"Holy shit, that is low," I answered.

"I'm sure he scored some points with conservative voters, though," Cam noted.

"That will be the line played over and over again by all the national news outlets," Janet predicted.

"Very true. It just seems a little out of character," I said. "What the hell was he thinking?"

The comment was picked up, but it didn't play the way we had anticipated. O'Connor played the women's rights–victim card by the following morning. McDermott's zinger was a headliner. It made all the news clips. And while the anti-immigration folks in the border states loved him, women across America hated him. The political battle between O'Connor and McDermott shot to a new level, and Jenkins was left behind as a third-tier candidate. He fell overnight from leader of the pack to the sleeper category.

Our bags were packed, and we were ready to jet back to Minnesota. The battleground of Iowa was next, and there was no time to look back on anything—not even pubic typos, Jenkins's tattooed floozy, or telling a right-wing Christian congresswoman that she's the equivalent of a hijab-wearing beauty queen. It was going to be a bumpy ride.

13
The Iowa Straw Poll

"I just can't believe it," Janet said as we flew back to Minnesota.

"I know. You'd think she could at least show up at the airport on time," I replied.

"Sleeping with the boss's married cousin is almost like fishing off your neighbor's dock," Cam said quietly and grinned. I didn't realize Cam knew that after the debate Heidi not only threw back about fifteen drinks, but she left the bar with the senator's married cousin.

Janet and I were both caught off guard the next morning when the senator called at 5:00 a.m. and asked if we'd seen his cousin

Rob. The senator said Rob's wife was trying to find him because he hadn't shown up for his morning radio show in Arizona. He asked us not to mention anything to Karma or Margot. Apparently, the married cousin was unaccounted for since 9:00 p.m. the night before, and had been expected home after the debate. Heidi was scheduled on our same flight back to Minnesota to help the senator with policy preparation for the Iowa Straw Poll.

"I mean, really, am I the only one who thinks she's not the least bit attractive?" Janet questioned.

"Oh, she's cute… until you get to know her," I answered.

"That ought to make for an interesting policy discussion with the senator: 'Before we talk about abortion and gay marriage, did you bang my cousin last weekend?'" Cam chimed in.

"Thank God I've never had that talk with him," I laughed.

"I just can't believe it," Janet repeated.

"When will you ever wake up and start seeing the real world?" I asked her.

"I like living in my own little bubble."

"Yeah, well, you'd think that little bubble of yours would burst after the antics of Jenkins," I said.

"Speaking of Jenkins," she asked, "why hasn't the press slammed the senator for saying in the debate that Jenkins was against the disabled because of his right-wing budget-cutting policies?"

"That is kind of hilarious. 'Chairman Jenkins is even against the blind,'" I announced using my best reporter's voice.

"He really needs to watch what he says," Janet said. "He may have been able to skate by this time, but as the campaign heats up, the press is going to be all over comments like that."

"I think the press is too busy chasing O'Connor around to notice anything else he said," Cam answered.

"They certainly do love her," I agreed. "Let me rephrase that: they love that she'll say anything to get a headline, some applause, or swing a vote."

"I just don't think America is ready for a female president," Janet said.

"Oh, I think America is ready for a female president, just not one who's worried about the next shoe sale or buying matching white gloves for her Easter dress," I said.

"I think she's a good candidate, and one we can't dismiss outright. She's got a following, and she is scarily popular," Cam noted. He continued, "If you don't give her credit as a viable candidate, I think she could be as dangerous as a shark in a tank full of guppies."

As soon as we were wheels down in Minnesota, Janet, Cam, and I turned on our mobile devices. My BlackBerry and iPhone vibrated for what seemed like hours as the new messages downloaded.

"Jesus, we should start calling you Ms. Hollywood," laughed Cam as he watched my devices vibrate.

"I'd take Hollywood messages over all these from the boss any day," I answered, reading from the screen of my BlackBerry. I went through the messages quickly and then read them over more closely.

"Holy shit, I think O'Connor launched an ethics complaint against our office today," I exclaimed and kept reading.

"What? An ethics complaint? About what?" Janet asked.

"I'll get online and start reading," Cam stated.

"She's claiming McDermott moved out of his apartment and is living out of the Senate gym to save money," I told them as I continued to read.

"That must have happened before the August recess," Janet said.

Cam added, "He does play an awful lot of tennis."

"Living out of the Senate gym is weird, but is it illegal?" I asked. "And besides, you can't live out of the gym. Where would he sleep? Plus, we've been to his apartment!"

"Allison, he has that big-ass couch and a bathroom in his office. And he easily could have gotten out of his lease," Janet reminded me, and I looked at her in shock. Before I left, he had somehow always managed to beat me to the office when he was in town, no matter how early I arrived.

"This could play well to the conservative folks who believe Anders spends money like a drunken liberal," Janet stated.

"Or play well to his scheduler who can't afford her rent and needs a raise to keep working for him. We finally have something in common—the boss and I are both broke!" I laughed.

"Good luck with that one." Janet laughed. "I can't believe the national press is on this complaint already."

"Welcome to the brave new world of campaigning. You can't take a shit without it being broadcast," Cam said as we stood to deplane.

"Don't play in the pool if you don't want to be splashed," I offered with a shrug.

We went into the office together and saw Charles slam his office door as we arrived.

"Great, this ought to be a wonderful afternoon," Janet sighed.

"He's under a lot of pressure. Charles has the senator's whole career on his shoulders, plus he has to deal with all of the McDermotts' countless hours of shit," I said, defending him.

"Well, ladies, we need to focus on Ames, Iowa, home of the Iowa State University Cyclones and Saturday's straw poll," Cam said, trying to refocus our energies.

"Did you all know that Iowa is the food capital of the world?" Janet asked us.

"You would know that," I said, shaking my head. "We won't be eating, we'll be working and entertaining the McDermott clan!"

"Not my idea of entertaining," Janet answered.

"Not my idea of going to the food capital of the world," laughed Cam.

"I'm crossing my fingers—and I'm nervous to say this out loud—but I think we're all set. We've responded to every event and we have detailed advance memos with all of the information the senator could possibly need," I stated.

"We better double, I mean, triple check our work," Cam said.

I shot him a smile. "Good idea."

"I wonder when Heidi will make an appearance," Janet offered absently.

"Right after she zips up her pants," I couldn't resist saying.

"Ouch, not like you two haven't had a one-night stand," Cam said.

"Well, actually..." laughed Janet.

Just then, Trista came into my office. "Looks like the pre-Iowa party is happening in here. Did you get a chance to call Karma, Janet?" she asked.

"I didn't know Karma was expecting a call. I'm on it right now," Janet said, leaving my office.

"Trista, Cam and I had an in-depth talk about Iowa. We feel comfortable with our advance work and preparation," I updated her.

"We can't predict the weather," laughed Trista.

"The boss thinks we can—or at least I had better be able to," I responded.

Janet returned to my office in a huff, obviously distraught. "What's up?" Trista asked her.

Janet rolled her eyes. "Karma's agent has booked her on a bunch of national interviews in Ames. Not only does she want me to escort her to all the interviews, but she wants me to do her makeup all weekend," Janet complained.

"Just add makeup artist to your growing list of job titles," laughed Trista.

"What kind of interviews?" I asked. I was curious to know what Karma would have to say, considering the most extensive conversation we had ever had was about fashion.

"I didn't really understand what she was talking about. All I can tell you is that she was all fired up, and she wants to talk about the role of a stay-at-home mother as a full-time job. She was attacking Congresswoman O'Connor for leaving her fifteen children at home while she went off and worked in an office job," Janet told us.

"Are we forgetting that Karma jets off to Los Angeles all the time to book modeling gigs?" I asked.

"She also has a full-time live-in nanny," Trista pointed out.

Janet said, "Actress."

"What?" asked Trista.

"Actress," she repeated. "Karma is an actress; she's not a model. I've been corrected a million times. Actress. She is an actress."

"Oh sorry. Actress!" Trista said, laughing.

"I'm not sure attacking Congresswoman O'Connor for juggling work with motherhood is good for the boss," Cam pointed out.

"She has fifteen kids, is a sitting congresswoman, and is running for president. Karma thinks she should be home playing arts and crap with the kiddies?" I summarized. "Who does she think she is? She's never held down a real job!"

"Its arts and crafts," Janet corrected. I shot her a dirty look.

"Seems pretty prehistoric to think a woman's role is only in the home," argued Trista.

"This isn't the dark ages," I continued, infuriated. "Women are allowed to have a career *and* a family. Those things are not mutually exclusive."

"She's not the right messenger on this topic," Cam agreed.

Janet asked, "I wonder if Charles knows about this?"

"You wonder if Charles knows about what?" Charles asked as he entered my office and sat on my desk.

"Karma—," Janet started and was quickly interrupted by Charles.

"Remember, I don't want to know anything about Karma and what she's up to. That way I have plausible deniability. I can't referee the fights between the senator and his wife."

"I think you need to hear this one," Trista told him.

"Fine. Lay it on me." Charles sighed.

"Karma is doing interviews all weekend in Iowa about the importance of being a stay-at-home mom," Janet explained.

"But she's not one," he said. "I guess maybe being an unemployed model could be called being a stay-at-home mom."

"Actress," we all yelled, cutting him off.

"Since when is Karma an actress?" Charles asked, and then offered his own answer, "I don't want to know anything."

"Janet left out that she's planning on attacking O'Connor for working," Cam stated.

"And why would we do that?" Charles asked.

"I dunno. I thought you talked with her," Janet said.

"I'll talk with the boss, and we'll get Karma focused on something else," Charles reassured us. "Maybe there's a shoe sale at Macy's. Thanks for the heads-up, gang."

"Whew, at least I don't have to do her makeup all weekend," Janet said, relieved.

"Speaking of the whole gang, have any of you seen or heard from Heidi today?" Charles asked. We all laughed. "Did I miss the punch line to my own joke?" There was an uncomfortable silence. Charles didn't know about Heidi and the married cousin.

"She was supposed to be on our plane, but we didn't see her," I told him.

"Give her a call," Charles ordered. "Oh, um, Janet and Allison, the senator was hoping that you'd go clothes shopping tonight for the family."

"Clothes shopping?" Janet asked.

"Yes, just pick up some things that make them look like they're from the Midwest. For Iowa."

"Aren't we all from the Midwest?" I asked.

"We are. But you two look like it," Charles answered quickly.

"I can't imagine picking out clothes for Karma," I said in shock.

Janet cut in, "How do we know how much to spend, and whose credit card to use? Mine is maxed out from the South Carolina trip."

"Why is your card maxed out from South Carolina? I thought we had the campaign covering everything," Charles asked, looking at Trista.

"Your room and airfares should have been on the campaign credit card," she said.

I could tell Janet was floundering. She'd stuck her foot in her mouth yet again. She couldn't tell Charles about paying for Chairman Jenkins's hotel room in Charleston.

"It's been an expensive month," she finally said without going into any further detail.

"You girls figure this out," Charles told us. Then he turned and walked out of my office, followed by Cam.

"I'll give you guys the campaign credit card for tonight. It has a daily limit of $50,000. I'd suggest that you call a big department store and ask for a professional shopping service to help you," Trista suggested and then left my office too.

"What just happened?" Janet asked, looking at me.

"I think we were just asked to go on a shopping spree for the McDermotts and we have $50,000 to spend."

"You don't make $50,000 in a year."

"Correction: I don't make $50,000 in two years," I clarified.

"How on earth are we going to pick out clothes for Karma?" Janet asked.

"Shit, we are trendy and stylish. She loved my yellow dress," I answered.

"But apparently we're the only two who look like we're from the Midwest," she replied.

"That was a weird thing to say. What does he mean we look like we're from the Midwest?"

"There's never a dull moment around here," Janet said as she glanced at the clock.

"Never a dull moment and never a night off," I said wryly.

"This will be fun, though!" Janet exclaimed.

"We'll get the urge to shop out of our system," she continued.

"We'll never get the urge to shop out of our system!"

"I'll call and find us a professional shopper," Janet offered.

"I'm going to track down Heidi," I told her. "Let's get out of here right away."

I left several messages for Heidi and then walked next door to Janet's office. "Oh, shit. I know that typing," I said. "You aren't emailing Jenkins, are you?"

"Just a quick message," she told me. "I want him to know he did a good job in South Carolina and that I'm headed to Iowa," Janet continued to type.

"What is wrong with you? He brought some floozy to Charleston for a romp in the hotel room you paid for, and now you're telling him you'll be in Iowa? Please don't tell me something might be going down in Iowa," I said.

"What?" asked Janet.

"You'd better not plan on seeing him. He's bad news." Janet shot me a glare and finished up her message.

"God, I don't know what you see in him," I said as we left the office.

"He's funny and nice. I don't appreciate your poor humor," Janet stated.

"Poor humor?"

"Yes, you said you don't know what I *see* in him," she said.

"Oh Christ, you are *blinded* by love," I said.

We left the office to meet our personal shopper. He was a trendy gay man who reminded me of Martin Short's character, Frank, in *Father of the Bride*. He really knew his way around Nordstrom, and within an hour we found the perfect outfits for the McDermotts. It was a different kind of shopping experience for us. We didn't worry about price tags or check to see if anything was on sale.

"This is so easy and painless," Janet said.

"I could get used to letting someone else pick out clothes for me. It's tough fighting for bargains in the sales racks!" I agreed.

Our sales associate totaled our purchases and wrote the amount on a piece of paper instead of announcing it out loud. I could see Janet physically gag at the $27,500 total.

"God, I hope our credit card doesn't get denied," I said as I handed the associate the campaign's credit card.

"Grab that card before it bounces away," Janet joked with the associate.

The card was approved. My hand physically shook as I signed the receipt. The sales associate informed us they would deliver our purchases to the McDermott residence.

"Gosh, I've never flown in first class, but if it's anything like this, book my next ticket," Janet said as we left.

"We just spent the equivalent of my salary and we're leaving without bags," I laughed. I felt high.

"I'm in the mood to be creative tonight," Janet said.

"Creative?"

"Yes. I want to relax and get crafty—like normal Americans. We should find ourselves a hobby," she told me as we got into her car.

"*Hobby?* Can you tell me what that word means? We don't have time for a hobby," I reminded her.

"Real people have hobbies," Janet said.

"I'm just guessing here, but I don't think either of us can croquet a blanket," I said, checking my BlackBerry.

"It's called *crocheting*, and I don't want to crochet a blanket. I was thinking we should do something creative and fun," Janet said as she pulled into the parking lot of a strip mall with a Michaels craft store.

"Oh, I've heard about this store. Bringing you here is going to be like bringing fat kids to a candy store and letting them run loose," I said.

"Let's just go in and see if there's anything we can do tonight and this week," Janet insisted.

"You're the driver," I said as I got out of the car.

We walked around the store. "We could make jewelry," Janet suggested as she showed me sparkling beads and gems.

"Our jewelry would fall apart and we'd have beads dropping all over the place."

"Look, we could paint a little wooden stool for a kid," Janet said.

"Are you smoking what Margot's been snorting? We are working women, we don't do kids. Remember?"

We pushed our empty cart through each aisle and looked at the endless rows of crafting materials.

"Ah ha! I got it. Let's make autumn wreaths!" Janet shrieked.

"Wreaths?" I asked.

"Sure. We could suck up to the boss and Charles, and even make one for Trista," Janet said as she grabbed artificial flowers and straw.

I reluctantly agreed to indulge her in her newfound hobby and was drawn in by some colorful materials for our creations. I hoped this "hobby" would take her mind off Jenkins. In just a few minutes our cart was overflowing with stems and straw.

"Do you know how to make a bow out of ribbon?" Janet asked as she pushed our cart to the checkout.

"Shit, it can't be too hard. I mean a little fold here and there," I said as I grabbed some ribbon.

The cashier totaled up our hobby supplies and we both cringed: $197.43.

"I guess hobbies aren't cheap," I said.

"We can make at least three wreaths with all that and we'll have hours of entertainment. It's cheaper than going to the mall," she replied pulling out her debit card.

"Yeah, but if we had gone to the mall, at least we'd come back with cute outfits."

As Janet began to envision immaculate Martha Stewart–style wreaths, we unloaded her car and dragged our bags of supplies into our hotel room. We began to create our autumn-themed wreaths, and as she indulged her inner crafter, she seemed to forget about Jenkins. The finished products didn't look half bad, and our hotel room looked like Martha Stewart vomited all over it. Ribbon, flowers, straw, and stems were strewn about the room, while three uniquely decorated straw wreaths laid in the center.

"I'm not sure these are worth $200," I said, laughing at the finished product.

"I wonder if we can market these," Janet stated.

"I don't know about that," I answered, thinking she was overly optimistic.

The night flew by and not once did we think about the boss, Charles, Heidi, or Karma.

"I could get into making wreaths and this hobby thing," Janet laughed.

"What time is it?" I asked.

Janet looked at her watch. "Almost 10:30 p.m."

"Wow. Do you realize Heidi still hasn't called me back?"

"Gosh, I actually do hope she's alright."

"She made her bed, now she's got to lie in it," I answered.

"Speaking of beds you sleep in," Janet said, as she crawled into her bed.

"I'm right behind you," I said as I brushed my teeth.

I woke up to Janet's violent coughing a few hours later.

"Are you okay?" I asked.

"I think I'm getting a cold," she answered, wheezing.

"Drink some water," I suggested.

All I heard the rest of the night was Janet's deep breathing and wheezy gasping. Janet had asthma and she was prone to have sudden attacks. But this was unusual. I didn't get much sleep; I kept watching her to make sure she was alright.

When Janet woke up, she could barely talk without hacking or wheezing. Her lungs were out of commission and she was miserable.

"I don't know what I'm allergic to," she said as she looked around the room.

"I don't know either, but maybe you should go to the ER," I suggested.

"N—n—n-oo, I'll be fine," she said haltingly and began to cough.

"You sound terrible."

"You think it's the wreaths?" she asked.

"You think?" I asked.

"They are straw, and I have really bad hay fever," Janet said as she coughed.

"Why did we buy straw then?" I asked, exasperated with her.

"Because we wanted to make autumn wreaths," she said as she hacked and coughed even more.

"Where is your inhaler?" I asked.

"I don't know," she spit out as she coughed. She sounded like a lung cancer patient.

"I think you should go to the emergency room," I suggested again.

"I'm fine, and we have work to do," she said.

"Well, let's at least get these damn wreaths out of here before we end up laying a wreath on your casket."

"Let's bring them into the office. We can hand them out there," Janet said as she gasped for breath.

"Okay, deal. But you shouldn't talk all day," I ordered, worried about her.

We arrived to the office early and strategically placed a wreath on Trista's, Charles's, and the senator's desks.

"Remember, no talking today. And if you need to get to a doctor, I'm a great ambulance driver," I said. She looked miserable.

Charles came into the office whistling and stopped just outside of our offices. "You two must be the ones I need to thank for the fancy wreath."

"We had fun making them, but I think they made Janet sick," I told him.

"Sick?" he asked.

"I'm fine," Janet whispered as she tried to convince Charles that she could breathe freely.

"Jesus, do we need to get the office defibrillator?"

"I'm fine," she reassured him.

"Say, Janet, we need a good Somali constituent story. Anything good you been working on?" he asked.

"I actually just got contacted yesterday about a five-year-old

little girl from St. Paul who is stuck in a Kenyan prison because the US Embassy doesn't believe she's the same kid in the passport photo. I'll follow up to see if it's legit and email you," Janet whispered.

"Sounds good," Charles whispered back and left.

I went straight to Janet's office and shut the door. "Can you believe how we operate?" I asked.

"What?" she whispered.

"That was all about O'Connor and the Muslim comment," I stated. Janet looked at me in disbelief.

"Oh, it totally is. He asked specifically about a Somali story. They're all Muslim, and the senator needs to trump O'Connor's glory in the press about his stupid Muslim immigration comment and yesterday's ethics complaint."

"I think you're grasping at straws," she whispered.

"Just you watch," I said as I left her office.

I caught up on my emails and sorted through the scheduling requests that were rolling in for September and October. My phone rang and the caller ID indicated that the call was coming from the McDermott residence. I took a deep breath before I answered and wondered what the new crisis would be. "This is Allison."

"Allison, did you pick out my clothes for Iowa or did Charles?" Karma asked without greeting me.

"Janet and I used a professional shopper. We thought the clothes were cute, trendy, and flattering. "Is there a problem?"

"They'll do. But I'm exchanging them all for two sizes smaller," Karma explained.

"I'm glad they'll work," I said, still wondering why she called me.

"I'm going to pack a few other items for all my interviews though. I don't want to look my age, and I certainly don't want to look like our past First Ladies."

"You will be a great First Lady," I assured her, surprised to hear she was still planning interviews. "Is there anything else I can help you with, Mrs. McDermott?" I asked, hoping to get her off the line.

"Yes, but I hate to ask you," she said.

"Ask away."

"Did Anders go fishing in International Falls last year with a reporter?" she asked.

I didn't know how to answer. There was a slight pause.

"Your silence is my answer, Allison."

"Yes, I believe he did," I replied.

"One more thing, Allison," she went on.

"Yes?" I asked.

"Can you put some outfits together for Janet in Iowa? I'm going to do a lot of interviews, and I need her to look more Hollywood and less small-town Minnesota," she stated.

I answered carefully. "I'll try to help her, but I think Janet always looks good."

"She does, but I need her more Hollywood," she said again. "You know what I mean Allison, you're trendy."

I ended the call and felt sick. I hoped that I hadn't just let the cat out of the bag and ruined their dysfunctional marriage by verifying Karma's suspicions about the senator's "fishing" trip.

Janet came in and shut my office door. She whispered, "I think the State Department is wrong about this five-year-old kid from St. Paul. I talked to her teacher and grandmother. The consulate staff is convinced it's not her in the passport photo. But the picture was taken when she was three years old. Kids change a lot in two years. I think she's a US citizen and they're detaining her in prison."

"She's in a Kenyan prison at five years old?" I asked, alarmed.

"Yes. She went to Kenya with her grandmother and was stopped when she tried to board her return flight."

"What did Charles say?" I asked.

"He said we need to tread lightly. He thinks the Embassy staff is right," she whispered.

"They might be. We hear about child trafficking constantly," I reminded her.

Janet shook her head and whispered, "No, her parents are here on refugee status. I don't think they would risk deportation for some other kid. She's the kid in the passport photo, I just know it."

"Why did they travel to Kenya anyway?" I asked.

"All of her extended family is there; this is the kid's third trip."

"God, I can't imagine being five years old, sitting in some prison in Kenya. It's like dirt floors, right?" I asked.

"I don't know. But the grandmother has a cell phone, and she called me from inside," Janet whispered.

"Maybe we can blow up pictures and see if she's the same kid ourselves," I suggested.

"Good idea, and maybe we can get dental x-rays scanned into the computer and we could email them to the US Embassy?" Janet whispered.

"That seems complicated but worth doing if you really think it's her. You'd better run all this past Charles," I suggested. I could tell Janet was on a mission to free the five-year-old, and she wasn't going to rest until the kid was back home in St. Paul.

Janet coughed all day. By that evening, she had the child's dental records, which she emailed to the US Embassy. We enlarged her passport photo and last school picture to compare them.

"Boy, it is tough to tell," I said.

"She's just older now," whispered Janet.

"When will the Embassy check the dental records?"

"Tonight," she told me.

"I'm curious to hear what they discover." Then, thinking this was as good a time as any to bring it up, I told her, "Oh, Karma called and she wants you to dress a bit more 'Hollywood' in Iowa," I said.

"Hollywood?" she coughed.

"You guys are going to lots of interviews and she wants you to look more Hollywood."

"I can look Holywood, but Hollywood is a stretch," she whispered with a grin.

"Let's head out. You need a full night's sleep before we head to Ames tomorrow," I ordered.

As we pulled into the hotel's parking lot, I noticed that my BlackBerry was vibrating and buzzing. I checked my messages and saw five unread from the senator. I read through them quickly.

6:29 p.m.	Did u tell Karma I went fishing in I-Falls?
6:31 p.m.	Don't talk to her unless I give u permission!
6:33 p.m.	U work 4 me. Get it? Do I need to explain it 2 u?
6:37 p.m.	Get me the number for CNN.
6:42 p.m.	I miss Blair. Where r u? Need number now. Not later. Now.

"Now I'm not supposed to talk to Karma without permission from the senator," I told Janet as I reread the messages. I wondered how to respond.

"He has you call her all the time about stuff. You're their bridge of communication."

"Oh trust me, I know! I forgot to tell you with all the crazy Kenya stuff today. When she called about your clothes she asked me about Anders's fishing trip to I-Falls," I stated.

"I-Falls from last year with that reporter?" she asked.

"Yup! That I-Falls."

"Are all politicians dirty?"

"God, they can't be," I answered. I quickly responded to the senator:

6:58 p.m.	Mrs. McDermott called today about the clothes we picked out for her and during that call she asked me about you fishing last year in International Falls. I told her you did.
7:00 p.m.	I'll find you the CNN number ASAP. We just got to our hotel from the office.

We went to our hotel room and I noticed another round of messages:

7:00 p.m.	Need CNN number now.
7:01 p.m.	My fishing trip is my personal business.
7:03 p.m.	Why are u at hotel? We don't have money for hotels. Stay with a volunteer or here.
7:06 p.m.	Need to talk to Heidi.

"The senator doesn't seem very happy. He just told me he needs to talk with Heidi." I updated Janet as she plopped onto the bed.

"The shit is going to hit the fan," she whispered.

"I'd love to be a fly on that wall," I said as I tried to call Heidi again. I left her a detailed message and told her to call me back.

"No answer?" Janet asked.

"If she was around she'd answer my call, knowing it would be about the boss," I answered. I got the CNN numbers for the senator and messaged him.

"Are you surprised that neither he nor Trista said anything about our wreaths?" Janet asked.

"Surprised? No, are you?" I asked.

"Kind of," Janet said. She sounded disappointed.

"Holy shit—Rose is going into labor," I read out loud as I checked my messages.

"Are you shitting me! Isn't that way early? She's only six months along, and she's here in Minnesota!" Janet said.

"Right, perfect timing, hours before Iowa," I stated loudly. "I really hope she's okay. Can you even have a baby that early?"

"If anyone can do it, it's Rose," Janet said. "Man, the senator will be lost without her."

"She's been mostly checked out for the past few months, and I've been doing all his scheduling and assistant work, really."

"That is true. I bet she's bummed out that the little bambino couldn't wait until after the straw poll, though," Janet said.

"Maybe they'll name it Ames," I said laughing.

"Or Anders," Janet said as she tried not to let her laugh turn into a cough.

"Jenkins, O'Connor, or Heidi," I laughed back.

"This is crazy, she's having a baby right now!" Janet exclaimed.

"Thankfully, we don't have to add obstetrician to our job titles," I laughed. "Oh, Heidi is calling! This ought to be interesting," I said as I answered my phone. I spoke with Heidi briefly, and asked her to call the senator.

"Wouldn't it be weird to sleep with the boss's married cousin and then have to talk to him about everyday matters?" Janet asked.

"Um, look who's talking!" I laughed.

"What do you mean?"

"Sleeping with his cousin is nothing compared to sleeping with the enemy," I scolded.

"I was not going to sleep with him. I'm a virgin, for God's sake!" she corrected me.

"A virgin in heat."

"Speaking of Jenkins, he hasn't written anything about Iowa," Janet told me.

"Thank God. You're already flat broke. At least Iowa hotel rooms are cheap. Maybe in Iowa you can wear a McDermott T-shirt and Jenkins underwear!"

"Shit, they could be O'Connor panties, he wouldn't know," she laughed.

"Oh, here we go, Charles is calling," I said as my phone rang.

"Hey, Charles," I answered.

"Rose is in labor, and I'm driving to the hospital. I'm going to be in the delivery room because her husband is still in DC and my better half is working. Can you guys come over and play with the kids until I'm home?" he asked quickly without taking a breath.

"Um, sure," I said, feeling pressured. Charles hung up without another word. I'd never cared much for children. Janet, on the other hand, adored them and wanted about a million of her own. With her help, watching three crazy kids would be doable.

"We're off to play nanny," I told her as I gathered our things together.

"What?" Janet asked as she rolled over in bed.

"Look, I'm no preschool teacher. I need you for this one. Get your ass out of bed," I ordered.

"Why are we babysitting?" she asked.

"Charles is going to be in the delivery room with Rose," I answered as if it was no big deal.

"Charles is going to be in the delivery room with Rose's legs spread eagle as a doctor stares up her crotch?!" Janet asked in shock.

"Yeah, it's nasty," I answered.

"Nasty? It's super awkward!" Janet responded.

As we walked out to our car, Janet asked, "Who would you want in the delivery room?"

"I'm not having kids, remember?"

"Come on, play along," she pushed.

"God, I have no idea. Hopefully my husband."

"Well no shit. I mean if your husband wasn't there."

"You and your questions. Well, I wouldn't want my mom or dad in the room. Geez, I don't know. You, I guess?" I answered, hoping to pacify her. "What about you?"

"Jenkins would be worthless," she said and we laughed.

"'Ah, doctor, can you tell me if the baby has a little wiener or a bun?'" I laughed.

"'Um, doctor, are Janet's legs in the air and are you pulling out a baby in this direction?'" She laughed as she pointed in different directions.

"Gross. I am not having kids and this *Romper Room* duty tonight is one of the many reasons why," I replied.

"It won't be that bad. Plus, Rose really needs Charles," Janet said. "Can you imagine?"

"Charles in the delivery room is a little too up close and personal for me," I answered.

When we arrived at Charles's house, he sprinted out the door. As he ran past us he hollered, "Thanks again! I'm off to personally welcome the newest member of Anders's campaign team!" Then he jumped in his car and left.

As we walked into his house, we found his four-year-old daughter on top of the kitchen table dancing and shaking her bottom. His three-year-old daughter was in her bedroom playing "FBI agent" and his ten-year-old son was downstairs planning his next model ship. Janet continued to cough so I told her to chill as I checked on each of the kids.

"Holy shit!" Janet yelled.

"I didn't know you could yell today," I answered.

"Look at this," she said as she shoved a staff salary sheet at me. It had been left out on the living room table.

"Why would Charles leave this out? He had to know we'd see it."

"Maybe he wanted us to?" Janet speculated.

"Lindsay is making $75,000 a year to brew tea and stir in honey! Heidi is making less than her and—holy shit!—Rose got a $45,000 raise last year," I said as I studied the numbers carefully.

"Blair didn't make much," Janet stated.

"He must be paid in ego worship," I remarked.

"Shit, this says I'm going to get a $7,500 raise next year!" Janet said as she found her salary and projected raise.

I looked at the figures next to my name and threw down the salary sheet. "Are you kidding me? I'm only getting a $1,000 raise. When will I hit the $30,000 mark? When I'm ninety?" I asked.

"$1,000 is pretty minimal when you look at everyone else's salary, especially Lindsay," Janet pointed out. "You're getting ripped off," Janet said as she picked up the paper and continued to study the salaries.

"God, why wouldn't Charles put this away before we showed up?" I asked again. "I am so pissed right now. I can't even tell you."

"I'm telling you, he wanted us to see it," Janet reinforced.

"That doesn't make any sense," I shot back as I poured juice for Charles's youngest daughter. "Why would he want a disgruntled employee? He had to know this would piss me off. He must have just forgotten it was out in the midst of jetting off to the hospital."

"We should play a game of hide and seek," Janet suggested in an attempt to change the subject. The three kids began to howl with joy at the suggestion.

"I'll hide for sure," I snarked.

"You need an attitude adjustment," Janet said as she split us into teams. I tried to put on a happy face for the kids, and we played for quite a while. We made the kids graham crackers with frosting in the middle for an evening snack, and they thought we were amazing chefs.

"We'd better get these kids into bed and hope Rose gives birth soon," I said as I licked my fingers.

"God, I just love these," Janet stated.

"Easy does it, those are carb central and you're going to be hanging out with Ms. Hollywood in less than a day," I teased.

"Don't remind me," she said as she went to read a book to the youngest.

After we put them all to bed, we fell asleep to some late-night television. Janet woke up as her BlackBerry chimed. Seconds later, I could hear her on the phone.

"Who are you talking to?" I asked as I woke up.

"The Embassy in Kenya," she said as she gestured for me to zip my lips. When she hung up I watched her smile from ear to ear.

"They just thanked us for sending the dental records and pictures. They checked her teeth, and it's the same child. They were wrong. They held that poor kid for no good reason."

"I cannot believe it," I said.

"At least they apologized. Her mother and grandmother are super happy and relieved," Janet said. She sounded proud.

"God, that is crazy. Can you imagine if we'd just given up and not challenged them?" I asked.

"I know. That family really needed the senator's voice and power. Without it they wouldn't have gotten anywhere, and that kid would still be detained," Janet said.

"You may have used the senator's name and power, but we both know it's because of your determination, compassion, and skill that a five-year-old from St. Paul is coming back home," I said as I looked her in the eye.

"I just hope Charles comes home soon too," Janet replied.

I checked my BlackBerry and saw a new message: "We have a baby. I'll be home soon."

Within a few minutes Charles arrived home and looked like a proud new papa. "It's a girl!" he announced proudly.

"That's awesome!" I replied.

"I love it!" Janet exclaimed as she began to collect our things.

"How were my rascals?" he asked.

"Perfect," I answered.

"We had lots of fun, especially playing FBI agent," Janet laughed.

"That's the new one lately," Charles giggled.

"Aren't you going to share your big news?" I prompted Janet.

"Oh yeah," Janet said, trying to sound like it wasn't a big deal. "Our five-year-old from St. Paul really was the child being held in the Kenyan jail. The Embassy just called to say thanks for the boss's hard work and for sending the dental records."

"Wow—that is awesome news! Be sure to email Anders about it right away. He might want to go to the airport to greet the family before he heads to Iowa," Charles stated.

"I'll send him a message," Janet told him.

"Thanks again for coming to the team's rescue tonight," Charles stated as we walked out.

We drove back to the hotel where Janet informed the senator about the terrific news. Then we set our alarm to catch at least four hours of sleep.

✳   ✳   ✳   ✳   ✳   ✳

"I think we need to write 'Iowa or bust!' on the back of our car," I laughed as Cam volunteered to drive Janet's car to Ames so we could work on the way.

"Don't write anything. Where's some wood for me to knock on?" Janet said as she suddenly became nervous about the trip.

Cam said, "We should write, 'Honk for Anders, wave for O'Connor, and—"

"—and blow a kiss for Jenkins!" Janet interrupted with a laugh.

"It should be 'and moon us for Jenkins,'" I laughed.

"The last thing I want to see is a bunch of Iowa ass," Cam stated.

As we started the four-hour drive, I was pumped to sit in the front next to Cam.

"Where's the CD player in this rig?" he asked.

"We provide our own music," Janet told him and began to belt out a Broadway show tune.

"I know, right?" I said quietly, and shot him a glance. I surreptitiously pulled out my iPhone and the new car adapter I had purchased, which didn't require the use of the cigarette outlet. I wouldn't make the same mistake twice. Road trips called for music.

"Did you get ahold of Heidi yesterday?" Cam asked.

"She called back but we didn't get the scoop. Did you hear Rose had a baby girl last night?" I asked.

"Yes, that's awesome. I heard you guys were nannies to the rescue." He laughed.

"Not sure *nanny* is the right term, but we went to the rescue," I responded.

✳   ✳   ✳   ✳   ✳   ✳

When we arrived in Ames the streets were lined with political signs.

"I can feel the energy!" exclaimed Janet.

"Man, it looks like O'Connor barfed all over the place," I commented as I counted lawn sign after lawn sign emblazoned with her name.

"I haven't seen one McDermott sign yet," Cam said.

"This is going to be a ground game between Jenkins and O'Connor. It doesn't look good for the boss."

"Who was in charge of bringing McDermott signs?" Janet asked.

"I'm not really sure," I replied as I messaged Trista.

"Hopefully they'll bring the senator in on a different highway. He'll flip if he sees the O'Connor domination," Cam predicted.

"Good point, Cam. I'll suggest that to Charles," I said.

"We need some signs! I feel like the hockey player who brought a baseball to the game," Janet stated.

"Do you really think lawn signs matter?" I asked them.

"I think they generate momentum," Janet stated.

"Name recognition is usually their sole purpose. Everyone knows the three candidates this weekend, but there's something to the ground game as a gauge of the momentum of supporters," Cam stated.

"I guess that's a good point. When people vote on Saturday they don't want to vote for the loser. Everyone wants to be on the winning team," I said.

"By the looks of this, we're going to be blown away by O'Connor," Janet said as we continued to pass waves of posted O'Connor signs.

We spent the afternoon checking in to our hotel rooms and working to ensure a successful arrival for everyone else. We informed Charles that he needed to increase the number of lawn signs they'd planned to bring along and encouraged him to come with additional boxes of T-shirts. We were going to need all the help we could get.

Early in the evening, we shopped our way through political book fairs, T-shirts, and bumper stickers. Ames felt like a political county fair. It was energizing. Trista was coming to Iowa to replace Rose. The senator, Karma, Charles, and the rest of the McDermott family were scheduled to arrive at various times throughout the evening.

The following day would be spent politicking at event after event. Each candidate's camp was competing for headlines and word-of-mouth popularity before the straw poll on Saturday.

Janet got word from Karma that their first interview was at 7:00 a.m. the next morning. She asked Janet to meet her in her hotel room at 6:00 a.m. to apply makeup.

"My makeup application skills are just about as good as my volleyball prowess: zilch," Janet said.

"You'll be fine," I reassured her. "Just pretend you know what you're doing."

"Easy for you to say." Janet laughed.

"Did the senator say anything to you about getting the kid out of the Kenyan prison?" I asked her.

"He wrote back: 'Awesome.'"

"That's it?" I asked.

"Yup, that's it," she said. "Charles told me the state office would handle the follow-up and issue a press release."

"Boom! I told you!"

"What?" she asked.

"I told you they needed to kill the O'Connor-in-a-hijab story with good news. Shit. We're almost ready for one of us to run for office and the other to be the chief of staff." I laughed.

*   *   *   *   *   *

The next morning I heard Janet wake up early for her appointment with Karma. After she left our room I was feeling nosy. When I heard them leave Karma's room, I peered through the peephole and saw them heading down the hall toward the exit to the parking lot. I darted over to the window and watched as Karma stopped short on their way to the car. Janet turned toward her, looking worried, and then Karma began to throw up. Janet appeared momentarily confused and then went to hold Karma's hair. Suddenly Karma regained her composure and walked over to the car as if nothing had happened. Janet seemed a little stunned but then got in the driver's seat and drove off. I had a feeling it was going to be a long day for Janet.

I was wide awake, so I turned my laptop on. Little did I know then that I'd be glued to that laptop for the next nine hours. I spent the entire morning and early afternoon answering messages from Cam,

Charles, and the senator about event logistics and details.

The most frustrating part was that all the answers they wanted were provided in the advance binder. I answered their questions anyway, resisting the urge to write back, "READ THE ADVANCE MEMO, IT IS IN YOUR BINDER!" I felt bad for Cam, because I knew no matter how bad I had it, he had it worse. He had to field their questions on his own, without Rose's help.

Throughout the day, I also got concise updates from Janet about the day's events. I decided to keep a list of her best messages:

pukinginbathroomfromnerves
actressafuckinactress
applymakeuptoforeheadforshadowduhjanet
shesnotshakinghandsofdelegateselectionover
nojokewearethrowingapartyforstafftonight!!

That last message worried me so I reread it. Apparently Karma wanted to throw a party for the staff after the straw poll, and Janet and I would be in charge of it. The only staffers we had on the ground in Iowa were Trista, Charles, Cam, Janet, and me. I didn't think Trista or Charles would want to hang out at a party with us lowlifes, and I figured a party for three would be easy to plan.

Before I knew it, Janet was back from Karma's interviews. She was gasping for breath. "I'm allergic to Iowa. I swear," she announced, breathing hard.

"Where's your inhaler?" I asked.

"In my purse," she told me as she collapsed on the hotel bed.

"I never thought about all the hay and straw in the air in Iowa," I said, feeling bad that I hadn't anticipated the problem after our wreath-making mishap.

"Neither did I," Janet said as she began to hack.

"Let me know if you need anything," I said as I watched to make sure she was still breathing.

"I need Jenkins," she mumbled.

"Like hell you do," I said.

"No, I really do," she whispered.

"What now, credit card declined?"

"Today Karma flat-out lied about Jenkins in all the interviews. She announced that Jenkins wants to change the legal term for victims of rape, stalking, and domestic violence to 'accuser.' But victims of other less gendered crimes, like burglary, would still be termed 'victims.' And she said that he has introduced a bill that would allow hospitals to let a woman to die rather than perform an abortion necessary to save her life."

"Are you kidding me? Did he?" I asked.

"Are you insane? Of course he didn't." She went on, "Oh, it gets worse. She attacked O'Connor like one witch hunting another. She claimed O'Connor believes that it's not enough to be abstinent with other people. You have to be abstinent alone. She claimed O'Connor has been preaching that the Bible says lust in your heart is committing adultery, and you can't masturbate without lust. She also said that Congresswoman O'Connor believes *The Lion King* is gay propaganda."

"Did you start to sing 'I Just Can't Wait to Be King' or 'Can You Feel the Love Tonight'?" I laughed.

"No. My head is still spinning. Charles is going to shit the bed. She spouted all day that her new platform is that as President, Anders will end all federal funding for low-income kids' preschool programs. Why, you might ask? No need for it—women should really be home with the kids, not out working," Janet reported between coughs.

"Charles is going to shit the bed," I agreed.

"Did you get my messages about our party for the staff tonight?" she asked.

"Yes, but the only staffers here are Trista, Charles, Cam, you, and me."

"Oh, well, she claimed today that O'Connor has the highest staff turnover because she's whacked out and nutty. So when asked what she and the senator do for his staff, she conveniently announced that we're having a staff appreciation party tonight," Janet replied.

"Remember that report. I bet we have a higher turnover than any Hill office," I said as I thought about the number of people who had quit in the short time the senator had been in office.

"I know, right?" Janet agreed. "I think we should just go out tonight and if any press asks, we're having our staff party. Bring on the campaign credit card!"

"You should take a nap. That wheezing is getting out of control again. I can take care of Lady Karma while I sit here and answer more questions via my trusty laptop," I instructed.

"I'm going to email Jenkins first," she said. But soon she had crashed out for an afternoon nap.

I decided to order room service since I couldn't leave my laptop for more than a few minutes. Janet slept for a few hours. When she woke up I was starving, and the day was almost over. I hadn't even showered because I was afraid of missing a message from Charles, Cam, or the boss.

"Charles wants to do dinner tonight with us," I told Janet as she took over laptop duty so I could take a shower.

"That'll be fun," Janet said quickly as she checked her messages to see if Jenkins had replied.

"So, any word from your blind lover?" I teased.

"Yes, he asked us to come to the Blue Jeans Ball tonight and say we're his guests," she said excitedly.

"I'm not going to any ball as his guest," I snapped. "How would that look?"

"Why not? It sounds fun," she said.

"First, you can barely breathe already. It's a country western party, and the event will be full of straw and hay. Second, he's our competitor!" I yelled from the bathroom.

"No one will know," she argued.

"The only ass I want to see in blue jeans is Cam's. If you can

convince him to go with us, I'm in," I told her, confident Cam wouldn't set foot in Jenkins's event.

"You can be so difficult," she hollered.

"And you can be so blind to reality," I yelled back.

We got ready and left for dinner with Charles and Cam. Charles just shook his head when he heard about Janet's day with Karma. "If this campaign doesn't kill me, the White House will," he laughed as we downed our second bottle of wine. Dinner was relaxing, and it was nice to see Charles upbeat and with his guard down again.

The senator called Charles five times during dinner. During one call Charles had the nerve to ask him about Karma's new platform. Janet, Cam, and I waited for him to share the boss's response. "He claims he knew that she was going to announce his support for ending all federal money for pre-K education programs. Way to get out the vote with women," Charles said with a smirk.

"How do you think we'll poll tomorrow?" Cam asked Charles.

"You can never count your chickens before they hatch—or your votes before they're tallied. But I think we'll be either first or second. I think O'Connor will bow out in the next few months," Charles predicted.

"O'Connor has a mean ground game, though," Cam pointed out.

"You can pay workers to put up your signs and distribute your literature, but you can't pay delegates to vote for you," Charles argued.

"Yeah, we're not Democrats," I quipped to mixed laughter.

"She's weird," Janet stated.

"That she is," Charles agreed. "So where are we heading tonight to paint this town?"

"Janet got us into the Blue Jeans Ball," I announced, causing Janet to almost choke on her ice.

"Really?" Charles asked and continued, "That's Jenkins's big event. I hear they have huge headliners tonight on stage. I think it sounds like fun. A little bootin' and scootin' would do us all some good," Charles said with a wink. "Plus it would be fun to see what the competition is up to."

"I'm game," Janet said still wheezing but grinning in triumph.

"I'm going to need a few more glasses of wine if I'm going to ride a cowboy," I said as I reached for our third bottle of wine.

"Should we really go?" Cam asked hesitantly.

"Why not?" Charles questioned and asked Janet, "You sure you can get us all in?"

"Absolutely," she answered.

Perhaps suspecting something, Charles sent me a questioning look.

"You think the boss would be okay with us going? Who will take care of him and the family?" I asked.

"Trista is with them. They're fine. Besides, Karma told me to take you all out on the town tonight," Charles told us.

"That's a first, you actually listening to her," I laughed.

"Trust me, it is a first!"

"I'm pretty excited to go to my first big presidential campaign concert!" Cam said.

"And it's right up your alley with all the country crooning," I teased.

"They usually have pretty awesome swag. Hopefully there'll be something good for the kids," Charles said.

"Yes, I'm sure they'd love to kick Jenkins balls around the house." I laughed.

"They know I already do that," he said back.

We all had another round of wine before we left for the hootenanny.

*　　*　　*　　*　　*　　*

"God, this place is packed! You can hardly move without rubbing up against someone," I said to Charles as he navigated our team to the dance floor.

"I love a good two-step," Cam said as he grabbed me to dance with him. Something had gotten into him. My heart began to beat out of my chest. I had longed to dance with Cam, but I had no idea how to do

a two-step. And at five foot ten I'd never been very coordinated when it came to dancing.

As Cam whisked me around the dance floor, I could see Janet skirting around the room as she searched for Jenkins. Cam surprised me with his moves. I'd always considered him a bit awkward, but he knew his way around the dance floor. He made me feel at ease even though I had no idea what I was doing.

Charles joined us for the next few fast songs, and as we left the dance floor to get some refreshments, he realized Janet was missing. "Where'd the wheezing blonde go?" he asked as his eyes darted around the room searching for her.

"Who knows," I answered back.

"Are all these folks delegates?" Cam asked Charles.

"Oh God no. Delegates don't dance. They don't know what fun is. These are lobbyists who make PAC donations. It's an exceptionally large turnout; I suspect that's because Jenkins is a committee chair," he answered.

"Why didn't we have a huge party?" I asked.

"At this point, the only thing we've got close to Hollywood or Nashville is Karma. Need I say more?" Charles asked. "Besides, we just got our PAC set up and we need to watch our campaign funds. At this point, we can't compete with an event like this. Jenkins has been around awhile. It's going to take some work to gain this kind of momentum."

"Talk about David vs. Goliath," Cam mumbled.

"We could have done an event with CROTCH," I joked.

"Don't remind me. I think we had enough CROTCH to last a lifetime," Charles answered back.

We danced for hours. Charles had all the right moves on the dance floor and encouraged others to dance with us.

"Maybe he can persuade some delegates to come to our side," Cam suggested.

"With those moves, I bet he could!" I exclaimed. "Don't look now, but he's getting frisky. I bet he could persuade all the soccer, hockey, and baseball moms to vote for Anders."

Just then Janet made her way back to us. "Well, well, well, look who has decided to finally join us," Charles said as he danced up to Janet. I could tell she was annoyed with Charles's energetic hips so close to her.

"You wanna grab everyone beers with me?" I invited her.

"Of course," she answered, backing away from Charles's slick moves.

"Where the hell have you been?"

"I was in Jenkins's hotel room," she answered.

I spit my mouthful of beer onto the floor. "Holy shit, please don't tell me...," I said as I grabbed the nearest glass of beer and gulped it down.

"He kissed me," she said without inflection.

I spit again. "Please, dear God, only a kiss?"

"Good girls never tell." She laughed.

"Knock it off! You are going to tell me everything that happened!" I insisted. "Only a kiss?"

"Well, we made out with our clothes on, and he asked me to purr like a kitty," she replied.

"Oh my God, that's so grade school! So you dry humped him?" I asked.

"Yes, he made the move, and I didn't know what to do," she said.

I took a deep breath. "Holy shit, I can't believe my best friend just dry humped a presidential candidate at his campaign event." I laughed and gave her a high five.

"What's so funny?" she asked.

"Think about it. He's running for president, and you work for his competition. He can't see you and you dry humped. You can't make shit like this up," I howled. Then I composed myself long enough to purr at her for added effect.

"I think he actually likes me. You know, a small-town Minnesota girl with a big heart and a contagious giggle," she answered.

"Is blindness contagious?" I asked and she glared at me. "Because you've certainly become blind—blind to being played."

"He must really like pussy." She laughed.

"Not only did you hump, I think you're drunk," I said.

"Wasted. He got me wasted. Or my allergy medicine doesn't mix with booze," she slurred. We walked back to the dance floor with beers in both of our hands. Charles, Cam, and I slammed our beers in a matter of minutes. Charles took Janet's hand and he started rockin' her to the music a bit too hard. I could see Janet's face turn white and I quickly jumped to her rescue.

"Charles, you'd better stop twirling Janet around before we have an asthma attack in Ames," I warned as I grabbed Janet's arm.

"Let's go to the ladies' room," she said urgently.

"Come with me," I said, trying to hold her up. Soon enough I was holding her hair as she vomited into the toilet. Tears began to roll down her face. "Why are you crying?" I asked.

"Jenkins is such an ass," she answered.

"What? Wait, you just made out with him and now he's an ass?"

"While we were making out he called out a name. It didn't sound like Janet so I ignored it the first time, but by the fourth time, it was clear he was yelling 'Samantha. Oh Samantha.' Who the hell is Samantha?" she asked.

"Probably the tattoo lady," I guessed. "I'm sorry."

"She's either the tattoo floozy or another online lover," she said. "I hope Anders and O'Connor beat his pompous ass tomorrow."

"Wow—strong words," I said as I helped her up. I was sorry she was in pain, but hoped that this was just the kick in the ass she needed to get over her fantasy.

"Can we just go home?" she asked. "I want nothing to do with Jenkins or his event."

I wanted to stay out so I could make a move on Cam, but my friend needed me. "Good plan," I agreed. "It's late and we need to be on our best game for the boss tomorrow."

We found Charles and Cam, who agreed to call it a night, and as we headed out we all grabbed several of the party's swag bags.

"Best part of the night is right here!" Charles roared as he rifled through his Jenkins campaign freebies.

"No way, boxes of macaroni and cheese with noodles shaped like elephants!" Cam laughed.

"The kids will love them. Grab some more," Charles asked.

"You can have my bag. I don't want anything with Jenkins's name on it," Janet said as she tossed her bag to Charles.

"Okay then," he replied, shooting me an odd look.

We made it back to our hotel without further incident and went right to bed so we'd be ready for the big day.

✳   ✳   ✳   ✳   ✳   ✳

"Do we have kosher hot dogs?" the senator asked me as we walked through our campaign's straw poll luncheon buffet line.

"I'm not sure, Senator. But since it's Iowa, I'm going to guess no," I answered.

Trista did a fantastic job organizing the McDermott campaign's straw poll events. They were themed around conservative, real-life folks. Hot dogs, beans, and corn on the cob with zero glitz—a bare-bones, working-man's campaign.

As I turned around, I noticed the senator was walking from table to table grabbing every woman's elbow with a hard, closed fist. He's still got it, I thought. Every woman he spoke to seemed to melt. He just had that kind of charisma. There was a distinct energy about today, and you could feel the excitement in the air with political rallies, events, and chanting as the sole soundtrack in every corner of Ames.

"I love this!" Janet stated as she scarfed down a hot dog.

"Me too!" I answered.

"This is America!" Cam jumped into the conversation.

"Man, I hate to predict it this early, but I really think Anders is

pulling out a win here," Janet said as we looked around at our gathering of supporters.

"I feel it too," I agreed.

"Jenkins's camp seems a bit dead on arrival today," Cam said.

"Amen," Janet replied.

"Why the sudden change of heart?" Cam asked.

"Typical guy bullshit," she answered as Cam looked at me for hints.

"Maybe all of his supporters are hung over from last night," I theorized, turning back to the original topic.

The O'Connor camp was hosting Christian bands under their tent and giving away old-fashioned root-beer floats. Their tent was well attended, but nothing compared to the growing number of McDermott supporters.

"Oh boy. Say it ain't so," I said as Karma approached the microphone on stage.

"What in the world is she doing?" Cam asked, alarmed.

"Anders and I are very thankful for your love and support today and through this campaign. We all love America, and I can't think of a better place to sing the songs we all love," Karma said. Without music or apparently any practice, Karma began to sing iconic patriotic songs, encouraging everyone to join in. From "This Land Is My Land" to "The Battle Hymn of the Republic," the music was out of tune and the song leaders needed the lyrics—desperately.

"This is outrageously horrible," Janet stated.

"I think Karma's going to announce she has a record deal." I laughed.

"Or maybe she's thinking they'll drop by a recording studio on their way to 1600 Pennsylvania Avenue." Cam laughed.

"Who told her to do this?" Charles asked as he looked at Janet.

"I had nothing to do with this, nor did I know about it," she answered quickly.

"God, she's more trouble than my kids," he complained. "Does anyone here want to remind my favorite future First Lady of the

United States that this isn't her ticket to Hollywood fame, and she's going to go viral on the Internet as America's most untalented singer?" No one answered him.

He sighed. "On second thought, the supporters seem to like it. It's got a small-town feel," Charles said, assessing the room.

I looked around too, and noticed that most folks were swaying to the music and even singing along. But I still worried a video would end up on YouTube and then make the social-media leap to every national syndicated political show.

The senator came over to us and put his arm across my shoulders. "Alright, the straw poll will be in two hours. Let's get some sign waving happening and jump-start this crowd! We have a poll to win tonight. I can feel it," the senator said as he watched his wife struggle to sing.

I could feel the momentum of the straw poll shift toward the McDermott campaign. It looked as though the corniness of Karma's singing was actually working. Our supporter base was increasing tenfold, and donors were leaving checks and credit card transactions with us to process on Monday. It was an incredible shift—the shift we'd all dreamed could happen in a campaign. And today it was happening in our campaign.

*   *   *   *   *   *

"This night is surreal," Janet said as we watched the announcement of the straw poll results.

"Holy crap, he did it!" I belted out.

"We won! We won this thing," Cam said as he studied the results.

"Serves him right—Jenkins landed dead last," Janet snarled.

"Easy pitbull with lipstick," I laughed. "Can you believe we're in first by 452 votes?"

"O'Connor must be pissed. We stole this right out from under her," Charles howled and cheered. We all were hugging each other,

and I hugged Cam a little longer than everyone else. When we released each other, he looked me in the eyes and kissed me on the lips. I stood there paralyzed, and before I knew it, he was gone.

The senator, Karma, the kids, and Colonel gathered on the McDermott stage while our crowd of supporters got louder and louder. They were almost ballistic. Everyone started chanting, "Anders! Anders! Anders!" in unison, and Karma waved like a newly crowned beauty queen. The senator did an outstanding job of thanking our supporters and firing them up for the long campaign ahead.

As the senator was speaking, Margot came over to Janet and me. She stood there nervously and then whispered, "You guys know where I can get a hit?"

"God, I hope there isn't random drug testing at the White House," I said as I grabbed Janet's arm and turned away.

"Maybe you can be the new administrator of the Drug Enforcement Agency," Janet added as we walked away. Margot never ceased to surprise.

We repositioned ourselves close to the stage and joined in the cheering for our boss. We spotted the senator staring at us during his victory speech. "I need to thank two special women in my life. Two of the hardest workers I know—Allison and Janet. Our win tonight is dedicated to both of you," the senator said as he winked at us.

"God, that was awfully sweet and out of character," Janet said.

"He must be drunk," I replied.

"You two deserve a lot of credit," Cam said as he sneaked up behind us.

"Thank you—as do you," I answered as I began to blush.

"The senator finally got one thing right without me writing his speech," Charles said as he smiled at us and gave us each a big hug.

Later we went to a local pub to celebrate our victory. Before we left the McDermott tent Charles handed us the campaign's credit card. We were thrilled and not shy about using it.

I didn't get any more kisses from Cam, but we all had a blast. I was full of anticipation for what was in store. After a heavy night of drinking, Cam crashed in our hotel room again, though neither of us made any moves.

We woke up to a national press release issued by Charles. It announced the new McDermott campaign team and pre-endorsement leadership.

Charles Stanford (651) 555-1212
getcharles@mcdermott.com
McDermott Announces Presidential Campaign and Leadership Team

Fresh off his Iowa straw poll victory, US Senator Anders McDermott III is hitting the presidential campaign trail with new vision, energy, and momentum. The campaign and McDermott proudly announce our presidential campaign and leadership team.

"This phenomenal team we have assembled will help our campaign with strategic messaging, building a solid, unprecedented national ground game and grassroots political activities, and record-breaking national fundraising. I am proud of my team, who I know, without question, will work tirelessly to ensure victory," states McDermott.

The campaign announces the following members of the McDermott for President Executive Leadership Team:

Charles Stanford: Campaign Manager
Allison Amundson: Executive Director of Scheduling and Candidate External Affairs
Janet Johannson: Special Assistant for Strategic and Political Affairs

Ingrid Mohamed: Special Assistant for Cultural Affairs (Mohamed joins the campaign from the American Muslim Association.)
Cam Douglas: Special Assistant for Public Policy
Trista Woodrow: Special Assistant for Campaign Financial Development
Thao "Nick" Yang: Director of Communications (Yang joins the campaign from the Jenkins presidential campaign.)

Additionally, the campaign announces the following staff members of the McDermott for President team:

Blair Bloomberg II: Press Secretary (Bloomberg rejoins the McDermott team after a brief leave.)
Sarah Blackbird: Northwest Regional Political Director
L. L. Lopez: Southwest Regional Political Director
John Carlson: Midwest Regional Political Director

----End----

"Shouldn't we have at least known about this before it was announced? And who are some of these people?" Janet asked.

"I think I'm going to be sick—Blair?" I asked. Then, suddenly worried, I continued, "Does this mean we aren't employees of the United States Senate anymore?"

"Ah, ladies, we just landed ourselves on a presidential campaign! Let the games begin!" Cam stated.

As we drove back to St. Paul to pack our belongings for our next adventure, once again, everything had changed overnight. We had once-in-a-lifetime jobs.

Janet and I called our parents within the first mile and told them the big news about our new positions (which we still didn't know anything about). The pride in our parents' voices left us all choked up. They were instantly proud.

By mile twenty the senator had requested Chairman Jenkins's home telephone number. Thankfully, Janet had it on speed dial.

By mile 197 we had proclaimed: "1600 Pennsylvania Avenue or bust!"

Acknowledgements

T his has been an incredible journey. The story of *Capitol Hell* wouldn't have been possible without the help, talent, and generosity of so many. Together, we have revised, re-revised, laughed, and even cursed. But, in the end, we are tremendously thankful for the wisdom and guidance of our families, friends, and mentors. Without your unconditional love and encouragement, this book never would have been possible and we are infinitely grateful for your advice and support.

We would also like to recognize and thank our publisher, Beaver's Pond Press, and specifically the dynamic duo of Lily Coyle and Dara Beevas. Thank you for helping us to tell this story.

To our editor, Wendy Weckwerth, and our proofreader, Molly Miller: Thank you for your diligence, your ATD, and for helping us make this book something we can truly be proud of.

To the creative minds of Tiffany Laschinger, Carrie Keenan, and the keen eye of NHR Photography, your talents have helped give *Capitol Hell* a face, and we are thankful for your artistic abilities.

To our publicist, Bronwyn Schaefer-Pope, thank you for your energy, professional expertise, and for always being willing to push the envelope. We are also thankful for the dogged persistence of Sara Lien.

Finally, we would like to thank our former bosses for their dedication to public service, and for their leadership to our amazing country. We are incredibly thankful for the opportunities and chances you gave to two small-town young ladies, and we wouldn't trade our *Capitol Hell* experience for anything on Heaven or Earth!

J ayne Jones and Alicia Long, co-authors of *Capitol Hell* began their political careers by working for former Senator Norm Coleman (MN).

Jayne Jones, a graduate of William Mitchell College of Law, left Capitol Hill to work for the Minnesota House of Representatives, where she was the Executive Assistant to the Speaker of the House. Her favorite adventure is teaching others about the legislative process and how to draft legislation in her capacity as a political science professor at Concordia University. Jones is also in the process of starting a summer camp for teenagers interested in public policy.

Alicia Long, a South Dakota native and graduate of the University of St. Thomas School of Law, also worked for United States Senator John Thune (SD) as well as former United States Senator George Allen (VA). After graduating from law school, she obtained employment as a Presidential Management Fellow in the Department of Justice. In that capacity, she worked as a Special Assistant U.S. Attorney in the United States Attorney's Office in the District of Columbia. Currently she is an attorney working in Washington D.C.